KU-747-384

withdraw

EVERYMAN'S LIBRARY

EVERYMAN,
I WILL GO WITH THEE,
AND BE THY GUIDE,
IN THY MOST NEED
TO GO BY THY SIDE

LEO TOLSTOY

Childhood, Boyhood and Youth

Translated from the Russian by C. J. Hogarth
Revised by Nigel J. Cooper
with an Introduction by A. N. Wilson

EVERYMAN'S LIBRARY

13

This book is one of 250 volumes in Everyman's Library
which have been distributed to 4500 state schools
throughout the United Kingdom.
The project has been supported by a grant of £4 million
from the Millennium Commission.

First included in Everyman's Library, 1912
Revisions to the translation © Everyman Publishers plc, 2000
Introduction © A. N. Wilson, 1991
Bibliography and Chronology © Everyman Publishers plc, 2000
Typography by Peter B. Willberg

ISBN 1-85715-013-9

A CIP catalogue record for this book is available from the
British Library

Published by Everyman Publishers plc,
Gloucester Mansions, 140A Shaftesbury Avenue,
London WC2H 8HD

Distributed by Random House (UK) Ltd.,
20 Vauxhall Bridge Road, London SW1V 2SA

CONTENTS

INTRODUCTION

———

Tolstoy's childhood, as opposed to Tolstoy's *Childhood*, was troubled, and tempestuous and emotionally deprived. When he was barely two years old, his mother died. Tolstoy was to remain obsessed by this fact all his life, and even in old age would vainly try to recover the memory of his mother's face. His father died (perhaps of syphilis) when Tolstoy was nine. Thereafter, the little Lev Nikolayevich Tolstoy, with his sister and brothers, was brought up by aunts.

It left Tolstoy a profound emotional emptiness which he filled, as he grew up, with addictive sexual promiscuity. He first visited a brothel with his brothers when he was in his early teens, and by the time he was stationed in the Caucasus, a young soldier in 1851, he was suffering from gonorrhoea, and having to undergo the painful mercury treatment which was then the only hope of curing his condition.

Writing to his favourite aunt in the November of that year, he said, 'Do you remember, dear Aunt, a piece of advice you once gave me – to write novels? Well, I'm following your advice.' He had set to work on *Childhood*. In the previous year, he had been reading a quantity of Dickens, and in particular *David Copperfield* and *Dombey and Son*. These works reinforced Tolstoy's sense, already derived from Rousseau, his intellectual master, that childhood was a time of innocence. In those days before Freud, it was fashionable to suppose that the dark and dangerous passions which haunt our grown-up life were not buried in childhood experience, but imposed upon us by a corrupting grown-up world. Wordsworth shared this belief, and expressed it in his *Immortality* ode, when he said that

> Shades of the prison-house begin to close
> Upon the growing boy,
> But he beholds the light, and whence it flows,
> He sees it in his joy

Thus, at the age of twenty-three, when Tolstoy began to write *Childhood*, he did not so much draw on his own childhood memories as project a time of blissful innocence which, emotionally and imaginatively, he profoundly needed at the time of writing it.

It is possible to trace some of Tolstoy's creative processes at this time, and see this habit of projection at work. For example, as he was laid up with VD in Tiflis, Tolstoy was much preoccupied with a beautiful girl called Katya. It was very likely his devotion to her which had led to his painful medical condition. In his longing for innocence and purity, he converted Katya in his novel into the twelve-year-old child of a house-serf, also called Katya (or Katenka). She is a pre-pubescent girl in his fantasies, a *devochka* and not a *devushka*. And yet, the scene where the narrator, his brother Volodya, their sister Lyuba and Katenka are gathering caterpillars would have a feeling of *Lolita* about it unless the narrator were meant to be a ten-year-old boy, or unless the twenty-three-year-old novelist were actually thinking of the twenty-year-old Katya.

I peeped over Katya's shoulder as she was trying to pick up the caterpillar by placing another leaf in its way. I had observed before that many girls had a way of twitching their shoulders whenever they were trying to adjust a low-necked dress which had slipped out of place, and that Mimi always grew angry on witnessing this manœuvre and declared, '*C'est un geste de femme de chambre.*' As Katya bent over the caterpillar she made that very movement, while at the same instant the breeze lifted the kerchief on her white neck. Her shoulder-strap was at that moment within two inches of my lips. I was no longer looking at the caterpillar: I gazed and gazed, then with all my strength kissed Katya's shoulder...

We read in his diaries that Katya, his girl-friend of the time, used to like to sit on his lap, and tell him that he was the only man in her life; so her shoulder-blades would have been particularly vivid to him. Yet here he and she are, converted into two children, like David Copperfield and Little Em'ly on Yarmouth beach, the prison house of sexuality not yet descended upon them.

In so far as *Childhood* represents actual memories for Tolstoy, they are projected memories of another family, rather than actual memories of Tolstoy's own. During his late adolescence in Petersburg, Tolstoy had 'fallen in love' (his phrase) with a young man called Islavin. They had gone about together, and Tolstoy had confided to his diary that he had never loved a woman in the way that he loved this young man. The reason for this, of course, was that they did not give sexual expression to their feelings, and in Tolstoy's tortured mind there was an ineradicable connection between sex and corruption. Islavin was very 'corrupt' indeed, and when Tolstoy came to write his *Childhood* memories, he chose to do so not through his own memory, but through the imagined memory of this young man. The family in *Childhood*, *Boyhood* and *Youth*, the Irtenyevs, have far more in common with the Islavin family than they do with the Tolstoys. There is a strange biographical irony in all this. Tolstoy used to play with the Islavins from time to time when he was a little boy. On one occasion, he pushed one of the Islavin girls in the small of the back and she fell off the balcony where they were playing. In his memory, Tolstoy suggested that he pushed her (she was only ten) because he was afraid that the other little boys were paying her special attention, and he feared for her sexual purity. This little girl, Lyubov Islavin – her first name is not altered when she appears as the narrator's sister in *Childhood* – was destined to be Tolstoy's mother-in-law, though he could never have guessed this when he was writing his novella. As the three stories unfold, we encounter not merely the emotionally chaotic narrator – the figure that Tolstoy 'was' when he was in love with Islavin, but also the agonized moralist Nekhlyudov. 'It will be readily understood that Nekhlyudov's influence caused me to adopt his cast of mind, the essence of which lay in an enthusiastic reverence for the ideal of virtue and a firm belief in man's vocation to perpetual perfection.' Nekhlyudov, much transformed, is the hero of Tolstoy's last great novel, *Resurrection*, written when he was an old man whose desire to perfect himself had taken over from his desire to be an artist. But, as these early essays in fiction tell us, the moralist in Tolstoy was always there. So, too, was the aristocratic Christian Tolstoy, who shared with his pious Aunt Toinette a fascination with peasant piety and holy idiots. Grisha, the holy idiot in *Childhood*, is one of the most memorable characters in the book.

Tolstoy the novelist achieved his extraordinary effects of realism by being able to project himself into the minds and personalities of so many different human types – a general on the field of battle, a teenage girl going to her first ball, a penitent *roué* in a brothel, a monk struggling with lust, a peasant simpleton who has somehow managed to master the secret of how to live, a blundering idealist finding happiness on his farm, and with his wife and children, a tormented wife-hater who believes that marriage is the curse of the human race. So long as Tolstoy used this capacity of his for 'being' all such characters in his fictions, he was to be not merely a great writer, but also a comparatively good man. Once he had decided that fiction was a waste of time, and that the serious business of life was to be a moralist, making his own boots and living on a diet of beetroot and cucumber, he became a more tormented soul. The imaginative habit of projection could not be shed, but instead of inventing characters on the page, he became all of them in real life, so that his long-suffering wife found herself living not with one, albeit 'difficult' Lev Nikolayevich, but with a whole household of 'characters': Lev the peasant at his prayers; Tolstoy the social revolutionary; St Lev the Apostle of Universal Love; Lev Nikolayevich the hater of women, and so on.

At the age of twenty-three, when he first began to write fiction, all this lay ahead. Re-reading *Childhood*, *Boyhood* and *Youth*, some fifty years after they were first published, Tolstoy particularly hated them. 'I have re-read them, and regret that I wrote them, so ill, so artificially, and insincerely are they penned. It could not be otherwise; because what I aimed at was not to write my own history but that of friends of my youth and this produced an awkward mixture of the facts of their childhood and my own.' The remark is typical of the monstrous egotism of Tolstoy in his 'saintly' old age. The only virtue for him in a piece of prose with these titles, *Childhood*, *Boyhood* and *Youth*, would be if they provided him with a mirror of what he had been like as a child. But it was because he could not really remember his own childhood that he was able to write them. The stories which began with such a strange mixture of self-projection and obsession with other people – filtered through Rousseau and Dickens – came to be possessed of a tremendous realism. It was this realism of his art which Tolstoy was to come to hate. The characters in art have more reality, and more emotional depth, very often, than the characters in life. Once released by Prospero's wand, the characters in literature outsoar their creators. This, we can imagine, was a source of joy to Shakespeare precisely for the reason that it was a torment to Tolstoy, which is why, we may suppose, he hated Shakespeare above all writers. Shakespeare, in his life and works, remains a shadowy figure. Tolstoy was a man, in life, who craved the position of centre stage. His mysterious, Shakespearean gift, as an artist, was to create a world out of his own most deeply held personal obsessions and to lose self altogether. *Childhood* is the first hint of what is to come in his later masterpieces, *War and Peace* and *Anna Karenina*.

A. N. Wilson

SELECT BIBLIOGRAPHY

BIOGRAPHY

MAUDE, AYLMER, *The Life of Tolstoy*, 2 volumes, Oxford University Press, 1930 (revised version of the 1908–10 edition). Besides translating Tolstoy's writings, Maude was Tolstoy's friend and follower, and has insights not available to later biographers. This *Life* remains a classic.

SIMMONS, ERNEST J., *Leo Tolstoy*, 2 volumes, Vintage Books, Boston, 1945–6 (Vintage paperback edition, 1960); Routledge, London, 1973. A detailed and scholarly account by a distinguished American critic.

TROYAT, HENRI, *Tolstoy* (first published in French, 1965), Doubleday, New York, 1967; W. H. Allen, London, 1968; Penguin Books, Harmondsworth, 1970. A detailed and popular biography (denounced by Nabokov as 'a vile *biographie romancée*'). Highly readable but somewhat bland, and thin on the implications of Tolstoy's ideas.

WILSON, A.N., *Tolstoy*, Hamish Hamilton, London, 1988; Penguin Books, Harmondsworth, 1989. A stimulating, consciously un-reverential treatment which is very readable, and good on the ideas as well as the literary writings.

CRANKSHAW, EDWARD, *Tolstoy – The Making of a Novelist*, Weidenfeld & Nicolson, London, 1974. Less detailed and more idiosyncratic than the titles above, but a knowledgeable and well-illustrated study concentrating largely on Tolstoy before 1880.

AUTOBIOGRAPHICAL SOURCES

CHRISTIAN, R.F. (editor and translator), *Tolstoy's Letters*, 2 volumes, Athlone Press, London and Scribner's, New York, 1978.

CHRISTIAN, R.F. (editor and translator), *Tolstoy's Diaries*, 2 volumes, Athlone Press, London and Scribner's, New York, 1985.

These two comprehensive collections, clearly presented and well annotated, provide invaluable tools for the reader who wants to explore the connections between Tolstoy's life and his fictions.

LITERARY CRITICISM

CHRISTIAN, R.F., *Tolstoy, a Critical Introduction*, Cambridge University Press, 1969. A methodical and detailed survey of Tolstoy's writing which is particularly helpful on the beginnings of his fiction and on *Childhood, Boyhood and Youth*.

GREENWOOD, E.B., *Tolstoy – The Comprehensive Vision*, Dent, London, 1975; paperback edition Methuen, London, 1980. A densely written survey covering the full range of Tolstoy's fiction with an emphasis on psychology and ideas. Has a chapter on *Childhood, Boyhood and Youth*.

CAIN, T.G.S., *Tolstoy* (*Novelists and their World* series), Paul Elek, London, 1977. A survey of Tolstoy's work which foregrounds his ethical and spiritual struggles. Includes a chapter on *Childhood, Boyhood and Youth*.

BAYLEY, JOHN, *Tolstoy and the Novel*, Chatto & Windus, London, 1966 (paperback edition 1968). A distinguished and very personal appreciation with many insights. The main focus is on *War and Peace*, but the early work is not neglected.

EIKHENBAUM, B.M., *The Young Tolstoy*, tr. G. Kern, Ardis, Ann Arbor, Michigan, 1972. A translation of the great Soviet critic's 1922 study which has much to say about narrative technique, time and observation, and the influence of Dickens on the trilogy.

ORWIN, DONNA TUSSING, *Tolstoy's Art and Thought*, 1847–1880, Princeton University Press, 1993. An examination of the philosophical and intellectual influences on Tolstoy during his major creative period: particularly illuminating on the impact of Rousseau and Hegel on the trilogy.

WILLIAMS, GARETH, *Tolstoy's 'Childhood'*, Bristol Classical Press, 1995. A detailed study of the first part of Tolstoy's trilogy which raises issues relevant to the whole work and traces in detail the reactions of critics in Russia and elsewhere. Includes a large bibliography.

ZWEERS, A.F., *Grown-up Narrator and Childlike Hero*, Mouton, The Hague and Paris, 1971. A very detailed neo-formalist examination of the literary devices used in Tolstoy's trilogy.

DE HAARD, ERIC, *Narrative and anti-narrative Structures in Lev Tolstoj's Early Works*, Rodopi, Amsterdam and Atlanta, 1989. A formalist study which includes a discussion of alternative narrative conventions as exemplified within the trilogy.

WACHTEL, ANDREW BARUCH, *The Battle for Childhood: Creation of a Russian Myth*, Stanford University Press, 1990. A study of *Childhood* which concentrates on the psychology of the central character and the complex relationships between child, adult narrator, and author.

GIFFORD, HENRY (editor), *Leo Tolstoy – A Critical Anthology*, Penguin Books, Harmondsworth, 1971. An interesting anthology of reactions to Tolstoy's writing, from contemporaries and from later readers up to 1969.

KNOWLES, A.V. (editor), *Tolstoy – The Critical Heritage*, Routledge, London and Boston, 1978. A rich collection of criticism and comment on his works from Tolstoy's own lifetime.

CHRONOLOGY

DATE	AUTHOR'S LIFE	LITERARY CONTEXT
1828	Lev Nikolayevich Tolstoy born 28 August at Yasnaya Polyana, his father's estate 130 miles south of Moscow.	
1830	Death of his mother.	Stendhal: *Scarlet and Black*. Pushkin: *Boris Godunov*.
1832		
1833		Pushkin: *Eugene Onegin*.
1835		Balzac: *Old Goriot*.
1836	The family moves to Moscow.	Gogol: *The Government Inspector*.
1837	Death of his father.	Pushkin dies after a duel. Dickens: *Oliver Twist* (to 1838).
1838	Death of his grandmother.	
1840		Lermontov: *A Hero of Our Time*.
1841	On the death of their guardian (an aunt), the Tolstoy children move to Kazan to live with another aunt.	Lermontov killed in a duel.
1842	Loses his virginity. Starts to read Rousseau.	Gogol: *Dead Souls Part 1*, *The Overcoat*.
1843		Dickens: *Martin Chuzzlewit* (to 1844).
1844	Enters Kazan University.	Thackeray: *Barry Lyndon*.
1846		Dostoevsky: *Poor Folk*, *The Double*.
1847	Inherits Yasnaya Polyana and leaves Kazan University without graduating. Suffering from a venereal disease. Returns to Yasnaya Polyana and attempts to institute a programme of social reform directed at the peasants.	Herzen: *Who is to Blame?* Goncharov: *An Ordinary Story*. Belinsky: *Letter to Gogol*. Charlotte Brontë: *Jane Eyre*. Emily Brontë: *Wuthering Heights*. Thackeray: *Vanity Fair* (to 1848). Herzen: *From the Other Shore* (to 1851). Turgenev: *A Sportsman's Notebook* (to 1852).
1848	Goes to Moscow.	

France: July Revolution.
Rebellion in Poland (to 1831).
Great Britain: First Reform Act.
Great Britain: Factory Act.

Great Britain: Accession of Queen Victoria.
First Russian railway line constructed.

Ban on sale of individual peasants.

Tsar Nicholas I visits England.

Herzen leaves Russia.

Revolution in France: Second Republic declared.
First Californian Gold Rush.

DATE	AUTHOR'S LIFE	LITERARY CONTEXT
1849	Goes to St Petersburg, studies law for a time. Becomes local magistrate in Tula.	Dickens: *David Copperfield* (to 1850).
1850	Living in Moscow. Reads and translates Sterne.	Death of Balzac.
1851	First serious attempt at writing fiction: *A History of Yesterday* (fragment). Goes to the Caucasus with eldest brother Nikolai to serve as a volunteer in the army. Begins *Childhood*, first part of a projected tetralogy entitled *Four Periods of Growth*.	Melville: *Moby-Dick.* Stowe: *Uncle Tom's Cabin* (to 1852).
1852	Enlists officially in the army. *Childhood* published in *The Contemporary.*	Death of Gogol. Dickens: *Bleak House* (to 1853).
1853	During campaigns in the Caucasus writes *Boyhood* and stories of army life. Writes *A Christmas Night.* Publishes *The Raid.*	Ostrovsky's first play produced.
1854	Promoted to ensign and transferred to Crimea. *Boyhood* appears in *The Contemporary.*	
1855	Publishes *A Billiard-Marker's Notes, Sevastopol in December, Sevastopol in May, The Wood-Felling.* Returns to St Petersburg.	Trollope: *The Warden.*
1856	Death of his brother Dmitri. Publishes *Sevastopol in August, The Snowstorm, Two Hussars, Meeting a Moscow Acquaintance, A Landlord's Morning.* Resigns from the army, returns to Yasnaya Polyana.	Aksakov: *A Family Chronicle.* Turgenev: *Rudin.* Nekrasov: *Poems.*
1857	Visits France and Switzerland. Publishes *Youth, Lucerne.*	Flaubert: *Madame Bovary.* Trollope: *Barchester Towers.* Birth of Conrad.
1858	Visits St Petersburg. Publishes *Albert.*	Pisemsky: *A Thousand Souls.*
1859	Publishes *Three Deaths, Family Happiness.* Critical enthusiasm more muted than for his earlier works. Starts an experimental school for the peasants at Yasnaya Polyana.	Goncharov: *Oblomov.* Turgenev: *A Nest of the Gentlefolk.* Ostrovsky: *The Storm.* Eliot: *Adam Bede.* Darwin: *The Origin of Species.*

HISTORICAL EVENTS

Russian intervention in Hungary.
Dostoevsky sentenced to forced labour in Siberia.

Great Exhibition in London.
St Petersburg–Moscow Railway opened.

France: Second Empire established.

Turkey declares war on Russia.

Crimean War begins.

Death of Tsar Nicholas I. Accession of Alexander II.

Crimean War ends.

Indian Mutiny.

Committees set up to prepare the gentry for the Emancipation of the serfs
from private ownership.
Russia acquires Amur and Maritime Provinces from China.
Russian conquest of Caucasus completed: surrender of Shamil.

DATE	AUTHOR'S LIFE	LITERARY CONTEXT
1860	Second (and last) visit to western Europe. Death of his brother Nikolai, in France. Visits Rome.	Turgenev: *On the Eve, First Love.* Eliot: *The Mill on the Floss.* Dickens: *Great Expectations* (to 1861). Chekhov born.
1861	Visits Paris, London, Brussels. Back in Russia, quarrels with Turgenev. Serves as Arbiter of the Peace. Resumes school work at Yasnaya Polyana.	Dostoevsky: *The House of the Dead.* Herzen: *My Past and Thoughts* (to 1867).
1862	Starts publication of educational magazine. Gives up being Arbiter of the Peace. Police raid on his house. Marries Sofya Andreyevna Behrs, daughter of a court physician. Closes the school.	Turgenev: *Fathers and Children.* Hugo: *Les Misérables.* Flaubert: *Salammbô.*
1863	Publishes *The Cossacks, Polikushka.* Sergei born (first of thirteen children).	Death of Thackeray. Chernyshevsky: *What is to be Done?*
1864		Dostoevsky: *Notes from Underground.* Nekrasov: *Who can Live Happy in Russia?* (to 1876). Dickens: *Our Mutual Friend* (to 1865).
1865–6	Publishes *1805* (volumes 1 and 2 of *War and Peace*).	Leskov: *Lady Macbeth of Mtsensk.*
1866	Unsuccessful defence of soldier court-martialled for striking an officer.	Dostoevsky: *Crime and Punishment.*
1867	*War and Peace* volume 3 published.	Turgenev: *Smoke.*
1868	*War and Peace* volume 4 published.	Dostoevsky: *The Idiot.* Gorky born.
1869	*War and Peace* volumes 5 and 6 published. Experiences acute fear of death in a hotel room at Arzamas.	Goncharov: *The Precipice.*
1870	Begins a novel about Peter the Great. Starts learning Ancient Greek.	Death of Dickens, Herzen. Kuprin born.
1871		Dostoevsky: *Demons* (to 1872).
1872	Reopens Yasnaya Polyana school. Poor health. Reading philosophers, notably Schopenhauer. Writes *A Prisoner in the Caucasus, God sees the Truth but Waits.*	Leskov: *Cathedral Folk.*

CHRONOLOGY

DATE	AUTHOR'S LIFE	LITERARY CONTEXT
1873	Begins writing *Anna Karenina*.	Leskov: *The Enchanted Wanderer*.
1875	Publishes *New Primer, Russian Reader*. Increasingly preoccupied with religious problems, troubled by war with Turkey.	Saltykov-Shchedrin: *The Golovlyovs* (to 1880).
1875–7	*Anna Karenina* appears in instalments.	
1876	Begins to practise Orthodoxy.	James: *Roderick Hudson*. Twain: *Tom Sawyer*.
1877		Turgenev: *Virgin Soil*. Garshin: *Four Days*.
1878	*Anna Karenina* published in book form. Reconciliation with Turgenev. Moral crisis leads him into theological studies. Abandons practice of Orthodoxy.	Hardy: *The Return of the Native*.
1879	Begins writing *A Confession*.	Dostoevsky: *The Brothers Karamazov* (to 1880).
1880	Begins *Critique of Dogmatic Theology, Translation and Harmony of the Gospels*. 4th edition of *Collected Works* appears (11 vols).	Death of Flaubert. Blok, Bely born.
1881	Writes to the Tsar asking for a pardon for the assassins of Alexander II. Visits monastery of Optina Pustyn.	Death of Dostoevsky. James: *The Portrait of a Lady*.
1882	Finishes *A Confession* (banned in Russia). Studies Hebrew. Moves his family to Moscow.	
1883	Writes *What I Believe*. Hands over control of property to his wife. Chertkov arrives as a visitor, stays as a disciple.	Death of Turgenev. Korolenko: *Makar's Dream*. Garshin: *The Scarlet Flower*.
1884	*What I Believe* banned. Publishes fragments from *The Decembrists* (unfinished novel). Writes *Memoirs of a Madman*.	Huysmans: *Against Nature*. Zamyatin born.
1885	Renounces hunting, meat, tobacco and alcohol. Publishes 'popular' tales including *What Men Live By, Where Love is, God is, Ivan the Fool, Two Old Men*.	Zola: *Germinal*.

CHRONOLOGY

HISTORICAL EVENTS

Russian Populist movement begins.
Russia invades Chinese Turkestan.
Universal Exhibition in Vienna.

Land and Liberty movement formed in Russia.

Russia declares war on Turkey.

Russo-Turkish War ends. Congress of Berlin.
Afghan War.
Trial of Vera Zasulich.

People's Will party formed in Russia.
Governor of Kharkov assassinated.
Osip Vissarionovich Djugashvili (Stalin) born.

Alexander II assassinated. Accession of Alexander III.
Jewish residence in Russia severely restricted.

Great Britain: Married Women's Property Act.
University riots. Censorship laws strengthened.

Plekhanov and others form Marxist study groups.

DATE	AUTHOR'S LIFE	LITERARY CONTEXT
1886	*The Death of Ivan Ilych, How Much Land Does a Man Need?, The Godson* published. Tolstoy's play *The Power of Darkness* offends the Tsar and is forbidden. Finishes *What Then Must We Do?* Denounced as heretic by Archbishop of Kherson.	Chekhov: first volume of stories. James: *The Bostonians, The Princess Casamassima*.
1887		
1888	Publishes *Strider* (written 1861). *The Power of Darkness* performed in Paris.	Chekhov: *The Steppe*. Death of Garshin.
1889	Begins writing *Resurrection*. Publication of *Collected Works* (12 vols). Unauthorized copies of *The Kreutzer Sonata* in circulation.	Akhmatova born.
1890	Tsar gives permission for publication of an edited version of *The Kreutzer Sonata*. Writes *The Devil*.	Pasternak born. Wilde: *The Picture of Dorian Gray*.
1891	Renounces copyright on his works post-1881, divides property among family. Writes *Why do Men Stupefy Themselves?*	Ehrenburg, Bulgakov born.
1891–2	Engaged in famine relief work.	
1892	*The Fruits of Enlightenment* produced in Moscow.	Chekhov: *Ward No. 6*. Merezhkovsky: *Symbols*. Gorky publishes his first story. Mandelstam, Tsvetayeva born.
1893	Publishes *The Kingdom of God is within you*.	Death of Maupassant.
1894	Publishes *Christianity and Patriotism, Reason and Religion, Religion and Morality, How to Read the Gospels, Walk in the Light*.	Babel born.
1895	Publishes *Master and Man*. Intervenes to defend the Dukhobors against persecution.	
1896		Chekhov: *The Seagull*. Merezhkovsky: *Christ and Anti-Christ* (to 1905).
1897	Chertkov arrested and exiled.	
1898	Finishes *Father Sergius*. Publishes a censored version of *What is Art?*	Zola: *J'Accuse*. Blok: *Ante Lucem* (to 1900).

CHRONOLOGY

HISTORICAL EVENTS

Five students (including Lenin's brother) hanged for an attempt on the Tsar's life.

Second International founded.

Beginning of Trans-Siberian Railway construction.
Famine in southern Russia.

Witte becomes Finance Minister.

Famine in some Russian regions.
Massacres in Armenia.
Great Britain: Independent Labour Party founded.
Death of Tsar Alexander III. Accession of Tsar Nicholas II.
Great Britain: Greenwich bomb outrage.

Socialist Revolutionary Party founded in Russia.

Pobedonostsev urges the Tsar to imprison Tolstoy.

Spanish–American War. Curies discover radium.
Russian Social Democrat Party founded.

DATE	AUTHOR'S LIFE	LITERARY CONTEXT
1899	Publishes *Resurrection* (begun 1889). Son Sergei accompanies Dukhobors to Canada.	Leonov, Olesha, Nabokov born. Gorky: *Foma Gordeyev.* Chekhov: *The Lady with the Dog.*
1900		Freud: *The Interpretation of Dreams.* Chekhov: *In the Ravine.*
1901	Excommunicated by the Holy Synod of the Russian Orthodox Church. Writes *Reply to the Synod's Edict.* Convalescing in Crimea, meets Gorky, Chekhov.	Chekhov: *Three Sisters.* Fadeyev born.
1902	Writes to the Tsar about the evils of autocracy and private land ownership. Finishes *What is Religion?*	Gorky: *The Lower Depths.* Death of Zola.
1903	Protests against anti-Jewish pogroms in Kishinyov and contributes three short stories for a benefit anthology published in Warsaw. Writes *After the Ball.*	Kuprin: *The Duel.*
1903–6	Writes *Reminiscences.*	
1904	Death of brother Sergei. Finishes *Hadji Murad.* Writes a pamphlet against the war with Japan, *Bethink Yourselves!*, published in England. Writes *The Forged Coupon, Divine and Human.*	Chekhov: *The Cherry Orchard.* Death of Chekhov. Blok: *Verses about the Beautiful Lady.* Bely: *Gold in Azure.*
1905	Writes *Alyosha Gorshok, Fëdor Kuzmich. The One Thing Needful* seized by police.	Rilke: *The Book of Hours.* Sholokhov, Panova born. Sologub: *The Petty Demon* (to 1907).
1906	Writes *What For?* Wife seriously ill.	
1907	Police raid Yasnaya Polyana and seize books.	Gorky: *Mother.* Blok: *The Snow Mask.* Bryusov: *The Fiery Angel.*
1908	Writes *I Cannot be Silent*, a protest against the hanging of the 1905 revolutionaries. Tolstoy's secretary Gusyev arrested and exiled. Chertkov returns from exile to live nearby.	Andreyev: *The Seven who were Hanged.*

CHRONOLOGY

Student riots: temporary closure of universities.
Boer War begins.

Russia occupies Manchuria.
Social Democrat Party brings out newspaper *The Spark*.

Great Britain: Death of Queen Victoria; accession of Edward VII.

Wave of political assassinations in Russia.
Boer War ends.

Lenin's faction (Bolsheviks) prevails at Social Democrat Party congress in London.
Massacre of Jews in Kishinyov.

Lenin launches newspaper *Forward*.
Russo-Japanese War (to 1905); Russian fleet destroyed in Tsushima Straits.

First Russian Revolution: Bloody Sunday, general strike, Tsar's October Manifesto. Witte becomes First Minister.

Meeting of the first Duma (elected parliament).

Austria annexes Bosnia-Herzegovina.

DATE	AUTHOR'S LIFE	LITERARY CONTEXT
1908 *cont.*	Growing quarrels with his wife and Chertkov about mss. and copyright ownership.	
1909	Draws up will relinquishing copyright on his published works since 1881 and his unpublished works from before 1881. Chertkov expelled, goes to Moscow.	Bely: *The Silver Dove, Ashes, The Urn.* Wells: *Tono-Bungay.*
1910	More quarrels with wife (now seriously unbalanced) about wills and copyright. Tolstoy leaves home and sets out to visit the monastery at Optina Pustyn. Taken ill on a train, he dies at the station of Astapovo on 7 November, aged 82. His body is buried without religious rites on the edge of the forest near Yasnaya Polyana.	Kuprin: *The Pit.* Bunin: *The Village.* Forster: *Howards End.* Rilke: *Sketches of Malte Laurids Brigge.*

CHRONOLOGY

REVISER'S NOTE

The idea of automatic progress may not be relevant to the arts, but the process known as translation is science as well as art, and few readers today would doubt that over the past century English translations from European literature have, at least in terms of linguistic and technical competence, got better. This revision of C. J. Hogarth's 1912 translation of *Childhood, Boyhood and Youth* aims to correct, improve and complete his version, but without destroying its essential manner. When inaccuracies have been minimized, polysyllabicity pruned, and occasional flippancies toned down, what remains is a fluent and vigorous rendering whose patina of age may be a virtue, in that it helps to transport the modern reader to the world, already quite distant and strange, of a narrator who writes in the 1850s to recount his own and other people's experiences over the preceeding quarter of a century and more. The Hogarth version is, after all, almost contemporaneous with the death of Tolstoy.

Closeness in time to Tolstoy also involves closeness to the mahogany and plush of late Victorian and Edwardian English literary styles. Hogarth's vocabulary is often too heavily Latinate to suit Tolstoy's conscious simplicity of language, and without attempting to rewrite wholesale I have in many instances replaced long words by shorter ones, Latin derivatives by Anglo-Saxon ones. The heavy pseudo-Johnsonian or Dickensian style is often used by Hogarth for a comic effect alien to Tolstoy, and I have in general reduced it. The most extreme example of caricatural exaggeration occurs in Chapters VIII–X of *Boyhood*, where the German tutor Karl Ivanych relates his life story to Nikolai Irtenyev, the 'I' of Tolstoy's book. Despite the narrator's clear statement that he is transcribing Karl Ivanych's narrative *minus* all its oddities of speech and accent, Hogarth (not alone among English translators) cannot resist the temptation to make him into a *Comic Cherman* who would not be out of place on the music-hall stage. To render this passage with an eye to farce is untrue to Tolstoy, and undermines our sympathy for a character who, despite the sentimental-melodramatic manner of his discourse, is very human.

The most undeniable gain in revising the 1912 translation is the increase in accuracy. While errors of sense and detail in Hogarth's version are in the main minor, they are extremely numerous, and they have been remedied wherever I have detected them. Progress in lexicography has been considerable in this century, and obscure, technical or obsolete terms are far more adequately handled in Russian–English dictionaries now than they were in Hogarth's time. Occasionally, where Tolstoy becomes too technical for comfort – for example in details of agriculture, horses and carriages, or in some of the narrator's more convoluted excursions into psychology and metaphysics – Hogarth omits whole sentences. This may be regarded as discretion wisely triumphing over valour, but he also exercises from time to time a minor editorial function on Tolstoy's text. Most often this involves paring away a single adjective, or a phrase (very occasionally a whole sentence) from a description. In later life Tolstoy – the Wise Old Man disparaging the follies of his artistic youth – was to describe his earlier mode of literary realism as 'the method of superfluous detail'; but translators today would be humbler than those of Hogarth's generation in deferring to the author himself as the only competent arbiter of what is and is not superfluous.

The one major omission made good in this revised version is a three-page passage in *Youth*, chapter XLIV, which was not cut by the translator, but which was absent from his Russian text (as also from the text used for the Maudes' version published in 1930 in the *World's Classics* series). The missing pages recount a visit by the narrator Irtenyev and his friends to a military barracks to see their fellow student Semyonov who has dropped out of university, got himself into trouble with the law, and finally sold himself into the army as a private soldier in order to cover his debts. Tolstoy's friend Druzhinin, to whom he sent the manuscript of *Youth* for his comments, advised him that this section was 'unprintable', and the censor Vyazemsky subsequently took the same view: the passage did not appear in print in Tolstoy's lifetime. The original manuscript, including the offending section, was unearthed by Professor M. A. Shlyapkin in 1908, and the passage published the year after Tolstoy's death, but it was not restored to the text of the novel until 1928, whence it found its way into the second volume of the authoritative Jubilee Edition in 1935.

It is not hard to see why the censor disapproved. Semyonov's behaviour would have been seen in 1856 as scandalously subversive of the rigidly stratified system of ranks which separated the various orders of the gentry from each other, and the gentry as a whole from the lower classes in Russian society: an example emphatically not to be held up for approval, let alone for emulation. The incident remains particularly interesting in that it marks the farthest extent of Irtenyev's (and, one may say, Tolstoy's) alienation from the idea of social hierarchy, and his growing disillusion with the smugly insulated world of *Childhood* and *Boyhood*. And although the action of *Youth* may be dated to the mid 1840s, the whole account of the narrator's relations with Zukhin, Operov and the other less privileged students reads like a pre-echo of the world of the *déclassé* radicals (*raznochíntsy*) soon to be explored more fully by Turgenev, Chernyshevsky and Dostoevsky in the novels they produced in the first half of the 1860s. It also perhaps prefigures in miniature the deeply critical attitudes and the harsh documentary realism of the older Tolstoy some forty years later in his *Resurrection* – the novel which brings him closest to Maxim Gorky and to the canons of Soviet literary taste.

The other changes made in this revised version are relatively minor. Russian personal names have been transliterated in accordance with more modern practice in English-speaking countries, and given a more consistent treatment, dispensing with most of the diminutives which are famously confusing to Anglophone readers. An example of the first principle above, which none the less violates the second, is the name of Nikolai Irtenyev's brother, who is now referred to as Volodya, and not (curiously) *Woloda*.

Lastly, there is the matter of censorship by translator: we tend to forget that in his own day – though far more in his later years than in the early ones to which this book belongs

– Tolstoy was regarded as a shockingly frank writer. I have been assiduous in restoring those few passages on budding sexuality which Mr Hogarth toned down, judging them unsuitable for a mixed readership in the England of 1912. (One of these passages is quoted by A. N. Wilson in his Introduction above.)

In producing this version I have worked from a 1998 reprint (Izdatyelstvo AST, Kharkov and Moscow), of the Russian text printed in Volume 1 of the edition of Tolstoy's Collected Works (*Tolstoi L.N.: Sobraniye sochinyenii v 20 tomakh*), published in Moscow by Khudozhestvennaya Literatura, 1978–9. My particular thanks are due to Professor R.F. Christian for the information he kindly provided on the circumstances surrounding the missing pages of the penultimate chapter of *Youth*.

Nigel J. Cooper

CHILDHOOD,
BOYHOOD AND
YOUTH

PART I

CHILDHOOD

I

OUR TUTOR, KARL IVANYCH

ON the 12th of August, 18– (just three days after my tenth birthday, when I had been given such wonderful presents), I was awakened at seven o'clock in the morning by Karl Ivanych slapping the wall close to my head with a fly-swat made of sugar-paper and a stick. He did this so roughly that he hit the little ikon of my patron saint suspended from the oaken back of my bed, and the dead fly fell down on my head. I peeped out from under the coverlet, steadied the still shaking ikon with my hand, flicked the dead fly on to the floor, and gazed at Karl Ivanych with sleepy, wrathful eyes. He, in a parti-coloured wadded dressing-gown fastened about the waist with a wide belt of the same material, a red knitted cap adorned with a tassel, and soft boots of goat skin, went on walking round the walls and taking aim at, and slapping, flies.

'Suppose,' I thought to myself, 'that I *am* only a small boy, yet why should he disturb me? Why does he not go killing flies around Volodya's bed? No; Volodya is older than I, and I am the youngest of the family, so he torments *me*. That is what he thinks of all day long – how to tease me. He knows very well that he has woken me up and frightened me, but he pretends not to notice it. Horrid man! And his dressing-gown and cap and tassel too – they are all of them horrid!'

While I was thus inwardly venting my wrath upon Karl Ivanych, he had passed to his own bedstead, looked at his watch (which hung suspended in a little shoe embroidered with beads), and hung up the fly-swat on a nail. Then, evidently in the most cheerful mood possible, he turned round to us.

'*Auf, Kinder, auf!... s'ist Zeit. Die Mutter ist schon im Saal*,'[1] he exclaimed in his kindly German voice. Then he crossed over to me, sat down at my feet, and took his snuff-box out of his pocket. I pretended to be asleep. Karl Ivanych took a pinch of snuff, wiped his nose, flicked his fingers, and began amusing himself by teasing me and tickling my heels as he said with a smile, '*Nun, nun, Faulenzer!*'[2]

For all my dread of being tickled, I determined not to get out of bed or to answer him, but hid my head deeper in the pillow, kicked out with all my strength, and strained every nerve to keep from laughing.

'How kind he is, and how fond of us!' I thought to myself. 'Yet to think that I could be hating him so just now!'

I felt angry both with myself and with Karl Ivanych. I wanted to laugh and to cry at the same time, for my nerves were all on edge.

'*Ach, lassen Sie, Karl Ivanych!*'[3] I exclaimed, with tears in my eyes, as I raised my head from beneath the pillows.

Karl Ivanych was taken aback. He left off tickling my feet, and asked me anxiously what the matter was. Had I had a disagreeable dream? His good German face and the sympathy with which he sought to know the cause of my tears made them flow the faster. I felt conscience-stricken, and could not understand how, only a minute ago, I had been hating Karl Ivanych, and thinking his dressing-gown and cap and tassel horrid. On the contrary, they looked eminently lovable now, and even the tassel seemed another token of his goodness. I replied that I was crying because I had had a bad dream: Mamma was dead and they were taking her away to bury her. Of course it was a mere invention, since I did not remember having dreamt anything at all that night, but the truth was that Karl Ivanych's sympathy as he tried to comfort and reassure me had gradually made me

---

1 Get up children, get up!... your mother is already in the parlour.
2 Come along now, lazy-bones!
3 Oh, leave me alone, Karl Ivanych!

believe that I *had* dreamt such a horrible dream, and so weep the more – though from a different cause to the one he imagined.

When Karl Ivanych had left me, I sat up in bed and proceeded to draw my stockings over my little feet. The tears had somewhat dried now, yet the mournful thought of the invented dream was still haunting me a little. Presently Uncle[1] Nikolai came in – a neat little man who was always grave, methodical, and respectful, as well as a great friend of Karl Ivanych's. He brought with him our clothes and boots – at least, boots for Volodya, and for myself the old detestable, be-ribanded shoes. In his presence I felt ashamed to cry, and, moreover, the morning sun was shining so gaily through the window, and Volodya, standing at the washstand as he mimicked Marya Ivanovna (my sister's governess), was laughing so loud and so long, that even the serious Nikolai – a towel over his shoulder, the soap in one hand, and the basin in the other – could not help smiling as he said, 'Will you please wash yourself, Vladimir Petrovich?' I had cheered up completely.

'*Sind Sie bald fertig?*'[2] came Karl Ivanych's voice from the schoolroom. The tone of that voice sounded stern now, and had nothing in it of the kindness which had just touched me so much. In fact, in the schoolroom Karl Ivanych was altogether a different man from what he was at other times: there he was the tutor. I washed and dressed myself hurriedly, and, a brush still in my hand as I smoothed my wet hair, answered to his call.

Karl Ivanych, with spectacles on nose and a book in his hand, was sitting, as usual, between the door and one of the windows. To the left of the door were two shelves – one of them the children's (that is to say, ours), and the other one Karl Ivanych's own. Upon ours were heaped all sorts of books – lesson books and play books – some standing up and some lying flat. The only two standing decorously against the wall were two large volumes of an *Histoire des Voyages*, in red binding;

1 This term was often applied by children to old servants in Russia.
2 Are you nearly ready?

then came books thick and thin and books large and small, as well as covers without books and books without covers, since everything got crammed up together anyhow when playtime arrived and we were told to put the 'library' (as Karl Ivanych solemnly called these shelves) in order. The collection of books on his own shelf was, if not so numerous as ours, at least more varied. Three of them in particular I remember, namely, a German pamphlet (*minus* a cover) on manuring cabbages in kitchen-gardens, a *History of the Seven Years' War* (bound in parchment and burnt at one corner), and a complete *Course of Hydrostatics*. Though Karl passed so much of his time in reading that he had injured his sight by doing so, he never read anything beyond these books and *The Northern Bee*.

Another article on Karl's shelf I remember well. This was a round piece of cardboard fastened to a wooden upright, on which its height could be adjusted by little pegs, with a sort of comic picture of a lady and a hairdresser glued to the cardboard. Karl Ivanych was very clever at fixing pieces of cardboard together, and had devised this contrivance for shielding his weak eyes from any very strong light.

I can see him before me now – the tall figure in its wadded dressing-gown and red cap (a few grey hairs visible beneath the latter) sitting beside the table; the screen with the hairdresser shading his face; one hand holding a book, and the other one resting on the arm of the chair. Before him lie his watch, with a huntsman painted on the dial, a check cotton handkerchief, a round black snuff-box, a green spectacle-case, and a pair of candle snuffers on their little tray. The neatness and orderliness of all these articles show clearly that Karl Ivanych has a clear conscience and a quiet mind.

Sometimes, when tired of running about the *salon* downstairs, I would steal on tiptoe to the schoolroom and find Karl Ivanych sitting alone in his arm-chair as, with a grave and quiet expression on his face, he perused one of his favourite books. Yet sometimes, also, there were moments when he was not reading, and when the spectacles had slipped down his large aquiline nose, and the blue, half-closed eyes and faintly smiling lips seemed to be gazing before them with a curious expression.

All would be quiet in the room – not a sound being audible save his regular breathing and the ticking of the watch with the hunter painted on the dial.

He would not see me, and I would stand at the door and think: 'Poor, poor old man! There are many of us, and we can play together and be happy, but he sits there all alone, and has nobody to be fond of him. Surely he speaks truth when he says that he is an orphan. And the story of his life, too – how terrible it is! I remember him telling it to Nikolai. How dreadful to be in his position!' Then I would feel so sorry for him that I would go to him, and take his hand, and say, '*Lieber* Karl Ivanych!' and he would be delighted whenever I spoke to him like this, and would pet me and look visibly touched.

On the second wall of the schoolroom hung some maps – mostly torn, but expertly glued together again by Karl Ivanych's hand. On the third wall (in the middle of which stood the door to the stairs) hung, on one side of the door, a couple of rulers (one of them ours – much bescratched, and the other one his – quite a new one, his own personal ruler, used more for our encouragement than for the ruling of lines), with, on the further side of the door, a blackboard on which our more serious faults were marked by little circles and our lesser faults by crosses. To the left of the blackboard was the corner in which we had to kneel when naughty.

How well I remember that corner – the shutter on the stove, the ventilator in it, and the noise which it made when turned! Sometimes I would be made to stay in that corner till my back and knees were aching all over, and I would think to myself, 'Has Karl Ivanych forgotten me? He goes on sitting quietly in his soft arm-chair and reading his *Hydrostatics*, while I——!' Then, to remind him of my presence, I would begin gently opening and closing the ventilator or scratching some plaster off the wall; but if by chance an extra large piece fell upon the floor, the fright of it was worse than any punishment. I would glance round at Karl Ivanych, but he would still be sitting there quietly, book in hand, apparently noticing nothing.

In the middle of the room stood a table, covered with a torn black oil-cloth under which the edge of the table showed through, all cut about with penknives. Round the table stood unpainted stools which, through use, had attained a high degree of polish. The fourth and last wall contained three windows, from the first of which the view was as follows. Immediately beneath it there ran a high road on which every irregularity, every pebble, every rut was known and dear to me. Beside the road stretched a row of clipped lime-trees, through which glimpses could be caught of a wattled fence, with a meadow with a barn on one side of it and a wood on the other – and a keeper's hut far off in the wood. The next window to the right overlooked the part of the terrace where the 'grown-ups' of the family used to sit before luncheon. Sometimes, when Karl Ivanych was correcting our dictations, I would look out of that window and see Mamma's dark hair and the backs of some persons with her, and hear the murmur of their talking and laughter. Then I would feel vexed that I could not be there too, and think to myself, 'When am I going to be grown up, and to have no more lessons, but sit with the people whom I love instead of sitting over these horrid dialogues?' Then my anger would change to sadness, and I would fall into such a reverie that I never even heard Karl Ivanych when he scolded me for my mistakes.

At last, on the morning of which I am speaking, Karl Ivanych took off his dressing-gown, put on his blue frockcoat with its padding and gathers on the shoulders, adjusted his tie before the looking-glass, and took us down to greet Mamma.

II

MAMMA

MAMMA was sitting in the drawing-room and pouring out tea. In one hand she was holding the tea-pot, and the other was on the tap of the samover, from which the water was overflowing the tea-pot and trickling on to the tray. Yet, though she appeared to be looking intently at what she was doing, in reality she noted neither this fact nor our entry.

Such a host of memories springs up when one attempts to resurrect in one's imagination the features of a beloved being, that one's vision perceives them as through a mist of tears – dim and blurred. Those tears are the tears of the imagination. When I try to recall Mamma as she was then, I see, true, her brown eyes, expressive always of love and kindness, the small mole on her neck below where the short hairs grow, her white embroidered collar, and the delicate, fresh hand which so often caressed me, and which I so often kissed; but her general appearance escapes me altogether.

To the left of the sofa stood an old English piano, at which my rather sallow-complexioned sister Lyuba was sitting and playing with manifest effort (for her hands were rosy from a recent washing in cold water) Clementi's 'Etudes.' Then eleven years old, she was dressed in a short gingham frock and white lace-frilled drawers, and could take her octaves only in *arpeggio*. Beside her and half turned towards her was sitting Marya Ivanovna, in a cap adorned with pink ribbons and a blue jacket. Her face was red and cross, and it assumed an expression even more severe when Karl Ivanych entered the room. Looking angrily at him without answering his bow, she went on beating time with her foot and counting, 'un, deux, trois – un, deux, trois,' more loudly and commandingly than ever.

Karl Ivanych paid no attention to this rudeness, but went, as usual, with German politeness to kiss Mamma's hand. She came to herself, shook her head as though by the movement to chase away sad thoughts from her, and gave Karl Ivanych her hand, kissing him on his wrinkled temple as he kissed her hand.

'I thank you, dear Karl Ivanych,' she said in German, and then, still using the same language, asked, 'Did the children sleep well?'

Karl Ivanych was deaf in one ear, and the added noise of the piano now prevented him from hearing anything at all. He moved nearer to the sofa, leaned one hand upon the table while standing on one leg, and lifting his cap above his head, said with a smile which in those days always seemed to me the perfection of politeness: 'You will excuse me, will you not, Natalya Nikolayevna?'

The reason for this was that, to avoid catching cold, Karl Ivanych never took off his red cap, but invariably asked permission, on entering the drawing-room, to retain it on his head.

'Yes, pray replace it, Karl Ivanych,' said Mamma rather loudly, moving towards him and raising her voice. 'But I asked you whether the children had slept well?'

Still he did not hear, but, covering his bald head again with the red cap, went on smiling more amiably than ever.

'Stop a moment, Mimi,' said Mamma (now smiling also) to Marya Ivanovna. 'It is impossible to hear anything.'

Beautiful as Mamma's face already was, when she smiled it made her so infinitely more charming, and everything around her seemed to grow brighter! If in the more painful moments of my life I could have seen that smile before my eyes, I should never have known what grief is. In my opinion, it is in the smile of a face that the essence of what we call beauty lies. If the smile heightens the charm of the face, then the face is a beautiful one. If the smile does not alter the face, then the face is an ordinary one. But if the smile spoils the face, then the face is an ugly one indeed.

Having greeted me, Mamma took my head between her hands, tilted it gently back, looked at me gravely, and said: 'You have been crying this morning?'

I did not answer. She kissed my eyes, and said again in German: 'Why did you cry?'

When talking to us with particular intimacy she always used this language, which she knew to perfection.

'I cried in my sleep, Mamma,' I replied, remembering the invented dream in all its details, and trembling involuntarily at the recollection.

Karl Ivanych confirmed my words, but said nothing as to the subject of the dream. Then, after a little conversation on the weather, in which Mimi also took part, Mamma laid six lumps of sugar on the tray for some of the more privileged servants, and crossed over to her embroidery frame, which stood near one of the windows.

'Go along to Papa now, children,' she said, 'and ask him to come to me before he goes to the threshing-floor.'

Then the music, the counting, and the wrathful looks began again, and we went off to see Papa. Passing through the room which had been known ever since Grandpapa's time as 'the pantry,' we entered the study.

III
PAPA

HE was standing near his writing-table, and pointing angrily to some envelopes, papers, and little piles of coin upon it as he addressed some heated observations to the steward, Yakov Mikhailov, who was standing in his usual place (that is to say, between the door and the barometer) and rapidly closing and unclosing the fingers of his hands which he held behind his back.

The more angry Papa grew, the more rapidly did those fingers twirl, and when Papa ceased speaking they came to rest also. Yet, as soon as ever Yakov himself began to talk, they grew extremely agitated, flying here, there, and everywhere with lightning rapidity. These movements always appeared to me an index of Yakov's secret thoughts, though his face was invariably placid, and expressive alike of dignity and submissiveness, as who should say, 'I am right, yet let it be as you wish.'

On seeing us, Papa said, 'Directly – wait a moment,' and looked towards the door as a hint for it to be shut.

'Gracious heavens! what can be the matter with you today, Yakov?' he went on with a hitch of one shoulder (a habit of his). 'This envelope here with the 800 roubles enclosed,' – Yakov adjusted his abacus to mark off '800,' and remained looking at some indefinite spot while he waited for what was to come next – 'is for expenses during my absence. Do you understand? From the mill you ought to receive 1000 roubles. Is not that so? And from the Treasury mortgage you ought to receive some 8000 roubles. From the hay – of which, according to your calculations, we shall be able to sell 7000 $poods$[1] at 45

1 The $pood$ = 36 lbs.

copecks apiece – there should come in 3000. Consequently the sum-total that you ought to have in hand soon is – how much? – 12,000 roubles. Is that right or not?'

'Just so, sir,' answered Yakov. Yet by the extreme rapidity with which his fingers were twitching I could see that he had an objection to make. Papa forestalled him:

'Well, of this money you will send 10,000 roubles to the Council for the Petrovskoye estate. As for the money already at the office,' continued Papa (Yakov abandoned the 12,000, he had registered on the abacus and marked off 21,000), 'you will remit it to me, and enter it as spent on this present date.' (Yakov ran his fingers over the abacus once more and turned it over – seeming, by his action, to imply that 12,000 roubles had been turned over in the same fashion as he had turned the tablet.) 'And this envelope with the enclosed money,' concluded Papa, 'you will deliver for me to the person to whom it is addressed.'

I was standing close to the table, and glanced at the address. It was 'To Karl Ivanych Mauer.' Perhaps Papa had an idea that I had read something which I ought not, for he touched my shoulder with his hand and made me aware, by a slight movement, that I must withdraw from the table. Not sure whether the movement was meant for a caress or a reprimand, I kissed the large, sinewy hand which rested upon my shoulder.

'Very well, sir,' said Yakov. 'And what are your orders about the accounts for the money from Khabarovka?' (Khabarovka was Mamma's property.)

'Only that it is to remain in my office, and not to be taken and used without my express instructions.'

For a second or two Yakov was silent. Then his fingers began to twitch with increased rapidity, and, changing the expression of deferential vacancy with which he had listened to his orders for one of shrewd intelligence, he drew the abacus to him and spoke.

'Will you allow me to inform you, Pyotr Alexandrych,' he said, with slow deliberation, 'that, however much you wish it, it is out of the question to repay the Council now. You enumerated some items, I think, as to what ought to come in from the mortgages, the mill, and the hay.' (He cast each of these items on to the abacus again as he spoke.) 'Yet I fear that we must have made a mistake somewhere in the accounts,' he added after a pause, and a grave look at Papa.

'How so?'

'Well, will you be good enough to look for yourself? Take the mill. The miller has been to me twice to ask for time, and he swore by the Lord Christ that he has no money whatever in hand. Why, he is here now. Would you perhaps like to speak to him yourself?'

'And what does he say?' replied Papa, showing by a movement of his head that he had no desire to have speech with the miller.

'Well, it is easy enough to guess what he says. He declares that there is no grinding to be got now, and that his last remaining money has gone to pay for the dam. What good would it do for us to turn him out? As to what you were pleased to say about the mortgage, you yourself are aware that your money there is locked up and cannot be recovered at a moment's notice. I was sending a load of flour to Ivan Afanassich today, and sent him a note as well, to which he replies that he would have been glad to oblige you, Pyotr Alexandrych, were it not that the matter is out of his hands now, and that all the circumstances show that it would take you at least two months to withdraw the money. From the hay you were pleased to say that you estimated a return of 3000 roubles?' (Here Yakov cast '3000' on his abacus, and then looked for a moment silently from the figures to Papa with a peculiar expression on his face as if to say: 'Well, surely you see for yourself how little that is? And even then we should lose if we were to sell the stuff now, for you must know that——')

It was clear that he would have had many other arguments to adduce had not Papa interrupted him.

'I cannot make any change in my arrangements,' said Papa. 'Yet if there should *really* have to be any delay in the recovery of these sums, it cannot be helped: you can take what is necessary from the Khabarovka funds.'

'Very well, sir.' The expression of Yakov's face and the way in which he twitched his fingers showed that this order had given him great satisfaction. He was a serf, and a most zealous, devoted man, but, like all good bailiffs, exacting and parsimonious to a degree in the interests of his master, though he had some queer notions of what was advantageous to his master. He was forever endeavouring to increase his master's property at the expense of his mistress's, and to prove that it would be impossible to avoid using the rents from her estates for the benefit of Petrovskoye (my father's village, and the place where we lived). This point he had now gained, and was delighted in consequence.

Papa then greeted us, and said that if we stayed much longer in the country we should become lazy boys; that we were growing quite big now, and must set about doing lessons in earnest.

'I suppose you know that I am starting for Moscow tonight?' he went on, 'and that I am going to take you with me? You will live with Grandmamma, but Mamma and the girls will remain here. You know, too, I am sure, that Mamma's one consolation will be to hear that you are doing your lessons well and pleasing everyone around you.'

The preparations which had been in progress for some days past had made us expect some unusual event, but this news left us thunderstruck. Volodya turned red, and, with a shaking voice, delivered Mamma's message to Papa.

'So this was what my dream foreboded!' I thought to myself. 'God send that there come nothing worse!' I felt terribly sorry to have to leave Mamma, but at the same time rejoiced to think that we should soon be grown up. 'If we are going today, we shall probably have no lessons to do, and that will be splendid. However, I am sorry for Karl Ivanych, for he will certainly be dismissed now. That was why that envelope had been prepared for him. I think I would almost rather stay and do lessons here than leave Mamma or hurt poor Karl Ivanych. He is miserable enough already.'

As these thoughts crossed my mind I stood looking sadly at the black bows on my shoes. After a few words to

Karl Ivanych about the depression of the barometer and an injunction to Yakov not to feed the dogs, since a farewell trial of the young hounds was to be held after dinner, Papa disappointed my hopes by sending us off to lessons – though he also consoled us by promising to take us out hunting later.

On my way upstairs I made a digression to the terrace. Near the door leading on to it Papa's favourite hound, Milka, was lying with screwed-up eyes in the sun.

'Milochka,' I cried as I caressed her and kissed her nose, 'we are going away today. Goodbye. We shall never see each other again.'

I was overcome by emotion and I burst into tears.

IV

LESSONS

KARL Ivanych was in a bad temper. This was clear from his contracted brows, and from the way in which he flung his frockcoat into a drawer, angrily donned his old dressing-gown again, and made deep dints with his nails to mark the place in the book of dialogues to which we were to learn by heart. Volodya began working diligently, but I was too distracted to do anything at all. For a long while I stared vacantly at the book of dialogues, but tears at the thought of the impending separation kept rushing to my eyes and preventing me from reading a single word. When at length the time came to repeat the dialogues to Karl Ivanych (who listened to us with narrowed eyes – a very bad sign), I had no sooner reached the place where someone asks, '*Wo kommen Sie her?*'[1] and someone else answers him, '*Ich komme vom Kaffeehaus*',[2] than I burst into tears and, for sobbing, could not pronounce, '*Haben Sie die Zeitung nicht gelesen?*'[3] at all. Next, when we came to our writing lesson, the tears kept falling from my eyes and

1 Where do you come from?
2 I come from the coffee-house.
3 Have you not read the newspaper?

making a mess on the paper, as though someone had written on wrapping-paper with water.

Karl Ivanych grew very angry. He ordered me to go down upon my knees, declared that it was all obstinacy and 'puppet-comedy playing' (a favourite expression of his) on my part, threatened me with the ruler, and commanded me to say that I was sorry. Yet for sobbing and crying I could not get a word out. At last – conscious, perhaps, that he was unjust – he departed to Nikolai's pantry, and slammed the door behind him. Nevertheless their conversation there carried to the schoolroom.

'Have you heard that the children are going to Moscow, Nikolai?' said Karl Ivanych as he entered.

'Yes, sir. I have heard.'

At this point Nikolai seemed to get up, for Karl Ivanych said, 'Sit down, Nikolai,' and then closed the door. However, I came out of my corner and crept to the door to listen.

'However much you may do for people, and however fond of them you may be, never expect any gratitude, Nikolai,' said Karl Ivanych with feeling. Nikolai, who was mending a boot by the window, nodded his head in assent.

'Twelve years have I lived in this house,' went on Karl Ivanych, lifting his eyes and his snuff-box towards the ceiling, 'and before God I can say that I have loved them, and worked for them, even more than if they had been my own children. You recollect, Nikolai, when Volodya had the fever? You recollect how, for nine days, I never closed my eyes as I sat beside his bed? Yes, at that time I was "the dear, good Karl Ivanych" – I was wanted then; but now' – and he smiled ironically – '*the children are growing up, and must go to study in earnest*. Perhaps they have not been learning anything with me, Nikolai? Eh?'

'How could they learn any more than that?' replied Nikolai, laying his awl down and pulling a piece of waxed thread through with both hands.

'No, I am wanted no longer, and am to be turned out. What good are promises and gratitude? Natalya Nikolayevna' – here he laid his hand upon his heart – 'I love and revere, but what

can *she* do here? Her will is powerless in this house.' He flung a
strip of leather on the floor with an angry gesture. 'Yet I know
who has been playing tricks here, and why I am no longer
wanted. It is because I do not flatter and toady as certain people
do. I am in the habit of speaking the truth in all places and to all
persons,' he continued proudly. 'God be with these children,
for my leaving them will benefit them little, whereas I – well,
by God's help I may be able to earn a crust of bread somewhere,
Nikolai, eh?'

Nikolai raised his head and looked at Karl Ivanych as though
to consider whether he would indeed be able to earn a crust of
bread, but he said nothing. Karl said a great deal more of
the same kind – in particular how much better his services
had been appreciated at a certain general's where he had for-
merly lived (I was upset to hear that). Likewise he spoke of
Saxony, his parents, his friend the tailor Schönheit, and so on.

I sympathised with his distress, and felt dreadfully sorry that
Papa and Karl Ivanych (both of whom I loved about equally)
had had a difference. Then I returned to my corner, crouched
down upon my heels, and fell to thinking how a reconciliation
between them might be effected.

Returning to the study, Karl Ivanych ordered me to get up
and prepare my exercise-book to write from dictation. When I
was ready he sat down with a dignified air in his arm-chair, and
in a voice which seemed to come from a profound abyss began
to dictate: '*Von al-len Lei-den-schaf-ten die grau-samste ist. Haben
Sie das geschrieben?*' He paused, slowly took a pinch of snuff,
and began again: '*Die grausamste ist die Un-dank-bar-keit*[1] – *ein
grosses U.*'

The last word written, I looked at him, for him to go on.

'*Punctum*,'[2] he concluded, with a faintly perceptible smile, as
he signed to us to hand him our copy-books.

Several times, and in several different tones, and always with
an expression of the greatest satisfaction, did he read out this

1 The cruellest of all passions is ingratitude. Have you written that? – with a
capital U.
2 Full stop.

dictum, which expressed his predominant thought at the moment. Then he set us to learn a lesson in history, and sat down near the window. His face did not look so depressed now, but, on the contrary, expressed eloquently the satisfaction of a man who had avenged himself for an injury dealt him.

By this time it was a quarter to one o'clock, but Karl Ivanych apparently had no thought of releasing us. He merely set us a new lesson to learn. My fatigue and hunger were increasing in equal proportions, so that I eagerly followed every sign of the approach of dinner. First came the housemaid with a cloth to wipe the plates. Next, the sound of crockery resounded in the dining-room as the table was moved and chairs placed round it. After that, Mimi, Lyuba, and Katya (Katya was Mimi's daughter, and twelve years old) came in from the garden, but Foka (the servant who always used to come and announce meals) was not yet to be seen. Only when he entered was it lawful to throw one's books aside and run downstairs, regardless of Karl Ivanych.

Hark! Steps resounded on the staircase, but they were not Foka's. Foka's I had learnt to study, and knew the creaking of his boots well. The door opened, and a figure quite unknown to me made its appearance.

V

A HOLY FOOL

THE man who now entered the room was about fifty years old, with a pale, attenuated face pitted with smallpox, long grey hair, and a scanty beard of a reddish hue. Likewise he was so tall that, on coming through the doorway, he was forced not only to bend his head, but to incline his whole body forward. He was dressed in something resembling a smock or a cassock that was much torn, and held in his hand a stout staff. As he entered he smote this staff upon the floor, and, contracting his brows and opening his mouth to its fullest extent, laughed in a dreadful, unnatural way. He had lost the sight of one eye, and its colourless pupil kept rolling about and imparting to his hideous face an even more repellent expression than it otherwise bore.

'Hullo, you are caught!' he exclaimed as he ran to Volodya with little short steps and, seizing him round the head, looked at it searchingly. Next he left him, went to the table, and, with a perfectly serious expression on his face, began to blow under the oil-cloth, and to make the sign of the cross over it. 'O-oh, what a pity! O-oh, how it hurts! They are angry! The little dears, fly from me!' he exclaimed in a tearful, choking voice as he gazed with emotion at Volodya and wiped away the streaming tears with his sleeve.

His voice was harsh and rough, all his movements hysterical and spasmodic, and his words devoid of sense or connection (for he used no pronouns). Yet the tone of that voice was so heartrending, and his yellow, deformed face at times so sincere and pitiful in its expression, that as one listened to him it was impossible to repress a mingled sensation of pity, fear, and grief.

This was the holy fool and pilgrim Grisha. Whence he had come, or who were his parents, or what had induced him to choose the strange life which he led, no one ever knew. All that I myself knew was that from his fifteenth year upwards he had been known as a saintly idiot who went barefooted both in winter and summer, visited monasteries, gave little ikons to anyone who cared to take them, and spoke meaningless words which some people took for prophecies; that nobody remembered him as being different; that at rare intervals he used to call at Grandmamma's house; and that by some people he was said to be the unfortunate son of rich parents and a pure, saintly soul, while others averred that he was a mere peasant and an idler.

At last the punctual and wished-for Foka arrived, and we went downstairs. Grisha followed us sobbing and continuing to talk nonsense, and knocking his staff on each step of the staircase. When we entered the drawing-room we found Papa and Mamma walking up and down arm in arm, and talking in low tones. Marya Ivanovna was sitting bolt upright in an arm-chair placed at right angles to the sofa, and exhorting in a stern but subdued voice the two girls sitting beside her. When Karl Ivanych entered the room she looked at him for a moment, and then turned her eyes away with an expression which seemed to say, 'You are beneath my notice, Karl Ivanych.' It was easy to see from the girls' eyes that they had important news to communicate to us as soon as an opportunity occurred (for to leave their seats and approach us first was contrary to Mimi's rules). It was for us to go to her and say, '*Bonjour, Mimi,*' and then click our heels; after which we should possibly be permitted to enter into conversation with the girls.

What an intolerable creature that Mimi was! One could hardly say a word in her presence without being found fault with. Also, whenever we wanted to speak in Russian, she would say, '*Parlez donc français,*'[1] as though on purpose to annoy us, while, if there was any particularly nice dish at dinner which we wished to enjoy in peace, she would keep on ejaculating, '*Mangez donc avec du pain!*'[2] or, '*Comment est-ce que vous tenez votre fourchette?*' 'What has *she* got to do with us?' I used to think to myself. 'Let her teach the girls. *We* have our Karl Ivanych.' I shared to the full his dislike of 'certain people.'

'Ask Mamma to make them take us hunting too,' Katya whispered to me as she caught me by the sleeve just when the elders of the family were making a move towards the dining-room.

'Very well, I will try.'

Grisha likewise ate in the dining-room, but at a little table apart from the rest. He never lifted his eyes from his plate, but kept on sighing and making horrible grimaces, as he muttered to himself: 'What a pity! Flown away! The dove will fly to heaven! Oh, the stone lies on the tomb!' and so forth.

Ever since the morning Mamma had been absent-minded, and Grisha's presence, words, and actions seemed to make her more so.

1 Come along, speak French.
2 Eat some bread with it.
3 How do you hold your fork?

'By the way, there is something I forgot to ask you,' she said, as she handed Papa a plate of soup.

'What is it?'

'That you will have those dreadful dogs of yours shut up. They nearly worried poor Grisha to death when he crossed the courtyard, and I am sure they will bite the children some day.'

No sooner did Grisha hear himself mentioned than he turned towards our table and began showing us his torn clothes, repeating over and over again, 'Would have let them tear me in pieces, but God would not allow! What a sin to let dogs loose – a great sin! But do not beat, master;[1] why beat! God will forgive! Times past now!'

'What does he say?' said Papa, looking at him gravely and sternly. 'I cannot understand him at all.'

'I think he is saying,' replied Mamma, 'that one of the huntsmen set the dogs on him, but that God would not allow him to be torn in pieces. Therefore he begs you not to punish the man.'

'Oh, is that it?' said Papa. 'How does he know that I intended to punish the huntsman? You know, I am not very fond of fellows like this,' he added in French, 'and this one offends me particularly. Should it ever happen that——'

'Oh, don't say so,' interrupted Mamma, as if frightened by some thought. 'How can you know what he is?'

'I think I have plenty of opportunities for studying people of his kind, since no lack of them come to see you – all of them the same sort, and probably all with the same story.'

I could see that Mamma's opinion differed from his, but that she did not mean to quarrel about it.

'Please hand me a patty,' she said to him. 'Are they good today or not?'

'Yes, I *am* angry,' he went on as he took a patty and held it where Mamma could not reach it, 'very angry at seeing supposedly reasonable and educated people let themselves be deceived,' and he struck the table with his fork.

---

1 He addressed all men as 'master.'

'I asked you to hand me a patty,' she repeated with out-stretched hand.

'And it is a good thing,' Papa continued as he put the hand aside, 'that the police run such vagabonds in. All they are good for is to play upon the nerves of certain people who are already not over-strong in that respect,' and he smiled, observing that Mamma did not like the conversation at all. However, he handed her the patty.

'All that I have to say,' she replied, 'is that one can hardly believe that a man who, though sixty years of age, goes barefooted winter and summer, and always wears chains of two *poods*' weight under his tunic, and never accepts the offers made to him to live a quiet, comfortable life – it is difficult to believe that such a man should act thus out of laziness.' Pausing a moment, she added with a sigh: 'As to predictions, *je suis payée pour y croire*.[1] I told you, I think, that Kiryusha prophesied the very day and hour of poor Papa's death?'

'Oh, what *have* you gone and done?' said Papa, smiling and putting his hand to his cheek on the side where Mimi was sitting (whenever he did this I used to look for something particularly comical from him). 'Why did you call my attention to his feet? I looked at them, and now can eat nothing more.'

The meal was nearly over, and Lyuba and Katya were winking at us, fidgeting about in their chairs, and generally showing great restlessness. The winking, of course, signified, 'Why don't you ask whether we too may go to the hunt?' I nudged Volodya with my elbow, and Volodya nudged me back, until at last he took courage, and began (at first shyly, but gradually with more assurance) to ask if, as we were going away that day, the girls too could be allowed to come and enjoy the sport. Thereupon a consultation was held among the elder folks, and eventually leave was granted – Mamma, to make things still more delightful, saying that she would come too.

1 I have good cause to believe in them.

VI
PREPARATIONS FOR THE HUNT

DURING dessert Yakov had been sent for, and orders given him to have ready the carriage, the hounds, and the saddle-horses – every detail being minutely specified, and every horse called by its own particular name. As Volodya's usual mount was lame, Papa ordered a 'hunter' to be saddled for him; which term 'hunter' sounded so strange to Mamma's ears that she imagined it to be some kind of a violent animal which would at once run away and bring about Volodya's death. Consequently, in spite of all Papa's and Volodya's assurances (the latter with remarkable bravura affirming that it was nothing, and that he liked his horse to run away with him), poor Mamma continued to exclaim that her pleasure would be quite spoilt for her.

When dinner was over, the grown-ups had coffee in the study, while we younger ones ran into the garden and went chattering and scuffling along the paths with their carpet of yellow leaves. We talked about Volodya's riding a hunter, and said what a shame it was that Lyuba could not run as fast as Katya, and what fun it would be if we could see Grisha's chains, and so forth; but of the impending separation we said not a word. Our chatter was interrupted by the sound of the trap driving up, with a house-serf boy perched on each of its springs. Behind the trap rode the huntsmen with the hounds, and they, again, were followed by the groom Ignat on the steed intended for Volodya, leading my old horse Kleper by his bridle. After running to the garden fence to get a sight of all these interesting objects, and indulging in a chorus of squealing and stamping, we rushed upstairs to dress – our one aim being to make ourselves look as much like huntsmen as possible. The obvious way to do this was to tuck one's breeches inside one's boots. We lost no time over it all, for we were in a hurry to run to the entrance steps again – there to feast our eyes upon the horses and hounds, and to have a chat with the huntsmen.

The day was exceedingly warm, while, though clouds of fantastic shape had been gathering on the horizon since morning and driving closer and closer before a light breeze across the sun, it was clear that, for all their menacing blackness, they did not really intend to gather into a thunderstorm and spoil our last day's pleasure. Moreover, towards evening some of them broke, grew pale and elongated, and sank to the horizon again, while others, just overhead, changed to the likeness of white transparent fish-scales. In the east, over Maslovka, a single lurid mass was louring, but Karl Ivanych (who always seemed to know where any cloud was going), explained that this cloud was on its way to Maslovka, that it was not going to rain, and that the weather would still continue to be fair.

In spite of his advanced years, it was in quite a sprightly manner that Foka came out to the entrance steps to give the order 'Drive up.' In fact, as he planted his legs firmly apart and took up his station between the lowest step and the spot where the coachman was to halt, his mien was that of a man who knew his duties and had no need to be reminded of them by anybody. Presently the ladies also came out, and after a little discussion as to seats and who should hold on to whom (though, to my way of thinking, there was no need to hold on), they settled themselves in the vehicle, opened their parasols, and started. As the wagonette was driving away, Mamma pointed to the hunter and asked nervously, 'Is that the horse intended for Vladimir Petrovich?' On the groom answering in the affirmative, she raised her hands in horror and turned her head away. As for myself, I was burning with impatience. Clambering on to the back of my steed (I was just tall enough to see between its ears), I proceeded to perform various evolutions in the courtyard.

'Mind you don't ride over the hounds, sir,' said one of the huntsmen.

'Never fear. It is not the first time I have been one of the party,' I retorted with dignity.

Although Volodya had plenty of pluck, he was not altogether free from apprehensions as he sat on the hunter. Indeed, he more than once asked as he patted it, 'Is he quiet?' He looked very well on horseback – almost a grown-up young man, and his tightly trousered thighs sat so well in the saddle that I envied him, since my shadow seemed to show that I could not compare with him in looks.

Presently Papa's footsteps sounded on the steps, the whipper-in collected the hounds, and the huntsmen with the borzois called them in and began to mount their steeds. Papa's horse came up in the charge of a groom, the hounds of his particular leash sprang up from their picturesque attitudes to fawn upon him, and Milka, in a collar studded with beads and a metal disc jingling at the end, came bounding joyfully from behind his heels. Whenever she came out, she would always greet the kennel dogs, sporting with some, sniffing and growling at others, and on others searching for fleas. Finally, as soon as Papa had mounted we rode away.

VII

THE HUNT

At the head of the cavalcade rode the whipper-in, nicknamed Turka, on a hook-nosed light grey horse. On his head he wore a shaggy cap, while, with a magnificent horn slung across his shoulders and a knife at his belt, he looked so cruel and inexorable that one would have thought he was going to engage in bloody strife with his fellow men rather than to hunt a small animal. Around the hind legs of his horse the hounds gambolled in a chequered, restless tangle. If one of them wished to lag behind, it was only with the greatest difficulty that it could do so, since not only had its leash-fellow also to be induced to halt, but at once one of the huntsmen would wheel round, crack his whip, and shout to the delinquent, 'Back to the pack, there!' Arrived at a gate, Papa told us and the huntsmen to continue our way along the road, and then rode off across a cornfield.

The harvest was at its height. On the further side of a large, shining, yellow stretch of corn-land lay a high purple belt of forest which always figured in my eyes as a distant, mysterious region behind which either the world ended or an uninhabited waste began. This expanse of corn-land was dotted with swathes and reapers, while along the lanes where the sickle had passed could be seen the back of a woman reaper or the swaying of the stalks as she grasped them in her fingers. In one shady corner a woman was bending over a cradle, and the whole stubble was studded with sheaves and cornflowers. In another direction peasants clad only in their shirts standing on waggons, stacking the sheaves for carrying, were covered in dust from the broken-up soil of the field. As soon as the village headman (dressed in a heavy coat thrown over his shoulders and high boots, and carrying tally-sticks in his hands) caught sight of Papa in the distance, he hastened to take off his lamb's-wool cap and, wiping his red head and beard with a towel, shouted something to the women. Papa's chestnut horse went trotting along with a prancing gait as it tossed its head and swished its thick tail to and fro to drive away the gadflies and other insects which clung thirstily to its flanks, while his two greyhounds – their tails curved like sickles – lifted their feet high and went springing gracefully over the tall stubble behind the horse's heels. Milka was always first, head down in search of the scent. The chatter of the peasants; the rumbling of horses and waggons; the joyous whistling of quails; the hum of insects as they hung suspended in motionless swarms; the smell of wormwood and straw and horses' sweat; the thousand different lights and shadows which the burning sun cast upon the yellowish-white stubble fields; the purple forest in the distance; the pale lilac clouds; the white gossamer threads which were floating in the air or resting on the stubble – all these things I observed and heard and felt to the core.

Arrived at the Kalina wood, we found the carriage awaiting us there, with, surpassing our expectations, a one-horse waggonette driven by the butler – a waggonette in which were a samovar, a tub and an ice-cream mould, and many other attractive boxes and bundles, all packed in straw! There was no mistaking these signs, for they meant that we were going to have tea, fruit, and ices in the open air. At the sight of the waggonette we gave expression to noisy delight, since to drink tea in a wood and on the grass and where none else had ever drunk tea before seemed to us a treat beyond expressing.

When Turka arrived at the little clearing where the carriage was halted he took Papa's detailed instructions as to how we were to divide ourselves and where each of us was to go (though, as a matter of fact, he never acted according to such instructions, but always followed his own inclinations). Then he unleashed the hounds, unhurriedly fastened the leashes to his saddle, remounted his horse and disappeared whistling among the young birch-trees. The liberated hounds at once expressed their satisfaction by wagging their tails and shaking themselves, and, having relieved themselves, trotted slowly off in different directions, sniffing one another and wagging their tails.

'Has anyone a pocket-handkerchief to spare?' asked Papa. I took mine from my pocket and offered it to him.

'Very well. Fasten it to this grey dog here.'

'Zhiran?' I asked, with the air of a connoisseur.

'Yes. Then run him along the road with you. When you come to a little clearing in the wood stop and look about you, and don't come back to me without a hare.'

Accordingly I tied my handkerchief round Zhiran's shaggy neck, and set off running at full speed towards the appointed spot, Papa laughing as he shouted after me, 'Hurry up, hurry up, or you'll be late!'

Every now and then Zhiran kept stopping, pricking up his ears, and listening to the hallooing of the huntsmen. Whenever he did this I was not strong enough to move him, and could do no more than shout, 'Tally-ho! Tally-ho!' Then he would set off so fast that I could not restrain him, and I encountered more than one fall before we reached our destination. Selecting there a level, shady spot near the roots of a great oak-tree, I lay down on the turf, made Zhiran crouch beside me, and waited. As usual, my imagination far outstripped reality. I fancied that I was pursuing at least my third hare when, as a matter of fact, the first hound was only just giving tongue in the wood. Presently, however, Turka's voice began to sound through the wood in ever louder and more excited tones, the baying of a hound came more and more frequently, and then another deep throat, and then a third, and then a fourth, joined in. Their voices now fell silent, now broke in one on another . . . The sounds gradually grew louder and more sustained, finally blending to form a single, ringing, uproarious din. 'The island was loud with voices and the hounds seethed like boiling pitch.'

On hearing this, I was rooted to the spot. I fastened my gaze on the edge of the forest. My lips parted themselves as though smiling, the perspiration poured from me in streams, and, in spite of the tickling sensation caused by the drops as they trickled over my chin, I never thought of wiping them away. I felt that a great crisis was approaching. The tension was too unnatural to last. Soon the hounds came tearing along the edge of the wood, and then – behold, they were racing away from me again, and of hares there was not a sign to be seen! I looked in every direction and Zhiran did the same – pulling at his leash at first, and yelping. Then he lay down again by my side, rested his muzzle on my knees, and calmed down.

Among the naked roots of the oak-tree under which I was sitting I could see countless ants swarming over the parched grey earth and winding among the acorns, withered oak-leaves, dry twigs, yellow-green moss, and slender, scanty blades of grass. In serried files they kept pressing forward on the level tracks they had made for themselves – some carrying burdens, some not. I took a piece of twig and barred their way. Instantly it was curious to see how some of them, scorning the danger, made light of the obstacle by creeping underneath, or by climbing over it. A few, however, there were (especially those weighted with loads) who were nonplussed what to do. They either halted and searched for a way round, or returned whence they had come, or climbed up the twig, with the evident intention of reaching my hand and going up the sleeve of my jacket. From this interesting spectacle my attention was distracted by the yellow wings of a butterfly which was flutter-ing alluringly before me. Yet I had scarcely noticed it before it flew away to a little distance and, circling over some half-faded blossoms of wild white clover, settled on one of them. Whether it was the sun's warmth that delighted it, or whether it was busy sucking nectar from the flower, at all events it seemed thoroughly comfortable. It scarcely moved its wings at all, and pressed itself down into the clover until it became quite still. I sat with my chin on my hands and watched it with intense interest.

Suddenly Zhiran sprang up with a whine and gave me such a violent jerk that I nearly rolled over. I looked round. At the edge of the wood a hare had just come into view, with one ear bent down and the other one sharply pricked. The blood rushed to my head, and I forgot everything else as I shouted, slipped the dog, and rushed towards the spot. Yet hardly had I done so, than I began to regret it. The hare stopped, made a bound, and was lost to view.

How ashamed I felt when at that moment Turka stepped from the undergrowth (he had been following the hounds as they ran along the edges of the wood)! He had seen my mistake (which had consisted in my not biding my time), and now threw me a contemptuous look as he said, 'Ah, master!' And you should have heard the tone in which he said it! It would have been a relief to me if he had then and there suspended me to his saddle instead of the hare.

For a while I could only stand miserably where I was, without attempting to recall the dog, and exclaim as I slapped my knees, 'Good heavens! What have I done!'

I could hear the hounds retreating into the distance, and baying along the further side of the wood as they pursued and took a hare, while Turka summoned them back with blasts on his tremendous horn: yet I did not stir from the spot.

VIII
WE PLAY GAMES

THE hunt was over. A rug had been spread in the shade of some young birch-trees, and the whole party was disposed on it in a circle. The butler, Gavrilo, had stamped down the lush, green surrounding grass, wiped the plates in readiness, and unpacked from a box a quantity of plums and peaches wrapped in leaves. Through the green branches of the young birch-trees the sun glittered and threw little glancing balls of light upon the pattern of the rug, my legs, and the bald, perspiring head of

Gavrilo. A soft breeze played in the leaves of the trees above us, and, breathing softly upon my hair and heated face, refreshed me beyond measure.

When we had finished our share of the fruit and ices, there was nothing to be gained by sitting on the rug, so, despite the oblique, scorching rays of the sun, we rose and proceeded to play.

'Well, what shall it be?' said Lyuba, screwing up her eyes in the sunlight and skipping about the grass. 'Suppose we play Robinson?'

'No, that's a tiresome game,' objected Volodya, stretching himself lazily on the turf and chewing some leaves. 'Always Robinson! If you want to play at something, play at building a summer-house.'

Volodya was giving himself tremendous airs. Probably he was proud of having ridden the hunter, and so pretended to be very tired. Perhaps, also, he already had too much hard-headedness and too little imagination fully to enjoy the game of Robinson. It was a game which consisted of performing various scenes from *The Swiss Family Robinson*, a book which we had recently been reading.

'Come on please . . . Why not try and please *us* this time?' the girls answered. 'You can be Charles or Ernest or the father, whichever you like best,' added Katya as she tried to raise him from the ground by pulling at his sleeve.

'No, I'm not going to; it's a tiresome game,' said Volodya again, stretching and smiling as if secretly pleased.

'It would be better to sit at home than not to play at *anything*,' murmured Lyuba, tearfully. She was a great weeper.

'Well, come on, then. Only, please *don't* cry; I can't stand that sort of thing.'

Volodya's condescension gave us little satisfaction. On the contrary, his lazy, bored expression took away all the fun of the game. When we sat on the ground and imagined that we were sitting in a boat fishing, and rowing with all our might, Volodya persisted in sitting with folded arms in anything but a fisherman's posture. I commented upon it, but he replied that, whether we waved our arms or not, we should neither gain nor lose ground – certainly not advance at all, and I was forced to agree with him. Again, when I pretended to go out hunting, and, with a stick over my shoulder, set off into the wood, Volodya only lay down on his back with his hands under his head, and said that he would pretend to be going with me. Such behaviour and speeches cooled our ardour for the game and were very disagreeable – the more so since it was impossible not to confess to oneself that Volodya was right.

I myself knew that it was not only impossible to kill birds with a stick, but to shoot at all with such a weapon. It was just a game. And if we were once to begin reasoning thus, it would become equally impossible for us to go for drives on chairs. I think that even Volodya himself cannot at that moment have forgotten how, in the long winter evenings, we used to cover an arm-chair with a shawl and make a carriage of it – one of us being the coachman, another one the footman, the two girls the passengers, and three other chairs the trio of horses abreast – and off we went. With what adventures we used to meet on the way! How gaily and quickly those long winter evenings used to pass! If we were always to judge from reality, there would be no games; but if there were no games, what else would there be left to do?

IX

SOMETHING RESEMBLING FIRST LOVE

PRETENDING to gather some 'American fruit' from a tree, Lyuba suddenly plucked a leaf upon which was a huge caterpillar, and throwing the insect with horror to the ground, lifted her hands and sprang away as though afraid it would spit at her. The game stopped, and we crowded our heads together as we stooped to look at this curiosity.

I peeped over Katya's shoulder as she was trying to pick up the caterpillar by placing another leaf in its way. I had observed before that many girls had a way of twitching their shoulders whenever they were trying to adjust a low-necked dress which had slipped out of place, and that Mimi always grew angry on witnessing this manœuvre and declared, '*C'est un geste de femme*

de chambre.'[1] As Katya bent over the caterpillar she made that
very movement, while at the same instant the breeze lifted the
kerchief on her white neck. Her shoulder-strap was at that
moment within two inches of my lips. I was no longer looking
at the caterpillar: I gazed and gazed, then with all my strength
kissed Katya's shoulder. She did not turn round, but I saw that
she blushed to her very ears. Volodya remarked scornfully,
without raising his head, 'What spooniness!' I felt the tears
rising to my eyes.

I could not take my gaze from Katya. I had long been used to
her fair, fresh little face, and had always been fond of her, but
now I looked at her more closely, and felt more fond of her,
than I had ever done or felt before. When we returned to the
grown-ups, Papa informed us, to our great joy, that, at
Mamma's entreaties, our departure was to be postponed until
the following morning.

We rode home beside the waggonette – Volodya and
I galloping near it, and vying with one another in our exhibition
of horsemanship and daring. My shadow looked longer now
than it had done before, and from that I judged that I had grown
into rather a fine rider. Yet my complacency was soon marred by
an unfortunate occurrence. Desiring to captivate the audience in
the carriage, I dropped a little behind. Then with whip and heels
I urged my steed forward, and at the same time assumed a natural,
graceful attitude, with the intention of shooting past the carriage
on the side on which Katya was seated. My only doubt was
whether to gallop past in silence, or to halloo as I did so. In the
event, my infernal horse stopped so abruptly when just level with
the carriage horses that I was pitched forward out of the saddle on
to its neck and very nearly tumbled off.

X

WHAT SORT OF MAN WAS MY FATHER?

PAPA was a gentleman of the last century, with all the discreetly
chivalrous character, enterprise, self-reliance, and gallantry of
the youth of that time. Upon the men of the present day

1 It's a chambermaid's trick.

he looked with a contempt arising partly from inborn pride and partly from a secret feeling of vexation that, in this age of ours, he could no longer enjoy the influence and success which had been his in youth. His two principal passions were gambling and gallantry, and he had won or lost, in the course of his career, several millions of roubles, and had had relations with innumerable women of all classes.

Tall and of imposing figure, he walked with a curiously quick, mincing gait, and had a habit of hitching one of his shoulders. His eyes were small and perpetually twinkling, his nose large and aquiline, his lips irregular and rather oddly (though pleasantly) shaped, his articulation slightly defective and lisping, and his head quite bald. Such was my father's exterior from the days of my earliest recollection. It was an exterior which not only brought him success and made him a man *à bonnes fortunes,*[1] but one which pleased people of all ranks and stations. Especially did it please those whom he desired to please.

At all junctures he knew how to take the lead, for, though not deriving from the highest circles of society, he had always mixed with them, and knew how to win their respect. He understood to the most precise degree that measure of pride and self-confidence which, without giving offence, maintains a man in the opinion of the world. He had much originality, as well as the ability to use it in such a way that it benefited him as much as actual breeding or fortune could have done. Nothing in the universe could surprise him, and in whatever dazzling social situation he might find himself, he seemed born to it. He understood so perfectly how to make both himself and others forget and keep at a distance the dark side of life which we all experience, with its petty troubles and vicissitudes, that it was impossible not to envy him. He was a connoisseur in everything which could give ease and pleasure, as well as knowing how to make use of such knowledge. His chief delight lay in the brilliant connections which he had formed through my mother's family or through friends of his youth, and he was secretly jealous of them for having risen to a higher rank than

1 Lady-killer.

himself – anyone, that is to say, of a rank higher than a retired lieutenant of the Guards. Moreover, like all ex-officers, he had no talent for dressing himself in the prevailing fashion, though he attired himself both originally and artistically – his invariable wear being light, loose-fitting suits, very fine shirts, and large collars and cuffs. Everything seemed to suit his upright figure, his bald head and quiet, assured air. He was sensitive to the pitch of sentimentality, and, when reading a pathetic passage, his voice would begin to tremble and the tears to come into his eyes, until he had to lay the book aside in vexation. He was fond of music, and could accompany himself on the piano as he sang the love-songs of his friend A—— or gipsy songs or themes from operas; but he had no love for serious music, and would frankly flout received opinion by declaring that, whereas Beethoven's sonatas wearied him and sent him to sleep, his ideal of beauty was 'Do not wake me, a young girl' as Semyonova sang it, or 'Not alone' as the gipsy girl Tanyusha rendered that ditty. His nature was essentially one of those which require an audience for their good deeds, and consider good only that which the public declares to be so. God only knows whether he had any moral convictions. His life was so full of amusement that probably he never had time to form any, and was too successful ever to feel the lack of them.

As he grew to old age he looked at things always from a fixed point of view, and cultivated fixed rules – but only so long as that point or those rules coincided with practicality. The mode of life which offered him some passing degree of interest or pleasure – that, in his opinion, was the right one and the only one that men ought to affect. He had great fluency of argument; and this, I think, increased the adaptability of his principles and enabled him to speak of one and the same act, now as an endearing prank, and now, as a piece of abject villainy.

XI
IN THE DRAWING-ROOM AND THE STUDY

TWILIGHT had set in when we reached home. Mamma sat down to the piano, and we to the round table, there to paint and draw in colours and pencil. Though I had only one cake of colour, and it was blue, I determined to draw a picture of the hunt. In exceedingly vivid fashion I painted a blue boy on a blue horse, and – but here I stopped, for I was uncertain whether it was possible also to paint a blue *hare*. I ran to the study to consult Papa, and as he was busy reading he never lifted his eyes from his book when I asked, 'Can there be blue hares?' but at once replied, 'There can, my boy, there can.' Returning to the round table I painted in my blue hare, but subsequently thought it better to change it into a blue bush. Yet the blue bush did not wholly please me, so I changed it into a tree, and then the tree into a rick and the rick into a cloud, until, the whole paper having now become one blur of blue, I tore it angrily in pieces, and went off to meditate in the large high-backed arm-chair.

Mamma was playing Field's second concerto. Field had been her master. As I dozed, the music brought up before my imagination a kind of luminosity, with transparent shapes of memory. She began to play the 'Sonate Pathétique' of Beethoven, and my memories turned sad, dark and oppressive. Mamma often played those two pieces, and therefore I well recollect the feelings they awakened in me. Those feelings were like reminiscences – but of what? Somehow I seemed to remember something which had never been.

Opposite to me was the study door, and presently I saw Yakov enter it, accompanied by several bearded men in *kaftans*. Then the door shut again.

'Now they are going to begin some business or other,' I thought. I believed the affairs transacted in that study to be the most important ones on earth. This opinion was confirmed by the fact that people only approached the door of that room on tiptoe and speaking in whispers. Presently Papa's resonant voice sounded within, and I also scented cigar smoke – for some reason always a very attractive thing to me. As I dozed, I suddenly heard a creaking of boots that I knew in the pantry, and, sure enough, saw Karl Ivanych go on tiptoe, and with a depressed but resolute expression on his face and some papers in his hand, to the study door and knock softly. He was admitted, and then the door shut again behind him.

'I hope nothing dreadful is going to happen,' I mused. 'Karl Ivanych is angry, and might be capable of anything——' and again I dozed off.

However nothing *did* happen. An hour later I was disturbed by the same creaking of boots, and saw Karl Ivanych come out, and disappear up the stairs, wiping away a few tears from his cheeks with his pocket-handkerchief as he went and muttering something between his teeth. Papa came out behind him, and turned aside into the drawing-room.

'Do you know what I have just decided to do?' he asked gaily as he laid a hand upon Mamma's shoulder.

'What, my love?'

'To take Karl Ivanych with the children. There will be room enough for him in the britzka. They are used to him, and he seems greatly attached to them. Seven hundred roubles a year cannot make much difference to us, *et puis au fond c'est un très bon diable.*'[1] I could not understand why Papa should speak of him so disrespectfully.

'I am delighted,' said Mamma, 'and as much for the children's sake as his own. He is a worthy old man.'

'I wish you could have seen how moved he was when I told him that he might look upon the 500 roubles as a present! But the most amusing thing of all is this account which he has just handed me. It is worth seeing,' and with a smile Papa gave Mamma a paper inscribed in Karl Ivanych's handwriting. 'Is it not capital?' he concluded.

The contents of the paper were as follows:[2]

'For the children two fishing rod – 70 copeck.
Coloured paper, gold border, gloo and dummy for making box, as presents – 6r.55c.
Book and bow, present for children – 8r.16c.

---

1 And then he is not such a bad fellow at heart.
2 The joke of this bill consists chiefly in its being written in very bad Russian, with continual mistakes as to plural and singular, prepositions, etc.

Trousers for Nikolai – 4r. Promissed by Pyotr
Alexandrovych from Moscow in the year 18.., a gold
watch, price 140 roubles.

Total due to receive Karl Mauer, in addition to salary – 159
roubles and 79 copecks.

If people were to judge only by this account (in which Karl
Ivanych demanded repayment of all the money he had spent on
presents, as well as the value of a present promised to himself),
they would take him to have been a callous, mercenary egotist:
yet they would be wrong.

It appears that he had entered the study with the paper in his
hand and a set speech in his head, for the purpose of declaiming
eloquently to Papa on the subject of the wrongs which he
believed himself to have suffered in our house, but that, as
soon as ever he began to speak in that touching voice and with
the expressive intonations which he used in dictating to us, his
eloquence wrought upon himself more than upon Papa; with
the result that, when he came to the point where he had to say,
'however sad it will be for me to part with the children,' he lost
his self-command utterly, his voice became choked, and he was
obliged to draw his chequered pocket-handkerchief from his
pocket.

'Yes, Pyotr Alexandrovych,' he said, weeping (this formed
no part of the prepared speech), 'I am grown so used to the
children that I cannot think what I should do without them.
I would rather serve you without salary than not at all,' and
with one hand he wiped his eyes, while with the other he
presented his bill.

Although I am convinced that at that moment Karl Ivanych
was speaking with absolute sincerity (for I know how good
his heart was), I confess that never to this day have I been
able quite to understand how he reconciled his words with
the bill.

'Well, if the idea of leaving us grieves you, you may be sure
that the idea of dismissing you grieves me even more,' said Papa,
patting him on the shoulder. Then, after a pause, he added, 'But
I have changed my mind, and you shall not leave us.'

Just before supper Grisha entered the room. Ever since he had entered our house he had never ceased to sigh and weep – a portent, according to those who believed in his prophetic powers, that misfortune was impending for the household. He had now come to take leave of us, for tomorrow (so he said) he must be moving on. I winked at Volodya, and moved towards the door.

'What is it?' he said.

'If you want to see Grisha's chains we must go upstairs at once to the men-servants' quarters. Grisha is to sleep in the second room, so we can sit in the store-room and see everything.'

'Fine! Wait here, and I'll call the girls.'

The girls ran out at once, and we ascended the stairs, though the question as to which of us should first enter the store-room gave us some little trouble. Then we settled down to wait.

XII
GRISHA

WE all felt a little uneasy in the darkness, so we pressed close to one another and said nothing. Before long Grisha arrived with his soft tread, carrying in one hand his staff and in the other a tallow candle set in a brass candlestick. We scarcely ventured to breathe.

'Lord Jesus Christ! Holy Mother of God! Father, Son, and Holy Ghost!' he kept repeating, drawing in his breath and speaking with the different intonations and abbreviations which gradually become peculiar to those accustomed to pronounce the words with great frequency.

Still praying, he placed his staff in a corner and inspected the bed; after which he began to undress. Unfastening his old black girdle, he slowly divested himself of his torn nankeen *kaftan*, and deposited it carefully on the back of a chair. His face had now lost its usual disquietude and obtuseness. On the contrary, it had in it something composed, thoughtful, and even impressive, while all his movements were deliberate and thoughtful.

He lay down quietly in his shirt and undergarment on the bed, made the sign of the cross towards every side of him, and adjusted his chains beneath his shirt – an operation which, as we could see from his face, occasioned him considerable effort. He sat for a while, looking gravely at his ragged shirt, then rose and taking the candle, lifted it towards the glass case where there were several irons. That done, he made the sign of the cross again, and turned the candle upside down. It went out with a hissing noise.

Through the window (which overlooked the wood) the moon, nearly full, was shining in such a way that one side of the tall white figure of the holy fool stood out in the pale, silvery moonlight, while the other side was lost in the dark shadow which covered the floor, walls, and ceiling. In the courtyard the watchman was tapping at intervals upon his iron sheet.

For a while Grisha stood silently before the images breathing heavily, with his large hands pressed to his breast and his head bowed. Then with difficulty he knelt down and began to pray.

At first he softly recited some well-known prayers, and only accented a word here and there. Next, he repeated the same prayers, but louder and with increased animation. Then he began to pray in his own words, with an evident effort to pronounce them in the Old Church Slavonic manner. Though disconnected, his prayers were very touching. He prayed for all his benefactors (so he called everyone who had received him hospitably), with, among them, Mamma and ourselves. He prayed for himself, and besought God to forgive him his grievous sins, in addition repeating, 'God forgive also my enemies!' Then, moaning with the effort, repeating the same words over and over again, he rose from his knees – only to fall to the floor. At last he regained his feet, despite the weight of the chains, which rattled loudly whenever they struck the floor.

Volodya pinched me painfully in the leg, but I took no notice of that (except that I involuntarily rubbed the place with my hand), as I observed with a feeling of childish astonishment, pity, and respect the words and gestures of Grisha. Instead of the laughter and amusement which I had expected on entering the store-room, I felt shaken and overcome.

Grisha continued for some time in this state of religious ecstasy as he improvised prayers. Now he repeated again and yet again, 'Lord, have mercy upon me!' each time pronouncing the words with added earnestness and emphasis. Now he said several times over: 'Forgive me, O Lord, instruct me how to live, instruct me how to live, O Lord,' with such depth of expression that he might have been expecting an immediate answer to his petition, and then fell to sobbing and moaning once more. Finally, he rose on his knees again, folded his arms upon his breast, and was silent.

I ventured to put my head round the door (holding my breath as I did so), but Grisha still made no movement except for the heavy sighs which heaved his breast. In the moonlight I could see a tear glistening on the white patch of his blind eye.

'Thy will be done!' he exclaimed suddenly, with an inimitable expression, as, prostrating himself with his forehead on the floor, he fell to sobbing like a child.

Much sand has run out since then, many recollections of the past have faded from my memory or become blurred in indistinct visions, and poor Grisha himself has long since reached the end of his pilgrimage; but the impression which he produced upon me and the feelings which he aroused in my breast will never leave my mind.

O truly Christian Grisha, your faith was so strong that you could feel the nearness of God; your love so great that the words fell of themselves from your lips. You had no reason to submit them to reason. And what lofty praise you offered to his greatness when, lacking more words, you fell to the ground in tears!

Nevertheless the sense of awe with which I had listened to Grisha could not last for ever. I had now satisfied my curiosity, and, my legs being numbed with sitting in one position so long, I desired to join in the whispering and commotion which I could hear going on in the dark store-room behind me. Someone took my hand and whispered, 'Whose hand is this?' Despite the darkness, I knew by the touch and the low voice in my ear that it was Katya. Almost involuntarily, I took hold of her bare elbow and pressed my lips to it. I suppose Katya must have been surprised, for she withdrew her arm and, in doing so, pushed a broken chair which was standing near. Grisha lifted his head, looked quietly about him, and, muttering a prayer, rose and made the sign of the cross towards each of the four corners of the room. Whispering to one another, we noisily scampered from the store-room.

XIII
NATALYA SAVISHNA

In the middle of the last century there used to run about the homesteads of the village of Khabarovka a girl called Natashka. She always wore a homespun linen dress, went barefooted, and was rosy-cheeked, plump, and gay. It was at the request and entreaties of her father, the clarinet player Savva, that my grandfather had 'taken her upstairs' – that is to say, made her one of his wife's female servants. As chambermaid, Natashka so distinguished herself by her zeal and amiable temper that when Mamma arrived as a baby and required a nurse Natashka was honoured with the charge of her. In this new office the girl earned still further praises and rewards for her activity, trust-worthiness, and devotion to her young mistress. Soon, how-ever, the powdered head and buckled shoes of the young and active footman Foka (who had frequent opportunities of court-ing her, since they were in the same service) captivated her unsophisticated but loving heart. At last she ventured to go and ask my grandfather if she might marry Foka, but her master took the request as proof of ingratitude, flew into a passion, and punished poor Natashka by exiling her to a cattle farm which he owned in a remote village of the steppes. At length, when she had been gone six months and nobody could be found to replace her, she was recalled to her former duties. Returning in her coarse linen dress from exile, she fell at Grandpapa's feet, and besought him to restore her his favour and kindness, and to forget the folly of which she had been guilty – folly which, she swore, should never recur again. And she kept her word.

From that time forth she called herself, not Natashka, but Natalya Savishna, and took to wearing a cap like a married woman. All the love in her heart was now bestowed upon her young lady.

When Mamma had a governess appointed for her education, Natalya was awarded the keys as housekeeper, and henceforth had the linen and provisions under her care. These new duties she fulfilled with equal fidelity and zeal. She lived only for her master's advantage. Everything in which she could detect fraud, damage, or waste she endeavoured to remedy to the best of her power.

When Mamma married and wished in some way to reward Natalya Savishna for her twenty years of care and labour, she sent for her and, voicing in the tenderest terms her attachment and love, presented her with a stamped charter of her freedom, telling her at the same time that, whether she continued to serve in the household or not, she should always receive an annual pension of 300 roubles. Natalya Savishna listened in silence to this. Then, taking the document in her hands and regarding it with a frown, she muttered something between her teeth, and darted from the room, slamming the door behind her. Not understanding the reason for such strange conduct, Mamma followed her presently to her room, and found her sitting with streaming eyes on her trunk, crushing her pocket-handkerchief between her fingers, and looking mournfully at the remains of the letter of enfranchisement, which was lying torn to pieces on the floor.

'What is the matter, dearest Natalya Savishna?' said Mamma, taking her hand.

'Nothing, ma'am,' she replied; 'only – only I must have displeased you somehow, since you wish to dismiss me from the house. Well, I will go.'

She withdrew her hand and, with difficulty restraining her tears, rose to leave the room, but Mamma stopped her, and they wept a while in one another's arms.

Ever since I can remember anything I can remember Natalya Savishna and her love and tenderness; yet only now have I learnt to appreciate them at their full value. In early days it never occurred to me to think what a rare and wonderful being this old domestic was. Not only did she never talk, but she seemed never even to *think*, of herself. Her whole life was compounded of love and self-sacrifice. Yet so used was I to her affection and singleness of heart that I could not picture things otherwise. I never thought of being grateful to her, or of asking myself, 'Is she happy? Is she contented?'

Often on some pressing pretext or other I would leave my lessons and run to her room, where, sitting down, I would begin to muse aloud as though she were not there. She was forever busy knitting a stocking, or tidying the shelves which lined her room, or making a list of linen, so that she took no heed of the nonsense which I talked – how that I meant to become a general, to marry a beautiful woman, to buy a chest-nut horse, to build myself a house of glass, to invite Karl Ivanych's relatives to come and visit me from Saxony, and so forth; to all of which she would only reply, 'Yes, my love, yes.' Then, on my rising and preparing to go, she would open a blue trunk which had pasted on the inside of its lid – I can see them now – a coloured picture of a hussar which had once adorned a pomade bottle and a sketch made by Volodya, and take from it an aromatic pastille, which she would light and wave about in the air for my benefit, saying:

'This, dear, is one of the Ochakov pastilles which your late grandfather (now in Heaven) brought back from fighting against the Turks.' Then she would add with a sigh: 'But this is nearly the last one.'

The trunks which filled her room seemed to contain almost everything in the world. Whenever anything was wanted, people said, 'Oh, go and ask Natalya Savishna for it,' and, sure enough, it was seldom that after some little rummaging she did not produce the object required and say, 'What a good thing that I put it by!' Her trunks contained thousands of things which nobody in the house but herself would have known or cared about.

Once I lost my temper with her. This was how it happened. One day after luncheon I poured myself out a glass of *kvass*, and then dropped the decanter, and so stained the tablecloth.

'Go and call Natalya Savishna, that she may come and see what her darling has done,' said Mamma.

Natalya Savishna arrived, and shook her head at me when she saw the damage I had done; but Mamma whispered something in her ear, and she threw a threatening look at me, and left the room.

I was just skipping away after lunch into the drawing-room, in the sprightliest mood possible, when Natalya Savishna darted out upon me from behind the door with the tablecloth in her hand, and, catching hold of me, rubbed my face hard with the wet part of it, repeating, 'Don't thou go spoiling tablecloths any more, don't thou go spoiling tablecloths any more!'

I was so offended that I roared with temper.

'What?' I said to myself as I paced the drawing-room choking with tears. 'To think that Natalya Savishna – just plain Natalya – should say "*thou*" to me and hit me in the face with a wet tablecloth as though I were a mere serf-boy! It is abominable!'

Seeing my fury, Natalya Savishna ran off, while I continued to strut about and plan how to punish the impudent Natalya for her offence. Yet not more than a few moments had passed when Natalya Savishna returned and, stealing to my side, began to admonish me.

'Hush, then, my love. Do not cry. Forgive me, fool that I am. It was wrong of me. You *will* pardon me, my darling, will you not? Here's something for you,' and she took from under her shawl a *cornet* of red paper containing two caramels and a grape, and offered it me with a trembling hand. I could not look the kind old woman in the face, but, turning aside, took the present, while my tears flowed the faster – though from love and shame now, not from anger.

XIV

THE PARTING

ON the day after the events described, the barouche and the britzka drew up to the door towards noon. Nikolai, dressed for the journey, with his breeches tucked into his boots and an old overcoat belted tightly about him with a girdle, got into the cart and arranged greatcoats and cushions under the seat.

When he thought that they were piled too high he sat down on them, and by bouncing up and down succeeded in flattening them.

'For mercy's sake, Nikolai Dmitrich, could you not get master's dressing-case in with your things?' said Papa's valet, poking his head out of the carriage. 'It won't take up much room.'

'You should have told me before, Mikhei Ivanych,' answered Nikolai snappishly as he hurled a bundle with all his might to the floor of the cart. 'Good gracious! Why, when my head is going round like a whirlpool, there you come along with your dressing-cases!' and he lifted his cap to wipe away the large drops of perspiration from his sunburnt brow.

Men-servants, bareheaded, in long coats, *kaftans* or simple shirts, women clad in coarse linen frocks and wearing striped kerchiefs, with babies in their arms, and barefooted little ones – crowded round the entrance steps. All were chattering among themselves as they stared at the carriages. One of the postillions, a bent old man dressed in a winter cap and cloth coat, took hold of the pole of the carriage and tried it carefully, while the other postillion (a young man in a white blouse with red calico gussets on the sleeves and a black lamb's-wool cap which he kept cocking first on one side and then on the other as he scratched his fair, curly hair) laid his overcoat upon the box, slung the reins over it, and cracked his thonged whip as he looked now at his boots and now at the coachmen where they stood greasing the wheels of the cart – one man straining to lift up each wheel in turn and the other, bent over the wheel, carefully greasing the axle and hub – and so as not to waste any surplus grease, smearing it on the rim below. Tired posthorses of various hues stood lashing away flies with their tails near the fence – some stamping their great shaggy legs, blinking their eyes, and dozing, some rubbing wearily against their neighbours, or cropping the leaves and stalks of coarse dark-green fern which grew near the entrance-porch. A number of borzoi dogs were lying panting in the sun, while others were slinking under the vehicles to lick the grease from the axles. The air was filled with a sort of dusty mist, and the horizon was lilac-grey in colour, though no clouds were to be seen. A strong wind from the west was raising columns of dust from the roads and fields, shaking the poplars and birch-trees in the garden, and whirling their yellow leaves away. I myself was sitting at a window and waiting impatiently for these various preparations to come to an end.

When we were all sitting together by the round table in the drawing-room, to pass the last few moments *en famille*, it never occurred to me that a sad moment was impending. On the contrary, the most trivial thoughts were filling my brain. Which driver was going to drive the carriage and which the cart? Which of us would sit with Papa, and which with Karl Ivanych? Why must I be kept forever muffled up in a scarf and wadded coat?

'Am I so delicate? Am I likely to be frozen?' I thought to myself. 'I wish it would all come to an end, and we could take our seats and start.'

'To whom shall I give the list of the children's linen?' asked Natalya Savishna of Mamma as she entered the room with a list in her hand and her eyes red with weeping.

'Give it to Nikolai, and then return to say goodbye to the children,' replied Mamma.

The old woman seemed about to say something more, but suddenly stopped short, covered her face with her handkerchief, and with a wave of her hand left the room. Something seemed to prick at my heart when I saw that gesture of hers, but impatience to be off soon drowned all other feeling, and I continued to listen indifferently to Papa and Mamma as they talked together. They were discussing subjects which evidently interested neither of them. What must be bought for the house? What would Princess Sophie or Madame Julie say? Would the roads be good?

Foka entered, and in the same tone and with the same air as he announced dinner said, 'The horses are ready.' I saw Mamma tremble and turn pale at the announcement, just as though it were something unexpected.

Next, Foka was ordered to shut all the doors of the room. This amused me highly. As though we needed to be concealed from someone! When everyone else was seated, Foka sat down on the edge of a chair. Scarcely, however, had he done so when the door creaked and everyone looked that way. Natalya Savishna entered hastily, and, without raising her eyes, sat down near the door on the same chair as Foka. I can see them before me now – Foka's bald head and wrinkled, set face, and, beside him, a bent, kind figure in a cap from beneath which a few grey hairs showed. The pair huddled together on the one chair, both looking distinctly uncomfortable.

I continued unconcerned and impatient. In fact, the ten seconds during which we sat there with closed doors seemed to me an hour. At last everyone rose, made the sign of the cross, and began to say goodbye. Papa embraced Mamma, and kissed her several times.

'Do not upset yourself, my dear,' he said presently. 'We are not parting for ever.'

'No, but it is – so – so sad!' replied Mamma, her voice trembling with emotion.

When I heard that faltering voice, and saw those quivering lips and tear-filled eyes, I forgot everything else in the world. I felt so sad and ill and wretched that I would gladly have run away rather than bid her farewell. I felt, too, that when she was embracing Papa she was taking leave of us all. She clasped Volodya to her several times and kissed him, and made the sign of the cross over him; after which I approached her, thinking that it was my turn. But she took him again and again to her heart, and blessed him. Finally I flung my arms round her, and, clinging to her, wept – wept, thinking of nothing in the world but my grief.

As we passed out to take our seats, the servants pressed importunately round us in the hall to say goodbye. Yet their requests to kiss our hands, their resounding kisses on our shoulders,[1] and the odour of their greasy heads only excited in me a feeling akin to irritable impatience with these tiresome people. The same feeling made me bestow nothing more than a very cross kiss upon Natalya Savishna's cap when she approached in tears to take leave of me. It is strange that I

1 The fashion in which inferiors saluted their superiors in Russia.

should still retain a perfect recollection of these servants' faces, and be able to draw them with the most minute accuracy in my mind, while Mamma's face and attitude escape me entirely. It may be that it is because at that moment I had not the heart to look at her closely. I felt that if I did so our mutual grief would burst forth too unrestrainedly.

I was the first to jump into the carriage and to take one of the hinder seats. The high back of the carriage prevented me from actually seeing anything, yet I knew by instinct that Mamma was still there.

'Shall I look at her again or not?' I said to myself. 'Well, just for the last time,' and I leaned out towards the entrance-steps. Exactly at that moment Mamma, moved by the same impulse, came to the opposite side of the carriage, and called me by name. Hearing her voice behind me, I turned round, but so hastily that our heads knocked together. She gave a sad smile, and kissed me convulsively for the last time.

When we had driven away a few yards I determined to look at her once more. The wind was lifting the blue kerchief from her head as, bent forward and her face buried in her hands, she moved slowly up the steps. Foka was supporting her.

Papa said nothing as he sat beside me. I felt breathless with tears – felt a sensation in my throat as though I were going to choke. Just as we came out on to the open road I saw a white handkerchief waving from the balcony. I waved mine in return, and the action of so doing calmed me a little. I still went on crying, but the thought that my tears were a proof of my sensitive nature helped to soothe and comfort me.

By the time we had gone a verst I began to recover, and to look with interest at the nearest object which presented itself to my view – the hind-quarters of the trace-horse which was trotting on my side. I watched how it would swish its tail, how it would strike one hoof against the other, how the driver's plaited whip fell upon its back, and how all its hooves would then seem to leap together and the harness, with the rings on it, to leap too. And I went on gazing until the breech-band near the animal's tail was quite covered with lather. Then I looked about me, at the rolling stretches of ripe rye, at the dark fallow fields where I could see a plough, a peasant and a horse with a foal. I looked at the mile-posts, even at the box of the carriage to see who was driving us; until, though my face was still wet with tears, my thoughts had strayed far from her with whom I had just parted – perhaps for ever. Yet ever and again something would recall her to my memory. I remembered too how, the evening before, I had found a mushroom in the birch avenue, how Lyuba had quarrelled with Katya as to whose it should be, and how they had both of them cried when taking leave of us.

I felt sorry to be parted from them, and from Natalya Savishna, and from the birch avenue, and from Foka. Yes, even the horrid Mimi I longed for. I longed for everything at home. And poor Mamma! – The tears rushed to my eyes again; but it was not for long.

XV
CHILDHOOD

HAPPY, happy, never-returning time of childhood! How can we help loving and dwelling upon its recollections? They cheer and elevate the soul, and become a source of one's sweetest enjoyments.

Tired out with running about, I have sat down, as of old, in my high arm-chair by the tea-table. It is late, and I have long since drunk my cup of milk with sugar in it. My eyes are heavy with sleep as I sit there and listen. How could I not listen, seeing that Mamma is speaking to somebody, and that the sound of her voice is so melodious and kind? How much its very sound conveys to my heart! With my eyes veiled with drowsiness I gaze at her wistfully. Suddenly she seems to grow smaller and smaller, her face no bigger than a button; yet I can still see it – can still see her as she looks at me and smiles. Somehow it pleases me to see her grown so small. I screw up my eyes tighter still, until now she looks no larger than a tiny boy reflected in the pupil of an eye. But I have moved, and the spell is broken. Once more I half-close my eyes, change my position, casting about to try and recall the dream, but in vain.

I get down from the table and settle myself comfortably, legs tucked under me, in an arm-chair.

'There! You are falling asleep again, little Nikolai,' says Mamma. 'You had better go upstairs.'

'No, I won't go to sleep, Mamma,' I reply, and pleasant, vague reveries are filling my mind, the healthful sleep of childhood is weighing my eyelids down, and for a few moments I sink into slumber and oblivion until awakened by someone. I feel in my sleep as though a soft hand were caressing me. I know it by the touch, and though still asleep I seize hold of it and press it to my lips.

Everyone else has gone to bed, and only one candle remains burning in the drawing-room. Mamma has said that she herself will wake me. She sits down on the arm of the chair in which I am asleep, with her soft hand stroking my hair, and I hear her beloved, well-known voice say in my ear:

'Get up, my darling. It is time to go to bed.'

Unconstrained now by the indifferent gaze of others, she is not afraid to shed upon me the whole of her tenderness and love. I do not move, but I kiss and kiss her hand.

'Get up, then, my angel.'

She passes her other arm round my neck, and her slender fingers tickle me as they move across it. The room is quiet and in half-darkness, but the tickling has touched my nerves and I begin to awake. Mamma is sitting near me; she touches me; I am conscious of her scent and her voice. This at last rouses me to spring up, to throw my arms around her neck, to hide my head in her bosom, and to say with a sigh:

'Ah, dear, darling Mamma, how much I love you!'

She smiles her sad, enchanting smile, takes my head between her two hands, kisses me on the forehead, and draws my head on to her lap.

'Do you love me so much, then?' she says. Then, after a few moments' silence, she continues: 'And you must love me *always*, and never forget me. If your mamma should no longer be here, will you promise never to forget her – *never*, my little Nikolai?' and she kisses me more fondly than ever.

'Oh, but you must not speak so, darling Mamma, my own darling Mamma!' I exclaim as I kiss her knees, and tears of joy and love fall from my eyes.

After scenes like this, I would go upstairs, and stand in my little quilted dressing-gown before the ikons, and say with what rapturous feeling, 'O Lord, save Papa and Mamma!' and repeat the prayers which my childish lips had learnt to lisp after my beloved mother – the love of her and of God blending strangely in a single emotion.

After saying my prayers I would wrap myself up in the bedclothes. My heart would feel light, peaceful, and happy, and one dream would follow another. Dreams of what? They were all of them elusive, but all of them full of pure love and of a sort of expectation of radiant happiness. Sometimes I would think about Karl Ivanych and his sad lot (he was the only unhappy being whom I knew), and so sorry would I feel for him, and so much did I love him, that tears would trickle from my eyes as I thought, 'May God give him happiness, and enable me to help him and to lessen his sorrow. I could make any sacrifice for him!' Usually, also, there would be some favourite toy – a china dog or hare – stuck into the bed-corner behind the pillow, and it would please me to think how warm and comfortable and well cared-for it was there. I would pray again to God to make everyone happy, so that everyone might be contented, and also to send fine weather tomorrow for our outing. Then I would turn myself over on to the other side, and thoughts and dreams would become jumbled and entangled together until at last I slept soundly and peacefully, my face still wet with tears.

Do in after life the freshness and lightheartedness, the craving for love and for strength of faith, ever return which we experience in our childhood's years? What better time is there in our lives than when the two best of virtues – innocent gaiety and a boundless yearning for affection – are our sole driving forces in life?

Where now are our ardent prayers? Where now are our best gifts – the pure tears of emotion which a guardian angel dries with a smile as he sheds upon us lovely dreams of innocent childish joy? Can it be that life has left such heavy traces upon one's heart that those tears and ecstasies are for ever vanished? Can it be that there remains to us only the recollection of them?

XVI
VERSE-MAKING

RATHER less than a month after our arrival in Moscow I was sitting upstairs in my grandmamma's house and doing some writing at a large table. Opposite to me sat the drawing master, who was giving a few finishing touches to the head of a turbaned Turk, executed in black crayon. Volodya, craning his neck, was standing behind the drawing master and looking over his shoulder. The head was Volodya's first production in crayon, and today – Grandmamma's name-day – it was to be presented to her.

'Aren't you going to put a little more shadow there?' said Volodya to the master as he raised himself on tiptoe and pointed to the Turk's neck.

'No, it is not necessary,' the master replied as he put crayon and holder into a box with a sliding lid. 'It is just right now, and you need not do anything more to it. As for you, young Nikolai,' he added, rising and still looking at the Turk out of the corner of his eye, 'won't you tell us your great secret at last? What are you going to give your grandmamma? I think another head would be your best gift. But goodbye, gentlemen,' and taking his hat and the ticket which would bring him payment he departed.

At that moment I too was thinking that a head would have been preferable to what I had been working on. When we were told that Grandmamma's name-day was soon to come round and that we must each of us have a present ready for her, I had taken it into my head to write some verses in honour of the occasion, and had forthwith composed two rhyming lines, hoping that the rest would soon materialise as rapidly. I really do not know how the idea – one so peculiar for a child – came to occur to me, but I know that I liked it vastly, and answered all questions on the subject of my gift by declaring that I should soon have something ready for Grandmamma, but was not going to say what it was.

Contrary to my expectation, I found that, after the first two lines executed in the initial heat of enthusiasm, even my most strenuous efforts refused to produce another one. I began to read the various poems in our books, but neither Dmitriev nor Derzhavin could help me. On the contrary, they only confirmed my sense of incompetence. Knowing, however, that Karl Ivanych was fond of writing out verses, I burrowed furtively among his papers, and found, among a number of German poems, some in the Russian language which seemed to have come from his own pen:

'To Madame L —— Petrovskaya, 3rd June 1828.

'Remember near,
Remember far,
Remember me.
Henceforth, and for ever –
Aye, still beyond the grave – remember
How truly I can love.

'KARL MAUER.'

This poem, written in a fine round hand on thin letter-paper, pleased me by the touching sentiment with which it was imbued. I forthwith learnt it by heart, and decided to take it as a model. The thing was much easier now. By the time the name-day had arrived I had completed a twelve-line congratulatory ode, and sat down to the table in our schoolroom to copy it out on vellum.

Two sheets were soon spoiled – not because I found it necessary to alter anything (the verses seemed to me perfect), but because, after the third line, the tail-end of each successive one would go curving upward, making it plain even from a distance that the whole thing had been written crookedly and simply would not do.

The third sheet also came out as crooked as the others, but I decided that I would not copy it out again. In my poem

I congratulated Grandmamma, wished her many happy returns, and concluded thus:

> 'Endeavouring you to please and cheer,
> We love you like our mother dear.'

This seemed to me not bad, yet the final line somehow offended my ear.

'Lo-ve you li-ike our Mo-ther dear,' I repeated to myself. 'What other rhyme could I use instead of "dear"? Fear? Steer? Well, it must go at that. At least the verses are better than Karl Ivanych's.'

Accordingly I added the last line to the rest. Then I went into our bedroom and recited the whole poem aloud with much feeling and gesticulation. Some of the lines were altogether guiltless of metre, but I did not dwell on them. Yet the last one displeased me more than ever. As I sat on my bed I thought:

'Why on earth did I write "like our mother dear"? She is not here, and therefore she need never have been mentioned. True, I love and respect Grandmamma, but she is not quite the same as — Why *did* I write that? What did I go and tell a lie for? It may be just poetry, yet I needn't quite have done *that*.'

At that moment the tailor arrived with new suits for us.

'Well, so be it!' I said in much vexation as I crammed the verses hastily under my pillow and ran down to try on the new Moscow garments.

They were splendid – both the brown jackets with bronze buttons (a garment made skin-tight and not 'to allow room for growth,' as in the country) and the black trousers, also close-fitting, so that they displayed our muscular legs and lay smoothly over the boots.

'At last I have real trousers with straps!' I thought as I looked at my legs from every angle with the utmost satisfaction. I concealed from everyone the fact that the new clothes were horribly tight and uncomfortable but, on the contrary, said that they fitted comfortably and that if there *were* a fault it was that they were not tight enough. For a long while I stood before the looking-glass as I brushed and combed my abundantly pomaded head, but, try as I would, I could not reduce the topmost tufts of hair to order. As soon as to test their obedience I left off combing them, they sprang up again and radiated in different directions, thus giving my face a ridiculous appearance.

Karl Ivanych was dressing in another room, and someone came through the schoolroom bearing his blue frockcoat and under-linen. Then at the door leading downstairs I heard a maid-servant's voice, and went to see what she wanted. In her hand she held a stiffly starched shirt-front which she said was for Karl Ivanych: she had been up all night to get it washed in time. I undertook to deliver it, and asked if Grandmamma was up yet.

'Oh yes, sir, she has had her coffee, and the arch-priest has come. My word, but you look a fine little fellow!' added the girl with a smile at my new clothes.

This observation made me blush, so I whirled round on one leg, snapped my fingers, and gave a little skip, in the hope that by these manœuvres I should make her sensible that even yet she had not realised quite what a fine fellow I was.

However, when I took the shirt-front to Karl Ivanych I found that he did not need it, having put on another one. Stooping before a small looking-glass which stood on the table, he was holding the imposing knot of his cravat with both hands – trying to see whether his smoothly shaven chin would move comfortably in and out over it. After straightening our clothes and asking Nikolai to do the same for him, he took us down to see Grandmamma. To this day I cannot help laughing when I remember what a smell of pomade the three of us left behind us on the staircase as we descended.

Karl Ivanych was carrying a little box which he had made himself, Volodya his drawing, and I my verses, while each of us also had a form of words ready with which to present his gift. Just as Karl Ivanych opened the door, the priest put on his vestment and the first words of prayer rang out.

Grandmamma was already in the drawing-room: she stood leaning over the back of a chair by the wall, with her head bent down, praying devoutly. Near her stood Papa. He turned and smiled at us as we hurriedly thrust our presents behind our backs and tried to remain unobserved by the door. The whole effect of a surprise, upon which we had been counting, was entirely lost.

When at last everyone started to go up and kiss the cross I became intolerably oppressed with a sudden, invincible, and deadly attack of shyness, so that the courage to offer my present completely failed me. I hid myself behind Karl Ivanych, who congratulated Grandmamma in the choicest phrases and, transferring his little box from his right hand to his left, presented it to her. Then he withdrew a few steps to make way for Volodya. Grandmamma seemed highly pleased with the box (which was adorned with a gold border), and smiled in the most friendly manner in order to express her gratitude. Yet it was evident that she did not know where to set the box down, and probably for this reason she handed it to Papa, bidding him observe how beautifully it was made.

His curiosity satisfied, Papa handed the box to the archpriest, who also seemed particularly delighted with it, and looked with curiosity, first at the article itself, and then at the craftsman who could make such wonderful things. Then Volodya presented his Turk, and received similarly flattering praises on all sides. It was my turn now, and Grandmamma turned to me with an encouraging smile.

Those who have experienced what shyness is know that it is a feeling which grows in direct proportion to delay, while one's resolve decreases in inverse proportion. In other words, the longer the condition lasts, the more invincible does it become, and the smaller does the power of decision come to be.

My last remnants of nerve and resolution had forsaken me while Karl Ivanych and Volodya were offering their presents, and my shyness now reached its culminating point. I felt the blood rushing from my heart to my head, one blush succeeding another across my face, and drops of perspiration beginning to stand out on my brow and nose. My ears were burning, I trembled and perspired from head to foot, and, though I kept shifting from one foot to the other, I remained rooted where I stood.

'Well, Nikolai, show us what you have brought?' said Papa. 'Is it a box or a drawing?'

There was no help for it. With a trembling hand I held out the crumpled, fatal scroll, but my voiced failed me completely, and I stood before Grandmamma in silence. I could not get rid of the dreadful idea that, instead of a display of the expected drawing, my totally inadequate verses were about to be read aloud before everyone, and that the words 'our Mother dear' would clearly prove that I had never loved but had only forgotten her.

How shall I describe my sufferings when Grandmamma began to read my poem aloud? – when, unable to decipher it, she stopped in the middle of a line and looked at Papa with a smile (which I took to be one of ridicule)? – when she did not pronounce it as I had meant it to be pronounced? – and when, her weak sight not allowing her to finish it, she handed the paper to Papa and requested him to read it all over again from the beginning? I fancied that she must have done this last because she did not like to read such a lot of stupid, crookedly written stuff herself, yet wanted to point out to Papa that last line which was such obvious evidence of my utter lack of feeling. I expected him to rap me on the nose with the verses and say, 'You horrid boy! So you have forgotten your mamma! Take that for it!' Yet nothing of the sort happened. On the contrary, when the whole had been read, Grandmamma said, '*Charmant!*'[1] and kissed me on the forehead.

Then our presents, together with two cambric pocket-handkerchiefs and a snuff-box engraved with Mamma's portrait, were laid on the adjustable side flap of the great Voltairian arm-chair in which Grandmamma always sat.

'The Princess Varvara Ilyinishna!' announced one of the two enormous footmen who used to stand behind Grandmamma's carriage when she drove out, but Grandmamma was looking thoughtfully at the portrait on the tortoise-shell snuff-box, and returned no answer.

'Shall I show her in, your ladyship?' repeated the footman.

1 Charming!

XVII
PRINCESS KORNAKOVA

'Yes, show her in,' said Grandmamma, settling herself as far back in her arm-chair as possible.

The Princess was a woman of about forty-five, small and delicate, with a shrivelled skin and disagreeable, greyish-green eyes, the expression of which contradicted the unnaturally suave look of the rest of her face. Underneath her velvet bonnet, adorned with an ostrich feather, was visible some reddish hair, while against the unhealthy colour of her skin her eyebrows and eyelashes looked even lighter and redder than they would otherwise have done. Yet, for all that, her animated movements, small hands, and peculiarly dry features communicated something aristocratic and energetic to her general appearance.

The Princess talked a great deal and, to judge from her eloquence, belonged to that class of persons who always speak as though someone were contradicting them, even though no one else may be saying a word. First she would raise her voice, then lower it, and then take on a fresh access of vivacity as she looked at the persons present, but not participating in the conversation, with an air of endeavouring to gain support merely by looking at them.

Although the Princess kissed Grandmamma's hand and repeatedly called her '*ma bonne tante*,'[1] I could see that Grandmamma did not care much for her, for she kept raising her eyebrows in a peculiar way while listening to the Princess's excuses why Prince Mikhailo had been prevented from calling and congratulating Grandmamma 'as he would like so much to have done.' She answered the Princess's French with Russian, curiously drawing out certain words.

'I am much obliged to you, my dear, for your kindness,' she said. 'As for Prince Mikhailo's absence, pray do not mention it. He has so much else to do. Besides, what pleasure could he find in coming to see an old woman like me?' Then, without

1 My kind aunt.

allowing the Princess time to contradict her, she went on: 'And how are your children, my dear?'

'Well, thank God, *ma tante*, they grow and do their lessons and get into mischief – particularly my eldest one, Etienne, who is so wild that it is almost impossible to keep him in order. Still, he is very clever – *un garçon qui promet*.[1] Would you believe it, *mon cousin*' (this last to Papa, since Grandmamma, altogether uninterested in the Princess's children but desiring to brag about her own grandchildren, had turned to us, taken my verses out from beneath the presentation box, and was starting to unfold them again), 'would you believe it, *mon cousin*, one day not long ago——' and leaning over towards Papa, the Princess related something or other with great vivacity. Then, her tale concluded, she laughed, and with a questioning look at Papa went on:

'What a boy, *mon cousin*! He ought to have been whipped, but the trick was so spirited and amusing that I let him off, *mon cousin*.' Then the Princess looked fixedly at Grandmamma and continued to smile, though she said nothing.

'Ah! So you *whip* your children, my dear, do you?' said Grandmamma, with a significant lift of her eyebrows, and laying a peculiar stress on the word '*whip*.'

'Alas, *ma bonne tante*,' replied the Princess in a sweet tone and with another swift glance at Papa, 'I know your views on the subject, but must beg to be allowed to differ with them in this one particular. However much I have thought over and read and talked about the matter, I have always been forced by experience to come to the conclusion that children must be ruled through *fear*. To make anything of a child, you must make it *fear* something. Is it not so, *mon cousin*? And what, *je vous demande un peu*,[2] do children fear so much as the birch?'

As she spoke she seemed to look inquiringly at Volodya and myself, and I confess that at that moment I did not feel altogether comfortable.

1 A promising boy.
2 I will just ask you.

'Whatever you may say,' she went on, 'a boy of twelve, or even of fourteen, is still a child, and should be whipped as such; but with girls, perhaps, it is another matter.'

'How lucky it is that I am not her son!' I thought to myself.

'Yes, that is all very fine, my dear,' said Grandmamma, folding up my verses and replacing them beneath the box (as though, after that exposition of views, the Princess was unworthy of the honour of listening to such a production). 'That is all very well, my dear, but please tell me how, in return, you can look after that for any delicate sensibility from your children?'

Evidently Grandmamma thought this argument unanswerable, for she cut the subject short by adding:

'However, it is a point on which people must follow their own opinions.'

The Princess did not choose to reply, but smiled condescendingly, and as though out of indulgence to the strange prejudices of a person whom she so greatly revered.

'Oh, by the way, pray introduce me to your young people,' she went on presently as she threw us another gracious smile.

Thereupon we rose and stood looking at the Princess, without in the least knowing what we ought to do to show that we were being introduced.

'Kiss the Princess's hand,' said Papa.

'Well, I hope you will love your old aunt,' she said to Volodya, kissing his hair, 'even though we are not near relatives. But I value friendship far more than I do degrees of relationship,' she added principally to Grandmamma. But Grandmamma remained displeased, and replied:

'Eh, my dear? Does anyone set store by such relationships nowadays?'

'This is going to be my young man of the world,' put in Papa, indicating Volodya; 'and here is my poet,' he added as I kissed the small, dry hand of the Princess, with a vivid picture in my mind of that same hand holding a rod, and a bench beneath the rod, and so on.

'*Which* one is the poet?' asked the Princess, holding on to my hand.

'This little one,' replied Papa, smiling cheerfully; 'the one with the tufts of hair on his top-knot.'

'Why need he bother about my tufts?' I thought to myself as I retired into a corner. 'Is there nothing else for him to talk about?'

I had strange ideas on manly beauty. I considered Karl Ivanych one of the handsomest men in the world, and myself not at all good-looking, so that I had no need to deceive myself on that point. Therefore any remark on the subject of my exterior offended me extremely.

I well remember how, one day at dinner (I was then six years of age), the talk fell upon my personal appearance, and how Mamma tried to find good features in my face, and said that I had clever eyes and a charming smile; how, nevertheless, when Papa had examined me and proved the contrary, she was obliged to confess that I was ugly; and how, when the meal was over and I went to pay her my respects, she said as she patted my cheek: 'You know, my little Nikolai, nobody will ever love you for your face alone, so you must try all the more to be a good and clever boy.'

These words of hers not only confirmed in me my conviction that I was not handsome, but also confirmed in me the determination to be without fail a good and clever boy. Yet I had my moments of despair at my ugliness, for I thought that no human being with such a large nose, such thick lips, and such small grey eyes as mine could ever hope to attain happiness on this earth. I used to ask God to perform a miracle by changing me into a handsome man, and would have given all that I possessed, or ever hoped to possess, to have a handsome face.

XVIII
PRINCE IVAN IVANYCH

WHEN the Princess had heard my verses and overwhelmed the writer of them with praise, Grandmamma softened to her a little. She began to address her in French and to cease calling her 'you, my dear.' Likewise she invited her to return that evening with her children. This invitation having been accepted, the Princess stayed a little longer, then took her leave. After that, so many other callers came to congratulate Grandmamma that the courtyard was crowded all morning with carriages.

'*Bonjour, chère cousine*,'[1] was the greeting of one guest in particular as he entered the room and kissed Grandmamma's hand. He was a man of seventy, with a stately figure clad in a military uniform and adorned with large epaulettes, an embroidered collar, and a white cross round the neck. His face, with its quiet and open expression, as well as the simplicity and ease of his movements, greatly pleased me, for in spite of the thin half-circle of hair which was all that was now left to him and the want of teeth disclosed by the set of his upper lip, his face was still a remarkably handsome one.

Thanks to his fine character, handsome exterior, remarkable valour, distinguished and influential relatives, and, above all, good fortune, Prince Ivan Ivanych had early made himself a career at the end of the last century. As that career in the Service progressed, his ambition had met with a success which left nothing more to be sought for in that direction. From his earliest youth upward he had prepared himself to fill the exalted station in the world to which fate eventually called him; consequently, although in his brilliant and somewhat vainglorious life (as in the lives of all) there had been failures, misfortunes, and cares, he had never lost his quietness of character, his elevated tone of thought, or his peculiarly moral, religious bent of mind. Consequently, though he had won the universal esteem of his fellows, he had done so less through his important position than through his perseverance and integrity. While not of specially distinguished intellect, the eminence of his station (whence he could afford to look down upon all petty agitations of life) had caused him to adopt high points of view. Though in reality he was kind and sympathetic, in manner he appeared cold and haughty – probably for the reason that he had forever to be on his guard against the endless claims and petitions of

1 Good day, dear cousin.

people who wished to profit through his influence. Yet even then his coldness was mitigated by the polite condescension of a man well accustomed to move in the highest circles of society. Well-educated and well-read, his education had stopped short at what he had acquired as a young man, at the end of the last century. He had read everything, whether philosophy or *belles lettres*, which the eighteenth century had produced in France. He was thoroughly familiar with the best of French literature, and loved to quote from Racine, Corneille, Boileau, Molière, Montaigne, and Fénelon. Likewise he had gleaned an adequate grasp of history from Ségur, his knowledge of mythology was outstanding and he had studied to good effect the ancient monuments of epic poetry in French translations: but of mathematics he was ignorant beyond the realm of arithmetic and ignorant likewise of physics and modern literature. However, he knew how to be silent in conversation, as well as when to make general remarks on authors whom he had never read – such as Goethe, Schiller, and Byron. Moreover, despite his French classical education of which there are few surviving examples to be found nowadays, he was simple in conversation and this simplicity both concealed his ignorance of certain things and demonstrated his good breeding and his tolerant nature. He hated any kind of eccentricity, which he called the mark of an untutored nature. Wherever he lived society was a necessity to him, and in Moscow or abroad he kept open house and had his reception days, on which practically 'all the town' called upon him. His standing was such that an introduction from him was a passport to every drawing-room; few young and pretty ladies in society objected to offering him their rosy cheeks for a paternal salute; and people even in the highest positions felt flattered beyond words by invitations to his parties.

The Prince had few friends left now like Grandmamma – that is to say, few friends who were of the same circle as himself, who had had the same sort of education, were of the same age, and who saw things from the same point of view: therefore he greatly valued his intimate, long-standing friendship with her, and always showed her the highest respect.

I could not gaze enough at the Prince: the honour paid him on all sides, the huge epaulettes, the peculiar pleasure with which Grandmamma received him, and the fact that he alone seemed in no way afraid of her, but addressed her with perfect freedom (even being so daring as to call her '*ma cousine*'), awakened in me a feeling of reverence for his person almost equal to that which I felt for Grandmamma herself.

On being shown my verses, he called me to his side and said: 'Who knows, *ma cousine*, but that he may prove to be a second Derzhavin?' Thereupon he pinched my cheek so hard that I was prevented from crying only by the thought that it must be meant as a caress.

Gradually the other guests dispersed, and with them Papa and Volodya. Thus only Grandmamma, the Prince, and I were left in the drawing-room.

'Why has our dear Natalya Nikolayevna not come today?' asked the Prince suddenly after a silence.

'Ah, *mon cher*,' replied Grandmamma, lowering her voice and laying a hand upon the sleeve of his uniform, 'she would certainly have come if she had been at liberty to do what she likes. She wrote to me that Pierre had proposed bringing her with him to town, but that she had refused, since their income had been non-existent this year, and she could see no real reason why the whole family need come to Moscow this year, seeing that Lyuba was as yet very young and that the boys were living with me – a fact, she said, which made her feel as safe about them as though she had been living with them herself.

'True, it is good for the boys to be here,' went on Grandmamma, yet in a tone which showed clearly that she did not think it *was* so very good, 'since it was more than time that they should be sent to Moscow to study, as well as to learn how to comport themselves in society. What sort of an education could they have got in the country? The eldest boy will soon be thirteen, and the second one eleven. You have noticed, *mon cousin*, they are veritable savages, and do not know even how to enter a room.'

'Nevertheless,' said the Prince, 'I cannot understand these complaints of straitened circumstances. *He* has a very handsome income, and Natalya has Khabarovka, where we used at one time to act plays together, and which I know as well as I do my own hand. It is a splendid property, and ought to bring in an excellent return.'

'Well,' said Grandmamma with a sad expression on her face, 'I do not mind telling *you*, as my most intimate friend, that all this seems to me a mere pretext on *his* part for living alone, for strolling about from club to club, for attending dinner-parties, and for resorting to – well, who knows what? She suspects nothing; you know her angelic sweetness and her implicit trust of *him* in everything. He had only to tell her that the children must go to Moscow, and that she must be left behind in the country with a stupid governess for company, for her to believe him! I almost think that, if he were to say that the children must be whipped just as the Princess Kornakova whips hers, she would believe even that!' And Grandmamma twisted round in her arm-chair with an expression of contempt. Then, after a moment of silence, during which she took one of her two handkerchiefs to wipe away a tear which had stolen down her cheek, she went on:

'Yes, my friend, I often think that he cannot value and understand her properly, and that, for all her goodness and love of him and her endeavours to conceal her grief (which, however, as I know only too well, exists), she cannot really be happy with him. Mark my words if he does not——' Here Grandmamma buried her face in the handkerchief.

'Ah, *ma bonne amie*,' said the Prince reproachfully, 'you have not grown a whit more reasonable. Why grieve and weep over imagined evils? That is not right. I have known *him* a long time, and feel sure that he is an attentive, kind, and excellent husband, as well as (which is the chief thing of all) a perfectly honourable man, *un parfait honnête homme.*'[1]

At this point, having been an involuntary auditor of a conversation not meant for my ears, I stole on tiptoe out of the room, in a state of great agitation.

1 A complete gentleman.

XIX
THE IVINS

'Volodya, Volodya! The Ivins are here!' I shouted on seeing from the window three boys in blue overcoats with beaver collars, advancing behind their fashionably dressed young tutor along the pavement opposite our house.

The Ivins were related to us, and of about the same age as ourselves. We had made their acquaintance soon after our arrival in Moscow. The second brother, Seriozha, had dark curly hair, a turned-up, strongly pronounced nose, very fresh red lips which, never being quite shut, showed a row of white teeth, beautiful dark-blue eyes, and an uncommonly bold expression of face. He never smiled, but was either wholly serious or laughing a clear, merry, and exceptionally agreeable laugh. His striking good looks had captivated me from the first, and I felt an irresistible attraction towards him. Only to see him filled me with pleasure, and at one time my whole mental faculties used to be concentrated in the wish that I might do so. If three or four days passed without my seeing him I felt listless and ready to cry. Awake or asleep, I was forever dreaming of him. On going to bed I used to see him in my dreams, and when I had shut my eyes and called up a picture of him I hugged the vision as my choicest delight. So much store did I set upon this feeling for my friend that I could never have mentioned it to anyone. Nevertheless, it must have annoyed him to see my admiring eyes constantly fixed upon him, or else he must have felt no reciprocal attraction, for he always preferred to play and talk with Volodya. Still, even with that I felt satisfied, and wished and asked for nothing better than to be ready at any time to make any sacrifice for him. Likewise, over and above the strange fascination which he exercised upon me, I always felt another sensation, namely, a dread of making him angry, of offending him, of displeasing him. Was this because his face bore such a haughty expression, or because I, despising my own exterior, over-rated the beautiful in others, or, lastly (and most probably), because this sort of dread is a common sign of affection? At all events, I felt as much fear of him as I did love. The first time Seriozha spoke to me I was so overwhelmed with sudden happiness that I turned pale, then red, and could not utter a word. He had an ugly habit of fixing his eyes on one particular spot when considering anything seriously and blinking, as well as of twitching his nose and eyebrows. Consequently everyone thought that this habit marred his face. Yet I thought it such a nice one that I involuntarily adopted it for myself, until, a few days after I had made his acquaintance, Grandmamma suddenly asked me whether my eyes were hurting me, since I was winking like an owl! Never a word of affection passed between us, yet he felt his power over me, and unconsciously but tyrannically exercised it in all our childish dealings with one another. I used to long to tell him all that was in my heart, yet was too much afraid of him to be frank in any way, and, while submitting myself to his will, tried to appear merely careless and indifferent. Although at times his influence seemed irksome and intolerable, to throw it off was beyond my strength.

I often think with regret of that fresh, beautiful feeling of boundless, disinterested love which came to an end without having ever found self-expression or return.

It is strange how, when a child, I always longed to be like grown-up people, and yet how I have often longed, since I ceased to be a child, to be like one. Many times, in my relations with Seriozha, this wish – not to behave like a child – put a rude check upon the love that was waiting to be poured out, and made me conceal it. Not only was I afraid of kissing him, or of taking his hand and saying how glad I was to see him, but I did not even dare to call him 'Seriozha,' but always said 'Sergei' as everyone else did in our house. Any expression of affection would have seemed like evidence of childishness, and anyone who indulged in it a *baby*. Not having yet passed through those bitter experiences which enforce upon older years circumspection and coldness, we deprived ourselves of the pure delight of a fresh, childish attachment for the absurd purpose of trying to resemble grown-up people.

I met the Ivins in the ante-room, welcomed them, and then ran to tell Grandmamma of their arrival with an expression as happy as though she were certain to be equally delighted. Then, never taking my eyes off Seriozha, I followed the visitors to the drawing-room, eagerly watching every movement of my favourite. When Grandmamma said how much he had grown, and fixed her penetrating glance upon him, I experienced that mingled sensation of pride and solicitude which an artist might feel when waiting for a revered critic to pronounce a judgement upon his work.

With Grandmamma's permission, the Ivins' young tutor, Herr Frost, accompanied us into the front garden, where he seated himself upon a green bench, arranged his legs in a tasteful attitude, rested his bronze-headed cane between them, lit a cigar, and assumed the air of a man well-pleased with himself.

Herr Frost was a German, but of a very different sort to our good Karl Ivanych. In the first place, he spoke Russian correctly and French with a bad accent. Indeed, he enjoyed – especially among the ladies – the reputation of being a very learned fellow. In the second place, he wore a reddish moustache, a large ruby pin in his black satin cravat, the ends of which were tucked into his braces, and light-blue trousers of a shiny material, with straps. Lastly, he was young, with a handsome, self-satisfied face and fine muscular legs. It was clear that he set the greatest store upon the latter, and thought them beyond compare, especially as regards the favour of the ladies. Consequently, whether sitting or standing, he always tried to exhibit them in the most favourable light. He was the very type of the young German-Russian whose main desire is to be thought a perfect gallant and a gentleman.

In the garden merriment reigned. In fact, the game of 'robbers' never went better. Yet an incident occurred which came near to spoiling it. Seriozha was the robber, and in pouncing upon some travellers he stumbled and knocked his leg so hard against a tree that I thought his leg must be smashed to fragments. Consequently, though I was the gendarme and therefore bound to apprehend him, I only asked him anxiously, when I reached him, if he had hurt himself very much. This threw him into a passion, and made him exclaim with fists clenched and in a voice which showed by its faltering what pain he was enduring, 'Why, whatever is the matter? Is this playing the game properly? You ought to arrest me. Why on earth don't you do so?' This he repeated several times, and then, with a sidelong glance seeing Volodya and the elder Ivin (who were taking the part of the travellers) jumping and running about the path, he suddenly threw himself upon them with a yell and loud laughter to effect their capture.

I cannot express my wonder and delight at this valiant behaviour of my hero. In spite of the severe pain, he had not only refrained from crying, but had repressed the least symptom of suffering and kept his eye fixed upon the game!

Shortly after this occurrence another boy, Ilyenka Grap, joined our party. We went upstairs, and Seriozha gave me an opportunity of still further appreciating and taking delight in his manly bravery and fortitude.

Ilyenka Grap was the son of a poor foreigner who had been under certain obligations to my grandpapa, having once lived in his house, and now thought it incumbent upon him to send his son to us as frequently as possible. Yet if he thought that the acquaintance would procure his son any advancement or plea-sure, he was entirely mistaken, for not only were we anything but friendly to Ilyenka, but it was seldom that we noticed him at all except to laugh at him. He was a boy of thirteen or so, tall and thin, with a pale, bird-like face, and a submissive, good-tempered expression. Though poorly dressed, he always had his head so thickly pomaded that we used to declare that on warm days the pomatum melted and ran down his neck. When I think of him now, it seems to me that he was a very quiet, obliging, and good-natured boy, but at the time I thought him a creature so contemptible that he was not worth either atten-tion or pity.

When we had concluded our game of robbers we went upstairs and set ourselves to astonish each other with gymnastic feats. Ilyenka watched us with a faint smile of admiration, but refused an invitation to attempt a similar feat, saying that he had not the strength for it. Seriozha looked extremely captivating.

He had taken his jacket off, and his face and eyes glowed with laughter as he surprised us with tricks which we had never seen before. He jumped over three chairs put together, turned somersaults right across the room, and finally stood on his head on a pyramid of Tatishchev's dictionaries, waving his legs in the air with such comical rapidity that it was impossible not to burst with laughter. After this last trick he pondered for a moment (blinking his eyes as usual), and then went up to Ilyenka with a very serious face.

'Try and do that,' he said. 'It is not really difficult.'

Ilyenka, observing that the general attention was fixed upon him, blushed, and said in an almost inaudible voice that he could not do it.

'Well, what does he mean by doing nothing at all? What a girl the fellow is! He has just *got* to stand on his head,' and Seriozha seized him by the hand.

'Yes, on your head at once! This instant, this instant!' everyone shouted as we ran upon Ilyenka and dragged him towards the dictionaries, despite his being visibly pale and frightened.

'Leave me alone! I'll do it myself! You are tearing my jacket!' cried the unhappy victim, but his exclamations of despair only encouraged us the more. We were dying with laughter, while the green jacket was parting at every seam.

Volodya and the eldest Ivin pushed his head down on to the dictionaries, while Seriozha and I seized his poor, thin legs kicking out wildly in all directions, rolled up his trousers to the knee, and with boisterous laughter held them upright – the youngest Ivin superintending his general balance.

Suddenly a moment of silence occurred amid our boisterous laughter – a moment during which nothing was to be heard in the room but the heavy panting of the miserable Ilyenka. It occurred to me at that moment that, after all, there was nothing so very comical and pleasant in all this.

'Now, *that's* a boy!' cried Seriozha, giving Ilyenka a smack with his hand. Ilyenka said nothing, but kicked out with his legs. With one of these desperate efforts he managed to catch Seriozha in the eye with his heel with the result that, letting go of Ilyenka's leg and covering the wounded eye, filled with involuntary tears, with one hand, Seriozha pushed Ilyenka as hard as he could with the other one. Ilyenka, no longer supported by us, came crashing to the floor and could only stammer out through his tears:

'Why do you bully me so?'

The poor fellow's miserable figure, with his tear-stained face, dishevelled hair, and crumpled trousers revealing the unblacked tops of his boots, touched us, and we stood silent and trying to smile.

Seriozha was the first to recover himself.

'What a girl! What a cissy!' he said, giving Ilyenka a slight tap with his foot. 'He can't take things in fun a bit. Well, get up, then.'

'I told them you are an utter beast! That's what *you* are!' said Ilyenka in fury, turning miserably away and bursting into loud sobs.

'Oh, oh! Would it still kick and show temper, then?' cried Seriozha, seizing a dictionary and flourishing it over the unfortunate boy's head. Apparently it never occurred to Ilyenka to take refuge from the missile; he merely guarded his head with his hands.

'Well, that's enough now,' added Seriozha with a forced laugh. 'He *deserves* to be hurt if he can't take things in fun. Now let's go downstairs.'

I could not help looking with some compassion at the miserable creature on the floor as, his face buried in the dictionaries, he lay there sobbing almost as though he might die of the convulsions which shook his whole body.

'Oh, Sergei!' I said. 'Why did you do this?'

'That's good! *I* did not cry this afternoon when I knocked my leg and nearly broke it.'

'True enough,' I thought. 'Ilyenka is a poor whining sort of a chap, while Seriozha is a fine fellow – a *real* boy.'

It never occurred to my mind that possibly poor Ilyenka was crying far less from bodily pain than from the thought that five companions for whom he may have felt a genuine liking had, for no reason at all, combined to hurt and humiliate him.

I cannot explain to myself my cruelty on this occasion. Why did I not step forward to comfort and protect him? Where was the feeling of sympathy which often made me burst into tears at the sight of a young jackdaw fallen from its nest, or of a puppy being thrown over a fence, or of a chicken being killed by the cook for soup?

Can it be that the better instinct in me was overshadowed by my affection for Seriozha and the desire to appear before him as fine a fellow as he was himself? If so, how contemptible were both the affection and the desire! They form the only dark spots on the pages of my youthful recollections.

XX
THE GUESTS ASSEMBLE

To judge from the extraordinary activity in the pantry, the brilliant lighting which imparted such a new and festal guise to the long familiar articles in the drawing-room and the ball-room and the arrival of some musicians whom Prince Ivanych would certainly not have sent for nothing, no small amount of company was to be expected that evening.

At the sound of every vehicle which chanced to pass the house I ran to the window, leaned my head upon my hands, and peered with impatient curiosity into the street. From the darkness which at first hid everything outside the window, there gradually emerged the familiar little shop opposite with its lamp post, diagonally across the street a large house with two illuminated windows on the ground floor, and in the middle of the street some cabby with a couple of passengers or an empty carriage on its way home at walking pace. At last a carriage drove up to our door, and, in the full belief that this must be the Ivins, who had promised to come early, I at once ran downstairs to meet them in the hall. But, instead of the Ivins, I beheld from behind the liveried arm of the footman who opened the door two female figures – one tall and wrapped in a blue coat trimmed with sable, and the other one short and wrapped in a green shawl from beneath which a pair of little feet in fur boots peeped forth.

Without paying any attention to my presence in the hall (although I thought it my duty, on the appearance of these persons, to bow to them), the shorter one moved towards the taller, and stood silently in front of her. Thereupon the tall lady unwound the shawl which enveloped the head of the little one, and unbuttoned the cloak which hid her form; until, by the time that the footmen had taken charge of these articles and removed the fur boots, there emerged from the muffled figure a charming little girl of twelve, dressed in a short low-necked muslin frock, white pantaloons, and tiny black satin shoes. Around her white neck she wore a narrow black velvet ribbon, while her head was covered with chestnut curls which so perfectly suited her beautiful face in front and her bare neck and shoulders behind that I would have believed nobody, not even Karl Ivanych, if he or she had told me that they only hung so nicely because, ever since the morning, they had been screwed up in fragments of the *Moscow News* and then warmed with a hot iron. To me it seemed as though she must have been *born* with those curls.

The most prominent feature in her face was a pair of unusually large, half-veiled eyes, which formed a strange but pleasing contrast to the small mouth. Her lips were closed, while her eyes looked so grave that the general expression of her face gave one the impression that a smile was never to be looked for from her: so that, when a smile did come, it was all the more enchanting.

Trying to escape notice, I slipped through the door of the ball-room, and then thought it necessary to be seen pacing to and fro, seemingly engaged in thought, as though unconscious of the arrival of guests. By the time, however, that the ladies had advanced to the middle of the ball-room, I seemed suddenly to awake from my reverie, bowed and brought my feet together and told them that Grandmamma was in the drawing-room. Madame Valakhina, whose face pleased me extremely (especially since it bore a great resemblance to her daughter Sonya's), nodded graciously in my direction.

Grandmamma seemed delighted to see little Sonya. She invited her to come to her, put back a curl which had fallen over her brow, and looking earnestly at her said, '*Quelle charmante enfant!*'[1] Sonya blushed, smiled, and, indeed, looked so charming that I myself blushed as I looked at her.

'I hope you are going to enjoy yourself here, my love,' said Grandmamma. 'Pray be as merry and dance as much as ever you can. See, we have one lady and two *beaux* for her already,' she added, turning to Madame Valakhina and stretching out her hand to me.

This coupling of Sonya with myself pleased me so much that I blushed again.

Feeling, presently, that my shyness was increasing, and hearing the sound of another carriage approaching, I thought it wise to retire. In the hall I encountered Princess Kornakova, her son, and an incredible number of daughters. They had all of them the same face as their mother, and were very plain. None of them arrested my attention. They talked in shrill tones as they took off their cloaks and boas, and laughed as they bustled about – probably at the fact that there were so many of them. Etienne was a boy of about fifteen, tall and plump, with a sharp face, deep-set eyes with dark shadows beneath them, and very large hands and feet for his age. He was awkward, and had a harsh, unpleasing voice. Nevertheless he seemed very pleased with himself, and was in my opinion precisely the sort of boy who could well bear being beaten with birch rods.

For some time we confronted one another without speaking as we took stock of each other. Then we approached one another, probably to exchange a kiss, but on looking again at one another's eyes, for some reason thought better of it. When the flood of his sisters' dresses had swept past I made shift to begin a conversation by asking him whether it had not been crowded in the carriage.

'I don't know,' he answered indifferently. 'I never ride inside it, for it makes me feel sick directly, and Mamma

1 What a charming child!

CHILDHOOD CHILDHOOD   75

knows that. Whenever we are driving anywhere at night-time I always sit on the box. I like that, for then one sees everything. Philip gives me the reins, and sometimes the whip too, and then the passers-by sometimes, you know, get a touch of it, get a regular – well, you know,' he added with a significant gesture. 'It's splendid then.'

'Your highness,' said a footman, entering the hall, 'Philip wishes me to ask you where you put the whip.'

'Where I put it? Why, I gave it back to him.'

'But he says that you did not.'

'Well, I laid it across the carriage-lamp.'

'No, sir, he says that you did not do that either. You had better confess that you took it and mislaid it, or I suppose poor Philip will have to make good your mischief out of his own pocket,' continued the angry footman, getting increasingly animated.

The footman, who looked a grave and honest man, seemed much put out by the affair, and determined to sift it to the bottom on Philip's behalf. Out of delicacy I pretended to notice nothing and turned aside, but the other footmen present gathered round and looked approvingly at the old servant.

'Hm – well, if I lost it, I lost it,' at length confessed Etienne, shrinking from further explanations. 'However, I will pay for it. Did you ever hear anything so absurd?' he added to me as he drew me towards the drawing-room.

'But excuse me, sir; *how* are you going to pay for it? I know your ways of paying. You have owed Marya Vasilyevna twenty copecks these seven months or more, and you have owed *me* something for over a year, and Petrushka for——'

'Hold your tongue, will you!' shouted the young prince, pale with rage. 'I shall report you for this.'

'Oh, you may do so,' said the footman. 'Yet it is not fair, your highness,' he added, with a peculiar stress on the title, as he departed with the ladies' wraps to the cloak-chest. We ourselves entered the ball-room.

'Quite right, footman,' remarked someone approvingly from the hall behind us.

Grandmamma had a peculiar way of employing, now the second person singular, now the second person plural, in order to indicate her opinion of people. Although she used the pronouns 'you' and 'thou' quite differently from the accepted manner, these distinctions acquired a peculiar significance on her lips. When the young Prince Etienne went up to her she addressed him as '*you*,' and altogether looked at him with such an expression of contempt that, had I been in his place, I should have been utterly crestfallen. Etienne, however, was evidently not a boy of that sort, for he not only took no notice of her reception of him, but none of her person either. In fact, he bowed to the company at large in a way which, though not graceful, was at least free from embarrassment. Sonya now claimed my whole attention. I remember that, as I stood in the *salon* chatting with Etienne and Volodya, at a spot whence we could both see and be seen by Sonya, I took great pleasure in talking, and when I happened to say something which I considered amusing or clever I raised my voice and glanced towards the door of the drawing-room, but that, as soon as we happened to move to another spot whence we could neither see nor be seen by her, I fell silent and took no further pleasure in the conversation.

The drawing-room and the *salon* gradually filled with people – among them (as at all children's parties) a number of older children who wished to dance and enjoy themselves very much, but who pretended to do everything merely in order to give pleasure to the mistress of the house.

When the Ivins arrived I found that, instead of being as delighted as usual to meet Seriozha, I felt a kind of vexation that he should see Sonya and be seen by her.

XXI
BEFORE THE MAZURKA

'Aha! So we are going to dance tonight,' said Seriozha, issuing from the drawing-room and taking out of his pocket a brand-new pair of kid gloves. 'I suppose I had better put my gloves on.'

'Goodness! What shall I do? We have no gloves,' I thought to myself. 'I must go upstairs and look for some.' Yet, though I rummaged in every chest of drawers, I only found, in one of them, my green travelling mittens, and in another a single kid glove, a thing which could be of no use to me, firstly, because it was very old and dirty, secondly, because it was too large for me, and thirdly (and principally), because the middle finger was wanting – Karl Ivanych having long ago cut it off to wear on a sore finger. However, I put on this remnant of a glove – and gazed in fascination at that section of my middle finger which was always ink-stained.

'If only Natalya Savishna had been here,' I reflected, 'we should certainly have found some gloves. I can't go downstairs in this condition, for, if they ask me why I am not dancing, what am I to say? However, I can't remain here either, or they will be sending upstairs to fetch me. What on earth am I to do?' and I swung my arms back and forth.

'What are you up to here?' asked Volodya, running into the room. 'Go and engage a partner. The dancing will be beginning directly.'

'Volodya,' I said despairingly, as I showed him my hand with two fingers thrust into a single finger of the dirty glove, 'Volodya, you never thought of this.'

'Of what?' he said impatiently. 'Oh, of gloves,' he added with a careless glance at my hand. 'That's nothing. We can ask Grandmamma what she thinks about it,' and without further ado he departed downstairs.

I felt a trifle relieved by the coolness with which he had met a situation which seemed to me so grave, and hastened back to the drawing-room, completely forgetful of the unfortunate glove which still adorned my left hand.

Cautiously approaching Grandmamma's arm-chair and gently touching her dress, I asked her in a whisper:

'Grandmamma, what are we to do? We have no gloves.'

'What, my love?'

'We have no gloves,' I repeated, coming closer to her and laying both hands on the arm of her chair.

'But what is that?' she cried as she caught hold of my left hand. '*Voyez ma chère*,' she continued, turning to Madame Valakhina. '*Voyez comme ce jeune homme s'est fait élégant pour danser avec votre fille!*'[1]

As Grandmamma persisted in keeping hold of my hand and gazing with an air of gravity and interrogation at all around her, curiosity was soon aroused, and a general roar of laughter ensued.

I should have been infuriated at the thought that Seriozha was present to see this, as I scowled with embarrassment and struggled to free my hand, had it not been that somehow Sonya's laughter (and she was laughing to such a degree that the tears came to her eyes and the curls danced about her lovely face) took away my feeling of humiliation. I felt that her laughter was not satirical, but only natural and free; so that, as we laughed together and looked at one another, there seemed to begin a kind of sympathy between us. Instead of turning out badly, therefore, the episode of the glove served only to set me at my ease among the dreaded circle of drawing-room guests, and to make me cease to feel oppressed with shyness in the *salon*.

The sufferings of shy people proceed only from the doubts which they feel concerning the opinions of their fellows. No sooner are those opinions clearly expressed (whether flattering or the reverse) than the agony disappears.

How lovely Sonya Valakhina looked when she was dancing the French quadrille opposite me, with, as her partner, the awkward Prince Etienne! How charmingly she smiled when, *en chaîne*, she gave me her hand! How gracefully the brown curls around her head nodded to the rhythm, and how artlessly she executed the *jeté assemblé* with her little feet! In the fifth figure, when my partner had to leave me for the other side and I, counting the beats, was getting ready to dance my solo, she pursed her lips gravely and looked in another direction; but her fears for me were groundless. Boldly I performed the *chassé en*

1 Look, my dear! See how smart this young man has made himself to dance with your daughter!

avant and *chassé en arrière* and my *glissade* until, when it came to my turn to move towards her and I, with a comic gesture, showed her the poor glove with its fingers sticking out, she laughed heartily and seemed to move her tiny feet more enchantingly than ever over the parquet floor. I remember too how we joined hands to form the circle, and how, without withdrawing her hand from mine, she bent her head down and rubbed her little nose with her glove. All this I can see before me still, and I can still hear the quadrille from 'The Maid of the Danube' to whose strains all this occurred.

The second quadrille I danced with Sonya herself; yet when we went to sit down together I felt overcome with shyness, and as though I had nothing to say. At last, when my silence had lasted so long that I began to be afraid that she would think me a fool, I decided at all hazards to counteract such a notion.

'*Vous êtes une habitante de Moscou?*' I began, and on receiving an affirmative answer, continued, '*Et moi, je n'ai encore jamais fréquenté la capitale*'[1] (relying particularly on the effect of the word '*fréquenté*'). Yet I felt that, brilliant though this introduction might be as evidence of my profound knowledge of the French language, I could not long keep up the conversation in that manner. Our turn for dancing had not yet arrived and silence again ensued between us. I kept looking anxiously at her in the hope both of discerning what impression I had produced and of her coming to my aid.

'Where did you get that ridiculous glove of yours?' she asked me all of a sudden, and the question afforded me immense satisfaction and relief. I replied that the glove belonged to Karl Ivanych, and then went on to speak ironically of his appearance, and to describe how comical he looked when he took off his red cap, and how he and his green coat had once fallen plump off a horse into a puddle.

The quadrille passed unnoticed. This was all very well, yet why had I spoken ironically of poor Karl Ivanych? Should I, really, have sunk in Sonya's esteem if, on the contrary, I had

---

1 Do you live in Moscow? For my part, I have never before frequented the capital.

spoken of him with the love and respect which I undoubtedly bore him?

The quadrille ended, Sonya said, '*Merci*,' with as lovely an expression on her face as though I had really conferred upon her a favour. I was delighted. In fact I hardly knew myself for joy, and could not think whence I derived such ease and confidence and even daring.

'Nothing in the world can abash me now,' I thought as I wandered carelessly about the ball-room. 'I am ready for anything.'

Just then Seriozha came and requested me to be his *vis-à-vis*.

'Very well,' I said. 'I have no partner as yet, but I can soon find one.'

Glancing round the room with a confident eye, I saw that every lady was engaged save one – a tall girl standing near the drawing-room door. A tall grown-up young man was approaching her – probably for the same purpose as myself! He was but two steps from her, while I was at the further end of the room! Doing a *glissade* over the polished floor, I covered the intervening space, and clicking my heels, in a brave, firm voice asked the favour of her hand in the quadrille. Smiling with a protecting air, the young lady accorded me her hand, and the tall young man was left without a partner.

I felt so conscious of my strength that I paid no attention to his irritation, though I learnt later that he had asked somebody who the tousled-headed boy was who had rushed past and snatched away the lady from under his nose.

XXII

THE MAZURKA

LATER the same young man formed one of the first couple in a mazurka. He sprang to his feet, took his partner's hand, and then, instead of executing the *pas de Basques* which Mimi had taught us, glided forward till he arrived at a corner of the room, stopped, divided his feet, stamped his heel, and, with a spring, glided back again. I, who had found no partner for this particular dance and was sitting on the arm of Grandmamma's chair, thought to myself:

'What on earth is he doing? That is not what Mimi taught us. She always insisted that the mazurka was danced on tiptoe with smooth circular foot movements; but it seems that is not at all how it is done. And there are the Ivins and Etienne all dancing in the same way – without the *pas de Basques*! Ah! and there is Volodya as well! He too is adopting the new style, and not so badly either. And there is Sonya too, what a darling! Yes, there she comes!' I felt immensely happy at that moment.

The mazurka came to an end, and already some of the adult guests were saying goodbye to Grandmamma. Footmen, avoiding the dancers, were carefully carrying plates and glasses into the back rooms. Grandmamma was evidently tired, and spoke slowly, as if with an effort. The musicians carelessly struck up the same tune for the thirtieth time when the young lady whom I had danced with before, and who was just about to join in another mazurka, caught sight of me, and with a perfidious smile led me to Sonya and one of the innumerable Kornakova princesses, at the same time asking me, '*Rose ou ortie?*'[1]

'Ah, so it's *you!*' said Grandmamma turning round in her arm-chair. 'Go and dance, then, my boy.'

Although I would gladly have taken refuge behind the arm-chair rather than leave its shelter, I could not refuse; so I got up, said 'Rose,' and glanced timidly at Sonya. Before I had time to realise it, however, a hand in a white glove laid itself on mine, and the Kornakova girl stepped forth with a pleased smile and evidently no suspicion that I was ignorant of the steps of the dance.

I only knew that the *pas de Basques* (the only figure of it which I had been taught) would be out of place and unsuitable, and might even bring me ridicule. However, the familiar strains of the mazurka falling upon my ears, and imparting their usual impulse to my acoustic nerves (which, in their turn, imparted their usual impulse to my feet), I involuntarily, and to the

[1] Rose or nettle?

amazement of the spectators, began executing on tiptoe the circular gliding steps which I had been taught.

So long as we went straight ahead we got on reasonably well, but when it came to turning I saw that I could easily get ahead of my partner. Accordingly, to avoid any appearance of awkwardness, I stopped short, with the intention of imitating the same figure which I had seen the young man in the first couple perform so neatly. Unfortunately, just as I divided my feet and prepared to make a spring, the Princess Kornakova circled quickly round me and looked sharply at my legs with such an expression of stupefied amazement and curiosity that the glance undid me. Instead of continuing to dance, I remained marking time on the spot, in an extraordinary fashion which bore no relation whatever either to form or rhythm. At last I stopped altogether. Everyone was looking at me – some with curiosity, some with astonishment, some with disdain, and some with compassion. Grandmamma alone seemed unmoved.

'*Il ne fallait pas danser, si vous ne savez pas,*'[1] said Papa's angry voice in my ear as, pushing me gently aside, he took my partner's hand, completed the figures with her in the old style to the admiration of everyone, and finally led her back to her place. The mazurka was at an end.

'Oh Lord, why dost thou punish me so severely?'

. . . .

'Everyone despises me, and will always despise me,' I thought to myself. 'The way is closed for me to friendship, love, and honours! All, all is lost!'

Why had Volodya made signs to me which everyone saw, yet which could in no way help me? Why had that disgusting princess looked at my legs like that? Why had Sonya – she was a darling, of course! – yet why, oh why, had she smiled at that moment? Why had Papa turned red and seized me by the arm? Can it be that even he was ashamed of me? Oh, this is dreadful! Alas, if only Mamma were here she would never have blushed for her little Nikolai!

1 You should not dance if you don't know the step.

On the instant, that dear image led my imagination far away to where I could see her beloved figure. I seemed to see once more the meadow before our house, the tall lime-trees in the garden, the clear pond with the swallows swooping above it, the blue sky dappled with motionless transparent white clouds, the sweet-smelling ricks of new-mown hay. How those memories – and many another quiet, beloved recollection – floated through my troubled imagination.

XXIII
AFTER THE MAZURKA

AT supper the young man who had danced in the first couple seated himself beside me at the children's table, and treated me with an amount of attention which would have flattered my self-esteem had I been able, after the occurrence just related, to give a thought to anything beyond my failure in the mazurka. However, the young man seemed determined to cheer me up at all costs. He jested, called me a fine fellow and finally, when none of the elder folks were looking at us, began to help me to wine, first from one bottle and then from another, and made me drink it off quickly. By the time (towards the end of supper) that the butler had poured me out a quarter of a glass of champagne from a bottle wrapped in a napkin, and the young man had straightway bid him fill it up and urged me to drink it off at a draught, I had begun to feel a grateful warmth diffusing itself through my body. I also felt particularly well-disposed towards my cheery patron, and burst out laughing.

Suddenly the music of the *Grossvater* dance struck up, and everyone began to get up from the table. My friendship with the young man had now outlived its day; so, whereas he joined a group of the older folk, I, not venturing to follow him, approached Madame Valakhina to hear what she and her daughter had to say to one another.

'Just *half* an hour more?' Sonya was imploring her.

'Impossible, my angel.'

'Only to please me – just this *once*?' Sonya went on persuasively.

'Well, will it make you happy if I should be ill tomorrow?' rejoined her mother, and was incautious enough to smile.

'There! You *do* consent, and we *can* stay after all!' exclaimed Sonya, jumping for joy.

'What is to be done with such a girl?' said Madame. 'Well, run away and dance. See,' she added on perceiving me, 'here is a cavalier ready waiting for you.'

Sonya gave me her hand, and we ran into the *salon*. The wine, added to Sonya's presence and gaiety, had at once made me forget all about the unfortunate end of the mazurka. I kept executing the most splendid feats with my feet – now imitating a horse as he throws out his hoofs in the trot, now stamping like a ram infuriated at a dog, and all the while laughing regardless of appearances. Sonya also laughed unceasingly, whether we were holding each other's hands and whirling round in a circle or whether we stood still to watch an old gentleman slowly lifting his feet to step over a handkerchief, giving the impression that this was a most difficult manœuvre. Finally Sonya nearly died of merriment when I jumped half-way to the ceiling in proof of my skill.

As I passed a mirror in Grandmamma's boudoir and glanced at myself I could see that my face was all in a perspiration and my hair dishevelled – the tufts on top, in particular, sticking up more than ever. Yet my general appearance looked so happy, healthy, and good-tempered that I felt wholly pleased with myself.

'If I were always as I am now,' I thought, 'I might yet be able to please people with my looks.' Yet as soon as I glanced at my partner's lovely face again, and saw there not only the expression of happiness, health, and freedom from care which had just pleased me in my own, but also a fresh and enchanting beauty besides, I felt dissatisfied with myself again. I understood how silly of me it was to hope to attract the attention of such a wonderful being.

I could not hope that she might return my feelings – could not even think of it, yet my heart was overflowing with happiness. I could not imagine that the feeling of love which was filling my soul so pleasantly could require any happiness still greater, or wish for more than that this happiness should never cease. I felt perfectly contented. My heart beat like that of a dove, with the blood constantly rushing back to it, and I almost wept for joy.

As we passed through the corridor and peered into a little dark store-room beneath the staircase I thought: 'What bliss it would be if I could pass the rest of my life with her in that dark corner, and never let anybody know that we were there!'

'It *has* been a delightful evening, hasn't it?' I asked her in a low, tremulous voice. Then I quickened my steps – not so much out of fear of what I had said as out of fear of what I had meant to imply.

'Yes, *very*!' she answered, and turned her face to look at me with an expression so open and kind that I ceased to be afraid. I went on:

'Particularly since supper. Yet if you could only know how I regret' (I had nearly said 'how miserable I am at') 'your going, and to think that we shall see each other no more!'

'But why *shouldn't* we?' she asked, looking gravely at the toes of her slippers, and running her fingers over a latticed screen which we were passing. 'Every Tuesday and Friday I drive with Mamma on Tverskaya Street. I suppose you go for walks sometimes?'

'Well, certainly I shall ask to go for one next Tuesday, and if they won't take me I shall go by myself – even without my hat, if necessary. I know the way all right.'

'Do you know what I have just thought of?' she went on. 'You know, I call some of the boys who come to see us *thou*. Shall you and I call each other *thou* too? Wilt *thou*?' she added, bending her head towards me and looking me straight in the eyes.

At this moment we entered the ball-room, where a more lively section of the *Grossvater* dance was beginning.

'Give me your hand,' I said, under the impression that the music and noise would drown my exact words, but she, laughing, replied, '*Thy* hand, not *your* hand.' Yet the dance was over before I had succeeded in saying *thou*, even though I kept running over phrases in which the pronoun could be employed several times – and employed more than once. But I lacked the courage to say it. 'Wilt *thou*?' and '*thy* hand' sounded continually in my ears, and caused in me a kind of intoxication. I could hear and see nothing but Sonya. I watched her mother take her curls, push them back behind her ears (thus disclosing portions of her forehead and temples which I had not yet seen), and wrap her up so completely in the green shawl that nothing was left visible but the tip of her nose. Indeed, I could see that, if her little rosy fingers had not made a small opening near her mouth, she would have been unable to breathe. Finally I saw her, as she came down the staircase behind her mother, turn and nod to us quickly before she disappeared through the doorway.

Volodya, the Ivins, the young Prince Etienne, and I were all of us in love with Sonya, and all of us standing on the staircase followed her with our eyes. To whom in particular she had nodded I do not know, but at the moment I firmly believed it to be myself.

In taking leave of the Ivins I spoke quite unconcernedly and even coldly to Seriozha before I finally shook hands with him. Though he tried to appear absolutely indifferent, I think that he understood that from that day forth he had lost both my affection and his power over me, and I think he regretted it.

For the first time in my life I had proved faithless in love, and for the first time had experienced the sweetness of that sensation. I was delighted to exchange the outworn feeling of a habitual devotion for the first excitement of a love which was full of mystery and the unknown. Moreover, to fall out of love and to fall in love at one and the some moment is to love twice as powerfully as before.

XXIV

IN BED

'How could I have managed to be so long and so passionately devoted to Seriozha?' I asked myself as I lay in bed that night. 'He never either understood, appreciated or deserved my love. But Sonya! What a darling *she* is! "Wilt *thou*?" – "*Thy* hand"!'

I jumped up on all fours in bed, vividly picturing to myself her lovely face, covered my head over with the bedclothes, tucked the counterpane in on all sides and, thus snugly covered, lay quiet and enjoying the warmth until I became wholly absorbed in sweet fancies and reminiscences.

If I stared fixedly at the lining of the quilt above me I found that I could see her as clearly as I had done an hour ago. I could talk to her in my thoughts, and though it was a quite senseless conversation I derived the greatest delight from it, seeing that '*thou*' and '*thine*' and 'for *thee*' and 'to *thee*' occurred in it incessantly.

These fancies were so vivid that I could not sleep for the sweetness of my emotion, and felt as though I must commun-icate my superabundant happiness to someone.

'The darling!' I said, half-aloud, as I suddenly turned over on to my other side; then, 'Volodya, are you asleep?'

'No,' he replied in a sleepy voice. 'What's the matter?'

'I am in love, Volodya – terribly in love with Sonya.'

'Well? What of it?' he replied, stretching himself.

'Oh, but you cannot imagine what I feel. Just now, as I lay tucked up in the counterpane, I could see her and talk to her so clearly that it was marvellous! And do you know, while I lie thinking about her – I don't know why, but all at once I feel so sad that I want to cry!'

Volodya made a movement of some sort.

'One thing only I wish for,' I continued; 'and that is that I could always be with her and always be seeing her. Just that. You are in love too, I believe. Confess that you are.'

It was strange, but somehow I wanted everyone to be in love with Sonya, and everyone to tell me so.

'What has it to do with you?' said Volodya, turning round to me. 'Well, perhaps.'

'I can see that you cannot sleep,' I remarked, observing by his bright eyes that he was anything but drowsy, and pushed back the quilt. 'Then let us talk about her properly.

Isn't she splendid? If she were to say to me, "dear Nikolai, jump out of the window," or "jump into the fire," I swear I should do it at once and rejoice in doing it. Oh, how glorious she is!'

I went on picturing her again and again to my imagination, and, to enjoy the vision the better, turned over on my side and buried my head in the pillows, murmuring, 'Oh, I want to cry, Volodya.'

'What a fool you are!' he said with a slight laugh. Then, after a moment's silence, he added: 'I am not like you. I think I would rather sit and talk with her.'

'Ah! Then you *are* in love with her!' I interrupted.

'And then,' went on Volodya, smiling tenderly, 'kiss her dear little fingers and eyes and lips and nose and feet – kiss *all* of her.'

'How stupid!' I exclaimed from beneath the pillows.

'Ah, you don't understand things,' said Volodya with contempt.

'I *do* understand. It's *you* who don't understand things, and talk rubbish,' I replied through my tears.

'Well, there is nothing to cry about,' he concluded. 'You're a real girl.'

XXV

THE LETTER

On the 16th of April, nearly six months after the day just described, Papa entered our schoolroom and told us that that night we must start with him for our country house. I felt a pang at my heart when I heard the news, and my thoughts at once turned to Mamma. The cause of our unexpected departure was the following letter:

'Petrovskoye, 12*th April*.

'Only this moment, at ten o'clock in the evening, have I received your dear letter of the 3rd of April, but, as usual, I answer it at once. Fyodor brought it yesterday from town, but, as it was late, he did not give it to Mimi till this morning, and Mimi on the pretext that I was unwell kept it from me all day. I have been a little feverish. In fact, to tell the truth, this is the fourth day that I have been unwell and stayed in bed.

'Yet do not be uneasy. I feel almost myself again now, and if Ivan Vasilyevich should allow me, I think of getting up tomorrow.

'On Friday last I took the girls for a drive, and close to the little bridge by the turning on to the high road (the place which always makes me nervous), the horses stuck fast in the mud. Well, the day being fine, I thought that we would walk a little up the road until the carriage should be extricated, but no sooner had we reached the chapel than I felt obliged to sit down, I was so tired, but half an hour passed before help arrived to get the carriage dug out. I began to feel cold, for I had only thin boots on, and they were wet through. After dinner, I had alternate cold and hot turns, yet continued to follow our ordinary routine. When tea was over I sat down to the piano to play duets with Lyuba (you would be astonished to hear what progress she has made!), but imagine my surprise when I found that I could not count the beats. Several times I began to do so, yet always felt confused in my head, and kept hearing strange noises in my ears. I would begin "One – two – three –" and then suddenly go on "– eight – fifteen," and so on, and worst of all, I realised that I was talking nonsense and could not help it. At last Mimi came to my assistance and virtually forced me to retire to bed. That, my dear, was exactly how my illness began, and it was all through my own fault. The next day I had a good deal of fever, and our kind old Ivan Vasilyevich came. He has not left us since, but promises soon to restore me to the world. What a wonderful old man he is! While I was feverish and delirious he sat the whole night by my bedside without once closing his eyes; and at this moment (since he knows I am busy writing) he is with the girls in the sitting-room, and I can hear him telling them German fairy-tales, and them laughing as they listen to him.

' "*La Belle Flamande*," as you call her, is now spending her second week here as my guest (her mother having gone to pay a visit somewhere), and she is most attentive and attached to me.

She even tells me her secret affairs. Under different circumstances her beautiful face, good nature and youth might make a
most excellent girl of her, but in the society in which – according to her own account – she moves, she will be wasted. The
idea has more than once occurred to me that, had I not had so
many children of my own, it would have been a deed of mercy
to have adopted her.

'Lyuba had meant to write to you herself, but she has torn up
three sheets of paper, saying: "I know what a mocker Papa
always is. If he were to find a single fault in my letter he would
show it to everybody." Katya is as sweet as usual, and Mimi,
too, is good, but tiresome.

'Now let me speak of more serious matters. You write to me
that your affairs are not going well this winter, and that you
wish to break into the Khabarovka revenues. It seems to me
strange that you should think it necessary to ask my consent.
Surely what belongs to me belongs no less to you?

'You are so kind-hearted, my dear one, that, for fear of
worrying me, you conceal the real state of things, but I can
guess that you have lost a great deal at cards, but I assure you
there is no need to be afraid of my being angry at that. So long as
you can tide over this crisis, pray do not think much of it, and
do not torment yourself unnecessarily. I have grown accustomed to no longer relying, so far as the children are concerned,
upon your winnings, nor yet – excuse me for saying so – upon
your fortune. Therefore your losses cause me as little anxiety as
your gains give me pleasure. What I really grieve over is your
unhappy *passion itself* for gambling – a passion which bereaves
me of part of your tender affection and obliges me to tell you
such bitter truths as (God knows with what pain) I am now
telling you. I never cease to beseech Him that He may preserve
us, not from poverty (for what is poverty?), but from the
terrible juncture which would arise should the interests of the
children, which I am called upon to protect, ever come into
collision with our own. Hitherto God has listened to my
prayer. You have never yet overstepped the limit beyond
which we should be obliged either to sacrifice our property,
which no longer belongs to us, but to the children, or—— It is

terrible to think of, but the dreadful misfortune at which I hint is forever hanging over our heads. Yes, it is a heavy cross which God has given us both to carry!

'Also, you write about the children, and come back to our old point of difference by asking my consent to your placing them at a boarding-school. You know my objection to that kind of upbringing.

'I do not know, dear, whether you will accede to my request, but I nevertheless beseech you, by your love for me, to give me your promise that never so long as I am alive, nor yet after my death (if God should see fit to separate us), shall such a thing be done.

'You write that our affairs render it indispensable for you to visit St Petersburg. May Christ go with you, my dearest. Go, and return as soon as possible. We all of us miss you so much! Spring is coming in beautifully. The double door of the balcony has already been taken down, while the path to the orangery has been dry for the past four days and the peach-trees are in full blossom. Only here and there is there a little snow remaining. The swallows have returned, and today Lyuba brought me the first spring flowers. The doctor says that in about three days' time I shall be well again and able to take the open air and to enjoy the April sun. Now, *au revoir* my dearest one. Do not be alarmed, I beg of you, either on account of my illness or on account of your losses. Finish your business as soon as possible, and then return here with the children for the whole summer. I am making wonderful plans for our passing of it, and I only need your presence to realise them.'

The next part of the letter was written in French, as well as in a fluent but uneven hand, on another scrap of paper. I translate it word for word:

'Do not believe what I have just written to you about my illness. It is more serious than anyone knows. I only know that I shall never leave my bed again. Do not, therefore, delay a minute in coming here with the children. Perhaps it may yet be permitted me to embrace and bless them. It is my last wish that it should be so. I know what a terrible blow this will be to you, but you would have had to hear it sooner or later – if not from me, from others. Let us try to bear the calamity with fortitude, and place our trust in the mercy of God. Let us submit ourselves to His will.

'Do not think that what I am writing is some delusion of my sick imagination. On the contrary, I am perfectly clear at this moment, and absolutely calm. Nor must you comfort yourself with the false hope that these are the unreal, confused forebodings of a timid spirit, for I feel – indeed, I *know*, since God has deigned to reveal it to me – that I have now but a very short time to live.

'Will my love for you and the children cease with my life? I know that that can never be. At this moment I am too full of that love to be capable of believing that such a feeling (which constitutes a part of my very existence) can ever perish. My soul cannot exist without its love for you, and I know that that love will exist for ever, since such a feeling could never have been awakened if it were not to be eternal.

'I shall no longer be with you, yet I firmly believe that my love will cleave to you always; and from that thought I glean such comfort that I await the approach of death calmly and without fear.

'Yes, I am calm, and God knows that I have ever looked, and do look now, upon death as no more than the passage to a better life. Yet why do tears blind my eyes? Why should the children lose a mother who is so dear to them? Why must you, my husband, experience such a heavy and unlooked-for blow? Why must I die when your love was making life so boundlessly happy for me?

'But His holy will be done!

'The tears prevent my writing more. It may be that I shall never see you again. I thank you, my darling beyond all price, for all the happiness with which you have surrounded me in this life. Soon I shall appear before God Himself to pray that He may reward you. Farewell, my dearest! Remember that, if I am no longer here, my love will none the less *never and nowhere* abandon you. Farewell, Volodya – farewell, my angel! Farewell, my Benjamin, my little Nikolai! Surely they will never forget me?'

With this letter was enclosed a note in French from Mimi, the contents of which were as follows:

'The sad presentiments of which she has written to you are but too surely confirmed by the words of the doctor. Yesterday evening she ordered the letter to be posted at once, but, thinking that she did so in delirium, I waited until this morning, and then decided to open it. Hardly had I broken the seal, than Natalya Nikolayevna asked me what I had done with the letter, and told me to burn it if not yet despatched. She is forever speaking of it, and saying that it will kill you. Do not delay your departure for an instant if you wish to see the angel before she leaves us. Pray excuse this scribble, but I have not slept now for three nights. You know how much I love her.'

Later I heard from Natalya Savishna, who passed the whole of the night of the 11th April at Mamma's bedside, that after writing the first part of the letter Mamma laid it down upon the little table beside her and settled down to sleep.

'I confess,' said Natalya Savishna, 'that I too dozed off in the arm-chair, and let the stocking I was knitting slip from my hands. Suddenly, some time after midnight, I thought I heard her saying something; I opened my eyes and looked at her. My darling was sitting up in bed, with her hands clasped together like this, and streams of tears gushing from her eyes.

'I sprang to my feet, and asked what the matter was.

' "Ah, Natalya Savishna, if you could only know what I have just seen!" she said; yet, for all my asking, she would say no more, beyond telling me to move the bedside table closer. She added something to her letter, ordered me to seal it in her presence, and said that it must be sent off directly. From that moment she grew rapidly worse.'

XXVI
WHAT AWAITED US AT THE COUNTRY-HOUSE

ON the 18th of April we descended from the carriage at the front door of the house at Petrovskoye. All the way from Moscow Papa had been preoccupied, and when Volodya had asked him 'whether Mamma was ill' he had looked at him sadly and nodded an affirmative. Nevertheless he had grown more composed during the journey, and it was only when we were actually nearing home that his face again began to grow more and more sorrowful, until, as he leaped from the carriage and asked Foka (who had run breathlessly to meet us), 'How is Natalya Nikolayevna now?' his voice was trembling and his eyes had filled with tears. The good old Foka looked at us evasively, and then lowered his gaze again. Finally he said as he opened the hall-door and turned his head aside: 'It is the sixth day since she has not left her bed.'

Milka who, as we afterwards learned, had never ceased to whine from the day when Mamma was taken ill, came leaping joyfully to meet Papa and barking a welcome as she licked his hands, but Papa pushed her aside and went first to the drawing-room and then into the sitting-room, from which a door led into the bedroom. The nearer he approached the bedroom, the more did his movements express the agitation that he felt. Entering the sitting-room, he crossed it on tiptoe, hardly daring to breathe. Even then he had to stop and make the sign of the cross before he could summon up courage to turn the handle of the door. At that moment Mimi, with dishevelled hair and eyes red with weeping, came hastily out of the corridor.

'Ah, Pyotr Alexandrych!' she said in a whisper and with a marked expression of despair. Then, observing that Papa was about to open the door, she whispered again:

'Not this way. This door is locked. You must go in through the maids' room.'

Oh, how terribly all this wrought upon my imagination, racked as it was by grief and terrible forebodings!

So we went round to the maids' room. In the corridor we met the idiot boy, Akim, who had been wont to amuse us with his grimaces, but at this moment I could see nothing comical in him. Indeed, the sight of his vacant indifferent face struck me more painfully than anything else. In the maid-servants' room, through which we had to pass, two maids were sitting at their needlework, but rose to salute us with an expression so mournful that I felt really frightened. Passing next through Mimi's room, Papa opened the door of the bedroom, and we entered. The two windows on the right were curtained over with shawls, and close to them sat Natalya Savishna, spectacles on nose and engaged in knitting a stocking. She did not approach us to kiss me as she had been used to do, but just rose and looked at us through her spectacles, her tears beginning to flow afresh. Somehow it disturbed me to see everyone, on beholding us, begin to cry, although they had been calm enough before.

To the left of the door stood a screen, and behind it the bed and the bedside table, a small medicine chest, and a great arm-chair in which the doctor lay asleep. Beside the bed a young, fair-haired and remarkably beautiful girl in a white house-coat, the sleeves pushed up a little, was applying ice to Mamma's head, but Mamma herself I could not see.

This girl was '*la belle Flamande*' of whom Mamma had written, and who afterwards played so important a part in our family life. As we entered she disengaged one of her hands, straightened the pleats of her dress on her bosom, and whispered, 'She is only partly conscious.'

Though I was in deep distress, I observed automatically at that moment every little detail.

It was almost dark in the room, and very hot, while the air was heavy with the mingled scent of mint, eau-de-cologne, camomile, and Hoffmann's drops. This smell caught my attention so strongly that even now I can never smell it, or even recall it, without my imagination carrying me back to that dark, close room, and all the tiniest details of that dreadful time.

Mamma's eyes were wide open, but she saw nothing...Never shall I forget the terrible expression in them – the expression of so much suffering!

Then we were taken away.

When, later, I was able to ask Natalya Savishna about Mamma's last moments she told me the following:

'After you were taken out of the room, my beloved one struggled for a long time, as though someone were trying to suffocate her. Then at last her head slipped off the pillows, and she fell into a doze, peacefully, like an angel from heaven. I went

out for a moment to see about her drink, and just as I entered
the room again my darling was throwing the bedclothes from
off her and beckoning for your dear papa to come to her. He
stooped over her, but strength failed her to say what she wanted
to. All she could do was to open her lips and gasp, "O God, O
Lord! The children, the children!" I would have run to fetch
you, but Ivan Vasilyevich stopped me, saying that it would only
excite her more – it were best not to do so. After that she would
just stretch her arms out, and drop them again. What she meant
by that gesture the good God alone knows, but I think that in it
she was blessing you – you the children she could not see. God
did not grant her to see her little ones before her death. Then
she raised herself up – did my little love, my darling – yes, just *so*
with her hands, and spoke out in a voice which I cannot bear to
remember, "Mother of God, never forsake them!"

'Then the pain mounted to her heart, and from her eyes it
was plain that she suffered terribly, poor dear! She sank back
upon the pillows, tore at the sheet with her teeth, and wept,
young master, wept———'

'Yes, and what then?' I asked; but Natalya Savishna could say
no more. She turned away and cried bitterly.

Mamma had expired in terrible agonies.

XXVII

GRIEF

LATE the following evening I thought I would like to look at
her once more; so, conquering an involuntary sense of fear,
I gently opened the door of the *salon* and entered on tiptoe.

In the middle of the room, on a table, lay the coffin, with tall
silver candlesticks in which the wax candles had burnt low. In
the further corner sat the chanter, reading the Psalms in a low,
monotonous voice.

I stopped at the door and tried to look, but my eyes were so
weak with crying, and my nerves so terribly on edge, that
I could distinguish nothing. The light, the brocade, the velvet,
the great candlesticks, the pink pillow trimmed with lace, the
paper frontlet, the ribboned cap, and – something else of a

translucent, wax-like colour: everything seemed to mingle together in a strange blur. I mounted a chair to see her face, yet where it should have been I could see only that pale yellow wax-like, translucent something. I could not believe it to be her face. Yet, as I stood gazing at it, I at last recognised the familiar, beloved features. I shuddered with horror to realise that this was she. Why were those closed eyes so sunken? What had laid that dreadful paleness upon her cheeks and stamped the black spot beneath the transparent skin on one of them? Why was the expression of the whole face so cold and severe? Why were the lips so pale, and their outline so beautiful, so majestic, so expressive of an unearthly calm that, as I looked at them, a chill shudder ran through my hair and down my back?

Somehow, as I gazed, an irrepressible, incomprehensible power seemed to compel me to keep my eyes fixed upon that lifeless face. I could not turn away, yet my imagination began to picture before me scenes of her active life and happiness. I forgot that the corpse lying before me now – the *thing* at which I was gazing unconsciously as at an object which had nothing in common with my memories – was *she*. I fancied I could see her – now here, now there, alive, happy, and smiling. Then some feature in the pale face at which I was gazing would suddenly arrest my attention, and in a flash I recalled the terrible reality and shuddered – though still unable to turn my eyes away. Then again the dreams would replace the reality – then again the reality shattered the dreams. At last my imagination grew weary and ceased to deceive me; the consciousness of the reality also vanished, and for a while I became insensible.

How long I remained in that condition I do not know, nor yet what it contained. I only know that for a time I lost all sense of my existence, and experienced a kind of vague blissfulness which, though grand and sweet, was also sad.

It may be that, as it ascended to a better world, her beautiful soul had looked down with longing at the world in which she had left us – that it had seen my sorrow, and pitying me had returned to earth on the wings of love to console and bless me with a heavenly smile of compassion.

The door creaked as the chanter entered who was to relieve his predecessor. The noise roused me, and my first thought was that, seeing me standing on the chair, not weeping but in a posture which had nothing touching in its aspect, he might take me for an unfeeling boy who had climbed on to the chair out of compassion or mere curiosity: and so I hastened to make the sign of the cross, to bend down my head, and to burst out crying.

As I recall my impressions of that episode now, I find that it was only during my moments of self-forgetfulness that my grief was whole-hearted. True, both before and after the funeral I never ceased to cry and to look miserable, yet I feel conscience-stricken when I recall that grief of mine, seeing that always present in it there was an element of self-love – of a desire to show that I was more grieved than anyone else, of an interest which I took in observing the effect produced upon others by my tears, and of an idle curiosity leading me to remark Mimi's bonnet and the faces of all present. The mere circumstance that I despised myself for not feeling grief to the exclusion of everything else, and that I endeavoured to conceal all other emotions, shows that my sadness was insincere and unnatural. I took a delight in feeling that I was unhappy and in trying to feel more so; and this egotistic consciousness completely annulled any element of real sincerity in my woe.

That night I slept calmly and soundly (as is usual after any great emotion), and awoke with my tears dried and my nerves restored. At ten o'clock we were summoned to attend the vigil service which was celebrated before the body was borne away. The room was full of weeping servants and peasants who had come to bid farewell to their late mistress. During the service I myself wept a great deal, as befitted the occasion, made frequent signs of the cross, and bowed low to the ground, but I did not pray with my soul, and felt if anything almost indifferent. My thoughts were chiefly centred upon the new jacket which I was wearing (a garment which was tight under the arms) and upon how to avoid soiling my trousers at the knees when I knelt down. Also I took the most minute notice of all present. Papa stood at the head of the coffin. He was as white as a sheet, and only with difficulty restrained his tears. His tall figure in its black frockcoat, his pale, expressive face, the graceful, assured manner in which, as usual, he made the sign of the cross or bowed until he touched the floor with his fingers or took the candle from the priest or went to the coffin – all were exceedingly effective; yet for some reason or another I felt a grudge against him for that very ability to appear so effective at such a moment. Mimi stood leaning against the wall as though scarcely able to support herself. Her dress was all crumpled and had bits of fluff sticking to it, and her cap was cocked to one side, while her eyes were red with weeping, her head shaking, and she sobbed incessantly in a heartrending manner as ever and again she buried her face in her handkerchief or her hands. I imagined that she did this to check her forced sobbing without being seen by the spectators. I remembered too her telling Papa, the evening before, that Mamma's death had come upon her as a blow from which she could never hope to recover; that with Mamma she had lost everything; but that 'the angel,' as she called my mother, had not forgotten her when at the point of death, since she had declared her wish to render her and Katya's fortunes secure for ever. Mimi had shed bitter tears while relating this, and very likely her sorrow, if not wholly pure and disinterested, was in the main sincere. Lyuba, in a black dress trimmed with white muslin weepers, her face wet with tears, stood with her head bowed upon her breast. She rarely looked at the coffin, yet whenever she did so her face expressed a sort of childish fear. Katya stood near her mother, and, despite her lengthened face, looked as rosy as ever. Volodya's frank nature was frank also in grief. He stood looking grave and as though he were staring at some object with fixed eyes. Then suddenly his lips would begin to quiver, and he would hastily make the sign of the cross, and bow his head again. Such of those present as were strangers I found intolerable. In fact, the phrases of condolence with which they addressed Papa (such, for instance, as that 'she is better off now,' 'she was too good for this world,' and so on) awakened in me something like fury.

What right had they to weep over or to talk about her? Some of them, in referring to us, called us 'orphans' – just as though it were not a matter of common knowledge that children who have lost their mother are known as orphans! Probably (I thought) they liked to be the first to give us that name, just as some people find pleasure in being the first to address a newly-married girl as 'Madame.'

In a far corner of the room, and almost hidden by the open door of the butler's pantry, knelt a grey-haired, bent old woman. With hands clasped together and eyes lifted to heaven, she prayed only – not wept. Her soul went out to God, and she was asking Him soon to reunite her with the one whom she had loved beyond all beings on this earth, and whom she earnestly hoped that she would very soon meet again.

'There stands one who truly loved her,' I thought to myself, and felt ashamed.

The service was over. They uncovered the face of the deceased, and all present except ourselves went up to the coffin to give her the kiss of farewell.

One of the last to take leave of her departed mistress was a peasant woman who was holding by the hand a pretty little girl of five whom she had brought with her, God knows for what reason. Just at a moment when I chanced to drop my wet handkerchief and was stooping to pick it up again, a loud, piercing scream startled me, and filled me with such terror that, were I to live a hundred years, I should never forget it. Even now the recollection always sends a cold shudder through my frame. I raised my head. Standing on the chair near the coffin was the peasant woman, struggling to hold the little girl in her arms, and it was this same poor child who had screamed with such dreadful, desperate frenzy as, pushing with her little fists and straining her terrified face away, she still continued to gaze with dilated eyes at the face of the corpse. I too screamed in a voice perhaps more dreadful still, and ran headlong from the room.

Only now did I understand the source of the strong, oppressive smell which, mingling with the scent of the incense, filled the chamber, while the thought that the face which, but a few days ago, had been full of beauty and tenderness – the face which I loved more than anything else in all the world – was now capable of inspiring horror at length revealed to me, as though for the first time, the terrible truth, and filled my soul with despair.

XXVIII
LAST SAD RECOLLECTIONS

MAMMA was no longer with us, but our life went on as usual. We went to bed and got up at the same times and in the same rooms; morning and evening tea, dinner and supper continued to be at their usual hours; chairs and tables remained standing in their accustomed place; nothing in the house or in our mode of life was altered: only, *she* was not there.

Yet it seemed to me as though such a misfortune ought to have changed everything. Our ordinary mode of life appeared like an insult to her memory. It recalled too vividly her absence.

The day before the funeral I felt as though I should like to rest a little after dinner, and accordingly went to Natalya Savishna's room with the intention of installing myself comfortably under the warm, soft down of the quilt on her bed. When I entered I found Natalya Savishna herself lying on the bed and apparently asleep, but on hearing my footsteps she sat up, removed the woollen shawl which had been protecting her face from the flies, and adjusting her cap, sat forward on the edge of the bed. Since it frequently happened that I came to lie down in her room after dinner, she guessed my errand at once, and getting up, said:

'So you have come to rest here a little, have you? Lie down, then, my dearest.'

'Oh, but how can you think that, Natalya Savishna?' I exclaimed as I held her back by the arm. 'I did not come for that. I just came . . . No, you are tired yourself, so *you* lie down.'

'I am quite rested now, darling,' she said (though I knew that it was three nights since she had closed her eyes). 'Yes, I am indeed, and have no wish to sleep again,' she added with a deep sigh.

I felt that I wanted to speak to her of our misfortune, since I knew her sincerity and love, and thought that it would be a consolation to me to weep with her.

'Natalya Savishna,' I said after a pause, sitting down upon the bed, 'would you ever have thought of this?'

The old woman looked at me with astonishment and curiosity, for she probably did not quite understand my question.

'Yes, who would ever have thought of it?' I repeated.

'Ah, my darling,' she said with a glance of tender compassion, 'it is not only "Who would ever have thought of it?" but "Who, even now, would ever believe it?" I am old, and my bones should long ago have gone to rest rather than that I should have lived to see the old master, your Grandpapa of blessed memory Prince Nikolai Mikhailovich, two of my brothers, and my sister Anna all buried before me, though all younger than me – and now my darling, for my sins, no doubt, gone home before me! Yet it has been God's will. He took her away because she was worthy to be taken, and because He has need of the good ones in heaven.'

This simple thought seemed to me a consolation, and I pressed closer to Natalya Savishna. She laid her hands upon her bosom as she looked upward, her moist, sunken eyes expressive of a deep but resigned sorrow. In her soul was a sure and certain hope that God would not long separate her from the one upon whom the whole strength of her love had for many years been concentrated.

'Yes, my dear,' she went on, 'it is a long time now since I used to nurse and swaddle her, and she used to call me Nasha. She used to come jumping upon me, throwing her little arms around me and kissing me, and say, "*My* Nashik, *my* darling, *my* ducky," and I used to answer jokingly, "Well, my love, I don't believe that you *do* love me. You will be a grown-up young lady soon, and going away to be married, and will leave your Nasha forgotten." Then she would grow thoughtful and say, "I think I had better *not* marry if my Nasha cannot go with me, for I mean never to leave her." Yet, alas! she has left me now and didn't wait! Who was there in the world she did not love? Yes, my dearest, it must never be *possible* for you to forget your Mamma. She was not a creature of earth – she was an angel from heaven. When her soul has entered the heavenly kingdom she will continue to love you and to be proud of you even there.'

'But why do you say "when her soul has entered the heavenly kingdom," Natalya Savishna?' I asked. 'I should think it is there now.'

'No, my dearest,' replied Natalia as she lowered her voice and settled herself yet closer to me, 'her soul is still here,' and she pointed upwards. She spoke almost in a whisper, but with such an intensity of conviction that I too involuntarily raised my eyes and looked at the ceiling, as though expecting to see something there. 'Before the souls of the just enter Paradise they have to undergo forty trials, my dear, for forty days, and during that time they may hover around their earthly home.'

She went on speaking for some time in this strain – speaking with the same simplicity and conviction as though she were relating utterly common things which she herself had witnessed, and to doubt which could never enter into anyone's head. I listened almost breathlessly, and though I did not understand all she said, I never for a moment doubted her word.

'Yes, my darling, she is here now, and perhaps looking at us and listening to what we are saying,' concluded Natalya Savishna. Lowering her head, she fell silent. She needed a handkerchief to wipe away the tears which were streaming from her eyes; she got up, looked me straight in the face, and said in a voice trembling with emotion:

'Ah, through this trial God has brought me many steps nearer to Him. Why, indeed, am I still here? Who have I to live for? Who have I to love?'

'Do you not love *us*, then?' I asked reproachfully, and half-choking with my tears.

'Yes, God knows that I love you, my darlings; but to love anyone as I loved *her* – that I cannot do.'

She could say no more, but turned her head aside and sobbed loudly. As for me, I no longer thought of going to sleep, but sat silently with her and mingled my tears with hers.

Presently Foka entered the room, but, on seeing our emotion and no doubt not wishing to disturb us, stopped short at the door, looking at us timidly and without speaking.

'Do you want anything, my good Foka?' asked Natalya Savishna as she wiped away her tears.

'If you please, a pound and a half of raisins, four pounds of sugar, and three pounds of rice for the *kutya*.'[1]

'Yes, in one moment,' said Natalya Savishna as she took a pinch of snuff and hastened to the provision chest. All traces of the grief aroused by our conversation disappeared on the instant that she had duties to fulfil, for she looked upon those duties as of paramount importance.

'But why *four* pounds?' she objected as she got out the sugar and weighed it on the balance. 'Three and a half would be sufficient,' and she withdrew a few lumps from the scale pan. 'How is it, too, that, though I weighed out eight pounds of rice yesterday, more is wanted now? Say what you will, Foka, but I am not letting them have any more rice. I suppose Vanka is glad that there is confusion in the house just now, for he thinks that nothing will be noticed, but I am not going to have any careless extravagance with my master's goods. Who ever heard of such a thing? Eight pounds!'

'Well, what is to do? He says it is all gone.'

'Oh well, then, here it is. Let him take it.'

I was struck by the sudden transition from the touching sensibility with which she had just been speaking to me to this petty reckoning and captiousness. Yet, thinking it over afterwards, I recognised that it was merely because, in spite of what was lying on her heart, she retained the habit of duty, and that it was the strength of that habit which enabled her to pursue her functions as of old. Her grief was too strong and too true to require any pretence of being unable to fulfil trivial tasks, nor would she have understood that anyone could want so to pretend.

Vanity is a sentiment so entirely at variance with genuine grief, yet a sentiment so inherent in human nature, that even

1 A cake partaken of by the mourners at a Russian funeral.

the most poignant sorrow does not always drive it wholly forth. Vanity in sorrow shows itself in a desire to be *recognised* as unhappy or resigned or brave; and this ignoble desire – an aspiration which, for all that we may not acknowledge it, is rarely absent, even in cases of the utmost affliction – detracts greatly from the force, the dignity, and the sincerity of the most profound grief. Natalya Savishna had been so sorely smitten by her misfortune that not a single wish of her own remained in her soul – she went on living purely by habit.

Having handed over the provisions to Foka, and reminded him about the pasty which must be ready for the clergy, she took up her knitting and seated herself by my side again. The conversation reverted to the old topic, and we once more mourned and dried our tears together.

These talks with Natalya Savishna I repeated every day, for her quiet tears and words of devotion brought me relief and comfort. Soon, however, a parting came. Three days after the funeral we returned with all our things to Moscow, and I was destined never to see her again.

Grandmamma received the sad tidings only on our return to her house, and her grief was extraordinary. At first we were not allowed to see her, since for a whole week she was beside herself, and the doctors were afraid for her life. Not only did she decline all medicine whatsoever, but she refused to speak to anybody or to take nourishment, and never closed her eyes in sleep. Sometimes, as she sat alone in the arm-chair in her room, she would begin laughing and crying at the same time, with a sort of tearless grief, or else relapse into convulsions, and scream out dreadful, incoherent words in a horrible voice. It was the first dire sorrow which she had known in her life, and it reduced her almost to despair. She would begin accusing first one person, and then another, of bringing this misfortune upon her, and rail at and threaten them with the most extraordinary virulence. Finally she would rise from her arm-chair, pace the room for a while, and end by falling senseless to the floor.

Once, when I went to her room, she appeared to be sitting as usual quietly in her chair, yet with an air which struck me as curious. Though her eyes were wide open, their glance was vacant and meaningless, and she seemed to gaze in my direction without seeing me. Suddenly her lips parted slowly in a smile, and she said in a touchingly tender voice: 'Come here, then, my dearest one; come here, my angel.' Thinking that it was myself she was addressing, I moved closer, but it was not I whom she was beholding at that moment. 'Oh, my treasure,' she went on, 'if only you could know how tormented I have been, and how delighted I am that you have come back to me.' I understood then that she believed herself to be looking upon Mamma, and halted where I was. 'They told me you were gone,' she concluded with a frown; 'but what nonsense! As if you could die before *me*!' and she laughed a terrible, hysterical laugh.

Only those who can love strongly can experience an overwhelming grief. Yet their very need of loving sometimes serves to throw off their grief from them and to save them. The moral nature of man is more tenacious of life than the physical, and grief never kills.

By the end of a week Grandmamma's power of weeping had returned to her, and she began to recover. Her first thought when her reason returned was for us children, and her love for us was greater than ever. We never left her arm-chair, and she would talk of Mamma, and weep softly, and caress us tenderly.

Nobody who saw her grief could say that it was consciously exaggerated, for its expression was too strong and touching; yet for some reason or another my sympathy went out more to Natalya Savishna, and to this day I am convinced that nobody loved and regretted Mamma so purely and sincerely as did that simple-hearted, affectionate being.

With Mamma's death the happy time of my childhood came to an end, and a new epoch – the epoch of my boyhood – began; but since my memories of Natalya Savishna whom I never saw again, and who exercised such a strong and beneficial influence upon the bent of my mind and the development of my sensibility belong rather to the first period, I will add a few words about her and her death.

I heard later from servants who had stayed behind on the estate that, after our return to Moscow, she found time hang very heavy on her hands. Although the clothes-presses were still under her charge, and she never ceased to rummage in them and rearrange them – to take things out and hang them up and put them away again – she sadly missed the din and bustle of a country-house occupied by the family to which she had been accustomed from her childhood up. Consequently grief, the alteration in her mode of life, and her lack of activity soon combined to develop in her a malady of old age to which she had always been more or less subject. Scarcely a year after Mamma's death dropsy showed itself, and she took to her bed.

I can imagine how sad it must have been for her to go on living – still more, to die – alone in that great empty house at Petrovskoye, with no relations or friends near her. Everyone there esteemed and loved her, but she had formed no intimate friendships in the place, and was rather proud of the fact. That was because, enjoying her master's confidence as she did, and having so many chests full of all sorts of goods under her care, she considered that intimacies would lead to culpable partiality and indulgence. Consequently (and perhaps, also, because she had nothing really in common with the other servants) she kept them all at a distance, and used to say that she 'recognised neither kinsman nor cronies in the house, and would permit of no exceptions with regard to her master's property.'

Instead, she sought and found consolation in fervent prayer to God. Yet sometimes, in those moments of weakness to which all of us are subject, and when man's best solace is the tears and compassion of his fellow-creatures, she would take her little pug-dog on to her bed, and talk to it, and weep softly over it as it answered her caresses by licking her hands, with its yellow eyes fixed upon her. When the dog began to whine plaintively she would say as she quieted it: 'Enough, enough! I know without thy telling me that my time is near.'

A month before her death she took out of her trunk some fine white calico, white cambric, and pink ribbon, and with the help of the maid-servant who looked after her fashioned the garments in which she wished to be buried and arranged everything for her funeral down to the last detail. Next she put everything in her master's chests in order and handed them over to the bailiff's wife with an inventory which she had made out with scrupulous accuracy. All that she kept back was a couple of silk gowns, an ancient shawl which Grandmamma had given her at some time, and Grandpapa's gold-laced military uniform – things which had been presented to her absolutely, and which, thanks to her care and orderliness, were in an excellent state of preservation – particularly the handsome gold lace and embroidery on the uniform.

Just before her death she expressed a wish that one of the gowns (the pink one) should be made into a dressing-gown or a quilted jacket for Volodya; that the other one (with brown checks) should be made into a similar garment for me; and that the shawl should go to Lyuba. As for the uniform, it was to go either to Volodya or to me, according as the one or the other of us should first become an officer. All the rest of her property (save only forty roubles, which she set aside for the costs of her burial and for prayers for her soul) was to pass to her brother, a peasant who had received his freedom long since, and with whom, since he lived a dissipated life in a distant province, she had had no real contact during her lifetime.

When, eventually, he arrived to claim the inheritance, and found that its sum-total amounted only to twenty-five paper roubles, he refused to believe it, and declared that it was impossible that his sister – a woman who for sixty years had had sole charge in a wealthy house, as well as all her life had been stingy and averse to giving away even the smallest rag – should have left no more: yet it was a fact.

Natalya Savishna's last illness lasted for two months, and she bore her sufferings with truly Christian fortitude. Never did she fret or complain, but as usual appealed continually to God. An hour before the end came she made her final confession, received the sacrament with quiet joy, and was anointed with holy oil.

Then she begged forgiveness of everyone in the household for any wrong she might have done them, and requested her confessor Father Vasili to tell us that she did not know how to thank us for all our kindnesses to her, and that she begged our forgiveness if, in her ignorance, she had ever at any time by her stupidity given us offence. 'Yet a thief have I never been. Never have I taken so much as a piece of thread that was not my own.' Such was the one quality which she valued in herself.

Dressed in the cap and gown prepared so long beforehand, and propping her elbow on the pillow, she conversed with the priest up to the very last moment. Suddenly recollecting that she had left him nothing for the poor, she took out ten roubles, and asked him to distribute them in the parish. Lastly she made the sign of the cross, lay down, and breathed her last – pronouncing with a smile of joy the name of the Almighty.

She quitted life without a pang, and, so far from fearing death, welcomed it as a blessing. How often do we hear that said, and how seldom is it a reality! Natalya Savishna had no reason to fear death, for the simple reason that she died in a sure and certain faith and in strict obedience to the commands of the Gospel. Her whole life had been one of pure, disinterested love, of utter self-negation.

What if her convictions might have been of a more enlightened order, her life directed to a higher aim, was that pure soul any less worthy of love and reverence? She accomplished the highest and best achievement in this world: she died without regret and without fear.

They buried her where she had wished to lie – near the little chapel which still covers Mamma's grave. The little mound beneath which she sleeps is overgrown with nettles and burdock, and surrounded by a black railing, and I never forget, when leaving the chapel, to approach that railing, and to bow down reverently to the ground.

Sometimes, too, I stand thoughtfully between the railing and the chapel, and sad memories pass through my mind. The thought comes to me as I stand there: 'Did Providence really unite me to those two beings solely in order to make me mourn their loss my whole life long?'

PART II
BOYHOOD

I
A SLOW JOURNEY

ONCE again two vehicles are drawn up at the front door of the house at Petrovskoye. In one of them, a closed carriage, sit Mimi, Katya, Lyuba and their maid, with the steward Yakov on the box, while in the other – a britzka – sit Volodya, myself, and our servant Vasili, a serf recently taken into household service. Papa, who is to follow us to Moscow in a few days, stands bareheaded on the entrance-steps. He makes the sign of the cross at the windows of the carriages.

'Christ go with you! Off you go!'

Yakov and our coachman (for we are travelling with our own horses) lift their caps in answer, and also cross themselves.

'Gee up! God go with us!'

The carriage and the britzka jolt off along the uneven road-way, and the birch-trees of the great avenue file out of sight behind us.

I am not in the least depressed on this occasion, for my mind is not so much turned upon what I am leaving as upon what is awaiting me. In proportion as the various objects connected with the sad recollections which have recently filled my imagin-ation recede behind me, those recollections lose their power, and give place to a consolatory feeling of life, youthful vigour, freshness, and hope.

Seldom have I spent four days more – well, I will not say gaily, since I should still have shrunk from appearing gay – but more agreeably and pleasantly than those occupied by our journey. No longer were my eyes confronted with the closed door of

Mamma's room (which I had never been able to pass without a shudder), nor with the closed piano (which we did not go near now, and could not even look at without a pang of fear), nor with mourning garments (we had each of us on our ordinary travelling clothes), nor with all those other objects which recalled to me so vividly our irreparable loss, and forced me to abstain from any display of merriment lest I should unwittingly offend against *her* memory. Here, on the contrary, a continual succession of new and exciting objects and places now catches and holds my attention, and the charms of spring awaken in my soul a soothing sense of satisfaction with the present and of bright hope for the future.

Very early in the morning the merciless Vasili (who with new duties, is like most people zealous to a fault) comes and strips off my counterpane, affirming that it is time for us to be off, since everything is in readiness for us to continue our journey. Though I feel inclined to snuggle down and resist – though I would gladly spend another quarter of an hour in sweet enjoyment of my morning slumber – Vasili's inexorable face shows that he will grant me no respite, but is ready to tear away the counterpane twenty times more if necessary. Accordingly I submit to the inevitable, and run down into the courtyard to wash.

In the entrance-hall a samovar, on which Mitka the post-illion is blowing – his face as red as a crab – is already boiling. All is grey and misty out of doors, like steam from a smoking dunghill, but in the eastern sky the sun diffuses a clear, cheerful radiance, making the straw roofs of the sheds around the courtyard sparkle with dew. Beneath them stand our horses, tethered to their mangers, and I can hear the ceaseless sound of their chewing. A curly-haired house-dog which has been spending the night on a dry dunghill now lazily stretches itself and, wagging its tail, walks slowly across the courtyard. A bustling peasant-woman opens the creaking gates, turns her meditative cows into the street (whence come the stamping, lowing and bellowing of other cattle), and exchanges a word or two with a sleepy neighbour. Philip, with his shirt-sleeves rolled up, is working the windlass of a draw-well, and sending sparkling fresh water coursing into an oaken trough, while in a puddle beneath it some early-rising ducks are taking a bath. It gives me pleasure to watch his striking, thickly-bearded face, and the veins and muscles as they stand out upon his great powerful arms whenever he makes an extra effort.

In the room behind the partition-wall where Mimi and the girls have slept (yet so near to ourselves that we have exchanged confidences overnight) movements are audible, their maid Masha keeps running in and out with clothes which she conceals from our curious gaze by covering them with her skirt, and at last the door opens and we are summoned to drink our tea.

Vasili, however, in an access of superfluous zeal, runs into the room to fetch first one article and then another and urges Marya Ivanovna to hasten her preparations for an early start.

The horses are harnessed and show their impatience by now and then tinkling their bells. Cases, trunks, and boxes both large and small are replaced, and we set about taking our seats. Yet, every time that we get in, the mountain of luggage in the britzka seems to have grown larger than before, and we cannot conceive how things were arranged yesterday, and how we should sit now. A walnut tea-caddy with a three-cornered lid in particular greatly irritates me, but Vasili declares that 'things will soon right themselves,' and I have no choice but to believe him.

The sun has just risen above the dense white clouds which cover the eastern sky, and the surrounding countryside stands out in a cheerful, calm radiance. Everything looks so beautiful, and my heart feels so light and peaceful... Before us the road winds onward like a broad, dark-grey ribbon through fields of dry stubble and green meadows glittering with dew. Here and there a gloomy willow or young birch-tree with tiny sticky leaves casts a long motionless shadow over the dry clayey ruts and short green grass-tufts of the track...Yet even the monotonous din of our carriage-wheels and the tinkling of our collar-bells cannot drown the song of the lark soaring up from the very edge of the road, nor the combined odour of moth-eaten cloth, dust, and sourness peculiar to our britzka overpower the fresh scents of the morning. I feel in my heart that delightful impulse to be up and doing which is a sign of sincere enjoyment.

As I had not been able to say my prayers in the courtyard of the inn, but had nevertheless noticed more than once that on the very first day when I omit to perform that ceremony some misfortune overtakes me, I now hasten to make good the omission. Taking off my cap, and turning my face to a corner of the britzka, I duly recite my prayers, and unobtrusively cross myself beneath my coat so that no one can see me do it. Yet all the while a thousand different objects are distracting my attention, and more than once I absent-mindedly repeat a prayer twice over.

Soon on the little footpath winding along beside the road become visible some slowly moving figures. They are woman pilgrims. On their heads are dirty kerchiefs, on their backs knapsacks of birch-bark, their legs are swathed in dirty ragged bands of cloth, and on their feet are clumsy bast sandals. Moving their staffs in regular rhythm, and scarcely throwing us a glance, they press onwards in single file with heavy tread.

'Where are they going?' I wonder to myself, 'and for what purpose? Is it a long pilgrimage they are making? And how soon will the long shadows they cast on the road join the shadow of the willow which they must pass?'

Now a carriage with four posthorses can be seen swiftly approaching us. In two seconds the faces which looked out at us from it with smiling curiosity have vanished. How strange it seems that those faces should have nothing in common with me, and that in all probability they will never meet my eyes again.

Next come a pair of shaggy, sweating horses, galloping along the roadside in their collars, with the traces looped up to their harness. And behind them, his long legs in their big boots dangling on either side of his horse, on whose neck hangs a shaft bow with a tinkling bell, rides a young post-boy. His lamb's-wool cap is cocked over one ear and he is singing some long drawn-out ditty. His face and attitude seem to me to express such perfect carelessness and indolent ease that I imagine it to be the height of happiness to be a postillion bringing the horses home and singing melancholy songs. Over there beyond the ravine there stands out against the light-blue sky the green roof of a village church. Here is the village itself, together with the red roof of the manor-house and the green garden attached to it. Who lives in that house? Children, parents, a tutor? Why should we not call there and make the acquaintance of its owners?

Next we come up with a long file of enormous loaded waggons, each drawn by a team of three well-fed sturdy horses – a procession to which our vehicles have to yield the road.

'What have you got in there?' Vasili asks the first waggoner who dangles his great legs lazily over the splashboard of his conveyance, flicking his whip about as he gazes at us with a stolid, vacant look; but he only answers when we are already too far off to catch what he said.

'And what have *you* got?' asks Vasili of the second waggoner who is lying at full length under a piece of new matting on the enclosed front part of his vehicle. The light-brown poll and red face beneath thrust themselves up for a second from under the matting, measure our britzka with a cold, contemptuous look, and disappear again; whereupon I conclude that these drivers are probably wondering to themselves who we are, whence we have come, and whither we are going.

For about an hour and a half I am so absorbed in these various observations that I pay no need to the crooked figures on the verst-posts as we pass them in rapid succession. Now the sun begins to burn my head and back more fiercely, the road to become increasingly dusty, the triangular lid of the tea-caddy to make me more and more uncomfortable, and I myself to feel hot, cramped, and bored. Consequently I fall to devoting my whole faculties to the distance-posts and their numerals, and to making various calculations for reckoning the time when we should arrive at the next posting-house.

'Twelve versts are a third of thirty-six, and in all there are forty-one to Liptsy. We have done a third and how much, then?' and so forth, and so on.

'Vasili,' I remark, on observing that he is beginning to nod on the box-seat, 'suppose you let me sit on the box, there's a dear. Will you?' Vasili agrees, we change places, and no sooner has he stretched himself out in the body of the britzka, leaving no room for anyone else, than he begins to snore. To me on my new perch, however, a most interesting spectacle now presents itself – namely, our four horses Neruchinskaya, Sexton, Left-Shaft and Apothecary, all of whom are familiar to me down to the finest shade and detail.

'Why is Sexton on the right trace today, Philip, not on the left?' I asked somewhat timidly. 'And Neruchinskaya is not doing her proper share of the pulling.'

'There is no use in putting Sexton on the left,' says Philip, altogether ignoring my last remark. 'He is not the kind of horse to put on the left at all. On the left you must have the sort of horse that is, in a word, a horse – and he is not that sort of a horse.'

With these words Philip turns towards Sexton and, jerking hard on the reins, begins whipping poor Sexton on the tail and legs in a peculiar manner, from underneath, and although Sexton does his utmost, even pulling the britzka to one side, Philip ceases this activity only when he finds it necessary to breathe and rest himself awhile, and to settle his cap askew, though it looked well and secure enough before. I profit by the opportunity to ask Philip to let me have the reins to hold. He gives me first one, then a second, until, the whole six in my hand, as well as the whip, I have attained complete happiness. I attempt to imitate Philip in every respect, and several times I ask whether I am doing things right, but it generally ends with him being dissatisfied with me. He says one horse is pulling too hard, another not pulling at all, and at last he thrusts his elbow into my chest and takes the reins from me. The heat increases more and more. Fleecy clouds begin to expand in the sky like soap bubbles, higher and higher, then merge into one another, taking on a dark-grey tinge. A hand shows itself at the carriage window, waving a bottle and a package of eatables; whereupon Vasili leaps briskly from the britzka while it is still moving, and runs forward to bring us a bottle of *kvass* and some curd tarts.

Arriving at a steep descent we all get out and race down it to a little bridge, while Vasili and Yakov, having put a drag on the wheels, support the carriage on either side with their hands, as though to hold it up in the event of its threatening to upset. After that Mimi gives permission for a change of seats, and sometimes Volodya or I ride in the carriage, and Lyuba and Katya in the britzka. This arrangement greatly pleases the girls, since, as they rightly say, it is much more fun in the britzka. Sometimes, just when the day is at its hottest, we get out at a grove of trees and, breaking off some green branches, transform our vehicle into a bower. This travelling arbour then bustles on to catch up with the carriage, and has the effect of exciting Lyuba to one of those piercing shrieks which she is in the habit of emitting when the occasion gives her great delight.

At last we are drawing near the village where we are to dine and rest. Already we can perceive the smell of the place – the smell of smoke and tar and sheep – and distinguish the sound of voices, footsteps, and wheels. The bells on our horses' harness begin to ring differently than they did in the open country, and on both sides of the road we catch glimpses of huts – dwellings with straw roofs, carved wooden porches, and small red or green painted shutters to the little windows, through which here and there an old woman's face looks inquisitively out. Peasant boys and girls clad only in smocks stand staring open-eyed or, stretching out their arms to us, run barefoot through the dust in pursuit of our carriages, or, despite Philip's menacing gestures, attempt to clamber up on to the luggage lashed on behind. And now red-haired waiters come darting out around the carriages to invite us, with words and signs, to select their several hostelries as our halting-place. 'Whoa, there!'

Presently a gate creaks, the cross-bars of the harness array scrape against the gate-posts, and we drive into a courtyard. Four hours of rest and liberty now await us.

II
THE THUNDERSTORM

THE sun was sinking towards the west, and its long, hot rays were burning my neck and cheeks beyond endurance: it was impossible to touch the scorching sides of the britzka. Thick clouds of dust were rising from the road and filling the whole air. Not the slightest wind was there to carry it away. Ahead of us, at a constant distance, the tall dusty shape of the carriage rolled rhythmically along with our baggage on top of it, and beyond this we caught occasional glimpses of the whip flourished by the coachman, the coachman's hat, and the cap belonging to Yakov. I could not think what to do. Neither the dust-blackened face of Volodya dozing beside me, nor the motion of Philip's back, nor the long shadow of our britzka as it came bowling along behind us at an oblique angle brought me any diversion. I concentrated my whole attention upon the distance-posts ahead and the clouds which, hitherto dispersed over the sky, were now assuming a menacing blackness, and beginning to form themselves into a single dark storm-cloud.

From time to time the rumble of distant thunder could be heard – a circumstance which greatly increased my impatience to arrive at the coaching inn where we were to spend the night. A thunderstorm always communicated to me an inexpressibly oppressive feeling of fear and gloom.

Yet we were still ten versts or so from the next village, and in the meanwhile the large purple cloudbank – arisen from heaven knows where – was advancing steadily towards us, apparently without mind. The sun, not yet obscured, picks out its sombre shape with dazzling light, and illuminates the grey streaks running from it right down to the horizon. At intervals vivid lightning can be seen in the distance, followed by low rumbles which increase steadily in volume, growing ever nearer until they merge into broken peals which seem to embrace the entire heavens. At length Vasili gets up and raises the hood of the britzka, the coachmen wrap themselves up in their cloaks and lift their caps to make the sign of the cross at each successive thunderclap, and the horses prick up their ears and snort as though to drink in the fresh air, scenting the approaching storm-cloud. The britzka begins to roll more swiftly along the dusty road, and I feel uneasy, as though the blood is coursing more quickly through my veins. Soon the nearest clouds have veiled the face of the sun, and though it throws a last gleam of light to the dark and threatening region of the horizon, the sun is soon hidden. Suddenly everything around us seems changed, and assumes a gloomy aspect. A wood of aspen-trees which we are passing seems to be all in a tremble, with its leaves – showing white against the dark-lilac background of the clouds – rustling together in an agitated manner. The tops of the larger birch-trees begin to bend to and fro, and dried leaves and grass to whirl about in eddies over the road. Martins and white-breasted swallows, as if trying to stop us, come darting around the britzka, even passing in front of the forelegs of the horses, while jackdaws with ruffled wing feathers fly almost sideways on to the wind. Finally the flaps of the leather apron which cover us begin to rise up, letting in gusts of damp wind and beating against the sides of the conveyance. The lightning seems to flash right into the britzka as, blinding us and cleaving the obscurity for a second, it lights up the grey cloth and silk braid of the lining and Volodya's figure pressed back into a corner. At that very moment comes a terrible din resounding over our heads. Rising higher and higher, and spreading further and further, it increases until it reaches its climax in a deafening thunderclap which makes us tremble and hold our breaths. 'The wrath of God' – what poetry there is in that simple popular conception!

The wheels of the vehicle revolve faster and faster, and from Philip's and Vasili's backs (the former tugging furiously at the reins) I can see that they too are alarmed.

Bowling rapidly down an incline, the britzka rattles over a plank bridge at the bottom. I dare not stir, and expect our destruction every moment.

Whoa! A cross-bar has given way, and in spite of the cease-less, deafening thunderclaps, we are compelled to pull up on the bridge.

Leaning my head despairingly against the side of the britzka, I follow with bated breath and beating heart the movements of Philip's great black fingers as he slowly ties a loop and adjusts the traces, pushing the harness back into its place with his hand and with the handle of the whip.

My sense of anxiety and dread was increasing with the violence of the storm. Indeed, at the moment of supreme silence which generally precedes the climax of a storm, it mounted to such a height that I felt as though another quarter of an hour of this emotion would cause me to die of fright.

Just then there appears from beneath the bridge a human being who, clad in a torn, filthy smock, and supported on a pair of crooked shanks bare of muscles, thrusts an idiotic, bloated face, a tremulous, bare, shaven head, and a pair of red, shining stumps in place of hands into the britzka.

'M – my lord! A copeck for a cripple – for Christ's sake!' groans a feeble voice as at each word the beggar makes the sign of the cross and bows from the waist.

I cannot describe the chill feeling of horror which penetrated my soul at that moment. A shudder crept over my scalp, and my eyes stared in vacant terror at the mendicant. . .

Vasili (charged with the apportioning of alms during the journey) is busy giving Philip instruction about securing the cross-bar, and only when everything has been put straight and Philip has resumed the reins and climbed back on to the box has he time to get something out of his side pocket. Hardly has the britzka begun to move when a blinding flash fills the hollow with a blaze of light which brings the horses to their haunches. Then the flash is accompanied by such an ear-splitting roar that the very vault of heaven seems to be descending upon our heads. The wind blows harder than ever, and the manes and tails of the horses, Vasili's cloak, and the carriage-apron are all swept in one direction as they wave furiously in the violent blast. Upon the britzka's leather top there falls a large drop of rain – another, a third, a fourth; then suddenly, and as though a roll of drums were being beaten over our heads, the whole countryside resounds with the regular patter of falling rain.

From the movements of Vasili's elbow I can see that he is opening his purse, and that the poor outcast is still bowing and crossing himself as he runs beside the wheels of the vehicle, so that we expect him at any moment to be run over, and reiterating his plea, 'Give me something, in Christ's name!' At last a copper coin flies past us, and the miserable creature – in his soaking wet rags which cling to his emaciated arms – stops perplexed in the roadway, swaying in the wind, and vanishes from my sight.

The slanting rain, driven before the tempestuous wind, pours down in buckets, and, dripping from Vasili's thick frieze coat, forms a series of muddy pools on the apron. The dust, at first beaten into little pellets, now becomes changed to a liquid paste which clings to the wheels; the jolts become fewer and the ruts become transformed into muddy rivulets. The lightning grows paler and more diffuse, and the thunderclaps lose some of their terror amid the monotonous rattling of the downpour.

Then the rain also abates, and the storm-cloud begins to split up into fleecy cloudlets and to grow lighter in the region where the sun must be, and between the whitey-grey edges of clouds can be caught glimpses of an azure sky. A minute later a shy sunbeam sparkles in the pools on the road – shot through the threads of rain (now falling thin and straight, as from a sieve), and falls upon the glistening new-washed blades of the roadside grass. The great cloud is still louring black and threatening on the far horizon, but I no longer feel afraid of it – I feel only an inexpressibly pleasant hopefulness in proportion as trust in life rapidly replaces the late burden of fear. Indeed, my soul is smiling like refreshed, revivified Nature herself. Vasili turns down the collar of his cloak, takes off his cap and shakes it. Volodya flings back the apron, and I stand up in the britzka to drink in the new, fresh, balm-laden air. In front of us is the glistening, well-washed body of the carriage with its boxes and trunks, rolling along; the horses' backs, the harness and reins, the tyres on the wheels, all look as wet and resplendent in the sunlight as though they have just been varnished. On one side of the road a boundless field of winter grain – intersected in places by small gullies which now show bright with their moist earth and greenery – stretches to the far horizon like a shadowy carpet, while on the other side of us an aspen-grove, intermingled with hazel-bushes and bird-cherry, stands as though overwhelmed with happiness, no longer rustling and trembling, but slowly dropping rich, sparkling diamonds from its newly-bathed branches on to the withered leaves of last year. On all sides crested larks are circling with glad song and swiftly falling earthwards. Little birds bustle about among the dripping brushwood, while from the inmost depths of the wood sounds the clear voice of the cuckoo. So delicious is the wondrous scent of the wood after that early spring storm, the scent of birch-trees, violets, rotting leaves, mushrooms, and bird-cherry – that I can no longer remain in the britzka. Jumping from the step, I run to some bushes, and, regardless of the showers of drops discharged upon me, tear off a few wet branches of the flowering bird-cherry, and bury my face in them to revel in their glorious scent. Then, despite the lumps of mud sticking to my boots, as also the fact that my stockings are soaked, I go skipping through the mud to the window of the carriage.

'Lyuba! Katya!' I shout as I hand them some of the branches of bird-cherry. 'Just look how lovely this is!'

The girls squeal and exclaim, 'Ah!' 'A – ah!' but Mimi shrieks to me to go away, for fear I should be run over by the wheels.

'Oh, but smell how delicious it is!' I cry.

III

A NEW POINT OF VIEW

KATYA was with me in the britzka – her pretty head inclined as she gazed pensively at the dusty roadway running away beneath our wheels. I looked at her in silence, and wondered what had brought the unchildlike expression of sadness which I now observed for the first time on her rosy little face.

'We shall soon be in Moscow,' I said at last. 'What do you suppose it is like?'

'I don't know,' she replied reluctantly.

'Well, but how do you *imagine it*? As large as Serpukhov or not?'

'What do you say?'

'Nothing.'

Yet the instinctive feeling which enables one person to guess the thoughts of another and serves as a guiding thread in conversation soon made Katya feel that her indifference was disagreeable to me; she raised her head presently and, turning round, said:

'Did your papa tell you that we girls too were going to live at your grandmamma's?'

'Yes, he said that we should *all* live there.'

'*All* live there?'

'Yes, of course. We shall have one half of the upper floor, and you the other half, and Papa the wing; but we shall all of us dine together with Grandmamma downstairs.'

'But Mamma says that your grandmamma is such a grand lady and so easily made angry.'

'No, she only *seems* like that at first. She is grand, but not a bit bad-tempered. On the contrary, she is both kind and cheerful. If you could only have seen her name-day ball!'

'All the same, I am afraid of her. Besides, heaven only knows whether we——'

Katya stopped short, and once again became thoughtful.

'What?' I asked with some anxiety.

'Nothing. I only said that——'

'No. You said, "Heaven only knows whether we——" '

'And *you* were saying, that once there was *ever* such a ball at Grandmamma's?'

'Yes. It is a pity you were not there. There were heaps of guests – about a thousand people, and there was music, and generals, and I danced—— But, Katya,' I broke off, 'you are not listening.'

'Oh yes, I am listening. You said that you danced——?'

'Why are you so serious?'

'Well, one cannot *always* be gay.'

'But you have changed tremendously since Volodya and I returned from Moscow. Tell me the truth, now,' I continued in a resolute tone, turning towards her, 'why have you become so strange?'

'*Am* I so strange?' said Katya with an animation which showed me that my question had interested her. 'I don't see that I am so at all.'

'Well, you are not the same as you were before,' I continued. 'Once upon a time anyone could see that you were our equal in everything, and that you looked on us as relations, and loved us just as we do you; but now you are always serious, and keep yourself apart from us.'

'Oh, not at all.'

'But let me finish, please,' I interrupted, already conscious of a slight tickling in my nose – the precursor of the tears which usually came to my eyes whenever I had to vent any long-pent-up and deeply-felt thought. 'You avoid us, and talk to no one but Mimi, as though you had no wish for our further acquaintance.'

'But one cannot always remain the same – one *must* change a little sometimes,' replied Katya, who had an inveterate habit of pleading some such fatalistic necessity whenever she did not know what else to say.

I recollect that once, when having a quarrel with Lyuba, who had called her 'a stupid little girl,' Katya retorted that *everybody* could not be clever, seeing that a certain number of stupid people was needed in the world. However, on the present occasion, I was not satisfied that any such necessity for 'changing sometimes' existed, and questioned her further.

'*Why* must one change?'

'Well, you see, we shall not always go on living together as we are doing now,' said Katya, colouring slightly, and staring at Philip's back with a grave expression. 'My mamma was able to live with your late mother because she was her friend; but will a similar arrangement always suit the Countess, who, they say, is so easily offended? Besides, in any case, we shall have to part *some* day. You are rich – you have Petrovskoye, while we are poor – Mamma has nothing.'

'You are rich,' 'we are poor' – both the words and the ideas which they connoted seemed to me extremely strange. Hitherto I had conceived that only beggars and peasants were poor, and could not reconcile in my mind the idea of poverty and the graceful, charming Katya. I felt that Mimi and her daughter ought to continue to live with us *always*, and to share everything that we possessed. Things could not be otherwise. Yet at this moment a thousand new thoughts with regard to their lonely position came crowding into my head, and I felt so remorseful at the notion that we were rich and they poor that I coloured up and could not look Katya in the face.

'Yet what does it matter,' I thought, 'that we are well off and they are not? Why should that necessitate a separation? Why should we not share in common what we possess?' Yet I had a feeling that I could not talk to Katya on the subject, since a certain practical instinct, opposed to all logical reasoning, warned me that, right though she possibly was, it would not be appropriate for me to tell her my thoughts.

'It is impossible that you should leave us. How could we ever live apart?'

'Yet what else is there to be done? It hurts me, too. Yet, if it *has* to be done, I know what my plan in life will be.'

'Yes, to become an actress! How absurd!' I exclaimed, for I knew that to enter that profession had always been her favourite dream.

'Oh no. I only used to say that when I was little.'

'Well, then? What?'

'To go into a convent and live there, and wear a black dress and a velvet cap!'

Katya began to cry.

Has it ever befallen you, my reader, to become suddenly aware at some point in your life that your conception of things has altered – as though every object which had hitherto been before your eyes had unexpectedly turned a side towards you which was different and unfamiliar? Such a species of moral change occurred in me for the first time during this journey, and from it I date the beginning of my boyhood.

For the first time in my life I then envisaged the idea that we – that is our family – were not the only persons in the world; that not every conceivable interest was centred in ourselves; but that there existed numbers of people who had nothing in common with us, cared nothing for us, and even knew nothing of our existence. No doubt I had known all this before – only I had not known it then as I knew it now; I had never properly felt or understood it.

Thought merges into conviction through paths of its own, as well as, sometimes, with great suddenness and by methods wholly different from those which have brought other minds to the same conclusion. For me the conversation with Katya – striking deeply as it did, and forcing me to reflect on her future position – was such a path. As I gazed at the towns and villages through which we passed, in each house of which lived at least one family like our own, at the women and children who stared with momentary curiosity at our carriages and then became lost to sight for ever, and at the peasants and shopkeepers who did not even look at us, much less make us any obeisance as I was used to seeing them do at Petrovskoye, the question arose for the first time in my thoughts, 'What else can they care for if not about us?' And this question was followed by others, such as, 'How, and on what do they live?' 'How do they bring up their children?' 'Do they teach their children? Do they let them play?' 'How do they punish them?' and so forth.

IV

IN MOSCOW

FROM the time of our arrival in Moscow the change in my conception of objects, of persons, and of my relation to them became increasingly perceptible.

When at my first meeting with Grandmamma I saw her thin, wrinkled face and faded eyes, the mingled respect and fear she had hitherto inspired in me gave place to compassion; and when, laying her cheek against Lyuba's head, she sobbed as though she saw before her the corpse of her beloved daughter, my compassion even grew to love. I felt deeply sorry to see her grief at our meeting, even though I knew that in ourselves we represented nothing in her eyes, but were dear to her only as reminders of our mother – that every kiss which she imprinted upon my cheeks expressed the one thought, 'She is no more – she is dead, and I shall never see her again.'

Papa, who took little notice of us here in Moscow, and only appeared at dinner, his face perpetually preoccupied, and wearing his black frockcoat or dress suit, had, together with his turned-up ruffles, dressing-gown, village elders and stewards, and his expeditions to the threshing-floor and the hunt, lost much in my eyes at this period. Karl Ivanych – whom Grandmamma always called 'Uncle,' and who, Heaven knows why, had taken it into his head to adorn the bald pate of my childhood's days with a red wig with a fabric parting visible almost in the middle – now looked to me so strange and ridiculous that I wondered how I could ever have failed to observe the fact before.

Even between the girls and ourselves there seemed to have sprung up an invisible barrier. They, too, began to have secrets among themselves, as well as to evince a desire to show off their ever-lengthening skirts, even as we boys did our trousers with ankle-straps. As for Mimi, she appeared at dinner, the first Sunday, in such a gorgeous dress and with so many ribbons in her cap that it was at once clear that we were no longer in the country, and that everything was now going to be different.

V

MY ELDER BROTHER

I WAS only a year and some odd months younger than Volodya, and from the first we had grown up and studied and played together. Hitherto the difference between elder and younger brother had never been felt between us, but at the period of which I am speaking I began to have a notion that I was not Volodya's equal either in years, in tastes, or in capabilities. I even began to fancy that Volodya himself was aware of his superiority, and that he was proud of it, and though perhaps I was wrong, the idea was inspired by my own conceit – already suffering from each and every contact with him. He was my superior in everything – in games, in studies, in quarrels, and in deportment. All this brought about an estrangement between us, and occasioned me moral sufferings which I was unable to understand.

If, when for the first time Volodya wore Dutch pleated shirts, I had at once said that I was greatly put out at not being given similar ones, I am sure I should have felt happier and should not have thought each time he arranged his collar, that he was doing so on purpose to offend me.

But what tormented me most of all was the idea that Volodya could see through me, yet did not choose to show it.

Who has not observed those secret, wordless communications which spring from some barely perceptible smile or movement – from a casual glance between two persons who live as constantly together as do brothers, friends, man and wife, or master and servant – particularly if those two persons do not in all things cultivate mutual frankness? How many unexpressed wishes, thoughts, and meanings which one shrinks from revealing are made plain by a single accidental glance when eyes timidly and irresolutely meet!

However, in my own case I may have been deceived by my extreme sensitivity and my excessive tendency to analyse. Possibly Volodya did not feel at all as I did. Passionate and frank, but unstable in his likings, he was attracted by the most diverse things, and always surrendered himself wholly to such attractions.

For instance, he suddenly conceived a passion for pictures, himself took up painting, spent all his money on buying them, begged Papa, Grandmamma, and his drawing master to add to their number. Next came a sudden rage for curios, with which he covered his table and for which he ransacked the whole house. Following that, he might take to violent novel-reading – procuring such works by stealth, and devouring them day and night. Involuntarily I was influenced by his enthusiasms, for, though too proud to imitate him, I was also too young and too lacking in independence to choose my own way. Above all, I envied Volodya his happy, nobly open-hearted character, which showed itself most strikingly when we quarrelled. I always felt that he was behaving correctly, yet could not imitate him.

For instance, on one occasion when his passion for curios was at its height, I went to his table and accidentally broke an empty many-coloured smelling-bottle.

'Who asked to touch my things?' asked Volodya, chancing to enter the room at that moment and at once perceiving the disorder which I had occasioned in the symmetry of the various treasures on his table. 'And where is that smelling-bottle? Perhaps you——?'

'I accidentally let it fall, and it got smashed. But what does that matter?'

'Well, please do me the favour never to *dare* to touch my things again,' he said as he gathered up the broken fragments of the little flask and looked at them sorrowfully.

'And *you* please never *order* me to do anything,' I retorted. 'When a thing's broken, it's broken; there is no more to be said.' And I smiled, though I hardly felt like smiling.

'Oh, it may mean nothing to *you*, but to me it means a good deal,' said Volodya, with a jerk of his shoulder (a habit he had inherited from Papa). 'First of all he goes and breaks my things, and then he laughs. What an insupportable little brat he is!'

'Little brat, indeed? Then *you*, I suppose, are big, but you are stupid!'

'I do not intend to quarrel with you,' said Volodya, giving me a slight push. 'Go away.'

'Don't you push me!'

'Go away.'

'I say again – don't you push me!'

Volodya took me by the arm and tried to drag me away from the table, but I was excited to the last degree: I took hold of the leg of the table and overturned it, and brought china and crystal ornaments and everything else with a crash to the floor.

'You disgusting little brat!' exclaimed Volodya, trying to save some of his falling treasures.

'Well, now it is over between us,' I thought to myself as I strode from the room. 'We have fallen out now, for good.'

It was not until evening that we again exchanged a word. Yet I felt guilty, and was afraid to look at him, and remained at a loose end all day. Volodya, on the contrary, did his lessons as diligently as ever, and passed the time after dinner in talking and laughing as usual with the girls.

As soon, again, as afternoon lessons were over I left the room, for I was too fearful, awkward and ashamed to want to be alone with my brother. When, too, the evening class in history was ended I took my notebook and moved towards the door. As I passed Volodya, though in reality I should have liked to have made my peace with him I pouted and pulled an angry face. At that moment he lifted his head, and with a barely perceptible and good-humouredly satirical smile looked me full in the face. Our eyes met, and I saw that he understood me, while he, for his part, saw that I *knew* that he understood me; yet a feeling stronger than myself obliged me to turn away from him.

'Dear Nikolai,' he said in a perfectly simple and anything but mock-pathetic way, 'you have been angry with me long enough. I am sorry if I offended you,' and he held out his hand.

It was as though something welled up inside me, pressing on my chest and hindering my breathing; but this lasted only a second and the tears rushed to my eyes, and I felt better.

'Forgive – me, Vo-lo-dya!' I stammered, taking his hand. Yet he only looked at me with an expression as though he could not understand why there should be tears in my eyes.

VI

MASHA

NONE of the changes produced in my conception of things was so striking as the one which led me to cease to see in one of our chambermaids a mere servant of the female sex, but, on the contrary, a *woman* upon whom depended, to a certain extent, my peace of mind and happiness.

From the time of my earliest recollection I can remember Masha as an inmate of our house, yet never until the occurrence of which I am going to speak – an occurrence which entirely altered my impression of her – had I bestowed the smallest attention upon her. Masha was about twenty-five years old, when I was but fourteen. She was very pretty. But I hesitate to give a further description of her lest my imagination should once more picture the bewitching though deceptive image of her which filled my mind during the period of my passion. To be frank, I will only say that she was unusually fair-skinned, generously endowed, and a *woman* – as also that I was fourteen.

At one of those moments when, lesson-book in hand, I would pace the room, and try to keep strictly to one particular crack in the floor as I hummed some silly fragment of a tune or smeared the table edge with ink or mechanically repeated some dictum – in short, at one of those moments when the mind leaves off thinking and the imagination gains the upper hand and yearns for new impressions – I left the schoolroom, and turned, with no definite purpose in view, towards the landing.

Somebody in slippers was ascending the lower flight of stairs. Of course I felt curious to see who it was, but the footsteps ceased abruptly, and then I heard Masha's voice say:

'Now then, you and your monkey-tricks! What would Marya Ivanovna say if she were to come now?'

'Oh, but she will not come,' answered Volodya's voice in a whisper, and directly after there was a sound, as though he were trying to detain her.

'Well, just look where your hands are – for shame!' and Masha came running up, and fled past me with her kerchief awry and her plump white neck visible beneath it.

I cannot describe the way in which this discovery confounded me. Nevertheless the feeling of amazement soon gave place to a kind of sympathy with Volodya's conduct. I found myself wondering less at the action itself than how he had perceived that such an action would be so agreeable. Also, I found myself involuntarily desiring to imitate him.

Sometimes I would pace the landing for hours on end, with no other thought in my head than to watch for movements from above. Yet, although I longed beyond all things to do as Volodya had done, I could not bring myself to the point of copying him. At other times, filled with a sense of envious jealousy, I would conceal myself behind a door and listen to the noise which came from the maid-servants' room, until the thought would occur to my mind, 'How if I were to go upstairs now and, like Volodya, kiss Masha? What should I say when she asked me – *me* with my broad nose and the tufts on the top of my head – what I wanted?' Sometimes, too, I heard her saying to Volodya, 'What a plague you are! Why do you come pestering me? Go away, you naughty boy. Nikolai Petrovich never comes in here with such nonsense.' Alas! she did not know that Nikolai Petrovich was sitting on the staircase just below and feeling that he would give all he possessed to be in 'that naughty boy Volodya's' place!

I was shy by nature, and rendered worse in that respect by a consciousness of my own ugliness. I am certain that nothing so much influences the development of a man as his external appearance – though the appearance itself less than his opinion of its plainness or beauty.

Yet I was too conceited altogether to resign myself to my fate. I tried to comfort myself much as the fox did when he declared that the grapes were sour. That is to say, I tried to make light of the satisfaction which I thought Volodya gained from making such use of a pleasing exterior (satisfaction which I nevertheless envied him from my heart), and endeavoured with every faculty of my intellect and imagination to console myself with a pride in my isolation.

VII

SMALL SHOT

'GOOD gracious! Gunpowder!' screamed Mimi in a voice choking with alarm. 'Whatever are you doing? You will set the house on fire in a moment, and be the death of us all!' Upon that, with an indescribable expression of firmness, Mimi ordered everyone to stand aside, and, regardless of all possible danger from a premature explosion, strode with long and resolute steps to where some small shot was scattered about the floor, and began to stamp upon it. When, in her opinion, the peril was over, she called for Mikhei and commanded him to throw the 'gunpowder' away into some remote spot or, better still, to immerse it in water; after which with a toss of her cap she took herself to the drawing-room, murmuring as she went, 'At least I can say that they are well looked after.'

When Papa issued from his wing and took us in to see Grandmamma we found Mimi sitting by the window and glancing with a grave, mysterious, official expression towards the door. In her hand she was holding something carefully wrapped in several layers of paper. I guessed that that something was the small shot, and that Grandmamma had been informed of the occurrence.

In the room also were the maid-servant Gasha (who, to judge by her angry flushed face, was extremely upset) and Doctor Blumenthal, a little man pitted with smallpox, who was vainly endeavouring by tacit, pacificatory signs with his head and eyes to reassure Gasha.

Grandmamma was sitting slightly sideways on her chair and playing that variety of 'patience' which is called 'The Traveller' – an unmistakable sign of her displeasure.

'How are you today, Mamma?' said Papa as he kissed her hand respectfully. 'Have you had a good night?'

'Yes, excellent, my dear; you *know* that I always enjoy sound health,' replied Grandmamma in a tone implying that Papa's inquiry was out of place and highly offensive. 'Are you going to give me a clean pocket-handkerchief?' she added to Gasha.

'I *have* given you one, madam,' answered Gasha, pointing to the snow-white cambric handkerchief lying on the arm of Grandmamma's chair.

'No, no; it's a nasty, dirty thing. Take it away and bring me a *clean* one, my dear.'

Gasha went to the chiffonier, pulled out a drawer and slammed it back so violently that every window rattled. Grandmamma glared angrily at each of us, and continued to stare intently at the movements of the servant. After the latter had presented her with what I suspected to be the same handkerchief as before, Grandmamma continued:

'And when do you mean to rub me some snuff, my dear?'

'When I have time.'

'What do you say?'

'I will do it presently.'

'If you don't want to continue in my service, my dear, you had better say so. I would have sent you away long ago had I known that you wished it.'

'It wouldn't break my heart if you did!' muttered the woman in an undertone.

Here the doctor winked at her again, but she returned his gaze so firmly and wrathfully that he at once lowered his eyes and fiddled with his watch-key.

'You see, my dear, how people speak to me in my own house!' said Grandmamma to Papa when Gasha, still grumbling, had left the room.

'Well, Mamma, permit me to rub you some snuff myself,' replied Papa, though evidently at a loss how to proceed with this unexpected appeal.

'No, no, I thank you. Probably she is impudent because she knows that no one except herself can rub the snuff just as I like it. Do you know, my dear,' she went on after a pause, 'that your children very nearly set the house on fire this morning?'

Papa gazed at Grandmamma with respectful curiosity.

'Yes, they were playing with something or another. Show him,' she added to Mimi.

Papa could not help smiling as he took the shot in his hand.

'Why this is only small shot, Mamma,' he remarked, 'and could never be dangerous.'

'I thank you, my dear, for your instruction, but I am rather too old for that sort of thing.'

'Nerves, nerves!' whispered the doctor.

Papa at once turned to us and asked, 'Where did you get this? How dare you play with such things?'

'Don't ask *them*, ask that useless "Uncle," rather,' put in Grandmamma, laying a peculiarly scornful stress upon the word '*Uncle*.' 'What else is he for?'

'Voldemar says that Karl Ivanych gave him the *gunpowder* himself,' declared Mimi.

'Then you can see for yourself what use he is,' continued Grandmamma. 'And where *is* he – this precious "Uncle"? How is one to get hold of him? Send him here.'

'I allowed him to go and visit some friends,' said Papa.

'That is no excuse,' rejoined Grandmamma. 'He ought *always* to be here. True, the children are yours, not mine, and I have no right to give advice, seeing that you are so much cleverer than I am; yet all the same I think it is time we had a regular tutor for them, and not this "Uncle" of a German peasant – a stupid peasant who knows only how to teach them rude manners and Tyrolean songs! Is it necessary, I ask you, that they should learn Tyrolean songs? However, there is now no one to consider such things, and you may do just as you please.'

The word '*now*' meant '*now that they have no mother*,' and suddenly awakened sad recollections in Grandmamma's heart. She threw a glance at the snuff-box bearing Mamma's portrait and became lost in thought.

'I have long been thinking about all this,' said Papa hurriedly, 'and I intended taking your advice on the subject. How would you like St Jérôme to superintend their lessons – the man who now gives them lessons by the hour?'

'Oh, I think he would do excellently, my friend,' said Grandmamma in a mollified tone. 'He is at least a proper tutor, and knows how to instruct *des enfants de bonne maison.*[1] He is not a mere "Uncle" who is good only for taking them out for walks.'

'Very well; I will talk to him tomorrow,' said Papa. And, sure enough, two days later Karl Ivanych was forced to retire in favour of the young French dandy referred to.

1 Children of good family.

KARL IVANYCH'S HISTORY

LATE in the evening before the day when Karl Ivanych was to leave us for ever, he was standing (clad, as usual, in his wadded dressing-gown and red cap) near the bed in his room, and bending down over his portmanteau as he carefully packed his belongings.

His behaviour towards us had been very cool of late, and he had seemed to shrink from all contact with us. Consequently, when I entered his room on the present occasion, he only glanced at me for a second from under his brows and then went on with his task. Even though I proceeded to jump on to his bed (a thing hitherto always forbidden me to do), Karl Ivanych said not a word; and the idea that he would soon be scolding or forgiving us no longer – no longer having anything to do with us – brought home to me me vividly the impending separation. I felt grieved to think that he had ceased to love us, and wanted to show him my grief.

'Will you let me help you, Karl Ivanych?' I said, approaching him.

Karl Ivanych looked at me for a moment and turned away again. Yet even in this fleeting glance the expression of pain in his eyes showed that his coldness was not the result of indifference, but rather of sincere and concentrated sorrow.

'God sees and knows everything and His holy will be done in all things,' he said at length, raising himself to his full height and drawing a deep sigh. 'Yes, my dear Nikolai,' he went on, observing the expression of genuine sympathy on my face, 'my fate has been an unhappy one from the cradle, and will continue so to the grave. The good that I have done to people has always been repaid with evil; yet, though my reward is not here, I shall find one *there*' (he pointed upwards). 'Ah, if only you knew my whole story, and all that I have endured in this life! – I who have been a bootmaker, a soldier, a deserter, a factory hand, and a teacher! Yet now – now I am nothing, and, like the Son of God, have nowhere to lay my head.' Sitting down upon a chair, he shut his eyes.

Seeing that Karl Ivanych was in the introspective mood in which a man pays no attention to his listener as he voices for his own benefit his most secret thoughts, I remained silent and, seating myself upon the bed, continued to watch his kind face.

'You are no longer a child. You can understand things now, and I will tell you my whole story and all that I have undergone in this life. Some day, my children, you may remember the old friend who loved you so much.'

Karl Ivanych leant his elbow upon the small table by his side, took a pinch of snuff, rolled his eyes heavenwards and, in the peculiarly measured, guttural tone in which he used to dictate us our lessons, began the story of his career.

'I voss un'appy alreaty in my mother's vomb. *Das Unglück verfolgte mich schon im Schosse meiner Mutter!*' he repeated in German with still greater feeling.

Since Karl Ivanych many times in later years repeated the whole to me again – always in the same order, and with the same expressions and the same unvarying intonation – I think I can render it word for word, omitting of course the language errors, of which the reader may gain a fair impression from the first sentence. Whether it was really the history of his life, or whether it was the product of his imagination – that is to say, some narrative which he had conceived during his lonely residence in our house, and had at last from endless repetition come to believe in himself – or whether he was merely adorning with imaginary facts the true events of his life, I have never quite been able to make out. On the one hand, there was too much depth of feeling and practical consistency in its recital for it to be wholly incredible, while, on the other hand, the abundance of poetical beauty which it contained tended to raise doubts in the mind of the listener.

'In my veins flows the noble blood of the Counts of Sommerblat! *In meinen Adern fliesst das edle Blut des Grafen von Sommerblat!* I was born six weeks after the vedding. My mother's husband (I called him Papa) was a tenant farmer of the Graf von Sommerblat. He could not forget my mother's

shame and he did not love me. I had a younger brother Johann
and two sisters, but I was a stranger in my own family! *Ich war ein
Fremder in meiner eigenen Familie!* Whenever Johann got up to
silly tricks, Papa would say, "With this child Karl I shall never
have a moment's peace!" and then I was scolded and punished.
When my sisters quarrelled among themselves, Papa would say,
"That Karl will never be an obedient boy!", and they scolded
me and punished me. Only my dear kind mother loved me and
fondled me. Often she would say to me, "Karl! come here, in
my room," and she kissed me secretly. "Poor, poor Karl!" she
used to say, "nobody loves you, but I would not change you for
anyone else in the world. One thing only your little mother
begs you to remember," she said to me, "do your lessons well
and be always an honest man, and God will not forsake you!
*Trachte nur, ein ehrlicher Deutscher zu werden – sagte sie – und der
liebe Gott wird dich nicht verlassen!*" And I tried. When my four-
teenth year had come and I was able to take Holy Communion,
my mother said to my papa: "Karl is a big boy now, Gustav:
what are we going to do with him?" And Papa said: "I do not
know." Then Mama said: "Let us send him away to town to
Herr Schultz, let him become a shoemaker!" and my father said
"Good," *und mein Vater sagte "Gut"*. Six years and seven months
I lived in the town at the shoemaker's house, and my master
loved me. He said: "Karl is a good workman, and soon he shall
become my *Geselle!*",[1] but ... man proposes, and God disposes
... in the year 1796 there was a *Konscription*, and everyone who
was fit to serve, from eighteen to twenty-one years of age, was
obliged to gather in the town.

'My father and my brother Johann travelled to town, and
together we went to draw the *Los*[2] to decide who would be a
Soldat and who would not be a *Soldat*. Johann drew a bad
number – he had to be a *Soldat* – and I drew a good number
– I did not have to be a *Soldat*. And Papa said: "I had only one
son, and with him I have to part! *Ich hatte einen einzigen Sohn,
und von diesem muss ich mich trennen!*"

1 Assistant.
2 Lot.

'I took him by the hand and I said "Why do you say that, Papa? Come with me, and I will tell you something." And Papa came with me. Papa came and we sat at a little table in the tavern. "Give us a pair of *Bierkrug*,"[1] I said, and they brought them to us. We drank a glass together, and my brother Johann also drank a glass.

' "Papa!" I said, "do not say that 'you had only one son, and with him you have to part' – my heart wants to *jump out* when I hear you say this. My brother Johann shall not serve in the army – I shall be a *Soldat*! . . . Nobody here has need of Karl, and Karl shall be a *Soldat*."

' "You are an honourable man, Karl Ivanych!" said my father to me, and he kissed me. "*Du bist ein braver Bursche!" sagte mir mein Vater und küsste mich.*

'And I was a *Soldat*.'

IX
KARL IVANYCH'S NARRATIVE CONTINUED

'Then was a terrible time, my little Nikolai,' continued Karl Ivanych, 'the time of Napoleon. He wanted to conquer Germany, and we defended our native land to the last drop of our blood! *und wir verteidigten unser Vaterland bis auf den letzten Tropfen Blut!*

'I was at Ulm, I was at Austerlitz, I was at Wagram!'

'Did you really fight?' I asked, looking at him with aston-ishment. 'Did you really kill anyone?'

Karl Ivanych instantly reassured me on this point.

'Once a French grenadier lagged behind his comrades and fell down in the road. I ran forward with my rifle and was going to run him through, *aber der Franzose warf sein Gewehr hin und rief pardon*,[2] and I spared him.

'At Wagram Napoleon drove us on to an island and surrounded us, so that there was no escape. For three days we had no provisions, and we were standing in water up to our

1 Jugs of beer.
2 But the Frenchman threw away his rifle and cried out 'pardon.'

knees. That villain Napoleon neither took us prisoner nor let us go! *und der Bösewicht Napoleon wollte uns nicht gefangen nehmen und auch nicht freilassen!*

'On the fourth day, praise God, they took us prisoner and led us off to a fortress. I was wearing my blue trousers, a uniform of good cloth and I had fifteen thalers in money and a silver watch – a present from my father. A French *Soldat* took it all from me. For my good fortune I had on me three gold pieces which my mamma had sewn into my jersey. Nobody found them.

'I had no wish to stay long in the fortress and I decided to run away. One day, when it was a big holiday, I said to the sergeant who was keeping his eye on us: "Mr Sergeant, it is a big holiday today, I want to celebrate it. Please bring me here two bottles of Madeira, and we will drink together." When the sergeant had brought the Madeira and we had each drunk a little glass, I took his hand and said: "Mr Sergeant, perhaps you have a father and a mother?" He said, "So I have, Mr Mauer..." "My father and mother," I said, "have not seen me these eight years, and they do not know whether I am alive, or whether my bones are already lying in the dark earth. Oh, Mr Sergeant, I have two gold ducats which were sewn into my jersey, take them and let me go. Be my benefactor in this matter, and my mother will pray to God for you all her life."

'The sergeant drank off his glass of Madeira and said: "Mr Mauer, I greatly love and pity you, but you are a prisoner, and I am a *Soldat*!" I pressed his hand and said: "Mr Sergeant!" *Ich drückte ihm die Hand und sagte: "Herr Sergeant!"*

'And the sergeant said: "You are a poor man, and I will not take your money, but I will help you. When I go to bed, buy a pail of vodka for the soldiers, and they will sleep. I will not look in your direction."

'He was a good man. I bought the pail of vodka, and when the *Soldaten* were drunk I put on my boots and my old coat and crept quietly out of the door. I went up on to the rampart and would have jumped down, but there was water below and I did not want to ruin my last set of clothes, so I went towards the gates.

'The sentry was going with his rifle *auf und ab*,[1] and he noticed me. *"Qui vive?" sagte er auf einmal*,[2] and I said nothing. *"Qui vive?" sagte er zum zweiten Mal*,[3] and I said nothing. *"Qui vive?" sagte er zum dritten Mal*,[4] and I ran. I chump in the vater, climb up on the other side and I make off. *Ich sprang ins Wasser, kletterte auf die andere Seite und machte mich aus dem Staube.*

'The whole night I ran along the road, but when daylight came I was afraid I might be recognised, and I hid myself in some tall rye. There I knelt down and put my hands together, and thanked the Heavenly Father for saving me, and fell asleep with a peaceful feeling. *Ich dankte dem allmächtigen Gott für seine Barmherzigkeit und mit beruhigtem Gefühl schlief ich ein.*

'I awoke in the evening and went on further. All at once a large German waggon and two black horses came up with me. In the waggon sat a well-dressed man smoking a pipe, and he looked at me. I walked slowly so that the waggon would pass me by, but I walked slowly and the waggon went slowly too, and the man kept looking at me. I walked faster, and the waggon went faster, and the man looked at me. I sat down by the road, and the man stopped his horses and looked at me. "Young man," he said, "Where are you going so late?" I said, "I am going to Frankfurt." "Sit here in my waggon, there is room enough, and I will take you there ... But why have you no luggage, why is your beard not shaven, why are your clothes dirty?" he said to me as I took my seat with him. "I am a poor man," I said, "I hope to find work somewhere in a manufactory, and my clothes are muddy because I fell down in the road." "You are not telling the truth, young man," he said, "the road round here is quite dry now." I said nothing.

' "Tell me the whole truth," said this good man. "Who are

---

1 Up and down.
2 'Who goes there?' he asked all of a sudden.
3 'Who goes there?' he asked for the second time.
4 'Who goes there?' he asked for the third time.

you and where are you from? I like your face, and if you are an honest man I will help you."

'And I told him everything. He said: "Well, young man, we will go to my rope-factory, and I will give you work and clothes and money, and you shall live with me."

'We arrived at the rope-factory, and this kind man said to his wife: "Here is a young man who has fought for his fatherland and has run away from prison: he has neither home nor clothes nor bread. He will live in our house. Give him some clean linen and get him something to eat."

'I lived for a year and a half at the rope-factory, and my master was so fond of me that he did not want to let me go. And I was happy there. I was then a handsome young man, tall, with blue eyes and a roman nose . . . And Madame L— (I cannot tell you her name), my master's wife, was a young and pretty lady. She fell in love with me.

'When she saw me, she said: "Mr Mauer, what does your mother call you?" I said "Karlchen."

'And she said: "Karlchen, come and sit here by me."

'I sat down beside her and she said: "Karlchen, kiss me."

'I kissed her and she said: "Karlchen, I love you so much that I cannot bear it any longer," and she trembled all over.'

Here Karl Ivanych made a long pause and, screwing up his kindly blue eyes, shook his head a little and began to smile as people do at a pleasant memory.

'Yes,' he resumed, as he leant back in his arm-chair and drew his dressing-gown around him, 'I have experienced many good things and many bad things in my life, but here is my witness,' he said, pointing to a little ikon of the Saviour embroidered in wool on canvas which hung over his bed, 'that nobody can say that Karl Ivanych was ever a dishonourable man! I did not wish to repay with black ingratitude the good which Mr L— did me, and I decided to run away. In the evening, when everyone was going to bed, I wrote a letter to my master and put it on the table in my room. I took my clothes and three thalers in money, and went quietly out into the street. Nobody saw me and I walked off down the road.'

X
THE CONCLUSION OF KARL IVANYCH'S NARRATIVE

'For nine years I had not seen my mother, and did not know whether she was alive, or whether her bones were already lying in the dark earth. I came back to my own country and when I came to my home town I asked where Gustav Mauer lived, who used to be a tenant of Graf Sommerblat. And they answered me: "Graf Sommerblat is dead, and Gustav Mauer lives now in the main street and keeps a liquor shop." I put on my new waistcoat and a good coat which the factory owner had given me, brushed my hair carefully and went to my papa's liquor shop. My sister Mariechen was sitting in the little shop and asked me what I wanted. I said: "May I have a glass of liqueur?" – and she said: "*Vater!* This young man is asking for a glass of liqueur." And Papa said: "Give the young man a glass of liqueur." I sat at the little table drinking my glass of liqueur and smoking my pipe, and looking at Papa, Mariechen and Johann, who had also come into the shop. In the course of the conversation Papa said to me: "You know perhaps, young man, where stands now our *Armee?*" I said: "I myself have come from the *Armee*, and it stands now near Wien." "Our son," said Papa, "was a *Soldat*, and it is nine years now since he wrote to us, and we do not know whether he is alive or dead. My wife weeps continually for him . . ." I went on smoking my pipe, and said: "What was your son's name and where did he serve? Perhaps I may know him." "His name was Karl Mauer, and he served in the Austrian Jägers," said my papa. "He is a tall boy, and handsome like you," said my sister Mariechen. I said: "I know your Karl." *"Amalia!" sagte auf einmal mein Vater,*[1] "come here, there is a young man here and he knows our Karl." And my dear *Mütterchen* come out the back door. I knew her directly. "You know our Karl," she said and looked at me, and white all over, tre-e-mbled! "Yes, I have seen him," I said, and I did not

---

[1] 'Amalia!' said my father at once.

dare to look up at her: my heart wanted to jump out almost. "My Karl is alive!" said my little mamma, "Praise God! Where is he, my dear Karl? I would die in peace if I could see him once more, my darling son: but God will not have it so." Then she weep, and I could not stand it any longer. "Darling Mamma!" I said, "I am your Karl!" And she fall into my arms.'

Karl Ivanych closed his eyes, and his lips trembled.

' *"Mutter," sagte ich, "ich bin Ihr Sohn, ich bin Ihr Karl," und sie stürzte mir in die Arme,*'[1] he repeated, recovering himself a little and wiping away the large tears which flowed down his cheeks.

'But it was not God's will that I should end my days in my own native land. Misfortune was for me decreed! *das Unglück verfolgte mich überall!*[2] I lived in my own land only three months. One Sunday I was in the coffee-house drinking a jug of beer and smoking my pipe and talking with my friends of *Politik*, of the Emperor Franz, of Napoleon and of the war, and everyone was giving his opinion. But next to us was sitting an unknown gentleman in a grey *Überrock*,[3] drinking coffee and smoking a pipe and not talking to us. *Er rauchte sein Pfeifchen und schwieg still.* When the *Nachtwächter*[4] called ten o'clock, I took my hat, paid the money and went home. In the middle of the night someone knocked at the door. I woke up and called out: "Who is there?" "*Macht auf.*"[5] I said: "*Sagt wer Ihr seid, und ich werde aufmachen.*"[6] "*Macht auf im Namen des Gesetzes!*"[7] said the person outside the door. I opened it. Two *Soldaten* with rifles were standing outside, and into the room stepped the man in the grey *Überrock*, who had been sitting next to us in the coffee-house. He was a spy! *Es war ein Spion!* "Come with me," said the spy. "Very good," said I. I put on my boots and *Pantalon*, buckled on my braces and paced up and

1 'Mother,' I said, 'I am your son, I am your Karl!' and she fell into my arms.
2 Misfortune pursued me everywhere.
3 Greatcoat.
4 Night-watchman.
5 Open up.
6 Say who you are, and I will open up.
7 Open in the name of the law.

down the room. My heart was seething: I said to myself, "He is a scoundrel!" When I came to the wall where my sword was hanging, I seized it and said, "You are a spy – defend yourself! *Du bist ein Spion, verteidige dich!*" *Ich gab ein Hieb* to the right, *ein Hieb* to the left and one to the head.[1] The spy fell down! I snatched up my portmanteau and my money and jumped out of the window. *Ich nahm meinen Mantelsack und Beutel* and *sprang zum Fenster hinaus. Ich kam nach Ems.*[2] There I made the acquaintance of Yeneral Sazin. He took a liking to me, got me a passport from the envoy, and took me with him to Russia to teach his children. When Yeneral Sazin died, your mamma called me to her. She said: "Karl Ivanych! I am giving you my children. Love them, and I will never abandon you and I will take care of you in your old age." But now she is no more, and all is forgotten. For my twenty years of service I must go now in my declining years into the street and seek for a crust of dry bread . . . God sees this and knows this. His holy will be done! Only it grieves me to part from you, my children!' concluded Karl Ivanych, as he drew me to him by the arm and kissed me on the forehead.

XI

BOTTOM MARKS

THE year of mourning over, Grandmamma recovered a little from her grief, and once more took to receiving occasional guests, especially children, boys and girls of the same age as ourselves.

On the 13th of December – Lyuba's birthday – the Princess Kornakova and her daughters, with Madame Valakhina, Sonya, Ilyenka Grap, and the two younger Ivins, arrived at our house before dinner.

Though we could hear the sounds of talking, laughter, and running about going on from downstairs where all the company was assembled, we could not join them until our morning

---

1 I gave a blow to the right, one to the left . . .
2 I got to Ems.

lessons were finished. The timetable hanging in the school-room said, '*Lundi, de 2 à 3, Maître d'Histoire et de Géographie*,'[1] and this infernal *maître d'Histoire* we must await, listen to, and see the back of before we could gain our liberty. Already it was twenty minutes past two, and nothing was to be heard of the history tutor, nor yet anything to be seen of him in the street, although I kept looking up and down it with the greatest impatience and with an emphatic longing never to see the *maître* again.

'I believe Lebedev is not coming today,' said Volodya, looking up for a moment from his lesson-book, a text-book by Smaragdov.

'I hope he is not, please the Lord!' I answered, but in a despondent tone. 'I don't know a single bit of it. Yet there he *does* come, I believe, all the same!'

Volodya got up and went to the window.

'Not he! Why, that is a *gentleman*,' he said. 'Let us wait till half-past two,' he added, stretching and scratching the top of his head at the same time, as he generally did while taking a rest from his studies. 'If he has not come by them, we will ask St Jérôme if we may put away our books.'

'And why should he want to come, anyway?' I said, likewise stretching, and waving Kaydanov's text-book, clasped in my hands, over my head.

Having nothing better to do, I now opened the book at the place where the lesson was to begin, and started to read it over. It was a long and difficult passage. I knew nothing about it and could see that I should not be able to memorise any of it in time, especially since I was in the mood when one's thoughts refuse to be arrested by anything at all.

After our last lesson in history (which always seemed to me a peculiarly arduous and wearisome subject) the history master Lebedev had complained to St Jérôme of me and had given me a grade two in the mark-book, which was considered very poor. St Jérôme had then told me that if I gained less than a *three* at the next lesson I should be severely punished. The next

1 Monday, 2 to 3, History and Geography master.

lesson was now imminent, and I confess that I was in a real fright.

So absorbed, however, did I become in my reading that the sound of goloshes being taken off in the ante-room came upon me almost as a shock. I had just time to look up when there appeared in the doorway the pock-marked and (to me) very disagreeable face and all too familiar form of the master, clad in a blue swallow-tailed coat with brass buttons.

Slowly he set down his hat on the window-sill and the exercise-books on the table, separated the tails of his coat with both hands (as though such a thing were most necessary), and seated himself wheezing in his place.

'Well, gentlemen,' he said, rubbing his clammy hands together, 'let us first of all repeat the general contents of the last lesson: after which I will proceed to acquaint with you the succeeding events of the Middle Ages.'

This meant: 'Say over the last lesson.'

While Volodya was answering the master with the entire ease and confidence which come of knowing a subject well I went aimlessly out on to the landing, and, since I was not allowed to go downstairs, what more natural than that I should involuntarily turn towards the landing? Yet before I had time to establish myself in my usual coign of vantage behind the door I found myself pounced upon by Mimi – always the cause of my misfortunes!

'*You* here?' she said, looking severely, first at me, and then at the maid-servants' door, and then at me again.

I felt thoroughly guilty, firstly because I was not in the schoolroom, and secondly because I was in a forbidden place. So I remained silent, and, dropping my head, assumed a touching expression of contrition.

'Indeed, this is *too* bad!' Mimi went on. 'What are you doing here?' Still I said nothing.

'Well, the matter shall not rest here,' she added, tapping the banister with her knuckles. 'I shall inform the Countess.'

It was five minutes to three when I re-entered the school-room. The master, as though oblivious of my presence or absence, was explaining the next lesson to Volodya. When he had finished doing this, and was putting his books together (while Volodya went into the other room to fetch the ticket for the lesson), the comforting idea occurred to me that perhaps the whole thing was over now, and that the master would forget about me.

But suddenly he turned in my direction with a malicious smile, and said as he rubbed his hands anew, 'I hope you have learnt your lesson?'

'Yes, sir,' I replied.

'Would you be so kind, then, as to tell me something about St Louis's Crusade?' he went on, rocking himself on his chair and looking gravely at his feet. 'Firstly, tell me something about the reasons which induced the French king to take the cross' (here he raised his eyebrows and pointed to the inkstand); 'then explain to me the general characteristics of the Crusade' (here he made a sweeping gesture with his hand, as though to seize hold of something with it); 'and lastly, expound to me the influence of this Crusade upon the European states in general' (slapping down the exercise-books on the left side of the table) 'and upon the French monarchy in particular' (tapping the right-hand side of the table, and inclining his head in the same direction).

I swallowed a few times, coughed, bent my head to one side, and was silent. Then, taking a quill pen from the table, I began to pick it to pieces, yet still said nothing.

'Allow me the pen – I shall want it,' said the master, stretching out his hand. 'Well, sir?'

'Louis the – er – Saint was – was – a very good and wise tsar.'

'What, sir?'

'Tsar. He took it into his head to go to Jerusalem, and handed over the reins of government to his mother.'

'What was her name?'

'B – b – b – lanka.'

'What? Bulanka?'[1]

I grinned in a forced and awkward manner.

[1] A name given in Russia to a dun horse.

'Well, sir, is that all you know?' he asked with a sarcastic smile.

I had nothing to lose now, so I cleared my throat and began chattering the first thing that came into my head. The master remained silent as he flicked specks of dust from the table with the pen which he had taken from me, looked gravely past my ear at the wall, and repeated from time to time, 'Very well sir, very well.' Though I was conscious that I knew nothing whatever and was expressing myself all wrong, I felt much hurt at the fact that he never either interrupted or corrected me.

'What made him think of going to Jerusalem?' he asked at last, repeating some words of my own.

'Because – because – that is to say――'

My confusion was complete, and I relapsed into silence. I felt that, even if this disgusting history master were to go on putting questions to me, and gazing inquiringly into my face, for a year, I should never be able to enunciate another syllable. After staring at me for some three minutes, he suddenly assumed a mournful cast of countenance, and said in an agitated voice to Volodya (who was just re-entering the room):

'Be so good as to hand me the register. I must put down your marks.'

Volodya handed him the book, carefully placing the lesson ticket beside it.

The master opened the book thoughtfully, dipped his pen in the ink with some deliberation, and in his fine calligraphy marked *five* for Volodya for progress, and the same for behaviour. Then, his pen poised over the column where my report was to go, he looked at me, shook some ink from his pen-nib, and reflected.

Suddenly his hand made a barely perceptible movement – and, behold, against my name stood a clearly-marked *one*, with a full stop after it! Another movement – and in the behaviour column there stood another *one* and another full stop!

Quietly closing the mark-book, the master then rose, and moved towards the door as though unconscious of my look of entreaty, despair, and reproach.

'Mikhail Larionych!' I said.

'No!' he replied, as though knowing beforehand what I was about to say. 'It is impossible for you to learn in that way. I am not going to earn my money for nothing.'

He put on his goloshes and camlet overcoat, and then with great care tied a scarf about his neck. To think that he could care about such trifles after what had just happened to me! To him it was a mere stroke of the pen, but to me it meant the direst misfortune.

'Is the lesson over?' asked St Jérôme, entering.

'Yes.'

'And was the master satisfied with you?'

'Yes,' said Volodya.

'What marks did he give you?'

'Five.'

'And Nicholas?'

I was silent.

'I think four,' said Volodya. His idea was to save me for at least today. If punishment there must be, it need not be awarded while we had guests.

'*Voyons, Messieurs!*' (St Jérôme was forever prefacing his remarks with '*Voyons!*') '*Faites votre toilette, et descendons.*'[1]

XII
THE LITTLE KEY

WE had hardly descended and greeted all our guests when dinner was announced. Papa was in the highest of spirits, since for some time past he had been winning. He had presented Lyuba with an expensive silver tea-service, and suddenly remembered, at dinner, that he had forgotten the *bonbonnière* which she was to have too as a name-day gift.

'Why send a servant for it? *You* had better go, Koko,' he said to me jestingly. 'The keys are in the shell on the big table, you know? Take them, and with the largest one open the second drawer on the right. There you will find a little box and some sweets in a paper. Bring them all here.'

1 Come now, gentlemen, tidy yourselves, and let us go down.

'Shall I get you some cigars as well?' said I, knowing that he always sent for them after dinner.

'Yes, do; but don't touch any of my things!' he called after me.

I found the keys, and was about to unlock the drawer, when I was seized with a desire to know what the smallest of the keys on the bunch belonged to.

On the edge of the table I saw, among innumerable other things, an embroidered portfolio with a tiny padlock on it, and at once felt curious to see if *that* was what the smallest key fitted. My experiment was crowned with success. The portfolio opened and disclosed a whole sheaf of papers. Curiosity so strongly urged me also to ascertain what those papers contained that the voice of conscience was stilled, and I began to read their contents. . . .

. . . .

My childish feeling of unconditional respect for my elders, especially for Papa, was so strong within me that my intellect involuntarily refused to draw any conclusions from what I had seen. I felt that Papa was living in a sphere completely apart from, incomprehensible by, and unattainable for, me, as well as one that was in every way wonderful, and that any attempt on my part to penetrate the secrets of his life would constitute something like sacrilege.

For this reason the discoveries which I made almost by accident from Papa's portfolio left no clear impression upon my mind, but only a dim consciousness that I had done wrong. I felt ashamed and confused.

The feeling made me eager to shut the portfolio again as quickly as possible, but it seemed as though on this memorable day I was destined to experience every possible kind of adversity. I put the key back into the padlock and turned it round, but not in the right direction. Thinking that the portfolio was now locked, I pulled at the key – and, oh horror! found my hand come away with only the top half of the key in it! In vain did I try to put the two halves together, and by some magic to extract the portion that was sticking in the padlock. At last I had to resign myself to the dreadful thought that I had committed a new crime – one which would be discovered today as soon as ever Papa returned to his study!

First of all, Mimi's accusation on the staircase, and then that *one* mark, and then this little key! Nothing worse could happen now. This very evening I should be assailed successively by Grandmamma (because of Mimi's denunciation), by St Jérôme (because of the bad mark), and by Papa (because of the matter of this key) – yes, all in one evening!

'What on earth is to become of me? Oh, what have I done?' I exclaimed as I paced the soft carpet of the study. 'Well,' I went on with sudden determination, 'what *will be, will be* – that's all,' and, taking up the bonbons and the cigars, I ran back to the other part of the house.

The fatalistic formula with which I had concluded (and which was one that I often heard Nikolai utter during my childhood) always produced in me, at the more difficult crises of my life, a momentarily soothing, beneficial effect. Consequently, when I re-entered the dining-room I was in a rather excited, unnatural mood, yet one that was perfectly cheerful.

XIII

THE TRAITRESS

AFTER dinner we began to play at round games, in which I took a lively part. While playing 'Cat and Mouse' I happened to cannon rather awkwardly against the Kornakovs' governess, who was playing with us, and, stepping on her dress, tore it. Seeing that the girls – particularly Sonya – were anything but displeased at the spectacle of the governess angrily departing to the maid-servants' room to have her dress mended, I resolved to give them the satisfaction a second time. In pursuance of this amiable resolution I waited until the governess returned, and then began to gallop madly round her, until a favourable moment occurred for once more catching my heel in her skirt and tearing it again. Sonya and the young princesses had much ado to restrain their laughter, which excited my conceit the more, but St Jérôme, who had probably observed my tricks, came up to me with the frown which I could never abide in him, and said that my new-found cheerfulness was clearly not a good sign, and that if I did not moderate my behaviour he would give me cause to repent, holiday or no holiday.

However, I was in the desperate position of a person who, having lost more than he has in his pocket, is afraid to reckon up his account and continues to stake desperately on unlucky cards – not because he hopes to regain his losses, but because it will not do for him to stop and consider. So I merely smiled in an impudent fashion and strode away from my tutor.

After 'Cat and Mouse' someone organised another game which, as I recall, we know as '*Lange Nase*,'[1] in which the gentlemen sit on one row of chairs and the ladies on another, and choose each other for partners.

The youngest princess chose the younger Ivin every time, Katya chose either Volodya or Ilyenka, and Sonya chose Seriozha – nor, to my extreme astonishment, did Sonya seem at all embarrassed when Seriozha went and sat down opposite her. On the contrary, she only laughed her sweet, musical laugh, and made a sign with her head that he had chosen right. But nobody chose *me*. My vanity had the mortification that I found myself left out, unwanted, and heard them say, 'Who is left? Oh, Nikolai. Well, *do* take him, somebody.' Consequently, whenever it came to my turn to guess who had chosen me, I had to go either to my sister or to one of the ugly elder princesses and, alas, I was never mistaken. Sonya seemed so absorbed in Seriozha Ivin that in her eyes I clearly existed no longer. I do not quite know why I called her 'the traitress' in my thoughts, since she had never promised to choose me instead of Seriozha, but, for all that, I felt convinced that she was treating me in a very abominable fashion.

After the game was finished I actually saw 'the traitress' (from whom, despite my contempt, I could not withdraw my eyes) go with Seriozha and Katya into a corner, and engage in mysterious discussion. Stealing softly round the piano to discover their secret, I beheld the following: Katya was holding up

1 Long Nose.

a pocket-handkerchief by two of its corners, so as to form a screen for the heads of her two companions. 'No, you have lost! You must pay the forfeit!' cried Seriozha at that moment, and Sonya, who was standing in front of him, blushed like a criminal as she replied, 'No, I have *not* lost! *Have* I, Mademoiselle Catherine?' 'Well, I must speak the truth,' answered Katya, 'and say that you *have* lost the wager, *ma chère*.'[1]

Scarcely had she spoken the words when Seriozha bent down and kissed Sonya, right on her rosy lips! And Sonya laughed as though it were nothing, but merely something very amusing.

Horrors!!! '*O insidious traitress!*'

XIV

DESPERATION

INSTANTLY I began to feel a strong contempt for the female sex in general and Sonya in particular. I began to think that there was nothing at all amusing in these games – that they were fit only for silly little girls, and felt as though I should like to behave outrageously, or to do something of such extraordinary boldness that everyone would be forced to admire it. The opportunity soon arrived.

St Jérôme, after a brief exchange with Mimi, left the room. I could hear his footsteps ascending the staircase, and then passing overhead in the direction of the schoolroom, and the idea occurred to me that Mimi must have told him her story about my being found on the landing during lesson-time, and thereupon he had gone to look at the register. In those days, I believed that St Jérôme had no other aim in life than to punish me. Somewhere I have read that children of from twelve to fourteen years of age – that is to say, children just passing from childhood to adolescence – are particularly inclined to incendiarism, or even to murder. As I look back upon my boyhood, and particularly upon the state of mind in which I was on that (for myself) most unlucky day, I can quite

1 My dear.

understand the possibility of such terrible crimes being committed by children without any real aim in view – without any real intent, or desire to injure, but *just like that*, merely out of curiosity or under the influence of an unconscious necessity for action. There are moments when the human being sees the future in such gloomy colours that he shrinks from fixing his mental eye upon it, puts a check upon all his intellectual activity, and tries to feel convinced that the future will never be, and that the past has never been. At such moments – moments when the will is not served by any advance reflection of the mind, and the carnal instincts alone constitute the springs of life – I can understand that want of experience (which is a particularly predisposing factor in this connection) might very possibly lead a child, without fear or hesitation, but rather with a smile of curiosity, to set fire to the house (and even fan the flames) in which his parents and brothers, whom he tenderly loves, are lying asleep. It would be under the same influence of momentary absence of thought – almost absence of mind – that a peasant lad of seventeen might catch sight of the edge of a newly-sharpened axe reposing near the bench on which his aged father is lying face downwards asleep, and suddenly swing the implement, to observe with vacant curiosity how the blood trickles under the bench from the severed neck. It is under the same influence – the same absence of thought, the same instinctive curiosity – that a man finds a certain gratification in standing on the brink of a precipice and thinking to himself, 'How if I were to throw myself down?' or in holding to his brow a loaded pistol and wondering, 'What if I were to pull the trigger?' or in feeling, when he catches sight of some highly worthy personage who is held by all in servile respect, that he would like to go up to him, pull his nose hard, and say, 'Now then, how do you do, old boy?'

Under the spell, then, of this instinctive agitation and lack of reflection, when St Jérôme came down and told me that I had behaved so badly that day, as well as done my lessons so ill, that I had no right to be where I was, and must go upstairs directly, I was moved to put out my tongue, and to say that I would not move.

At first, from astonishment and anger, St Jérôme could not utter a word.

'*C'est bien!*'[1] he said, coming up to me. 'Several times have I promised to punish you, and you have been saved from it by your grandmamma, but now I see that nothing but the birch will teach you obedience, and today you have amply deserved it.'

This was said loud enough for everyone to hear. The blood rushed to my heart with such force that I could feel it beating violently – could feel the colour draining from my face and my lips trembling uncontrollably. Probably I looked horrible at that moment, for, avoiding my eye, St Jérôme stepped forward and caught me by the arm. But on feeling his touch, I immediately pulled away my arm in blind fury, and with all my childish might struck him.

'What is wrong with you?' said Volodya, who had seen my behaviour, and now approached me in alarm and astonishment.

'Let me alone!' I shouted at him through my tears. 'Not a single one of you loves me or understands how miserable I am! You are all of you odious and disgusting!' I added in a frenzy, addressing the company at large.

At this moment St Jérôme – his face pale, but determined – approached me again, and, with a movement too quick to admit of any defence, seized my arms as in a vice, and dragged me away. My head swam with excitement, and I can only remember that, so long as I had strength to do it, I fought with head and knees; that my nose several times collided with someone's thighs; that someone's coat got into my mouth; that all around me I could hear the shuffling of feet; and that I could smell dust and the scent of violets with which St. Jérôme used to perfume himself.

Five minutes later the door of the store-room closed behind me.

'Vasili,' said a triumphant but detestable voice, 'bring me the birch.'

[1] Very good.

XV
DREAMS

COULD I at that moment have supposed that I should ever live to survive the misfortunes of that day, or that there would ever come a time when I should be able to look back upon those misfortunes composedly?. . .

As I sat there thinking over what I had done, I could not imagine what would become of me. I only felt with vague despair that I was lost for ever.

At first the most profound stillness reigned around me – at least, so it appeared to me as compared with the violent internal agitation which I had been experiencing; but by and by I began to distinguish various sounds. Vasili came upstairs, threw down something, which sounded like a broom, on the window-sill and yawning, lay down on the chest outside. Below me I could hear St Jérôme's loud voice (probably speaking of me), and then children's voices and laughter and running feet; until in a few moments everything seemed to have regained its normal course in the house, as though nobody knew or cared to know that here was I sitting alone in the dark store-room!

I did not cry, but something lay heavy, like a stone, upon my heart. Ideas and pictures passed with extraordinary rapidity before my troubled imagination, yet through their fantastic sequence broke continually the remembrance of the misfortune which had befallen me as I once again plunged into an interminable labyrinth of conjectures as to the fate, the despair, and the fear that were awaiting me.

The thought occurred to me that there must be some reason for the general dislike – even contempt – which I fancied to be felt for me by others. (At that time I was firmly convinced that everyone, from Grandmamma down to the coachman Philip, hated me, and took pleasure in my sufferings.) 'Perhaps I am not the son of my father and mother at all, nor Volodya's brother, but only some unfortunate orphan adopted by them out of compassion,' I said to myself; and this absurd notion not only afforded me a certain melancholy consolation, but seemed to me quite probable. I found it comforting to think that I was unhappy, not through my own fault, but because I was fated to be so from my birth, and conceived that my destiny was very much like the unfortunate Karl Ivanych's.

'Why conceal the secret any longer, now that I have discovered it?' I reflected. 'Tomorrow I will go to Papa and say to him, "It is in vain for you to try and conceal from me the mystery of my birth. I know it already." And he will answer me, "What could I do, my good fellow? Sooner or later you would have found out that you are not my son, but were adopted. Nevertheless, so long as you remain worthy of my love, I will never cast you out." Then I shall say, "Papa, though I have no right to call you by that name, and am now doing so for the last time, I have always loved you, and shall always retain that love. At the same time, while I can never forget that you have been my benefactor, I cannot remain longer in your house. Nobody here loves me, and St Jérôme has sworn to bring about my ruin. Either he or I must leave your house, since I cannot answer for myself. I hate the man so that I could do anything – I could even kill him." Papa will begin to entreat me, but I shall wave my hand, and say, "No, no, my friend and benefactor! We cannot live together. Let me go" – and for the last time I shall embrace him, and say for some reason in French, "*O mon père, O mon bienfaiteur, donne-moi, pour la dernière fois, ta bénédiction, et que la volonté de Dieu soit faite!*" '[1] I sobbed bitterly at these thoughts as I sat on a trunk in that dark store-room. Then, suddenly recollecting the shameful punishment which was awaiting me, I found myself back again in actuality, and the dreams had fled.

Soon, again, I began to fancy myself far away from the house and alone in the world. I enter a hussar regiment and go to war. Surrounded by the foe on every side, I wave my sword, and kill one of them, wave my sword again and wound another – then a third. At last, exhausted with loss of blood and fatigue, I fall to

---

1 O my father, O my benefactor, give me for the last time your blessing, and God's will be done.

the ground with a cry of 'Victory!' The general rides up to look for me, asking, 'Where is he, where is our saviour?' whereupon *I* am pointed out to him. He embraces me, and, in his turn, exclaims with tears of joy, 'Victory!' I recover and, with my arm in a black sling, go to walk on the Tverskoy Boulevard. I am a general now! I meet the Emperor, who asks, 'Who is this young man who has been wounded?' He is told that it is the famous hero Nikolai; whereupon he approaches me and says, 'My thanks to you! Whatsoever you may ask for, I will grant it.' To this I bow respectfully, and, leaning on my sword, reply, 'I am happy, most august Emperor, that I have been able to shed my blood for my fatherland. I would gladly have died for it. Yet, since you are so generous as to grant any wish of mine, I venture to ask of you permission to annihilate my enemy, the foreigner St Jérôme.' And then I halt menacingly before St Jérôme and say, '*You* were the cause of all my fortunes – *à genoux!*'[1]

Unfortunately this recalled to my mind the fact that at any moment the *real* St Jérôme might be entering with the birch; so that once more I saw myself, not a general and the saviour of my country, but a wretched, pitiful creature.

Then the idea of God occurred to me, and I asked Him boldly why He was punishing me thus. 'I have never forgotten to say my prayers, morning or evening, so why am I suffering in this manner?' Indeed, I can positively declare that it was during that hour in the store-room that I took the first step towards the religious doubt which assailed me in my boyhood (not that mere misfortune could arouse me to murmuring and unbelief, but that the idea of the injustice of Providence, which entered my mind in that day-long period of complete spiritual confusion and isolation, took root in me as readily as bad seed germinates and takes root in soft earth well soaked with rain). Next, I imagined that I was going to die there and then, and drew vivid pictures of St Jérôme's astonishment when he entered the store-room and found a lifeless corpse there instead of myself! Likewise, recollecting what Natalya Savishna had

1 Down on your knees!

told me of the forty days during which the souls of the departed must hover around their earthly home, I imagined myself flying invisibly through the rooms of Grandmamma's house, and seeing Lyuba's bitter tears, and hearing Grandmamma's lament-ations, and listening to Papa and St Jérôme talking together. 'He was a fine boy,' Papa would say with tears in his eyes. 'Yes,' St Jérôme would reply, 'but a sad scapegrace and good-for-nothing.' 'But you should respect the dead,' Papa would say. '*You* were the cause of his death; *you* frightened him until he could no longer bear the thought of the humiliation which you were about to inflict upon him. Away from me, you villain!'

Upon that St Jérôme would fall upon his knees weeping and implore forgiveness, and when the forty days were ended my soul would fly to Heaven, and see there something wonderfully beautiful, white, transparent and tall, and know that it was Mamma. And that something surrounds and caresses me. Yet all at once I feel troubled, and seem not to know her. 'If it really is you,' I say to her, 'show yourself more distinctly, so that I may embrace you in return.' And her voice answers me, 'Here we are all thus, I cannot embrace you any better. Do you not feel happy like this?' and I reply, 'Yes, I do, but you cannot *really* tickle me, and I cannot *really* kiss your hands like this.' 'But it is not necessary,' she would say. 'It is wonderful here without that,' – and I feel that it is so, and together we ascend, ever higher and higher. Suddenly I seem to wake up, and find myself sitting on the trunk in the dark store-room, my cheeks wet with tears, and my thoughts in a mist, still repeating the words, 'Let us ascend together, higher and higher.' Indeed, it is a long, long while before I can remember where I am, for at that moment my mind's eye sees only a dark, dreadful, impenetrable vista. I try to renew the happy, consoling dreams which have been thus interrupted by the return to reality, but to my surprise I find that as soon as ever I attempt to re-enter my former reverie, its continuation is now impossible, and – still more astonishing – it no longer gives me any pleasure.

XVI
'KEEP ON GRINDING, AND YOU'LL HAVE FLOUR'

I PASSED the night in the store-room, and no one came to me, but on the following morning – a Sunday – I was moved to a small chamber adjoining the schoolroom, and once more locked in. I began to hope that my punishment was going to be limited to confinement, and found my thoughts growing calmer under the influence of a sound, soft sleep, the bright sunlight playing upon the frost crystals of the window-panes, and the familiar daytime noises in the street. Nevertheless, my solitude was extremely irksome. I wanted to move about, and to communicate to someone all that was lying upon my heart, but not a living creature was near me. The position was the more unpleasant because, willy-nilly, I could hear St Jérôme walking about in his room, and softly whistling fragments of some cheerful tune. Somehow I felt convinced that he was whistling not because he wanted to, but in order to torment me.

At two o'clock he and Volodya departed downstairs, and Nikolai brought me up some dinner. When I told him about what I had done and what was awaiting me he said:

'Pshaw, sir! Don't be alarmed. "Keep on grinding, and you'll have flour." '

Although this expression (which also in later days has more than once helped me to keep up my spirits) brought me a little comfort, the fact that I received not bread and water only but a whole dinner, and even dessert (a sweet pastry), gave me much to think about. If they had sent me no dessert it would have meant that my punishment was to be limited to confinement; whereas it was now evident that I was looked upon as not yet punished – that I was only being kept away from the others, as an evil-doer, until the due time of punishment. While I was still debating the question the key of my prison turned, and St Jérôme entered with a stern, official face.

'Come down and see your grandmamma,' he said without looking at me.

I should have liked first to have brushed the sleeves of my jacket, since it was smeared with chalk dust, but St Jérôme said that that was quite unnecessary, since I was in such a deplorable moral condition that my exterior was not worth considering.

As he led me through the *salon*, Katya, Lyuba, and Volodya looked at me with much the same expression as we were wont to look at the convicts who on Mondays filed past my grandmother's house. Likewise, when I approached Grandmamma's arm-chair to kiss her hand, she withdrew it, and thrust it under her mantilla.

'Well, my dear,' she began after a long pause, during which she regarded me from head to foot with an expression which made me uncertain where to look or what to do with my hands, 'I must say that you seem to value my love very highly, and afford me great consolation.' Then she went on, drawing out every word, 'Monsieur St Jérôme, who, at my request, undertook your education, says that he can no longer remain in the house. And why? Simply because of you.' Another pause ensued. Presently she continued in a tone which clearly showed that her speech had been prepared beforehand, 'I had hoped that you would be grateful for all his care, and for all the trouble that he has taken with you – that you would have appreciated his services; but you – you baby, you silly little boy! – you actually dared to raise your hand against him! Very well, very good. I am beginning to think that you cannot understand kind treatment, but require to be treated in a less dignified and more elementary fashion. Go now directly and beg his pardon,' she added in a stern and peremptory tone as she pointed to St Jérôme. 'Do you hear me?'

I followed the direction of her finger with my eye, but on catching sight of St Jérôme's coat I turned my head away and stood rooted to the spot, feeling my heart sink once more.

'What? Did you not hear me when I told you what to do?'

I was trembling all over, but I would not stir.

'Koko,' went on my grandmother, probably divining my inward sufferings, 'Koko,' she repeated in a voice tender rather than harsh, 'is this you?'

'Grandmamma, I cannot possibly beg his pardon for——'
and I stopped suddenly, for I felt the next word refuse to come
for the tears that were choking me.

'But I order you, I ask you, to do so. What is the matter with
you?'

'I – I – I will not – I cannot!' I gasped, and the tears, long
pent up and accumulated in my breast, burst forth like a stream
which breaks its dikes and goes flowing madly over the
country.

'*C'est ainsi que vous obéissez à votre seconde mère, c'est ainsi que
vous reconnaissez ses bontés!*' remarked St Jérôme in tragic tones.
'*A genoux!*'[1]

'Good God! If *she* had seen this!' exclaimed Grandmamma,
turning from me and wiping away her tears. 'If *she* had seen this!
It may be all for the best, for she could never have survived such
grief – never!' and Grandmamma wept more and more. I too
wept, but it never occurred to me to ask for pardon.

'*Tranquillisez-vous au nom du ciel, Madame la Comtesse,*'[2] said
St Jérôme, but Grandmamma had ceased to listen to him. She
covered her face with her hands, and her sobs soon passed to
hiccups and hysteria. Mimi and Gasha came running in with
frightened faces, salts and spirits were applied, and the whole
house was soon in a ferment of running feet and whispering.

'You may feel pleased at your work,' said St Jérôme to me as
he led me upstairs again.

'Good God! What have I done?' I thought to myself. 'What
a dreadful criminal I am!'

As soon as St Jérôme, bidding me go to my room, had
returned to Grandmamma, I, all unconscious of what I was
doing, ran towards the grand staircase leading to the front door.

Whether I intended to drown myself, or merely to run away
from home, I do not remember. I only know that I ran blindly
on down the staircase, my face covered with my hands that I
might see no one.

---

1 This is how you obey your second mother, this is how you repay her
kindnesses to you! . . . On your knees!
2 Calm yourself, in Heaven's name, Countess.

'Where are you going to?' asked a well-known voice. 'I want you, my boy.'

I would have passed on, but Papa caught hold of me, and said sternly:

'Come here, my good fellow. – How could you dare to do such a thing as to touch the portfolio in my study?' he went on as he dragged me into his small sitting-room. 'Oh! you are silent, eh?' and he pulled my ear.

'Yes, I *was* naughty,' I said. 'I don't know myself what came over me.'

'So you don't know what came over you – you don't know, you don't know, you don't know, you don't know?' he repeated as he pulled my ear at each repetition of the phrase. 'Will you go and put your nose where you ought not to again – will you, will you?'

Although my ear was hurting very badly indeed, I did not cry, but, on the contrary, felt a sort of morally pleasing sensation. No sooner did Papa let go of my ear than I seized his hand and covered it with tears and kisses.

'Please whip me!' I cried, sobbing. 'Please hurt me the more and more. I am a wretched, bad, miserable boy!'

'Why, what on earth is the matter with you?' he said, giving me a slight push from him.

'No, I will not go away!' I continued, clinging to his coat. 'Everyone else hates me – I know that, but do *you* listen to me and protect me, or else send me away altogether. I cannot live with *him*. He tries to humiliate me – he tells me to kneel before him, and wants to thrash me. I can't stand it. I'm not a baby. I can't stand it – I shall die, I shall kill myself. *He* told Grandmamma that I was worthless, and now she is ill – she will die through me. It is all his fault. I . . . can't . . . with him. Please Papa, you punish me.—— W-why . . . do . . . they – torment me?'

Tears choked my further speech. I sat down on the sofa, and, with my head buried on Papa's knees, sobbed until I thought I should die of grief.

'Come, come! Why are you such a water-pump?' said Papa compassionately, as he bent over me.

'He is such a bully! He torments me! I shall die! Nobody loves me at all!' I gasped almost inaudibly, and went into convulsions.

Papa lifted me up in his arms, and carried me to my bedroom, where I fell asleep.

When I awoke it was very late. Only a solitary candle burned in the room, while beside the bed there were seated Mimi, Lyuba, and our family doctor. In their faces I could discern anxiety for my state. But I felt so well and light of heart after my twelve hours' sleep that I could have got up directly, had I not disliked the thought of disturbing their conviction that I was very ill.

XVII
HATRED

YES, it was the real feeling of hatred that was mine now: not the hatred of which one reads in novels, and in which I do not believe – the hatred which finds satisfaction in doing harm to a fellow-creature – but the hatred which consists of an unconquerable aversion to a person who may be wholly deserving of your esteem, yet whose very hair, neck, walk, voice, limbs, movements, and whole person are disgusting to you, while all the while an incomprehensible force attracts you towards him, and compels you to follow his slightest acts with anxious attention. This was the feeling which I experienced towards St Jérôme.

St Jérôme had lived with us now for a year and a half. Judging coolly of the man now, I find that he was a true Frenchman, but a Frenchman to the highest degree of Frenchness. He was not a fool, he was fairly well educated, and fulfilled his duties to us conscientiously, but he had the peculiar features of shallow egotism, vanity, impertinence, and ignorant self-assurance which are common to all his countrymen, and entirely opposed to the Russian character. All this set me against him. Grandmamma had signified to him her dislike for corporal punishment, and therefore he dared not beat us, but he frequently *threatened* us, particularly me, with the cane, and would utter the word *fouetter*[1] as though it were *fouatter* in an expressive and detestable way which always gave me the idea that to whip me would afford him the greatest possible satisfaction.

I was not in the least afraid of the physical pain of the punishment, for I had never experienced it. It was the mere idea that St Jérôme could strike me that threw me into such paroxysms of suppressed wrath and despair.

True, Karl Ivanych sometimes (in moments of exasperation) had recourse to a ruler or to his braces, but that I can look back upon without the slightest anger. Even if he had given me a beating at the time of which I am now speaking (when I was fourteen years old), I should have submitted quietly to the correction, for I loved him, and had known him for as long as I could remember, and looked upon him as a member of our family; but St Jérôme was a conceited, opinionated fellow for whom I felt merely the automatic respect which I entertained for all *grown-ups*. Karl Ivanych was a comical old 'Uncle' whom I loved with my whole heart, but who, according to my childish conception of social distinctions, ranked below us.

St Jérôme on the other hand was a well-educated, handsome young dandy who was for showing himself the equal of anyone. Karl Ivanych had always scolded and punished us coolly, as though he thought it a necessary, but extremely disagreeable, duty. St Jérôme, on the contrary, always liked to emphasise his lofty role as mentor when correcting us, and clearly did it as much for his own satisfaction as for our good. He was carried away by his own importance. I always found his grandiloquent French phrases (which he pronounced with a strong emphasis on all the final syllables and on circumflex accents) inexpressibly disgusting. Karl Ivanych, when angry, had never said anything beyond, 'What a foolish puppet-comedy it is!' or 'You vicked poy', or 'You boys are as irritating as Spanish fly' (which he always called '*Champagne*' fly). St Jérôme, however, had names for us like '*mauvais sujet,*'

---

1 To whip.

'*vilain garnement*,'[1] and so forth – epithets which greatly offended my self-respect.

When Karl Ivanych ordered us to kneel in the corner with our faces to the wall, the punishment consisted merely in the bodily discomfort of the position, whereas St Jérôme, in such cases, always assumed a haughty air, made a grandiose gesture with his hand, and exclaiming in a pseudo-tragic tone, '*À genoux, mauvais sujet!*' ordered us to kneel with our faces towards him, and to crave his pardon. His punishment consisted in humiliation.

However, on the present occasion the punishment never came, nor was the matter ever referred to again. Yet I could not forget all that I had gone through – the despair, the shame, the fear, and the hatred of those two days. From that time forth St Jérôme appeared to give me up in despair, and took no further trouble with me, yet I could not bring myself to treat him with indifference. Every time that our eyes met I felt that my look expressed only too plainly my enmity, and though I tried hard to assume a careless air he seemed to divine my hypocrisy, until I was forced to blush and turn away.

In short, it was a terrible trial to me to have anything to do with him.

XVIII
THE MAID-SERVANTS' ROOM

I BEGAN to feel more and more lonely, until my chief solace lay in solitary reflection and observation. Of the subject of my reflections I shall speak in the next chapter, but the scene where I indulged in them was, for preference, the maid-servants' room, where what was for me an intriguing and touching romance was in train. The heroine of the romance was, of course, Masha. She was in love with Vasili, who had known her before she had become a servant in our house, and who had already promised to marry her some day.

1 Knave, bad lot.

Unfortunately, fate, which had separated them five years ago, and afterwards reunited them in Grandmamma's house, next proceeded to interpose an obstacle between them in the shape of Masha's uncle, our man Nikolai, who would not hear of his niece marrying that 'unsuitable and ungovernable fellow,' as he called Vasili.

One effect of the obstacle had been to make the otherwise slightly cool and indifferent Vasili fall as passionately in love with Masha as it is possible for a man to be who is a servant and a tailor, wears a pink shirt, and has his hair pomaded.

Although his methods of expressing his affection were odd and unsuitable (for instance, whenever he met Masha he always endeavoured to inflict upon her some bodily pain, either by pinching her, giving her a slap with his open hand, or squeezing her so hard that she could scarcely breathe), that affection was sincere enough, and he proved it by the fact that, from the moment when Nikolai finally refused him his niece's hand, his grief led him to drinking, and to frequenting taverns and caus-ing trouble, until he proved so unruly that more than once he had to be sent to undergo the humiliation of being shut up in a cell at the police-station. Nevertheless, these faults of his and their consequences only served to elevate him in Masha's eyes, and to increase her love for him. Whenever he was *in the hands of the police* she would sit crying the whole day without wiping her eyes, and complain to Gasha of her hard fate (Gasha played an active part in the affairs of these unfortunate lovers). Then, regardless of her uncle's anger and blows, she would stealthily make her way to the police-station, there to visit and console her swain.

Do not disdain, reader, this company into which I am introducing you. If the cords of love and compassion have not wholly snapped in your soul, you will find, even in that maid-servants' room, sounds which may cause them to vibrate again. So, whether you please to follow me or not, I will return to the landing on the staircase whence I can observe all that passes in that room. From my post I can see the stove-couch, with upon it an iron, a dressmaker's dummy made of paste-board with a broken nose, a wash-tub, and a basin. There, too, is the window-sill, and on it, in fine disorder, a piece of black wax, a skein of silk, a half-eaten green cucumber, a box of sweets. There, too, is the large red table with some unfinished needle-work lying on it beneath a calico-covered brick, at which *she* sits in the pink gingham dress which I admired so much and the blue handkerchief which always caught my attention so. She is sewing – though interrupting her work at intervals to scratch her head with her needle, or to snuff the candle – and I look at her and think to myself: 'Why was she not born a lady – she with her blue eyes, beautiful light-brown plait, and magnificent bosom? How splendid she would look if she were sitting in a drawing-room and dressed in a cap with pink ribbons and a raspberry silk gown – not one like Mimi's, but one like the gown which I saw the other day on the Tverskoy Boulevard! Yes, she would work at her embroidery-frame, and I would sit and look at her in the mirror, and be ready to do whatever she wanted – to help her on with her mantle or to hand her a dish at the dinner-table.

As for Vasili's drunken face and horrid figure in the scanty coat with the dirty pink shirt which he wears outside his trousers, well, in his every gesture, in his every twist of his back, I seem always to see signs of the disgusting chastisement which he has undergone.

'Ah, Vasya! *Again?*' cried Masha on one occasion as she stuck her needle into the pin-cushion, but without looking up at the person who was entering.

'Well, what of it? What is the good of a man like *him*?' was Vasili's first remark.

'Yes. If only he would say something *decisive* one way or the other! I am all at odds and ends, and through his fault, too.'

'Will you have some tea?' put in Nadezha, another of the housemaids.

'Thank you kindly. – But why does he hate me so, that old thief of an uncle of yours? Why? Is it because of the clothes I wear, or because I am smart, or is it the way I walk, or what? Well, confound him!' finished Vasili, snapping his fingers.

'We must be patient,' said Masha, biting off her thread. 'You are always so——'

'I just can't endure it, that's all.'

At this moment the door of Grandmamma's room banged, and Gasha's querulous voice could be heard as she came up the stairs.

'There!' she muttered, waving her arms. 'Try to please people when even they themselves do not know what they want, and it is a cursed life – sheer hard labour, and nothing else! If only a certain thing would happen! – though God forgive me my trespass for thinking it!'

'My respects, Agafya Mikhailovna,' said Vasili, rising to greet her.

'*You* here?' she answered brusquely as she stared at him. 'What need have I of your respects? What do you come here for? Is the maids' room a proper place for men?'

'I wanted to see how you were,' said Vasili timidly.

'I shall soon be breathing my last – *that's* how I am!' cried Gasha, still more incensed, at the top of her voice.

Vasili laughed.

'Oh, there's nothing to laugh at, and if I tell you to take yourself out of here, then quick march. Just look at the rascal! Marry her, would he? The scoundrel! Come, get out of here!' and, with a stamp of her foot on the floor, Gasha retreated to her own room, and banged the door behind her so that the window-panes rattled.

For a while she could be heard scolding at everything and everyone, cursing her own life, flinging dresses and other things about, and pulling the ears of her pet cat. Then the door opened a crack, and puss, mewing pitifully, was flung forth by the tail.

'I had better come another time for tea,' said Vasili in a whisper – 'at some better time for our meeting.'

'Don't you worry!' put in Nadezha. 'I'll go and see if the samovar is ready.'

'I mean to put an end to things soon,' went on Vasili, seating himself nearer to Masha as soon as ever Nadezha had left the room.

'Either I'll go straight to the Countess, and say, "It's like this, and like that" or I will throw up my situation and go off into the world. Oh dear, oh dear!'

'And am I to remain here?'

'Ah, there's the difficulty – that's what I feel so badly about. But for you my dearest I'd have gone off long ago to seek my fortune. Ah, deary me!'

'Why don't you bring me your shirts to wash, Vasya?' asked Masha after a pause. 'Just look how dirty this one is,' she added, taking hold of his shirt-collar.

At this moment Grandmamma's bell rang downstairs, and Gasha issued from her room again.

'What do you want with her, you impudent fellow?' she cried as she pushed Vasili (who had risen hastily at her entrance) before her towards the door. 'First you lead a girl on shamefully, and then here you are again troubling her. I suppose it amuses you to see her tears, you shameless fellow. There's the door, now. Off you go! Make yourself scarce. And what good can *you* see in him?' she went on, turning to Masha. 'Has not your uncle been laying into you enough today already on his account? No; she must have her own way, forsooth! "I will have no one but Vasili Gruskov." Fool that you are!'

'Yes, I *will* have no one but him! I'll never love anyone else, even if you beat me to death!' poor Masha burst out, the tears suddenly gushing forth.

For a while I stood watching her as she lay on a trunk, wiping away those tears with her kerchief. Then I fell to contemplating Vasili attentively, in the hope of discovering the point of view from which he appeared to her so attractive; yet, though I sympathised with her sincerely in her grief, I could not for the life of me understand how such a charming creature as I considered her to be could love a man like Vasili.

'When *I* become a man,' I thought to myself as I returned to my room, 'Petrovskoye shall be mine, and Vasili and Masha my serfs. Some day, when I am sitting in my study and smoking a pipe, Masha will chance to pass the door on her way to the kitchen with an iron, and I shall say, "Send Masha to me," and she will enter, and there will be no one else in the room. Then suddenly Vasili too will come in, and, on seeing her, will cry, "I am done for!" and Masha will begin to weep. Then *I* shall say, "Vasili, I know that you love her, and that she loves you. Here is a thousand roubles for you. Marry her, and may God grant you both happiness!" Then I shall depart into the sitting-room.'

Among the countless thoughts and fancies which pass without logic or sequence through the mind and the imagination, leaving no trace, there are always some which leave behind them a furrow so profound and so sensitive that, without remembering their exact subject, we can at least recall that something good has passed through our brain, we are conscious of the trace left by this thought and try to reproduce it. Such was the mark left upon my consciousness by the idea I had then of sacrificing my feelings to Masha's happiness, seeing that she believed that she could attain it only through marriage with Vasili.

XIX
BOYHOOD

PERHAPS people will scarcely believe me when I tell them what were the dearest, most constant, objects of my reflections during my boyhood, so little did those objects consort with my age and position. Yet, in my opinion, contrast between a man's actual position and his moral activity constitutes the most reliable sign of his genuineness.

For a whole year, when I was leading a solitary and self-centred moral life, I was much taken up with abstract thoughts on man's destiny, on a future life, and on the immortality of the soul, and with all the ardour of inexperience strove to make my youthful intellect solve those questions – the questions which constitute the highest level of thought to which the human intellect can tend, but a final decision of which the human intellect can never succeed in attaining.

I believe the human mind to take the same course of development in the individual as in whole generations, as also that the thoughts which serve as a basis for philosophical theories are an inseparable part of that mind, and that every man must be more or less conscious of those thoughts before he can know anything of the existence of philosophical theories.

To my own mind those thoughts presented themselves with such clarity and force that I even tried to apply them to life, in the fond belief that I was the first to have discovered such great and invaluable truths.

At one time it occurred to me that happiness depends, not upon external causes themselves, but only upon our attitude to them, and that provided a man can accustom himself to bearing suffering he need never be unhappy. To discipline myself to the task I would (despite the horrible pain) hold out a Tatishchev's dictionary at arm's length for five minutes at a time, or else go into the store-room and scourge my bare back with a rope so severely that the tears involuntarily came to my eyes!

Another time, suddenly bethinking me that death might find me at any hour or any minute, I came to the conclusion, wondering how people had never found it out before, that man could be happy only by using the present to the full and taking no thought for the future. Acting under the influence of the new idea, I laid my lesson-books aside for two or three days, and reposing on my bed gave myself up to novel-reading and the eating of gingerbread made with honey which I had bought with my last remaining coins.

Again, standing one day before the blackboard and drawing various figures on it with chalk, I was struck with the thought, 'Why is symmetry so agreeable to the eye? What *is* symmetry? Of course it is an innate sense,' I answered myself; 'yet what is its basis? Perhaps everything in life is symmetry? But no. On the contrary, *this* is life' – and I drew an oval on the board – 'and after life the soul passes to eternity, here is eternity' – here I drew a line from one end of the oval figure to the edge of the board. 'Why should there not be a corresponding line on the other side? If there be an eternity on one side, there must surely be a corresponding one on the other? We must have existed in a previous life, but have lost the recollection of it.'

This conclusion – which seemed to me at the time both clear and novel, but the arguments for which it would be difficult for me at this distance of time to piece together – pleased me extremely, so I took a piece of paper and tried to write it down. But at the first attempt such a rush of other thoughts came whirling though my brain that I was obliged to jump up and pace the room. At the window my attention was arrested by a driver harnessing a horse to a water-cart, and at once my mind concentrated itself upon resolving the question, 'Into what animal or human being will the spirit of that horse pass at death?' Just at that moment Volodya passed through the room, and smiled to see me absorbed in speculative thoughts. His smile at once made me feel that all that I had been thinking about was utter nonsense.

I have related this occasion, which for some reason I seem to remember, in order to show the reader the nature of my cogitations. But no philosophical theory attracted me so much as scepticism, which at one period brought me to a state of mind verging upon insanity. I took the fancy into my head that no one nor anything really existed in the world except myself – that objects were not objects at all, but images which became manifest only so soon as I turned my attention upon them, and vanished again directly that I ceased to think about them. In short, this idea of mine (that objects do not exist, but only one's conception of them) brought me the same conclusion as Schelling's. There were moments when the influence of this idea led me to such vagaries as, for instance, turning sharply round, in the hope that by the suddenness of the movement I should come in contact with the void (*néant*) which I believed to be existing where I myself was not.

What a pitiful spring of moral activity is the human mind! My faulty reason could not penetrate the impenetrable, but in an effort which was beyond my strength it lost one after another those convictions which, for the happiness of my life, I should never have dared to disturb.

From all this weary mental struggle I derived only a certain pliancy of mind, a weakening of the will, a habit of perpetual moral analysis, which destroyed both freshness of feeling and clearness of thought.

Usually abstract thoughts are generated through man's capacity for apprehending the bent of his mind at a certain moment and transferring that apprehension to his memory. But my inclination for abstract thought developed my consciousness to such an unnatural degree that often, when I began to consider even the simplest matter, I would lose myself in a labyrinthine analysis of my own thoughts concerning the matter in question. That is to say, I no longer thought of the matter itself, but only of what I was thinking about it. If I then asked myself, 'Of what am I thinking?' my answer would be, 'I am thinking of what I am thinking'; and if I had further asked myself, 'What, then, are the thoughts of which I am thinking?' I should have had to reply, 'They are attempts to think of what I am thinking concerning my own thoughts' – and so on. I was nearing my wits' end.

However, every philosophical discovery which I made so flattered my conceit that I often imagined myself to be a great man discovering new truths for the benefit of humanity. Consequently I looked down with proud dignity upon my fellow-mortals. Yet, strange to state, no sooner did I come in contact with those fellow-mortals than I became filled with a stupid shyness of them, and the higher I happened to be standing in my own opinion, the less did I feel capable of making others perceive my consciousness of my own dignity, or ridding myself of a sense of diffidence concerning even the simplest of my words and acts.

XX
VOLODYA

THE further I advance in the recital of this period of my life, the more painful and difficult does the task become for me. Too rarely do I find among the reminiscences of that time any moments full of the sincere warmth of feeling which so often and so brightly illumined my childhood. Gladly would I pass in haste over the desert waste of my lonely boyhood, the sooner to arrive at the happy time when once again a tender, sincere, and noble sentiment marked with a gleam of light at once the termination of that period and the beginning of a new phase which was full of the charm of poetry – the period of my youth.

Therefore I will not pursue my recollections from hour to hour, but only throw a cursory glance at the most prominent of them, from the time to which I have now carried my narrative to the moment of my first contact with the exceptional personality who was to exercise such a decisive and beneficial influence upon my character and ideas.

Volodya is soon to enter the University. Tutors come to give him lessons independently of myself, and I listen with envy and involuntary respect as he taps boldly on the blackboard with the chalk and talks about functions, sines, co-ordinates, and so forth – all of which seem to me terms pertaining to unattainable wisdom. At length, one Sunday after dinner all the tutors – and among them two professors – assemble in Grandmamma's room, and in the presence of Papa and some friends put Volodya through a rehearsal of his University examination – in which, to Grandmamma's delight, he gives evidence of no ordinary amount of knowledge. Questions on several subjects are also put to me, but on all of them I show complete ignorance, while the fact that the professors manifestly endeavour to conceal that ignorance from Grandmamma only embarrasses me the more. Yet, after all, I am only fifteen, and so have a year before me in which to prepare for the examinations. Volodya now comes downstairs for dinner only, and spends whole days and evenings over his studies in his own room – not from necessity, but because he prefers its seclusion. He is very ambitious, and means to pass the examinations, not by halves, but with flying colours.

But now the first day of the examination has arrived. Volodya puts on a new blue frockcoat with brass buttons, a gold watch, and shiny boots. Papa's phaeton is brought up to the door. Nikolai throws back the apron, and Volodya and St Jérôme set out for the University. The girls – particularly Katya – can be seen gazing with beaming faces from the window at Volodya's pleasing figure as he gets into the carriage. Papa says several times, 'God go with him!' and Grandmamma, who has also dragged herself to the window, continues with tears in her eyes to make the sign of the cross in Volodya's direction until the phaeton disappears round the corner of the street, and as long as the phaeton remains visible, murmurs something to herself.

When Volodya returns everyone eagerly crowds round him. 'How many marks? Were they good ones?' But his happy face is an answer in itself. He has received a five – the maximum! The next day he speeds on his way with the same good wishes and the same anxiety for his success, and is welcomed home with the same eagerness and joy. This goes on for nine days. On the tenth day comes the last and most difficult examination of all – the one in divinity, and we all stand at the window and watch for him with greater impatience than ever. Two o'clock, and still no Volodya.

'O Lord, goodness gracious, here they come, Papa! Here they come!' suddenly screams Lyuba, her face glued to the window.

Sure enough the phaeton is driving up with St Jérôme and Volodya – the latter no longer in his grey cap and blue frock-coat, but in the uniform of a student of the University, with its embroidered blue collar, three-cornered hat, and gilded sword at his side.

'Ah! If only *she* had been alive now!' exclaims Grandmamma on seeing Volodya in his uniform, and falls into a swoon.

Volodya runs into the ante-room with a beaming face, and embraces me, Lyuba, Mimi, and Katya – the latter blushing to her ears. He hardly knows himself for joy. And how smart he looks in that uniform! How well the blue collar suits his budding, dark moustache! What a tall, elegant figure is his, and what a distinguished walk!

On that memorable day we all dine together in Grand-mamma's room. Every face expresses delight, and with the dessert which follows the meal the butler, with a gravely formal but joyful expression on his face, brings in a bottle of champagne wrapped in a napkin. Grandmamma, for the first time since Mamma's death, takes the champagne, and drinks a full glass to Volodya's health, again weeping for joy as she looks at him.

Henceforth Volodya drives out by himself in his own turn-out, invites his own friends in, smokes, and goes to balls. On one occasion I even saw him sharing a couple of bottles of champagne with some companions in his room and the whole company drinking a toast with each glass to some mysterious personages, and then quarrelling as to who should have *le fond de la bouteille!*[1]

Nevertheless he always lunches at home, and after the meal stretches himself on a sofa as of old and talks confidentially to Katya: yet from what I overhear, while taking no part of course in their conversation, I gather that they are only talking of the heroes and heroines of novels which they have read, of jealousy and love. Never can I understand what they find so attractive in these conversations, nor why they smile so subtly and discuss things with such animation.

Altogether I can see that, in addition to the friendship natural to persons who have been companions from childhood, there exists between Volodya and Katya a relation which sets them apart from us, and unites them mysteriously to one another.

XXI
KATYA AND LYUBA

KATYA is now sixteen years old – quite a grown-up girl; and although at that age the angular figure, the bashfulness, and the *gaucherie* peculiar to girls passing from childhood to youth have given place to the comely freshness and grace of a budding flower, she has in no way altered. Still the same blue eyes with their merry glance, the well-shaped nose with firm nostrils and almost forming a line with the forehead, the little mouth with its charming smile, the tiny dimples in the rosy cheeks, and the small white hands . . . To her the epithet of 'girl,' pure and simple, is still pre-eminently applicable, for in her the only new features are a new and 'young-lady-like' arrangement of her thick light-brown hair worn in a plait, and a youthful bosom – an addition which at once causes her great joy and makes her bashful.

1 The bottom of the bottle!

Although Lyuba and she have grown up together and
received the same education, Lyuba is in all respects a very
different girl. Lyuba is not tall, and the rickets from which she
has suffered have shaped her feet in goose fashion and made her
figure very bad. The only pretty feature in her face is her eyes,
which are indeed wonderful, being large and black, and instinct
with such an extremely pleasing expression of mingled gravity
and *naïveté* that they attract everyone's attention. In everything
she is simple and natural, so that, whereas Katya always looks as
though she is trying to be like someone else, Lyuba looks
people straight in the face, and sometimes fixes them so long
with her splendid black eyes that she gets blamed for doing
what is thought to be improper. Katya, on the contrary, always
casts her eyelids down, screws up her eyes, and pretends that she
is short-sighted, though I know very well that her sight is
excellent. Lyuba hates being shown off before strangers, and
when anyone kisses her in the presence of visitors she invariably
pouts, and says that she cannot bear 'sentiment'; whereas, when
strangers are present, Katya is always particularly endearing to
Mimi, and loves to walk about the ball-room with her arm
round some other girl's waist. Likewise, though Lyuba is a
terrible giggler, and sometimes runs about the room in convulsions of gesticulating laughter, Katya always covers her mouth
with her hands or her pocket-handkerchief when she wants to
laugh. Lyuba invariably sits bolt upright and walks with her
arms hanging down, but Katya holds her head a little on one
side and walks with her hands folded together. Lyuba, again,
always loves to have grown-up men to talk to, and says that
some day she means to marry a hussar, but Katya always maintains that all men are horrid, and that she never means to marry
at all, and as soon as a male visitor addresses her she changes
completely, as though she is nervous of something. Lyuba is
continually at loggerheads with Mimi for lacing her stays so
tight that she connot breathe, and she is fond of eating; while
Katya, on the contrary, often inserts her finger into her
waistband to show us how loose it is, and always eats very
little. Lyuba likes drawing heads; Katya only flowers and but-
terflies. Lyuba plays Field's concertos and some of Beethoven's

sonatas excellently; Katya indulges in variations and waltzes, cannot keep time, thumps, and uses the pedal incessantly – not to mention the fact that, before she begins, she invariably strikes three chords in *arpeggio*.

Nevertheless, in those days I thought Katya much more grown-up of the two, and liked her the best.

XXII
PAPA

PAPA has been in particularly good humour ever since Volodya passed into the University, and comes much oftener to dine with Grandmamma. However, the reason for his good humour, as I learned from Nikolai, is that he has won a great deal lately at cards. Occasionally he comes and sits with us in the evening before going to the club. He sits down to the piano, gathers us around him, after which he beats time with his soft boots (he detests heels, and never wears them), and sings gipsy songs. At such times you should see the quaint enthusiasm of his beloved Lyuba, who adores him!

Sometimes, again, he will come to the schoolroom and listen with a grave face as I say my lessons; yet by the few words which he lets drop when correcting me I can see that he knows even less about the subject than I do. Not infrequently too, he winks slyly at us and makes secret signs when Grandmamma begins to scold us and find fault with us all round with no good reason. 'So much for us children!' he says afterwards. On the whole, however, the impossible pinnacle upon which my childish imagination had placed him has undergone a certain abasement. I still kiss his large white hand with the same feeling of love and respect, but I also allow myself to think about him and to criticise his behaviour, until involuntarily thoughts occur to me about him which alarm me by their presence. Never shall I forget one incident in particular which awakened thoughts of this kind, and caused me intense moral pain.

Late one evening he entered the drawing-room in his black dress-coat and white waistcoat, to take Volodya (who was still dressing in his bedroom) to a ball. Grandmamma was also in her bedroom, but had given orders that before setting out Volodya was to come and say goodbye to her (it was her invariable custom to inspect him before he went to a ball, and to bless him and direct him as to his behaviour). The room where we were was lighted by a solitary lamp. Mimi and Katya were walking up and down, and Lyuba was practising Field's Second Concerto (Mamma's favourite piece) at the piano.

Never was there such a family likeness as between Mamma and my sister – not so much in the face or the stature as in some elusive quality of the hands, the walk, the voice, the favourite expressions. When Lyuba was annoyed and said: 'They keep one waiting simply ages,' she pronounced the words 'simply ages,' a characteristic phrase of Mamma's, in a particular long drawn-out way – 'Si-i-imply a-a-ages' – so that one almost seemed to hear Mamma speaking. But most remarkable of all was the likeness in their ways of playing the piano and their whole demeanour at the instrument. Lyuba always smoothed her dress when sitting down just as Mamma had done, and turned the leaves from the top with her left hand like her, pounded the keys with her fist in vexation and said 'O Lord!' whenever she had not yet mastered a difficult passage, and, in particular, played with the same delicacy and exquisite purity of touch which in those days was known characteristically in the execution of Field's music as '*jeu perlé*' and which all the humbug of our modern *virtuosi* has not induced us to forget.

Papa entered the room with short, quick steps, and approached Lyuba. On seeing him she stopped playing.

'No, go on, Lyuba, go on,' he said as he made her sit down again. 'You know how I love to hear you play . . .' She went on playing, while Papa, his head on his hand, sat near her for a while. Then suddenly he gave his shoulders a sudden twitch and, rising, began to pace the room. Every time he approached the piano he halted for a moment and looked intently at Lyuba. By his walk and his every movement I could see that he was greatly agitated. After several turns round the room he stopped behind Lyuba, kissed her black hair, and then, wheeling quickly round, resumed his pacing. The piece finished, Lyuba went up to him and said, 'Was it well played?' whereupon, without answering, he took her head in his two hands, and began kissing her forehead and eyes with such tenderness as I had never before seen him display.

'Oh goodness, you are crying!' said Lyuba suddenly as she ceased to toy with his watch-chain and stared at him with her great black startled eyes. 'Pardon me, darling Papa! I had quite forgotten that it was dear Mamma's piece which I was playing.'

'No, no, my love; play it often,' he said in a voice trembling with emotion. 'Ah, if you only knew how much good it does me to share your tears!'

He kissed her again, then, mastering his feelings and with a jerk of his shoulders, went to the door leading to the corridor which ran past Volodya's room.

'Voldemar, shall you be ready soon?' he cried, halting in the middle of the passage. Just then Masha the maid came along and, confused at seeing her master, made as if to go round him. He stopped her.

'Why, you look prettier every day,' he said, leaning over her. She blushed and hung her head still lower. 'Please let me pass,' she whispered.

'Voldemar, shall you be ready soon?' he cried again, with a cough and a shake of his shoulders, just as Masha slipped away and he caught sight of me.

I loved Papa, but the intellect is independent of the heart, and often gives birth to thoughts which offend and are harsh and incomprehensible to the feelings. And it was thoughts of this kind that, for all I strove to put them away, arose at that moment in my mind.

XXIII
GRANDMAMMA

GRANDMAMMA is growing weaker every day. Her bell, Gasha's grumbling voice, and the slamming of doors are sounds of constant occurrence in her apartment, and she no longer receives us sitting in the Voltairian arm-chair in her boudoir, but lying on the high bed in her bedroom, supported on lace-trimmed pillows. One day when greeting her I notice a yellowish-white shiny swelling on her hand, and smell the same

oppressive odour which I smelt five years ago in Mamma's
room. The doctor comes three times a day, and there has
been more than one consultation. Yet the character of her
haughty, ceremonious bearing towards all who live with her,
and particularly towards Papa, has not changed in the least. She
still emphasises certain words, raising her eyebrows and saying
'my dear,' just as she has always done.

And now for several days we have not been allowed to see
her at all, and one morning during lessons St Jérôme proposes
to me that Volodya and I should take Katya and Lyuba for a
drive. Although I observe as I get into the sledge that the street
is strewn with straw under the windows of Grandmamma's
room, and that some men in blue jackets[1] are standing at our
gate, the reason never dawns upon me why we are being sent
out at that unusual hour. Throughout the drive Lyuba and I are,
for some reason, in that particularly merry mood when the least
trifle, the least word or movement, sets one off laughing.

A pedlar goes trotting across the road with a tray, and we
laugh. Some ragged cabman, brandishing his reins and driving
at full speed, overtakes our sledge, and we laugh again. Next,
Philip's whip gets caught in the sledge-runner, and the way in
which he turns round and says, 'Bother the thing!' as he strives
to disentangle it almost kills us with mirth. Mimi looks displeased, and says that only silly people laugh for no reason at all,
but Lyuba – her face purple with suppressed merriment – needs
but to give me a sly glance, and we again burst out into such
Homeric laughter when our eyes meet that the tears rush into
them and we cannot stop our paroxysms, although they nearly
choke us. Hardly, again, have we desisted a little when I look at
Lyuba once more, and give vent to one of the slang words
which we then affected among ourselves – words which always
called forth hilarity; and in a moment we are laughing again.

Driving up to the house on our way back I open my mouth
to make a splendid grimace at Lyuba when my eye falls upon a
black coffin-cover leaning against one panel of the front door –
and my mouth remains fixed in its gaping position.

1 Undertaker's men.

'*Votre grand'mère est morte*,'[1] says St Jérôme as he comes to meet us. His face is very pale.

Throughout the whole time that Grandmamma's body is in the house I am oppressed with the fear of death, for the corpse serves as a forcible and disagreeable reminder that I too must die some day – a feeling which people often mistake for grief. I have no sincere regret for Grandmamma, nor, I think, has any-one else, since, although the house is full of sympathising callers, nobody seems to mourn for her from their hearts except one mourner whose genuine grief surprises me unutterably. The mourner in question is her maid Gasha. She shuts herself up in the garret, weeps unceasingly, curses herself, tears her hair, and refuses all consolation, saying that, now that her beloved mistress is dead, the only consolation left her is to die herself.

I again assert that, in matters of feeling, it is the unexpected effects that constitute the most reliable signs of sincerity.

Though Grandmamma is no longer with us, reminiscences and gossip about her long continue in the house. Such gossip refers mostly to her will, which she made shortly before her death, and of which, as yet, no one knows the contents except her executor, Prince Ivan Ivanych. I notice a certain excite-ment among Grandmamma's serfs, and hear them making innumerable conjectures as to whose property they are likely to become: nor can I deny that the idea that we ourselves will receive an inheritance greatly pleases me.

Six weeks later, Nikolai – who acted as regular newsmonger to the house – informs me that Grandmamma has left the whole of her fortune to Lyuba, with, as her trustee until her marriage, not Papa, but Prince Ivan Ivanych.

XXIV

MYSELF

ONLY a few months remain before I am to matriculate for the University. I am making such good progress that I feel no apprehensions, and even take a certain pleasure in my studies.

1 Your grandmamma is dead.

I enjoy reciting clearly and accurately the lessons I have studied. I am preparing for entry to the mathematical faculty – probably, to tell the truth, just because the terms 'sines,' 'tangents,' 'differentials,' 'integrals,' and so forth please my fancy.

I am much shorter than Volodya, broad-shouldered and stocky, and my ugliness of face still remains and torments me as much as ever. I try to appear original. Yet one thing comforts me, namely, that Papa had said that I had 'an *intelligent* phiz.' I quite believe him.

St Jérôme is not only satisfied with me, but has actually taken to praising me, and I have ceased to hate him. In fact, when he sometimes says that, with my 'capacities' and my 'intellect,' it would be shameful for me not to accomplish this, that, or the other thing, I believe I almost like him.

I have long ago given up keeping observation on the maid-servants' room, for I am ashamed now to hide behind doors, and besides I confess that the knowledge of Masha's love for Vasili greatly cooled my ardour for her, and that my unfortunate passion has undergone a final cure by their marriage – to which I myself contributed by, at Vasili's request, asking for Papa's consent to the union.

When the newly-married couple bring trays of cakes and sweetmeats to Papa as a thanks-offering, and Masha, in a cap with blue ribbons, kisses each of us on the shoulder in token of her gratitude, I merely notice the scent of the rose pomade on her hair, but feel not the least emotion.

In general, I am beginning to get the better of my youthful defects, with the exception of the principal one – the one which is destined to do me considerable harm in the course of my life – namely, my penchant for philosophising.

XXV
VOLODYA'S FRIENDS

ALTHOUGH, when in the society of Volodya's friends, I had to play a part that hurt my pride, I liked sitting in his room when he had visitors, and silently watching all they did. The two who came most frequently to see him were a military adjutant called Dubkov and a student named Prince Nekhlyudov. Dubkov was a little dark-haired, wiry man who, though short of stature and no longer in his first youth, had a pleasing and invariably cheerful air. His was one of those limited natures which are agreeable through their very limitations – natures which cannot regard matters from every point of view, and which are constantly getting carried away. Usually the reasoning of such persons is false and one-sided, yet always genuine and taking; even their narrow egoism seems both amiable and excusable. There were two other reasons why Dubkov had charms for Volodya and me – namely, the fact that he was of military appearance, and secondly (and principally) the fact that he was of a certain age – an age with which young people are apt to associate that quality of 'gentlemanliness' which is so highly esteemed at their time of life. And in fact Dubkov was in very truth *un homme comme il faut.*[1] The only thing which I did not like about it all was that in his presence Volodya always seemed ashamed of my most innocent behaviour, and still more so of my youthfulness.

Prince Nekhlyudov was in no way handsome, since neither his small grey eyes, his low, straight forehead, nor his disproportionately long arms and legs could be called good features. The only good points about him were his unusually tall stature, his delicate colouring, and his splendid teeth. Nevertheless, his face was of such an original, energetic character (owing to his narrow, sparkling eyes and ever-changing smile – now stern, now vaguely childlike) that it was impossible to help noticing him.

To all appearances he was very shy, and would blush to the ears at the smallest trifle, but it was a shyness altogether different from mine, seeing that the more he blushed, the more determined-looking he grew, as though he were vexed at his own weakness.

Although he seemed to be on very good terms with Volodya and Dubkov, it was clearly chance alone which had united

1 The sort of man a man should be.

them thus, since their tastes were entirely dissimilar. Volodya
and Dubkov seemed to be afraid of anything like serious discussion or emotion, whereas Nekhlyudov was beyond all
things an enthusiast, and would often, despite their sarcastic
remarks, plunge into dissertations on philosophical matters or
matters of feeling. Again, the two former liked talking about
the fair objects of their adoration (they were often all of a
sudden in love with several ladies, and both of them with the
same ones), whereas Nekhlyudov invariably grew annoyed
when taxed with his love for a certain *red-haired lady*.

Volodya and Dubkov often permitted themselves to make
affectionate fun of their relatives, but Nekhlyudov was capable
of flying into a tremendous rage when anyone referred to some
weak point in the character of an aunt of his whom he positively
adored. Finally, after supper Volodya and Dubkov would
usually go off to some place whither Nekhlyudov would not
accompany them; for which they called him *a fair maiden*.

The first time I saw Prince Nekhlyudov I was struck with his
exterior and his conversation. Yet, though I could discern a
great similarity between his disposition and my own (or perhaps it was because I *could* so discern it), the impression which
he produced upon me at first was anything but agreeable.

I liked neither his quick glance, his firm voice, his proud
bearing, nor (least of all) the utter indifference with which he
treated me. Often, when conversing, I burned to contradict
him, to punish his pride by confuting him, to show him that I
was clever in spite of his unwillingness to pay me any attention.
But I was prevented from doing so by my shyness.

XXVI
DISCUSSIONS

VOLODYA was lying reading a French novel with his feet up on
the sofa when I paid my usual visit to his room after my evening
lessons. He looked up at me for a moment from his book, and
then went on reading. This perfectly simple and natural movement, however, caused me to blush. I felt that the glance
implied a question why I had come, and the quick lowering

of his head a wish to hide his thoughts from me (I may say that at that period a tendency to attach a meaning to the most insignificant of acts formed a prominent feature in my character). So I went to the table and also took up a book to read. Yet, even before I had actually begun reading, the idea struck me how ridiculous it was that, although we had never seen one another all day, we should have not a word to exchange.

'Are you going to stay in tonight, Volodya?'

'I don't know. Why?'

'Oh, because――' Seeing that the conversation did not promise to be a success, I took up my book again, and began to read. It was a strange thing that, though we sometimes passed whole hours together without speaking when we were alone, the mere presence of a third – even a taciturn – person sufficed to plunge us into the most varied and engrossing of discussions. The truth was that we felt we knew one another too well – and to know a person either too well or too little acts as a bar to intimacy.

'Is Volodya at home?' came Dubkov's voice from the anteroom.

'Yes!' said Volodya, setting his feet to the floor and putting his book down on the table.

Dubkov and Nekhlyudov entered wearing their overcoats and hats.

'Well, shall we go to the theatre, Volodya?'

'No, I have no time,' he replied, reddening.

'Oh, never mind that. Come along.'

'But I haven't got a ticket.'

'Tickets, as many as you like, at the door.'

'Very well, then; I'll be back in a minute,' said Volodya evasively as he left the room, twitching his shoulder. I knew very well that he wanted to go, but that he had declined because he had no money, and had now gone to borrow five roubles of the butler – to be repaid when he got his next allowance.

'How do you do, *diplomat*?' said Dubkov to me as he shook me by the hand. Volodya's friends had called me by that nickname since the day when Grandmamma had said after dinner that Volodya would go into the army, but that she would like to see me in the diplomatic service, dressed in a black frockcoat, and with my hair arranged *à la coq* (the two essential requirements, in her opinion, of the diplomatic calling).

'Where has Volodya gone to?' asked Nekhlyudov.

'I don't know,' I replied, blushing to think that nevertheless they had probably guessed his errand.

'I suppose he has no money? Am I right? Oh, you diplomat,' he added, taking my smile as an affirmative. 'Well, I have none, either. Have you any, Dubkov?'

'Let's see,' replied Dubkov, feeling for his purse, and rummaging gingerly about with his squat little fingers among his small change. 'Yes, here's five copecks – here's a twenty – but after that I'm stony,' he concluded with a comic gesture of his hand.

At this point Volodya re-entered.

'Are we going?'

'No.'

'What an odd fellow you are!' said Nekhlyudov. 'Why don't you say that you have no money? Here, take my ticket if you like.'

'But what are *you* going to do?'

'He can go to his cousins' box,' said Dubkov.

'No, I'm not going at all,' replied Nekhlyudov.

'Why?'

'Because as you know I hate sitting in a box.'

'And for what reason?'

'I don't know. Somehow I feel uncomfortable there.'

'Always the same! I can't understand a fellow feeling uncomfortable when he is sitting with people who are glad to see him. It is absurd, *mon cher.*'[1]

'But what else is there to be done *si je suis tant timide*?[2] I am sure you never blushed in your life, but I do all the time, at the least trifle,' and he blushed as he spoke.

1 My dear fellow.
2 If I am so shy.

'*Savez-vous d'où vient votre timidité?*'[1] said Dubkov in a patronising sort of tone. '*D'un excès d'amour propre, mon cher.*'[2]

'What do you mean by "*excès d'amour propre*"?' asked Nekhlyudov, highly offended. 'On the contrary, I am shy just because I have *too little amour propre*. I always feel as though I were being tiresome and disagreeable, that is why. . .'

'Well, get ready, Volodya,' interrupted Dubkov, taking my brother by his shoulders and pulling his jacket off. 'Ignat, get your master ready.'

'That is why,' continued Nekhlyudov, 'it often happens with me that——'

But Dubkov was not listening. 'Tra-la-la-ta-ra-ra-la-la,' and he hummed a popular air.

'Oh, but I'm not going to let you off,' went on Nekhlyudov. 'I mean to prove to you that my shyness is not the result of conceit.'

'You can prove it as we go along.'

'But I have told you that I am *not* going.'

'Well, then, stay here and prove it to the *diplomat*, and he can tell us all about it when we return.'

'Yes, that's what I *will* do,' said Nekhlyudov with boyish obstinacy, 'only hurry up with your return.'

'Well, *do* you think I am egotistic?' he continued, seating himself beside me.

True, I had a definite opinion on the subject, but I felt so taken aback by this unexpected question that at first I could make no reply.

'Yes, I *do* think so,' I said at length in a faltering voice, and colouring at the thought that at last the moment had come when I could show him that I was clever. 'I think that *everybody* is egotistic, and that everything we do is done out of self-love.'

'But what do you call self-love?' asked Nekhlyudov – smiling, as I thought, a little contemptuously.

'Self-love is a conviction that we are better and cleverer than anyone else,' I replied.

---

1 Do you know what that nervousness of yours proceeds from?
2 From an excess of self-esteem, my dear fellow.

'But how can we *all* be filled with this conviction?' he inquired.

'Well, I don't know if I am right or not – certainly no one but myself will ever confess it – but I am convinced that I am cleverer than anyone else in the world, and I am convinced that you too are sure of the same thing.'

'At least I can say for myself,' observed Nekhlyudov, 'that I have met people whom I believe to excel me in wisdom.'

'It is impossible,' I replied with conviction.

'Do you really think so?' he said, looking at me intently.

'Yes, really,' I answered, and an idea crossed my mind which I immediately proceeded to expound. 'Let me prove it to you. Why do we love ourselves better than anyone else? Because we think ourselves *better* than anyone else – more worthy of being loved. If we *thought* others better than ourselves, we should *love* them better than ourselves: but that is never the case. And even if it were so, I should still be right,' I added with an involuntary smile of complacency.

For a minute Nekhlyudov was silent.

'I never thought you were so clever,' he said with a smile so good-humoured and charming that I at once felt extraordinarily happy.

Praise exercises an all-potent influence, not only upon the feelings, but also upon the mind; so that under the influence of that agreeable sensation I straightway felt much cleverer than before, and thoughts began to rush with extraordinary rapidity through my head. From self-love we passed insensibly to the theme of love, which seemed inexhaustible. Although our reasonings might have sounded nonsensical to a listener (so vague and one-sided were they), for ourselves they had a lofty significance. Our minds were so perfectly in harmony that not a chord was struck in the one without awakening an echo in the other; and in this harmonious striking of different chords as we conversed we found the greatest delight. Indeed, we felt as though time and language were insufficient to express the thoughts which clamoured to be uttered.

XXVII
THE BEGINNING OF OUR FRIENDSHIP

FROM that time forth a rather strange but exceedingly pleasant relation was established between Dmitri and myself. Before other people he paid me scanty attention, but as soon as we were alone we would sit down together in some comfortable corner and, forgetful both of time and of everything around us, fall to reasoning.

We talked of a future life, of art, government service, marriage, and bringing up children; nor did the idea ever occur to us that very possibly all we said was the most awful nonsense. The reason why it never occurred to us was that the nonsense which we talked was good, sensible nonsense, and that, so long as one is young, one still values intellect and believes in it. In youth the powers of the mind are directed wholly to the future, and that future assumes such various, vivid, and alluring forms under the influence of hope – hope based not upon the experience of the past but upon an imagined possibility of happiness to come – that such dreams of expected felicity, when understood and shared by another, constitute in themselves the true happiness of that period of our life. How I loved those moments in our metaphysical discussions (discussions which formed the major portion of our talks together) when thoughts came thronging faster and faster, and succeeding one another at lightning speed, and growing more and more abstract, at length attained such a pitch of elevation that one felt powerless to express them, and said something quite different from what one had intended at first to say! How I liked those moments, too, when, carried higher and higher into the realm of thought, we suddenly felt that we could comprehend its immensity and realised the impossibility of proceeding any further.

At Carnival time Nekhlyudov was so much taken up with one festivity and another that, though he came to see us several times a day, he never addressed a single word to me. This offended me so much that once again I found myself thinking him a haughty, disagreeable fellow, and only awaited an opportunity to show him that I no longer valued his company or felt any particular affection for him.

Accordingly, the first time that he spoke to me after Shrovetide was over, I said that I had lessons to prepare and went upstairs, but a quarter of an hour later someone opened the schoolroom door and entered.

'Am I disturbing you?' he asked.

'No,' I replied, although I had at first intended to say that I had a great deal to do.

'Then why did you run away from Volodya's room just now? It is a long while since we had a talk together, and I have grown so accustomed to these discussions that I feel as though something were wanting.'

My anger had quite gone in a moment, and Dmitri stood before me the same good and lovable being as before.

'You know, perhaps, why I ran away?' I said.

'Perhaps I do,' he answered, taking a seat near me. 'However, though it is possible I know why, I cannot say it straight out, whereas *you* can.'

'Then I will do so. I came away because I was angry with you – well, not angry, but vexed. To put it simply I always have an idea that you despise me for being so young.'

'Well, do you know why *I* hit it off so well with you?' he replied, meeting my confession with a look of kind understanding, 'and why I like you better than any of the people I know better than you, and with whom I have more in common? It is because I found out at once that you have the rare and astonishing gift of outspokenness.'

'Yes, I always confess the things of which I am most ashamed – but only to people in whom I trust,' I said.

'Ah, but to trust a man you must be his friend *completely*, and we are not friends yet, Nikolai. Remember how, when we were speaking of friendship, we agreed that to be real friends, each needs to be sure of the other.'

'To be convinced that you would never repeat a word of what I might tell you,' I said. 'Yet perhaps the most interesting and important thoughts of all are just those which we would never for anything tell one another.'

'And what mean thoughts they sometimes are. The base thoughts which, if we only knew that we had to confess them to one another, would probably never have the hardihood to enter our minds. Well, do you know what I am thinking of, Nikolai?' he broke off, rising and rubbing his hands together with a smile. 'Let us do precisely that, and you will see how it will benefit us mutually. Let us pledge our word to one another to tell each other *everything*. We should then really know each other, and never have anything to be ashamed of. And, to guard against outsiders, let us also agree never to speak of one another to a third person. Suppose we do that?'

'I agree,' I replied. And we did it. What the result was shall be told in due course.

Karr[1] has said that every attachment has two sides: one loves, and the other allows himself to be loved; one kisses, and the other surrenders his cheek. That is perfectly true. In the case of our friendship it was I who kissed, and Dmitri who surrendered his cheek – though he, in his turn, was ready to pay me a similar salute. We loved equally because we knew and appreciated each other thoroughly, but this did not prevent him from exercising an influence over me, nor me from submitting to him.

It will readily be understood that Nekhlyudov's influence caused me to adopt his cast of mind, the essence of which lay in an enthusiastic reverence for the ideal of virtue and a firm belief in man's vocation to perpetual perfection. To raise mankind, to abolish vice and misery, seemed at that time a task offering no difficulties. To educate oneself to every virtue, and so to achieve happiness, seemed a simple and easy matter.

Only God Himself knows whether those blessed dreams of youth were ridiculous, or whose the fault was that they never became realised . . .

---

1 Alphonse Karr (1808–90), French novelist and editor of *Le Figaro*.

PART III

YOUTH

I

WHAT I CONSIDER TO HAVE BEEN THE BEGINNING OF MY YOUTH

I HAVE said that my friendship with Dmitri opened up for me a new view of life, and of its aim and relations. The essence of that view lay in the conviction that the destiny of man is to strive for moral improvement, and that such improvement is at once easy, possible, and lasting. Hitherto however I had found pleasure only in the new ideas which I discovered to arise from that conviction, and in the forming of brilliant plans for a moral, active future, while all the time my life had been continuing along its old petty, muddled, idle course.

The virtuous thoughts which I and my adored friend Dmitri ('my own marvellous Mitya,' as I used to call him to myself in a whisper) had been wont to exchange with one another so far pleased my mind, but left my sensibility untouched. Nevertheless there came a time when those thoughts swept into my head with a sudden freshness and force of moral revelation which left me aghast at the amount of time which I had been wasting, and made me feel as though I must at once – that very second – apply those thoughts to life, with the firm intention of never again betraying them.

It is from that time that I date the beginning of my youth.

I was then nearly sixteen. Tutors still attended to give me lessons, St Jérôme still acted as general supervisor of my education, and, willy-nilly, I was being prepared for the University. In addition to my studies, my occupations included certain vague solitary dreamings and ponderings, a number of gymnastic exercises to make myself the strongest man in the world, a good deal of aimless, thoughtless wandering through the rooms of the house (but more especially along the maid-servants' corridor), and much looking at myself in the mirror. From the latter, however, I always turned away with a vague feeling of depression, almost of repulsion. Not only did I feel sure that my outward appearance was ugly, but I could derive no comfort from any of the usual consolations in such cases. I could not say, for instance, that I had at least an expressive, clever, or noble face, for there was nothing whatever expressive about it. Its features were of the most humdrum, dull, and plain type, with small grey eyes which seemed to me, especially when I regarded myself in the mirror, to be stupid rather than clever. Of manly bearing I possessed even less, since although I was by no means small of stature and had moreover plenty of strength for my years, every feature in my face was of the meek, sleepy-looking, indefinite type. Even refinement was lacking in it, since on the contrary it precisely resembled that of a simple-looking peasant and I also had the same big hands and feet as he. At the time all this seemed to me very shameful.

II

SPRINGTIME

EASTER of the year when I entered the University fell quite late in April, so that the examinations were fixed for St Thomas's tide,[1] and I had to spend Holy Week not only in fasting but also in the final preparations for the ordeal.

Following upon wet snow (the kind of stuff which Karl Ivanych used to describe as 'a child following its father'), the weather had for three days been bright and mild and still. Not a clot of snow was now to be seen in the streets, and the dirty slush had given place to wet, shining pavements and coursing rivulets. The last icicles on the roofs were fast melting in the sunshine, buds were swelling on the trees in the little garden,

1 The week after Easter.

the path leading across the courtyard past a frozen heap of manure to the stables was dry, and mossy grass was showing green between the stones around the entrance-steps. It was just that particular time in spring when the season exercises the strongest influence upon the human soul – when clear sunlight illuminates everything yet sheds no warmth, when there are rivulets and thawed patches of earth beneath one's feet, when the air is charged with an odorous freshness, and when the bright blue sky is streaked with long, transparent clouds. For some reason or another the influence of this early stage in the birth of spring always seems to me more perceptible and more impressive in a great town than in the country. One sees less, but one feels the promise more. I stood near the window – through the double frames of which the morning sun was throwing its mote-flecked beams upon the floor of what seemed to me my intolerably wearisome schoolroom – working out a long algebraical equation on the blackboard. In one hand I was holding a ragged, long-suffering copy of Franker's 'Algebra,' and in the other a small piece of chalk which had already besmeared my hands, my face, and the elbows of my jacket. Nikolai, clad in an apron and with his sleeves rolled up, was picking out the putty from the window-frames with a pair of pincers, and bending back the nails of the inner window-frame, put in for the winter. The window looked out upon the garden. At length his occupation and the noise which he was making over it distracted my attention. At the moment I was in a very cross, dissatisfied frame of mind, for nothing seemed to be going right with me. I had made a mistake at the very beginning of my calculation, and so should have to work it out again; twice I had let the chalk drop; I was conscious that my hands and face were whitened all over; the sponge had rolled away into a corner; and the noise of Nikolai's operations was fast getting on my nerves. I felt as though I wanted to fly into a temper and grumble at someone, so I threw down chalk and 'Algebra' alike, and began to pace the room. Then suddenly I remembered that today was Wednesday of Holy Week and we were to go to confession, and that therefore I must refrain from doing anything wrong. Next, with equal suddenness I relapsed into a peculiarly gentle frame of mind, and walked across to Nikolai.

'Let me help you, Nikolai,' I said, trying to speak as pleasantly as I possibly could. The idea that I was performing a meritorious action in thus suppressing my ill-temper and offering to help him increased my chastened mood all the more.

By this time the putty had been chipped out, and the nails bent back, yet, though Nikolai pulled with might and main at the cross-pieces, the window-frame refused to budge.

'If it comes out as soon as he and I begin to pull at it together,' I thought, 'it will mean that it would be a sin to study any more today.'

Suddenly the frame yielded at one side, and came out.

'Where shall I put it?' I said.

'Let *me* see to it, if you please,' replied Nikolai, evidently surprised – as well as, seemingly, not over-pleased – at my zeal. 'They must not get mixed up: I keep all the frames stored and numbered in the lumber-room.'

'Oh, I will mark this one,' I said as I lifted it up. I verily believe that if the lumber-room had been a couple of versts away, and the frame twice as heavy as it was, I should have been the more pleased. I felt as though I wanted to tire myself out in performing this service for Nikolai. When I returned to the room the little bricks and pyramids of salt placed between the double windows to absorb the moisture had been transferred to the window-sill, and Nikolai was sweeping the *débris*, as well as a few torpid flies, out of the open window with a feather. The fresh, fragrant air was already rushing into and filling all the room, while with it came also the dull murmur of the city and the twittering of sparrows in the garden.

Everything was in brilliant light, the room looked cheerful, and a gentle spring breeze was stirring Nikolai's hair and the leaves of my 'Algebra.' Approaching the window, I sat down upon the sill, turned my eyes downwards towards the garden, and fell into a brown study.

Something new to me, something extraordinarily potent and unfamiliar, had suddenly invaded my soul. The wet ground

on which, here and there, a few yellowish stalks and blades of
bright-green grass were to be seen; the little rivulets glittering
in the sunshine and sweeping clods of earth and tiny chips of
wood along with them; the reddening twigs of the lilac with
their swelling buds which nodded just beneath the window;
the fussy twitterings of birds as they fluttered in the bush below;
the dark fence shining wet from the snow which had lately
melted off it; and, most of all, the moist, odorous air and radiant
sunlight – all spoke to me, clearly and unmistakably, of something new and beautiful – of something which, though I cannot
repeat it here as it was then expressed to me, I will try to
reproduce so far as I understood it. Everything spoke to me
of beauty, happiness, and virtue as three things which were
both easy and possible for me, and said that no one of them
could exist without the other two, since beauty, happiness,
and virtue were one and the same thing. 'How did
I never come to understand that before?' I said to myself.
'How did I ever manage to be so wicked? Oh, but how
good, how happy, I could have been – nay, I *will* be – in the
future! At once, at once – yes, this very minute – I will become
another being, and begin to live differently!' For all that, I
continued sitting on the window-sill – continued merely
dreaming, and doing nothing. Have you ever, on a summer's
day, lain down and fallen asleep in dull rainy weather and,
waking just at sunset, opened your eyes and seen through the
widening square space of the window – the space where the
linen blind is blowing up and down, and beating its rod upon
the window-sill – the rain-soaked, shadowy, purple vista of an
avenue of lime-trees, with a damp garden path lit up by the
clear, slanting beams of the sun, and suddenly heard the joyous
sounds of bird life in the garden, seen insects flying to and fro at
the open window, translucent in the sunlight, smelt the fra-
grance of the rain-washed air, and thought to yourself, 'Am I
not ashamed to be lying in bed on such an evening as this?' and,
leaping joyously to your feet, gone out into the garden and
revelled in all that welter of life? If you have, then you can
imagine for yourself the overpowering sensation which was
then possessing me.

III
DAY-DREAMS

'TODAY I will make my confession and purge myself of every sin,' I thought to myself. 'Nor will I ever again...' Here I recalled all the sins which most troubled my conscience. 'I will go to church regularly every Sunday, and afterwards read the Gospels for a whole hour. What is more, I will set aside out of the twenty-five-rouble note which I shall receive each month after I have gone to the University, two and a half roubles' (a tenth of my monthly allowance – a tithe) 'for people who are poor, but not for beggars, yet without letting anyone know anything about it. Yes, I will begin to look out for people like that – an orphan or an old woman whom nobody knows about.

'Also, I will have a room here of my very own (St Jérôme's, probably), and look after it myself, and keep it marvellously clean. I will never let anyone do anything for me, for everyone is just a human being like myself. Likewise I will *walk* every day, not drive, to the University. Even if someone gives me a drozhki[1] I will sell it, and devote that money too to the poor. Everything I will carry out exactly and without fail' (what that 'everything' meant I could not possibly have said, but at least I had a vivid consciousness of its connoting some kind of prudent, moral, and irreproachable life). 'I will get up all my lectures thoroughly, and go over all the subjects beforehand, so that at the end of my first course I may come out top and write a thesis. During my second course I will get up everything beforehand, so that I may soon be transferred to the third course, and at eighteen come out top in the examinations, and receive two gold medals, and go on to be Master of Arts, and Doctor, and the first scholar in Russia. Yes, even in all Europe I mean to be the first scholar. – Well, what next?' I asked myself at this point. Suddenly it struck me that day-dreams of this sort were a form of pride – a sin which I should have to

1 Russian phaeton.

confess to the priest that very evening, so I returned to the
original thread of my meditations. 'When getting up my lectures I will go to the Sparrow Hills and choose some spot under
a tree, and read my lectures over there. Sometimes I will take
with me something to eat – cheese or a pie from Pedotti's, or
something of the kind. I will rest a little, and then read some
good book or other, or else make landscape sketches or play on
some instrument (certainly I must learn to play the flute).
Perhaps *she* too will be walking on the Sparrow Hills, and will
come up to me one day and say, "Who are you?" and I shall look
at her, oh, so sadly, and say that I am the son of a priest, and that I
am happy only when I am there alone, quite alone. Then she
will give me her hand, and say something to me, and sit down
beside me. So every day we shall go to the same spot, and be
friends together, and I shall kiss her. But no! That would not be
right! On the contrary, from this day forward I never mean to
look at a woman again. Never, never again will I go into the
maids' room, nor even go near it if I can help it. Yet, of course,
in three years' time, when I have come of age, I shall marry. Also,
I mean to take as much exercise as ever I can, and to do
gymnastics every day, so that, when I have turned twenty-
five, I shall be stronger even than Rappeau. On my first day's
training I mean to hold out half a *pood*[1] at arm's length for five
minutes, and the next day a twenty-one-pound weight, and the
third day twenty-two pounds, and so on, until at last I can hold
out four *poods* in each hand, and be stronger even than any of the
servants. Then, if ever anyone should try to insult me or should
begin to speak disrespectfully of *her*, I shall take him so – by the
front of his coat, and lift him up an *arshin*[2] or two into the air
with one hand, and just hold him there, so that he may feel my
strength, and then release him. Yet that too would not be right.
No, no, it would not matter; I should not hurt him, merely
show him that I——'

    Let no one blame me because the dreams of my youth were
as foolish as those of my childhood and boyhood. I am sure that,

1   The *pood* = 40 pounds.
2   The *arshin* = 2 feet 3 inches.

even if it be my fate to live to extreme old age and to continue my story with the years, I, an old man of seventy, shall be found dreaming dreams just as impossible and childish as those I am dreaming now. I shall be dreaming of some lovely Marya who will fall in love with me, the toothless old man, as she fell in love with Mazeppa; of some feeble-minded son who, through some extraordinary chance, will suddenly become a minister of state; of my suddenly receiving a windfall of millions of roubles. I am sure that there exists no human being, no human age, to which that gracious, consolatory power of dreaming is totally a stranger. Yet, save for the one general feature of magic and impossibility, the dreams of each human being, of each age of man, have their own distinctive character. At the period upon which I look as having marked the close of my boyhood and the beginning of my youth four sentiments formed the basis of my dreams. The first was love for *her* – for an imaginary woman whom I always pictured the same in my dreams, and whom I constantly expected to meet some day, somewhere. This *she* of mine had a little of Sonya in her, a little of Masha, Vasili's wife, as Masha could look when she stood washing linen over the clothes-tub, and a little of a certain woman with pearls round her fair white neck whom I had once seen long, long ago at a theatre, in a box next to ours. My second sentiment was a craving for love. I wanted everyone to know me and to love me. I wanted to be able to utter my name – Nikolai Irtenyev – and at once to see everyone thunderstruck at it, and come crowding round me and thanking me for something or another, I hardly knew what. My third sentiment was the expectation of some extraordinary, glorious happiness that was impending – some happiness so strong and assured as to verge upon ecstasy. Indeed, so firmly persuaded was I that very, very soon some unexpected chance would suddenly make me the richest and most famous man in the world that I lived in constant, tremulous expectation of this magic good fortune befalling me. I was always thinking to myself that '*it* is about to begin,' and that I should go on thereafter to attain everything that a man could wish for. Consequently I was forever hurrying from place to place, in the belief that '*it*' must be 'beginning' just where I happened not to be. Lastly, my fourth and most important sentiment of all was abhorrence of myself, mingled with penitence – yet a penitence so blended with the expectation of happiness that it had in it nothing of sorrow. It seemed to me that it would be so easy and natural for me to tear myself free from my past and to remake it – to forget all that had been and to begin my life, with all its relations, anew – that the past never troubled me, never bound me at all. I even found a certain pleasure in detesting the past and in seeing it in a darker light than the true one. The darker the circle of my past recollections was, the more purely and brightly did the pure, radiant point of the present and the rainbow hues of the future stand out against it. This note of penitence and of a curious longing for perfection were the chief spiritual impressions which I gathered from that new stage of my growth – impressions which imparted new principles to my view of myself, of men, and of God's world. O blessed and consoling voice which in later days – in sorrowful days when my soul yielded silently to the sway of life's falseness and depravity – has so often raised a sudden, bold protest against all untruth, and mercilessly exposed the past, commanding, nay, compelling me to love only the bright spot of the present, and promising me all that was fair and happy in the future! O blessed and consoling voice! Surely the day will never come when you are silent?

IV
OUR FAMILY CIRCLE

PAPA was seldom at home that spring. Yet, whenever he was so, he seemed extraordinarily cheerful as he strummed his favourite pieces on the piano or looked roguishly at us and made jokes about us all, not excluding even Mimi. For instance, he would say that the Crown Prince of Georgia had seen Mimi out driving, and fallen so much in love with her that he had presented a petition to the Synod for divorce; or else that I had been granted an appointment as secretary to the ambassador in Vienna – and these pieces of news he imparted to us with a perfectly grave face. Next, he would frighten Katya with some spiders (of which she was very much afraid), engage in cordial conversation with our friends Dubkov and Nekhlyudov, and tell us and our guests over and over again his plans for the year. Although these plans changed almost from day to day, and were forever contradicting one another, they seemed so attractive that we were always glad to listen to them, and Lyuba in particular would glue her eyes to his lips so as not to lose a single word. One day his plan would be that he should leave my brother and me at the University and go and live with Lyuba in Italy for two years. Next, the plan would be that he should buy an estate on the south coast of the Crimea and take us there every summer; next, that we should migrate *en masse* to Petersburg; and so forth. Yet, in addition to this unusual cheerfulness of his, another change had come over him of late, which greatly surprised me. This was that he had had some fashionable clothes made – an olive-coloured frockcoat, smart trousers with straps at the sides, and a long wadded greatcoat which suited him to perfection. Often, too, there was a delightful smell of scent about him when he went visiting – more especially when he went to see a lady of whom Mimi never spoke but with a sigh and a face that seemed to say: 'Poor orphans! what an unfortunate passion! A good thing that *she* is gone now!' and so on, and so on. From Nikolai (for Papa never spoke to us of his gambling) I had learnt that Papa had been very fortunate in play that winter, and so had won an extraordinary amount of money, all of which he had deposited in the bank, and that he intended to play no more that spring. It was probably his fear of being unable to resist doing so again that was making him anxious to leave for the country as soon as possible. Indeed, he ended by deciding not to wait until I had entered the University, but to take the girls to Petrovskoye immediately after Easter, and to leave Volodya and me to follow them later.

All that winter, until early spring, Volodya had been insep-arable from Dubkov, while at the same time the pair of them had cooled greatly towards Dmitri. Their chief amusements (so I gathered from conversations overheard) were continual drinking of champagne, driving in a sledge past the windows of a lady with whom both of them appeared to be in love, and dancing *vis-à-vis* – not at children's parties, but at real balls. It was this last fact which, despite our love for one another, placed a vast gulf between Volodya and me. We felt that the distance between a boy still taking lessons at home with tutors and a man who danced at real grown-up balls was too great to allow of their exchanging confidences. Katya too seemed quite grown up now, and read innumerable novels; so that the idea that she might soon be getting married no longer seemed to me a joke. Yet though she and Volodya were thus grown up they did not get on well with one another, but on the contrary seemed to cherish a mutual contempt. In general, when Katya was at home alone nothing but novels amused her, and they but slightly; but as soon as ever a visitor of the opposite sex called, she at once grew lively and amiable, and used her eyes for saying things which I could not then understand. It was only later – when she one day informed me in conversation that the only coquetry a girl was allowed to indulge in was this coquetry of the eyes – that I understood those strange contortions of her features which to everyone else had seemed a matter for no surprise at all. Lyuba also had begun to wear what were almost long dresses – dresses which almost concealed her crooked legs; yet she still remained as much of a cry-baby as ever. She dreamed now of marrying, not a hussar, but a singer or a musician, and accordingly applied herself to her music with greater diligence than ever. St Jérôme, who knew that he was going to remain with us only until my examinations were over, and so had obtained for himself a new post in the family of some count or another, now looked with disdain upon the members of our household. He stayed at home very little, took to smoking cigarettes (then all the rage), and was forever whistling lively tunes on the edge of a card. Mimi daily grew more and more despondent, as though, now that we were beginning to grow up, she looked for nothing good from anyone or anything.

When, on the day of which I am speaking, I went in to dinner I found only Mimi, Katya, Lyuba, and St Jérôme in the dining-room. Papa was out, and Volodya in his own room, doing some preparation work for his examinations in company with a party of his comrades: he had ordered lunch to be sent to him there. Of late Mimi had usually taken the head of the table, and as none of us had any respect for her, dinner had lost most of its charm. That is to say, the meal was no longer what it had been in Mamma's or Grandmamma's time, namely a kind of rite which brought all the family together at a given hour and divided the day into two halves. We allowed ourselves to come in as late as the second course, to drink wine out of tumblers (St Jérôme himself set us the example), to loll about on our chairs, to depart before the meal was over, and so on. In fact, luncheon had ceased to be the agreeable family ceremony it once was. In the old days at Petrovskoye everyone had been used to wash and dress for the meal, and then to repair to the drawing-room as the appointed hour (two o'clock) drew near, and pass the time of waiting in lively conversation. Just as the clock in the butler's pantry was beginning to whirr before striking the hour, Foka, a napkin on his arm, would enter with noiseless footsteps, and assuming a dignified, rather severe expression would say in loud, measured tones: 'Dinner is ready!' Thereupon, with pleased, cheerful faces, we would form a procession – the elders going first and the juniors following, and with much rustling of starched petticoats and subdued creaking of boots and shoes would proceed to the dining-room, where, still talking in undertones, the company would seat themselves in their accustomed places. Or, again, at Moscow, we would all of us be standing before the table ready-laid in the dining-room, talking quietly among ourselves as we waited for our grandmother, whom the butler, Gavrilo, had gone to inform that dinner was ready. Suddenly the door would open, there would come the faint swish of a dress and the sound of footsteps, and our grandmother – dressed in a mob-cap trimmed with a quaint old lilac bow, and wearing either a smile on her face or looking gloomily askance, according as the state of her health inclined her – would sail forth from her room. Gavrilo would hasten to precede her to her arm-chair, the other chairs would make a scraping sound, and, with a feeling as though a cold shiver (the precursor of appetite) were running down one's back, one would seize upon one's damp, starched napkin, nibble a morsel or two of bread, and, rubbing one's hands softly under the table, gaze with eager, radiant impatience at the steaming plates of soup which the butler was beginning to dispense in order of ranks and ages or according to the favour of our grandmother.

Now, however, I was conscious of neither excitement nor pleasure when I went in to dinner.

Even the mingled chatter of Mimi, the girls, and St Jérôme about the horrible boots of our Russian tutor, the pleated dresses worn by the young Princesses Kornakova, and so forth (chatter which at any other time would have filled me with a frank contempt which I should have been at no pains to conceal − at all events so far as Lyuba and Katya were concerned), failed to shake my new, benevolent frame of mind. I was perfectly good-humoured, and listened to everything with a smile and a studied air of kindness. I asked politely for the *kvass* to be passed to me, and lost not a moment in agreeing with St Jérôme when he told me that it was undoubtedly more elegant to say '*Je puis*' than '*Je peux*.'[1] Yet I must confess to a certain disappointment at finding that no one paid any particular attention to my politeness and good-humour. After dinner Lyuba showed me a paper on which she had written down a list of her sins: upon which I observed that, although the idea was excellent so far as it went, it would be still better for her to write down her sins on her *soul* − 'a very different matter.'

'Why is it "a very different matter"?' asked Lyuba.

'Never mind: it is all right; you would not understand me,' and I went upstairs to my room, telling St Jérôme that I was going to work, but in reality purposing to occupy the hour and a half before confession time in writing down a list of tasks and duties which should last me all my life, together with a statement of my life's aim, and the rules by which I meant unswervingly to be guided.

1 I can.

V

MY RULES

I TOOK a sheet of paper and tried first of all to make a list of my tasks and duties for the coming year. The paper needed ruling, but as I could not find the ruler I had to use the Latin dictionary instead. The result was that when I had drawn the pen along the edge of the dictionary and removed the latter, I found that instead of a line I had only made an oblong smudge on the paper, since the dictionary was not long enough to reach across it and the pen had slipped round the soft, yielding corner of the book. I took another piece of paper, and by carefully manipulating the dictionary contrived to rule the paper after a fashion. Dividing my duties into three sections – my duties to myself, my duties to my neighbour, and my duties to God – I started to make a list of the first, but they seemed to me so numerous, and therefore requiring to be divided into so many kinds and subdivisions, that I thought I had better first of all write down the heading 'Rules of Life' before setting to work and writing them down. Accordingly I proceeded to write 'Rules of Life' on the outside of the six sheets of paper which I had made into a sort of folio, but the words came out so crooked and uneven that for a long time I sat debating the question, 'Shall I write them again?', and long sat in agonised contemplation of the ragged handwriting and disfigured title-page. Why was it that all the beauty and clarity which my soul then contained came out so misshapenly on paper, and in life itself, just when I was wishing put into practice something of those qualities I was thinking about at the moment?

'The priest is here, so please come downstairs and hear his directions,' announced Nikolai as he entered.

Hurriedly concealing my folio in the table-drawer, I looked at myself in the mirror, combed my hair upwards (I imagined this to give me a pensive air), and descended to the sitting-room where the table stood covered with a cloth, and with an ikon and candles placed upon it. Papa entered just as I did, but by another door: whereupon the confessor – a grey-headed old monk with a severe, elderly face – blessed him, and Papa kissed his small, broad, wizened hand. I did the same.

'Go and call Voldemar,' said Papa. 'Where is he? Wait a minute, though. Perhaps he is preparing for Communion at the University?'

'No, he is with the Prince,' said Katya, and glanced at Lyuba. Lyuba suddenly blushed for some reason or another, and then frowned. Finally, pretending that she was not well, she left the room, and I followed her. In the drawing-room she halted, and began to pencil something fresh on her paper of peccadillos.

'Well, what new sin have you gone and committed?' I asked.

'Nothing in particular,' she replied, colouring. All at once we heard Dmitri 's voice raised in the hall as he took his leave of Volodya.

'It seems to me you are always experiencing some new temptation,' said Katya, who had entered the room behind us, and now stood looking at Lyuba.

What was the matter with my sister I could not conceive, but she was now so agitated that the tears were starting from her eyes. Finally her confusion grew uncontrollable, and vented itself in anger against both herself and Katya, who was evidently teasing her.

'Anyone can see that you are a *foreigner*!' she cried (nothing offended Katya so much as to be called by that term, which is why Lyuba used it). 'Just at this solemn moment,' she went on, in a tone of great gravity, 'you purposely go and upset me! Please to understand that it is no joking matter.'

'Do you know what she has gone and written on her paper, Nikolai?' cried Katya, much infuriated by the term 'foreigner.' 'She has written down that——'

'Oh, I never could have believed that you could be so cruel!' exclaimed Lyuba, now bursting into open sobbing as she moved away from us. 'You chose that moment on purpose! You spend your whole time in trying to make me sin! I don't badger *you* about your feelings and your sufferings.'

VI
CONFESSION

WITH these and other disjointed impressions in my mind I
returned to the sitting-room. As soon as everyone had reas-
sembled, the priest rose and prepared to read the prayer before
confession. The instant that the silence was broken by the stern,
expressive voice of the monk as he recited the prayer — and
more especially when he addressed to us the words: 'Reveal
thou all thy sins without shame, concealment, or extenuation,
and let thy soul be cleansed before God: for if thou concealest
aught, then great will be thy sin' — the same sensation of
reverent awe came over me as I had felt during the morning
when thinking about the approaching sacrament. I even took a
certain pleasure in recognising this condition of mine, and
strove to preserve it by restraining all other thoughts from
entering my brain, and consciously striving to increase my
feeling of holy dread.

Papa was the first to go to confession. He remained a long,
long time in the room which had belonged to our grandmother, and during that time the rest of us kept silence in the
sitting-room, or whispered to one another on the subject of
who should precede whom. At length the voice of the priest
was heard through the door, again reading the prayer, and
then Papa's footsteps. The door creaked as he came out —
coughing a little and jerking his shoulder in his usual way,
and he did not look at any of us.

'*You* go now, Lyuba,' he said presently, as he gave her cheek
a mischievous pinch. 'Mind you tell him everything. You are
my great sinner, you know.'

Lyuba went red and pale by turns, took her little memor-
andum out of her apron, put it back again, and finally moved
towards the doorway with her head sunk between her
shoulders as though she expected to receive a blow upon it
from above. She was not long gone, but when she returned her
shoulders were shaking with sobs.

At length – after pretty little Katya (who came out with a smile on her face) – my turn arrived. I entered the dimly-lighted room with the same vague feeling of awe, the same conscious desire to arouse that feeling more and more in my soul, that had possessed me up to the present moment. The priest, standing in front of a reading-desk, slowly turned his face to me.

I was not more than five minutes in the room, but came out from it happy and (so I persuaded myself) entirely cleansed – a new, a morally regenerated individual. Despite the fact that the old surroundings of my life struck me as disagreeably unchanged (the rooms, the furniture, and my own appearance) – if only everything external to me could have undergone such a transformation as I believed had taken place within me – I remained in that blissful attitude of mind until bedtime.

Yet, no sooner had I begun to grow drowsy with the conning over of the sins from which I had been cleansed, than in a flash I recollected a particularly shameful sin which I had suppressed at confession. Instantly the words of the prayer before confession came back to my memory and began sounding in my ears. My peace was gone in an instant. 'For if thou concealest aught, then great will be thy sin.' Each time that the phrase recurred to me I saw myself a dreadful sinner for whom no punishment was adequate. Long did I toss from side to side as I considered my position, while expecting every moment to be visited with the divine wrath – to be struck with sudden death, perhaps! – a thought which cast me into indescribable terror! Then suddenly the reassuring thought occurred to me: 'Why should I not walk or drive out to the monastery as soon as morning comes, and see the priest again, and make a second confession?' Thereafter I grew calmer.

VII

MY EXPEDITION TO THE MONASTERY

SEVERAL times that night I woke, afraid that I might be over-sleeping, and by six o'clock was out of bed, although the dawn was hardly peeping in at the window. I put on my clothes and boots (all of which were lying tumbled and unbrushed beside the bed, since Nikolai, of course, had not been in yet to tidy them up), and without a prayer said or my face washed, emerged, for the first time in my life, into the street *alone*.

Over the way, behind the green roof of a large building, the misty, cold dawn was beginning to blush red. The keen frost of the spring morning which had frozen the puddles and mud and made them crackle under my feet now nipped my face and hands also. Not a cab was to be seen, though I had counted upon one to make the journey out and home the quicker. Only a file of waggons was rumbling along the Arbat, and a couple of bricklayers talking noisily together as they strode along the pavement. However, after walking a verst or so I began to meet men and women taking baskets to market or going with empty barrels to fetch the day's water supply, and a pieman who appeared at the crossroads. One baker had opened his shop, and at the Arbat Gate I espied an old cabman dozing as he swayed along on the box of his be-scratched old blue-painted, hobbledehoy wreck of a drozhki. He seemed barely awake as he asked twenty copecks as the fare to the monastery and back, but came to himself a moment afterwards, just as I was about to get in, and touching his horse with the spare end of the reins, started to drive off and leave me. 'My horse wants feeding,' he growled. 'Can't take you, sir.'

With some difficulty and a promise of *forty* copecks I persuaded him to stop. He eyed me narrowly as he pulled up, but nevertheless said: 'Very well. Get in, sir.' I must confess that I had some qualms lest he should drive me to a quiet alley somewhere and then rob me, but I caught hold of the collar of his ragged driving-coat, close to where his wrinkled neck showed sadly lean above his hunched-up back, and climbed on to the lumpy, blue-painted, rickety seat. As we set off along Vozdvizhenka Street I noticed that the back of the drozhki was covered with a strip of the same greenish material from which his coat was made. For some reason or another this reassured me, and I no longer felt nervous of being taken to a quiet alley and robbed.

The sun had risen to a good height and was brightly gilding the cupolas of the churches when we arrived at the monastery. In the shade the frost had not yet given, but in the open roadway muddy rivulets of water were coursing along, and it was through fast-thawing mire that the horse went clip-clopping his way. Alighting, and entering the monastery grounds, I inquired of the first person I met where I could find the father-confessor.

'His cell is over there,' replied the monk as he stopped a moment and pointed towards a little house with a flight of steps leading up to it.

'I respectfully thank you,' I said, and then fell to wondering what all the monks (who at that moment began filing out of the church) must be thinking of me as they glanced in my direction. I was neither a grown-up nor a child, while my face was unwashed, my hair unbrushed, my clothes covered with bits of fluff, and my boots unblacked and muddy. To what class of persons were the monks assigning me – for they stared at me hard enough? Nevertheless I proceeded in the direction which the young monk had pointed out to me.

An old man with bushy grey eyebrows, wearing a black cassock, met me on the narrow path to the cells, and asked me what I wanted. For a brief moment I felt inclined to say 'Nothing,' and then run back to the drozhki and drive away home; but for all its beetling brows the face of the old man inspired confidence, and I merely said that I wished to see the confessor (whom I named).

'Very well, young sir; I will take you to him,' said the old man as he turned round. Clearly he had guessed my errand at a stroke. 'The father is at matins at this moment, but he will soon be back,' and, opening a door, the old man led me through a neat passage and ante-room, all lined with clean linen matting, to a cell.

'Please to wait here,' he added, and then, with a kind, reassuring glance, departed.

The little room in which I found myself was very small, and extremely neat and clean. Its furniture consisted only of a small table covered with oil-cloth, placed between two casement-windows in which stood two pots of geraniums, a stand of ikons with a lamp suspended in front of them, an arm-chair, and two chairs. In one corner hung a wall clock, with little flowers painted on its dial, and brass weights to its chains, while upon two nails driven into a partition (which, joined to the ceiling with small whitewashed wooden posts, probably concealed the bed) hung a couple of cassocks.

The windows looked out upon a white wall, about five feet distant, and in the space between them there grew a small lilac-bush. Not a sound penetrated from without, and in the stillness the measured, friendly stroke of the clock's pendulum seemed to beat quite loudly. The instant that I found myself alone in this calm retreat all other thoughts and recollections left my head as completely as though they had never been there, and I subsided into an inexpressibly pleasing kind of torpor. That rusty nankeen cassock with its frayed lining, the worn black leather bindings of the books with their metal clasps, the dull-green plants with their carefully watered earth and well washed leaves, and above all the abrupt, regular beat of the pendulum, all spoke to me distinctly of some new life hitherto unknown to me – a life of solitude and prayer, of calm, restful happiness.

'The months, the years, may pass,' I thought to myself, 'but he remains alone – always at peace, always knowing that his conscience is pure before God, that his prayer will be heard by Him.' For fully half an hour I sat on that chair, trying not to move, not even to breathe loudly, for fear I should mar the harmony of the sounds which were telling me so much: and ever the pendulum continued to beat the same – a little louder to the right, a little softer to the left.

VIII

MY SECOND CONFESSION

THE sound of the priest's footsteps roused me from this reverie.

'Good morning to you,' he said, smoothing his grey hair with his hand. 'What can I do for you?'

I asked him to give me his blessing, and then kissed his small yellowish hand with great fervour. After I had explained to him my errand he said nothing, but moved away towards the ikons, and began to read the exhortation. When I had overcome my shame, and told him all that was in my heart, he laid his hands upon my head and pronounced in his even, resonant voice the words: 'My son, may the blessing of Our Heavenly Father be upon thee, and may He alway preserve thee in faithfulness, meekness, and humility. Amen.'

I was entirely happy. Tears of joy choked me as I kissed the fold of his cassock and then raised my head again. The face of the monk expressed perfect tranquillity. So keenly did I feel the joy of my emotion that, fearing in any way to dispel it, I took hasty leave of him, and without looking to one side of me or the other (that my attention might not be distracted), left the grounds and re-entered the rickety, jolting drozhki. Yet the bumpings of the vehicle and the variety of objects which flitted past my eyes soon dissipated that feeling, and I became filled with nothing but the idea that the priest must have thought me the finest-spirited young man he had ever met, or ever would meet, in the whole of his life. Indeed, I reflected, there could not be many such as myself – of that I felt sure, and the conviction produced in me the kind of exhilaration which craves for self-communication to another.

I had a great desire to unbosom myself to someone, and as there was no one else to speak to, I addressed myself to the cabman.

'Was I very long gone?' I asked him.

'No, not very long,' he replied. He seemed to have grown more cheerful under the influence of the sunshine. 'Yet now it is a good while past my horse's feeding-time. You see, I am a night cabman.'

'Well, it only seemed to me to be about a minute,' I went on. 'Do you know what I went to the monastery for?' I added, changing my seat to the well of the drozhki, so as to be nearer the elderly driver.

'What business is it of mine? I drive a fare where he tells me to go,' he replied.

'Yes, but, all the same, what do you think I went there for?' I persisted.

'I expect someone you know is going to be buried there, so you went to see about a plot for the grave.'

'No, no, my friend. Still, *do* you know what I went there for?'

'No, I cannot tell, sir,' he repeated.

His voice seemed to me so kind that I decided to edify him by relating the reason for my expedition, and even telling him of the feeling which I had experienced.

'Shall I tell you?' I said. 'Well, you see,' – and I told him all, including a description of my fine sentiments. To this day I blush at the recollection.

'Well, well!' said the cabman non-committally, and for a long while afterwards he remained silent and motionless, except that at intervals he adjusted the skirt of his coat each time that it was jerked from beneath his striped trousers by the joltings of his huge boot on the drozhki's step. I felt sure that he must be thinking of me even as the priest had done. That is to say, that he must be thinking that no such fine-spirited young man existed in the world as I. Suddenly he turned to me:

'I tell you what, *barin*. You ought to keep your own affairs to yourself.'

'What?' I said.

'Those affairs of yours – they are your business,' he repeated, mumbling the words with his toothless lips.

'No, he has not understood me,' I thought to myself, and said no more to him till we reached home.

Although it was not my original sense of tender reverence, but only a sort of complacency at having experienced such a sense, that lasted in me during the drive home (and that, too, despite the distraction of the crowds of people now scattered along the sunlit streets in every direction), I had no sooner reached home than even my complacency was shattered: for I found that I had not the forty copecks to pay the cabman! To the butler, Gavrilo, I already owed a small debt, and he refused to lend me any more. Seeing me twice run across the courtyard in quest of the money, the cabman must have divined the reason, for, climbing down from his drozhki, he – notwithstanding that he had seemed so kind – began to bawl aloud (with an evident desire to wound my vanity) that people who do not pay for their cab-rides are swindlers.

None of my family was yet out of bed, so that except for the servants there was no one from whom to borrow the forty copecks. At length, on my most sacred, sacred word of honour to repay (a word which, as I could see from his face, he did not trust at all), Vasili so far yielded to his fondness for me and his remembrance of the services I had done him as to pay the cabman for me. Thus all my beautiful feelings vanished like smoke. When I went upstairs to dress for church and go to Communion with the rest I found that my new clothes had not yet come home from being altered, and so I could not wear them. Then I fell headlong into sin. Donning my other suit, I went to Communion in a sad state of mental perturbation, and filled with a complete distrust of all my finer impulses.

IX

HOW I PREPARED FOR THE EXAMINATIONS

ON the Thursday in Easter week Papa, my sister, Katya, and Mimi went away to the country, and no one remained in my grandmother's great house but Volodya, myself and St Jérôme. The frame of mind which I had experienced on the day of my confession and during my expedition to the monastery had now completely passed away, and left behind it only a dim, though pleasing, memory which daily became more and more submerged by the impressions of the new emancipated life I was now leading.

The folio with the heading 'Rules of Life' lay concealed among my rough exercise-books. Although the idea of the possibility of framing rules for every occasion in my life and always letting myself be guided by them still pleased me (since it appeared an idea at once simple and magnificent, and I was determined to make practical application of it), I seemed somehow to have forgotten once again to put it into practice *at once*, and kept deferring doing so until such and such a moment. At the same time, I took pleasure in the thought that every idea which now entered my head could be allotted precisely to one or other of my three sections of tasks and duties – those to my neighbour, those to myself and those to God. 'I can always refer everything to them,' I said to myself, 'as well as the many, many other ideas which will occur to me later on that subject.' Yet today I often ask myself: 'Was I better and more righteous when I believed in the omnipotence of the human intellect, or am I more so now, when I have lost the faculty of developing that power, and am in doubt both as to its potency and as to its importance?' To this I can return no positive answer.

The sense of freedom, combined with the spring feeling of vague expectation which I have mentioned already, so unsettled me that I could not keep myself in hand – could make none but the sorriest of preparations for my University examination. Thus I would sit in the schoolroom of a morning, fully aware that I must work hard, seeing that tomorrow was the day of my examination in a subject of which I had two whole questions still to read up; yet no sooner had a breath of spring come wafting through the window than I felt as though there were something quite different that I wished to recall to my memory. My hands would lay down the book of themselves, my feet began to move automatically, and to set me walking up and down the room, and my head felt as though someone had suddenly touched in it a little spring and set some machine in motion – so easily and swiftly and naturally did all sorts of pleasing fancies, of which I could catch no more than the radiancy, begin coursing through it. Thus one hour, two hours, would elapse unperceived. Even if I sat down determinedly to my book and managed to concentrate my whole attention upon what I was reading, suddenly there would sound in the corridor the footsteps of a woman and the rustle of her dress. Instantly everything would escape my mind, and I would find it impossible to sit still any longer, however much I knew that the woman could only be Gasha, my grandmother's old sewing-maid, moving about in the corridor. 'Yet suppose it should be *she* all at once?' I would say to myself. 'Suppose *it* is beginning now, and I were to miss it?' and darting out into the corridor, I would find each time that it *was* only Gasha. Yet for long enough afterwards I could not recall my attention to my studies. A little spring had been touched in my head, and a strange mental ferment started afresh. Again, in the evening I might be sitting alone beside a tallow candle in my room. I would look up for a moment – to snuff the candle or to straighten myself in my chair – and at once became aware of the darkness in the corners and the blank of the open doorway. Then I also became conscious how still the house was, and felt as though I could do nothing else than go on listening to that stillness, and gazing into the black square of that open doorway, and gradually sinking into a brown study as I sat there without moving, or I would get up and go downstairs, and wander through the empty rooms. Often, too, in the evening I would sit a long while in the small drawing-room as I listened to Gasha playing 'The Nightingale' with two fingers on the piano in the large drawing-room, where a tallow candle burned. Later, when the moon was bright, I would feel obliged to get out of bed and to lean out of the window, so that I might gaze into the garden, and at the moonlit roof of the Shaposhnikov mansion, the slender bell-tower of our parish church, and the evening shadows of the fence and a bush where they lay black upon the path. So long did I remain there that, when I at length returned to bed, it was ten o'clock in the morning before I could rouse myself from sleep.

In short, had it not been for the tutors who came to give me lessons, and for St Jérôme (who at intervals, and very grudgingly, applied a spur to my self-conceit) and most of all, for the desire to figure as 'clever' in the eyes of my friend Nekhlyudov (who looked upon distinctions in University examinations as a matter of first-rate importance) – had it not been for all these things, the spring and my new freedom would have combined to make me forget everything I had ever learnt, and so to go through the examinations to no purpose what-soever.

X
THE EXAMINATION IN HISTORY

ON the 16th of April I entered, for the first time, and under the wing of St Jérôme, the great hall of the University. I had driven there with St Jérôme in our smart phaeton and wearing the first frockcoat of my life, while all my other clothes – even down to my socks and linen – were of a new and grander sort. When a doorkeeper downstairs relieved me of my overcoat, and I stood before him in all the beauty of my attire, I felt almost ashamed to dazzle him so. Yet I had no sooner entered the bright, parquet-floored, crowded hall, and caught sight of hundreds of other young men in gymnasium[1] uniforms or frockcoats (of whom a few threw me an indifferent glance), as well as, at the far end, of some solemn-looking professors who were seated in arm-chairs or walking carelessly about among the tables, than I at once became disabused of the notion that I should attract the general attention, while the expression of my face, which at home, and even in the vestibule of the University buildings, had denoted only a kind of vague regret that I should have to present so important and distinguished an appearance, was replaced by an expression of the most acute nervousness and dejection. However, I soon picked up again when I perceived sitting at one of the desks a very badly, untidily dressed gentleman who, though not really old, was almost entirely grey. He was occupying a seat quite at the back of the hall and a little apart from the rest, so I hastened to sit down beside him, and fell to looking at the candidates and forming conclusions about them. Many different figures and faces were to be seen there; yet, in my opinion, they all seemed to divide themselves into three categories.

First, there were youths like myself, attending for examination in the company of their parents or tutors. Among such I could see the youngest Ivin (accompanied by Frost, whom

1   The Russian gymnasium = the English grammar or secondary school.

I knew) and Ilyenka Grap (accompanied by his old father). All youths of this class had downy chins, sported prominent linen, sat quietly in their places, and never opened the books and notebooks which they had brought with them, but gazed at the professors and examination tables with evident nervousness. The second class of candidates were young men in gymnasium uniforms. Many of them had already begun to shave, and most of them knew one another. They talked loudly, called the professors by their names and patronymics, occupied themselves in getting their subjects ready, exchanged notebooks, stepped over the benches, fetched themselves pies and sandwiches from the vestibule, and consumed them then and there – merely lowering their heads to the level of a bench to eat them. Lastly, the third class of candidates (a small one) consisted of oldish men – some of them in frockcoats, but the majority in jackets, and with no linen to be seen. These preserved a serious demeanour, sat by themselves, and had a very gloomy look. The man who had afforded me consolation by being worse dressed than myself belonged to this class. Leaning forward upon his elbows, and running his fingers through his grey, dishevelled hair as he read a book, he had thrown me only a momentary glance – and that not a very friendly one – from a pair of glittering eyes. Then, as I sat down, he had frowned grimly, and stuck out a shiny elbow to prevent me from coming any nearer. The gymnasium men on the other hand, were *over*-sociable, and I felt rather afraid of their proximity. One of them did not hesitate to thrust a book into my hands, saying, 'Give that to that fellow over there, will you?' while another of them exclaimed as he pushed past me, 'By your leave, young fellow!' and a third made use of my shoulder as a prop when he wanted to scramble over a bench. All this seemed to me a little rough and unpleasant, for I looked upon myself as immensely superior to these gymnasium fellows, and considered that they ought not to treat me with such familiarity. At length the names began to be called out. The gymnasium men walked out boldly, answered their questions well on the whole, and came back looking cheerful. My own class of candidates were much more diffident, and appeared to answer worse. Of the oldish men, some answered well, and some very poorly. When the name 'Semyonov' was called out, my neighbour with the grey hair and glittering eyes jostled rudely past me, stepped over my legs, and went up to one of the examiners' tables. It was plain from the aspect of the professors that he answered well and with assurance, yet on returning to his place he did not wait to see where he was placed on the list, but quietly collected his note-books and departed. Several times I shuddered at the sound of the voice calling out the names, but my turn did not come in exact alphabetical order, though already names had begun to be called beginning with 'K.'

'Ikonin and Tenyev!' suddenly shouted someone from the professors' corner of the hall. A chill ran up my spine and through my hair 'Who did they call? Who is Bartenyev?' People were saying around me.

'Go on, Ikonin! You are being called,' said a tall, red-faced gymnasium student near me. 'But who is this *Bar*tenyev or *Mor*denyev or somebody? I don't know him. Show yourself!'

'It must be you,' said St Jérôme.

'*My* name is *Ir*tenyev,' I said to the red-faced student. 'Do you think that was the name they were calling out?'

'Yes. Why on earth don't you go up?' he replied. 'Lord, what a dandy!' he added under his breath, yet not so quietly that I failed to hear the words as they came to me from below the desk. In front of me walked Ikonin – a tall young man of about twenty-five, who was one of those whom I had classed as oldish men. He wore a tight olive frockcoat and a blue satin cravat, and had his long fair hair carefully brushed over his collar in the peasant style. His appearance had already caught my attention when we were sitting on the benches and had given me an impression that he was not bad-looking. Also I had noticed that he was very talkative. Yet what struck me most about him was a tuft of queer red hairs which he had allowed to grow under his chin, as well as the strange habit he had of continually unbut-toning his waistcoat and scratching his chest under his shirt.

Behind the table to which we were summoned sat three professors, none of whom acknowledged our bow. A young professor was shuffling a bundle of question slips like a pack of

cards; another one, with a star on his frockcoat, was gazing hard
at a gymnasium student, who was repeating something at great
speed about Charlemagne, and adding to each of his utterances
the word 'finally'; while a third one – an old man in spectacles –
proceeded to bend his head down as we approached, and
peering at us through his glasses, pointed silently to the question slips. I felt his glance go over both myself and Ikonin, and
also felt sure that something about us had displeased him
(perhaps it was Ikonin's red hairs), for after taking another
look at the pair of us he motioned impatiently to us to be
quick in taking our slips. I felt vexed and offended – firstly
because none of the professors had responded to our bows,
and secondly because they evidently coupled me with Ikonin
under the one denomination of 'candidates,' and so were con-
demning me in advance on account of Ikonin's red hairs. I took
my slip boldly and made ready to answer, but the professor's eye
passed over my head and alighted upon Ikonin. Accordingly
I occupied myself in reading my slip. The question printed on it
was familiar to me, so, as I silently awaited my turn, I gazed at
what was passing near me. Ikonin seemed in no way diffident –
rather the reverse, for in reaching for his slip he leaned his body
half-way across the table. Then he gave his long hair a shake and
rapidly read over what was written on his slip. I think he had
just opened his mouth to answer when the professor with the
star dismissed the gymnasium student with a word of commendation, and then turned and looked at Ikonin. Ikonin at once
seemed taken back, and stopped short. For about two minutes
there was a dead silence.

'Well?' said the professor in the spectacles.

Once more Ikonin opened his mouth, and once more
remained silent.

'Come! You are not the only one to be examined. Do you
mean to answer or do you not?' said the young professor, but
Ikonin did not even look at him. He was gazing fixedly at his
slip, and uttered not a single word. The professor in the spectacles scanned him through his glasses, then over them, then
without them (for, indeed, he had time to take them off, to
wipe their lenses carefully, and to replace them). Still not a

word from Ikonin. All at once, however, a smile flashed across his face, and he gave his hair another shake. Next he reached across the table again, laid down his slip, looked at each of the professors in turn and then at me, and finally, wheeling round on his heels, returned, arms swinging, to the benches. The professors exchanged glances with one another.

'Bless the fellow!' said the young professor. 'Studies at his own expense.'

I now moved towards the table, but the professors went on talking in undertones among themselves, as though they were unaware of my presence. At that moment I felt firmly persuaded that the three of them were engrossed solely with the question of whether I should merely *pass* the examination or whether I should pass it *well*, and that it was only swagger which made them pretend that they did not care either way, and behave as though they had not seen me.

When at length the professor in the spectacles turned to me with an air of indifference and invited me to answer my question, I felt ashamed for him, as I looked straight at him, to think that he should have so dissembled before me: and I answered brokenly at first. In time, however, things came easier to my tongue, and as the question was on Russian history (which I knew thoroughly), I ended brilliantly, and even went so far, in my desire to convince the professors that I was not Ikonin and that they must not in any way confound me with him, as to offer to draw a second slip. The professor in the spectacles, however, merely nodded his head, said 'That will do,' and marked something in his register. On returning to the benches I at once learnt from the gymnasium students (who, heaven knows how, seemed to have found out everything) that I had been given a five.

XI

THE EXAMINATION IN MATHEMATICS

AT the subsequent examinations I made several new acquaintances in addition to Grap (whom I considered unworthy of my notice) and Ivin (who for some reason avoided me). Some of these new friends already exchanged greetings with me, and Ikonin even seemed glad to see me, and plucked up sufficient courage to inform me that he would have to undergo re-examination in history – the reason for his failure this time being that the professor of that faculty had never forgiven him for last year's examination, when, he claimed, the professor had also put him off. Semyonov (who was destined for the same faculty as myself – the faculty of mathematics) avoided everyone up to the very close of the examinations. Always leaning forward upon his elbows and running his fingers through his grey hair, he sat silent and alone. Nevertheless, he did excellently in the examination, coming out second: the first place was taken by a student from the first gymnasium. He was a tall, dark, lanky, pale-faced fellow who wore a black scarf tied round his cheek, and his forehead was dotted all over with pimples. His hands were thin and red, with unusually long fingers, and their nails were so bitten to the quick that the finger-ends looked as though they had been tied round with strips of thread. All this seemed to me splendid, and wholly becoming to a student of the first gymnasium. He spoke to everyone just like anybody else, and I even made friends with him; his walk, his every movement, his lips, his dark eyes, all seemed to me to have in them something extraordinary and magnetic.

On the day of the mathematics examination I arrived earlier than usual at the hall. I knew the syllabus well, yet there were two questions in the algebra which I had somehow managed to avoid with my tutor, and which were therefore quite unknown to me. If I remember rightly, they were the theory of combinations and Newton's binomial theorem. I seated myself on one of the back benches and pored over the two questions, but as I was not accustomed to working in a noisy room and anticipated that I would not have enough time for preparation, I found it difficult to take in what I was reading.

'Here he is. This way, Nekhlyudov,' said Volodya's familiar voice behind me.

I turned and saw my brother and Dmitri – their coats unbuttoned, and their arms swinging – threading their way towards me between the benches. It was obvious that they were second-year students, to whom the University was as a second home. The mere look of their unbuttoned coats expressed at once their disdain for the candidates who were only matriculating, and inspired the candidates who were only matriculating with envy and admiration of them. I felt flattered to think that everyone near me could now see that I knew two real second-year students; and I quickly got up to meet them.

Volodya, of course, could not help vaunting his superiority a little.

'Hullo, you poor wretch!' he said. 'Haven't you been examined yet?'

'No.'

'Well, what are you reading? Aren't you sufficiently primed?'

'Yes, except in two questions. I don't understand them at all.'

'Eh, what? This bit here?' – and Volodya straightway began to expound to me Newton's binomial theorem, but so rapidly and unintelligibly that, reading in my eyes my misgivings as to the soundness of his knowledge, he glanced also at Dmitri's face. Clearly he saw the same misgivings there, for he blushed hotly, though still continuing his explanations, which I failed to understand.

'No; hold on, Volodya, and let me try and do it,' put in Dmitri, with a glance at the professors' corner as he seated himself beside me.

I could see that my friend was in that gently complacent frame of mind which always came upon him when he was satisfied with himself, and which was one of the things which I liked best about him. Since he knew mathematics well and could speak clearly, he hammered the question so thoroughly into my head that I can remember it to this day. Hardly had he finished when St Jérôme said to me in a loud whisper, '*À vous*, Nikolai,'[1] and I followed Ikonin out from among the benches without having had an opportunity of going through the *other* question of which I was ignorant. At the table which we now

1 Your turn.

approached were seated two professors, while before the blackboard stood a gymnasium student, who was animatedly working some formula, and snapping bits off the end of the chalk
against the board. He went on writing after one of the professors
had said to him 'Enough!' and bidden us draw our question
slips. 'Suppose I get the theory of combinations?' I thought to
myself as my tremulous fingers took a slip from among the soft
pile of slips of cut-up paper. Ikonin, for his part, reached across
the table with the same assurance and the same sidelong
movement of his whole body as he had done at the previous
examination. Taking the topmost slip without troubling to
make further selection, he just glanced at it, and then frowned
angrily.

'I always draw this kind of thing,' he muttered.

I looked at mine. Horrors! It was the theory of combinations! . . .

'What have *you* got?' whispered Ikonin at this point.

I showed him.

'Oh, *I* know that,' he said.

'Will you make an exchange, then?'

'No. Besides, it would be all the same for me if I did,' he
managed to whisper just as the professor called us up to the
blackboard. 'I don't feel up to *anything* today.'

'Then everything is lost!' I thought to myself. 'Instead of
doing brilliantly as I anticipated I shall be forever covered with
shame – more so even than Ikonin!' But suddenly, under the
very eyes of the professor, Ikonin turned to me, snatched
my slip out of my hands, and handed me his own. I looked at
his slip. It was Newton's binomial.

The professor was a youngish man, with a pleasant, clever
expression of face, due chiefly to the prominence of the lower
part of his forehead.

'What? Are you exchanging tickets, gentlemen?' he said.

'No. He only gave me his to look at, professor,' answered
Ikonin – and, again, the word 'professor' was the last word that
he uttered while standing there. Once again he stepped backwards towards me from the table, once again he looked at each
of the professors in turn and then at myself, once again he

smiled faintly, and once again he shrugged his shoulders as much as to say, 'It is no use, my friend.' Then he returned to the benches. Subsequently I learnt that this was the third year he had vainly attempted to matriculate.

I answered my question admirably, for I had just been going over it; and the professor, kindly informing me that I had done even better than was required, gave me a five.

XII

MY EXAMINATION IN LATIN

ALL went very well until my examination in Latin. So far, the gymnasium student with the scarf tied round his cheek stood first on the list, Semyonov second, and myself third. On the strength of it I had begun to swagger a little, and to think that, for all my youth, I was not to be underestimated.

From the first day of the examinations I had heard everyone speak with awe of the Professor of Latin, who appeared to be some sort of a wild beast who battened on the financial ruin of young men (of those, that is to say, who paid their own fees) and spoke only in the Greek and Latin tongues. However, St Jérôme, who had coached me in Latin, spoke encouragingly, and I myself thought that since I could translate Cicero and certain parts of Horace without the aid of a lexicon and had a thorough knowledge of Zumpt's grammar, I should do no worse than the rest. Yet things proved otherwise. All the morning the air had been full of rumours concerning the tribulations of candidates who had gone up before me: rumours of how one young fellow had been accorded a nought, another a one, a third greeted with abuse and threatened with expulsion, and so forth. Only Semyonov and the student from the first gymnasium had, as usual, gone up calmly, and returned to their seats each with a five credited to his name. Already I felt a prescience of disaster when Ikonin and I found ourselves summoned to the little table at which the terrible professor sat in solitary grandeur. The terrible professor turned out to be a little thin, bilious-looking man with long greasy hair and a face expressive of extraordinary thoughtfulness.

Handing Ikonin a volume of Cicero's *Orations*, he told him
to translate. To my great astonishment Ikonin not only read off
some of the Latin, but even managed to translate a few lines to
the professor's prompting. At the same time, conscious of
my superiority over such a feeble companion, I could not
help smiling a little, even rather contemptuously, when it
came to a question of analysis and Ikonin, as on previous
occasions, plunged into a silence which promised never to
end. I had hoped to please the professor by that knowing,
slightly sarcastic smile of mine, but I contrived to do quite
the contrary.

'Evidently you know better than he, since you are smiling,'
he said to me in bad Russian. 'Well, we shall see. Tell me the
answer, then.'

Later I learnt that the professor had taken Ikonin under his
wing, and that Ikonin actually lodged with him. I lost no time
in answering the question in syntax which had been put to
Ikonin, but the professor only pulled a long face and turned
away from me.

'Well, your turn will come presently, and then we shall see
how much you know,' he remarked, without looking at me,
and proceeding to explain to Ikonin the point on which he had
questioned him.

'That will do,' he added, and I saw him put down a four for
Ikonin in his register. 'Come!' I thought to myself. 'He cannot
be so strict as they made out.'

After Ikonin had taken his departure the professor spent fully
five minutes – which seemed to me five hours – in setting his
books and question slips in order, in blowing his nose, in
adjusting and sprawling about on his chair, in gazing down
the hall, and in looking here, there, and everywhere – but never
once at me. Yet even that amount of dissimulation did not seem
to satisfy him, for he next opened a book and pretended to read
it, as though I were not there at all. I moved a little nearer and
gave a cough.

'Ah, yes! You too, of course! Well, translate me something,'
he remarked, handing me a book of some kind. 'But no; you
had better take this,' and, turning over the leaves of a Horace,

he indicated to me a passage which I should never have imagined possible of translation.

'I have not prepared this,' I said.

'Oh! Then you only wish to answer on things which you have got by heart, do you? Indeed? No, no; translate me that.'

I started to grope for the meaning of the passage, but each questioning look of mine was met by a shake of the head, a profound sigh, and an exclamation of 'No, no!' Finally he nervously banged the book to with such a snap that he caught his finger between the covers. Angrily releasing it, he handed me a slip with a grammar question on it, and leaning back in his chair maintained a menacing silence. I tried to answer the question, but the expression of his face so clogged my tongue that nothing seemed to come from it right.

'No, no! That's not it at all!' he suddenly exclaimed in his horrible accent, as he shifted his position and leaned forward upon the table, playing with a gold signet-ring which hung loosely on one of the skinny fingers of his left hand. 'That is not the way to prepare for study in a higher education institution, my good sir. Fellows like yourself only want to wear a uniform with a blue collar; you pick up a few essentials, and you think you can be University students. No, no, my dear sir. A subject needs to be studied *fundamentally*,' and so on, and so on.

During this speech (which was uttered in the most mangled Russian) I went on staring dully at his lowered eyelids. Beginning with a fear lest I should lose my place as third on the list, I went on to fear that I might not pass at all. Next, these feelings became reinforced by a sense of injustice, injured self-respect, and unmerited humiliation, while the contempt which I felt for the professor as someone not quite (according to my ideas) '*comme il faut*' – a fact which I deduced from the shortness, strength, and roundness of his nails – flared up in me more and more and turned all my other feelings to sheer venom. Happening presently to glance at me and to note my quivering lips and tear-filled eyes, he seemed to interpret my agitation as a desire to be accorded my marks and dismissed: and so, with an air of relenting, he said (in the presence of another professor who had just come up):

'Very well; I will accord you a "pass"' (which signified a two), 'although you do not deserve it. I do so simply out of consideration for your youth, and in the hope that, when you begin your University career, you will learn to be less thoughtless.'

The concluding phrase, uttered in the hearing of the other professor (who at once turned his eyes upon me, as though remarking, 'There! You see, young man!') completed my discomfiture. For a moment a mist swam before my eyes – a mist in which the terrible professor seemed to be far away, as he sat at his table, while for an instant a wild idea danced through my brain. 'What if I *did* do such a thing?' I thought to myself. 'What would come of it?' However, I did not do the thing in question, but on the contrary, made a particularly respectful bow to each of the professors, and with a slight smile on my face – presumably the same smile as Ikonin's had been, left the table.

This piece of unfairness affected me so powerfully at the time that, had I been a free agent, I should have attended for no more examinations. My ambition was gone (since now I could not possibly be third), and I therefore let the other examinations pass without any exertion, or even agitation, on my part. My marks, however, averaged something over a four, but that failed to interest me, since I had reasoned things out to myself and come to the conclusion that to try for first place was stupid – even *mauvais genre*,[1] that in fact it was better to pass neither very well nor very badly, as Volodya had done. This attitude I decided to maintain throughout the whole of my University career, notwithstanding that it meant disagreeing for the first time with my friend Dmitri.

My thoughts were now only about my uniform, my three-cornered hat, and the possession of a drozhki of my own, a room of my own, and above all, my freedom.

1 Bad form.

XIII
I BECOME GROWN UP

And certainly, this prospect had its charm.

When on May 8th I returned home from the final examination, the one in divinity, I found the tailor's assistant from Rozanov's awaiting me. I knew him, for he had called once before to fit me for my uniform, as well as for a jacket of glossy black cloth which was only tacked together, and the lapels, as only marked in chalk; but today he had come to bring me the clothes in their finished state, with their shiny gilt buttons wrapped in tissue paper.

Donning the garments, and finding them splendid (notwithstanding that St Jérôme assured me that the back of the coat wrinkled), I went downstairs with a complacent smile which I was powerless to banish from my face and sought Volodya, trying the while to affect unconsciousness of the admiring looks of the servants, who came darting out of the ante-room and corridor to gaze upon me with great satisfaction. Gavrilo, the butler, overtook me in the ball-room, and after congratulating me on having passed into the University, handed me, according to instructions from my father, four twenty-five-rouble bank-notes, and informed me that Papa had also given orders that, from that day forth, the coachman Kuzma, a drozhki, and the bay horse Beauty were to be entirely at my disposal. I was so overjoyed at this almost unexpected good-fortune that I could no longer feign indifference in Gavrilo's presence, but, flustered and somewhat breathless, said the first thing which came into my head ('Beauty is a splendid trotter,' I think it was). Then, catching sight of the various heads protruding from the doors of the ante-room and corridor, I felt that I could restrain myself no longer, and set off at full speed across the ball-room, dressed as I was in the new tunic with its shining gilt buttons. Just as I burst into Volodya's room I heard behind me the voices of Dubkov and Nekhlyudov, who had come to congratulate me and to propose

a dinner somewhere and the drinking of champagne in honour
of my matriculation. Dmitri informed me that though he did not
care for champagne, he would nevertheless join us that evening
and drink to our friendship, while Dubkov remarked that I
looked almost like a colonel, and Volodya omitted to congratulate me at all – merely saying dryly that he supposed we should
now be able to leave for the country the day after tomorrow.
The truth was that Volodya, though pleased at my matriculation, did not altogether like my becoming as grown up as
himself. St Jérôme, who also joined us at this moment, said in a
very pompous manner that his duties were now ended, and that
although he did not know whether they had been well done or
ill, at least he had done his best, and must depart tomorrow to his
Count's. In replying to their various remarks I could feel, in spite
of myself, a pleased, agreeable, faintly complacent smile playing
over my countenance, and remarked that the smile communicated itself to those to whom I was speaking.

So here was I without a tutor, with my own private drozhki,
my name printed on the list of students, a sword and belt of my
own, and a chance of an occasional salute from policemen . . .
In short, I was grownup and, I suppose, happy.

We arranged to go out and dine at Yar's soon after four
o'clock, but since Volodya presently went off to Dubkov's and
Dmitri disappeared in his usual fashion (saying that there was
something he *must* do before dinner), I was left with two whole
hours still at my disposal. For a while I walked through the
rooms of the house and looked at myself in all the mirrors –
firstly with the tunic buttoned, then with it unbuttoned, and
lastly with only the top button fastened. Each time it looked
splendid. Then, though anxious not to show any excess of
delight, I found myself unable to resist going over to the
coach-house and stables to gaze at Beauty, Kuzma, and
the drozhki. Then I returned, and once more began my tour
of the rooms, where I looked at myself in all the mirrors as
before, and counted my money over in my pocket – still
smiling happily the while. Yet not an hour had elapsed before
I began to feel slightly bored – to feel a shade of regret that
no one was present to see me in my splendour. I began to desire

life and movement, and so sent out orders for the drozhki to be
got ready, since I had made up my mind to drive to the
Kuznetsky Bridge and make some purchases.

In this connection I recalled how, when Volodya had
entered the University, he had gone and bought himself some
lithographs of horses by Victor Adam and some pipes and
tobacco; and I felt that I too must do the same.

Amid glances from every side, and with the sunlight shining
brightly on my buttons, the cockade of my hat, and my sword, I
drove to the Kuznetsky Bridge, where I stopped at Dazziaro's
shop. I entered it and glanced all round. It was not precisely
horses by V. Adam which I meant to buy, since I did not wish to
be accused of copying Volodya; so, out of embarrassment at
causing the obsequious shopmen such agitation as I appeared to
be doing, I made a hasty selection, and pitched upon a gouache
of a woman's head which I saw displayed in the window – price
twenty roubles. Yet no sooner had I paid the twenty roubles
over the counter than my heart smote me for having put two
such beautifully dressed shop-assistants to so much trouble for
such a trifle. Moreover, I fancied that they were regarding me
rather too casually. Accordingly, in my desire to show them
what manner of man I was, I turned my attention to a little
silver object which I saw in a show-case, and, being told that it
was a *porte-crayon*[1] (price eighteen roubles), requested that it
should forthwith be wrapped in paper for me. Next, having
paid and been informed that splendid pipes and tobacco were to
be obtained in the tobacconist's next door, I bowed to the two
shopmen politely and went out into the street with the picture
under my arm. At the shop next door, which had painted on its
sign-board a negro smoking a cigar, I bought (likewise out of
a desire to imitate no one) not Zhukov, but some Turkish
tobacco, a Stamboul pipe, and two pipe-stems of limewood
and rosewood. I had come out of the shop, I was just approaching the drozhki when I caught sight of Semyonov, who was
walking hurriedly along the pavement in his everyday clothes
with his head bent down. Vexed that he should not have

1 Pencil holder.

recognised me, I called out to him pretty loudly, 'Hold on a minute!' and getting into the drozhki, soon overtook him.

'How do you do?' I said.

'My respects to you,' he replied, but without stopping.

'Why are you not in your University uniform?' I inquired.

He stopped short, screwing up his eyes and showing his white teeth as though the sun were hurting his eyes, but actually in order to show his indifference to my drozhki and uniform, looked at me without speaking and continued on his way.

From the Kuznetsky Bridge I drove to a confectioner's in Tverskaya Street and, much as I should have liked it to be supposed that it was the newspapers there which most interested me, I could not resist eating one sweet pastry after another. In fact, for all my bashfulness before a gentleman who kept regarding me with some curiosity from behind a newspaper, I ate with great swiftness a tartlet of each of the eight different sorts which the confectioner had in his shop.

On reaching home, I experienced a slight touch of heartburn, but paid no attention to it and set to work to inspect my purchases. Of these the picture so much displeased me that, instead of having it framed and hung in my room, as Volodya had done with his, I took pains to hide it behind a chest of drawers, where no one could see it. Likewise, though I also found the *porte-crayon* distasteful, I was able, as I put it away in my table-drawer, to comfort myself with the thought that it was at least a *silver* article – so much capital, as it were – and likely to be very useful to a student. As for the smoking things, I decided to put them into use at once, and try them out.

Unsealing the quarter-pound package and carefully filling the Stamboul pipe with some fine-cut, reddish-yellow Turkish tobacco, I applied a hot cinder to it, and taking the mouthpiece between my second and third fingers (a position of the hand which greatly caught my fancy), started to inhale the smoke.

The smell of the tobacco seemed delightful, yet there was a bitter taste in my mouth and the smoke took my breath away. Nevertheless I hardened my heart, and continued to draw abundant fumes into my interior. Then I tried blowing rings and inhaling. Soon the room became filled with bluish clouds of smoke, while the pipe started to crackle and the tobacco to bob up and down. Presently, also, I began to feel a smarting in my mouth and a giddiness in my head. I was on the point of stopping and going to look at myself and my pipe in the mirror, when, to my surprise, I found myself staggering about. The room was whirling round and round, and as I peered into the mirror (which I reached with some difficulty) I saw that my face was as white as a sheet. Hardly had I thrown myself down upon a sofa when such nausea and faintness swept over me that, making up my mind that the pipe had proved my death, I expected every moment to expire. Terribly frightened, I was on the point of calling out for someone to come and help me, and to send for the doctor.

However, this panic of mine did not last long, for I soon understood what the matter was, and remained lying on the sofa feeling quite weak and with a racking headache, as I stared dully at the trademark of Bostonzhoglo on the packet of tobacco, the pipe lying on the floor, and the odds and ends of tobacco and confectioner's tartlets which were littered about. 'Truly,' I thought to myself in my dejection and disillusionment, 'I cannot be quite grown up if I cannot smoke as other fellows do, and should be fated never to hold a *chibouk* between my second and third fingers, or to inhale and puff smoke through a brown moustache!'

When Dmitri called for me just after four he found me in this unpleasant predicament. After drinking a glass of water, however, I felt nearly recovered, and ready to go with him.

'So much for your trying to smoke!' said he as he gazed at the remnants of my smoking session. 'It is a silly thing to do, and a waste of money as well. I long ago promised myself never to smoke. But come along now; we have to go and call for Dubkov.'

HOW VOLODYA AND DUBKOV AMUSED THEMSELVES

THE moment that Dmitri entered my room I perceived from his face, manner of walking, and the signs which, in him, denoted ill-humour – a blinking of one eye and an awkward jerking of his head to one side, as though to straighten his tie – that he was in the coldly-correct frame of mind which was his when he felt dissatisfied with himself. It was a frame of mind, too, which always produced a chilling effect upon my feelings towards him. Of late I had begun to observe and appraise my friend's character a little more, but our friendship had in no way suffered from that, since it was still too young and strong for me to be able to look upon Dmitri as anything but perfect, no matter in what light I regarded him. In him there were two personalities, both of which I thought splendid. One, which I loved devotedly, was kind, mild, forgiving, gay, and conscious of being those various things. When he was in this frame of mind his whole exterior, the very tone of his voice, his every movement, appeared to say: 'I am kind and good-natured, and rejoice in being so, and everyone can see that I do.' The other of his two personalities – one which I had only just begun to apprehend, and before the majesty of which I bowed in spirit – was that of a man who was cold, stern to himself and to others, proud, religious to the point of fanaticism, and pedantically moral. At the present moment he was this second personality.

With that frankness which constituted an essential condition of our relations I told him, as soon as we had sat down in the drozhki, how much it depressed and hurt me to see him, on this day which was so happy for me, in a frame of mind so irksome and disagreeable to me.

'What has upset you so?' I asked him. 'Will you not tell me?'

'My dear Nikolai,' was his slow reply as he gave his head a nervous twitch to one side and blinked, 'since I have given you my word never to conceal anything from you, you have no reason to suspect me of secretiveness. One cannot always be in exactly the same mood, and if I seem at all put out, then I cannot myself account for it.'

'What a marvellously open, honourable character his is!' I thought to myself, and dropped the subject.

We drove the rest of the way to Dubkov's in silence. Dubkov's flat was an unusually fine one – or so it seemed to me. Everywhere were rugs, pictures, curtains, brightly patterned wallpaper, portraits, bentwood chairs and lounge chairs, while on the walls hung guns, pistols, tobacco pouches, and some papier mâché heads of wild beasts. It was the appearance of his study which made me aware who it was that Volodya had imitated in the scheme of his own room. We found Dubkov and Volodya engaged in cards, while seated also at the table and watching the game with close attention was a gentleman whom I did not know, but who appeared to be of no great importance, judging by the modesty of his attitude. Dubkov himself was in a silk dressing-gown and soft slippers, while Volodya – seated opposite him on a divan – was in his shirt-sleeves, as well as (to judge by his flushed face and the impatient, cursory glance which he gave us for a second as he looked up from the cards) much taken up with the game. On seeing me he reddened still more.

'Well, it is your deal,' he remarked to Dubkov. In an instant I divined that he did not altogether relish my knowing that he gambled. Yet his expression had nothing in it of confusion – only a look which seemed to say: 'Yes, I play cards, and if you are surprised at that, it is only because you are so young. There is nothing wrong about it – it is a necessity at our age.' Yes, I at once divined and understood that.

Instead of dealing, however, Dubkov rose and shook hands with us; after which he bade us be seated, and offered us pipes, which we declined.

'Here is our *diplomat*, then – the hero of our celebration!' he said to me. 'Good Lord! you do look like a colonel!'

'H – m!' I muttered in reply, though once more feeling a complacent smile overspread my countenance.

I stood in that awe of Dubkov which a sixteen-year-old boy naturally feels for a twenty-seven-year-old adjutant of whom all the grown-ups say that he is a very clever young man who can dance well and speak French, and who, though secretly despising my youth, endeavours to conceal the fact.

Yet despite my respect for him I somehow found it difficult and uncomfortable, throughout my acquaintance with him, to look him in the eyes. I have since remarked that there are three kinds of people whom I cannot easily look in the face, namely, those who are much better than myself, those who are much worse, and those between whom and myself there is a mutual determination not to mention some particular thing of which we are both aware. Dubkov may have been a much better fellow than myself, or he may have been a much worse; but the point was that he lied very frequently without admitting it, and that I was aware of this weakness of his, yet could not bring myself to mention it.

'Let us play one more hand,' said Volodya, jerking one shoulder after the manner of Papa, and shuffling the cards.

'How persistent he is!' said Dubkov. 'We can play all we want to afterwards. Well, all right then, one more round.'

During the play I watched their hands. Volodya's were large and well-shaped, while in the crook of the thumb and the way in which the other fingers curved themselves round the cards as he held them they so exactly resembled Papa's that now and then I could not help thinking that Volodya purposely held the cards thus so as to look the more like a grown-up. Yet the next moment, looking at his face, I could see that he had not a thought in his mind beyond the game. Dubkov's hands, on the contrary, were small, puffy, and inclined to clench themselves, extremely nimble and soft-fingered. They were just the kind of hands which generally display rings, and which are most to be seen on persons who are both inclined to use them and fond of beautiful things.

Volodya must have lost, for the gentleman who was watching looked at the cards he held and remarked that Vladimir Petrovich had terribly bad luck, while Dubkov reached for a notebook, wrote something in it, and then, showing Volodya what he had written, said: 'Is that right?'

'Yes,' said Volodya, glancing with feigned carelessness at the notebook. 'Now let us go.'

Volodya took Dubkov, and Dmitri gave me a lift in his phaeton.

'What game were they playing?' I inquired of Dmitri.

'Piquet. It is a stupid game. In fact, all such games are stupid.'

'And do they play for much?'

'No, not very much, but still, it's a bad idea.'

'Do you ever play yourself?'

'No; I swore never to do so; but Dubkov cannot resist winning from someone.'

'He ought not to do that,' I remarked. 'So Volodya does not play so well as he does?'

'Perhaps Dubkov ought not to, as you say, yet there is nothing especially bad about it all. He likes playing, and plays well, but he is a good fellow all the same.'

'Of course I didn't mean . . .' I said.

'We must not think ill of him,' concluded Dmitri, 'since he is a simply splendid fellow. I like him very much, and always shall like him, in spite of his weaknesses.'

For some reason or another the idea occurred to me that, just *because* Dmitri stuck up so stoutly for Dubkov, he neither liked nor respected him in reality, but was determined, out of stubbornness and a desire not to be accused of inconstancy, never to own to the fact. He was one of those people who love their friends their life long – not so much because those friends remain always dear to them, as because, having once – possibly mistakenly – liked a person, they look upon it as dishonourable to cease ever to do so.

XV
I AM FETED AT DINNER

DUBKOV and Volodya knew everyone at Yar's restaurant by name, and everyone, from the commissionaire to the proprietor, paid them great respect. No time was lost in showing us into a private room, where a bottle of iced champagne – upon which I tried to look with as much indifference as I could – stood ready waiting for us, and where we were served with a most wonderful repast selected by Dubkov from a French *menu*. The meal went off most gaily and agreeably, although Dubkov, as usual, told us the strangest tales of doubtful veracity (among others, a tale of how his grandmother once shot dead with a blunderbuss three robbers who were attacking her – a recital at which I blushed, closed my eyes, and turned away from the narrator), and although Volodya reddened visibly whenever I opened my mouth to speak – which was the more uncalled-for on his part, seeing that never once, so far as I can remember, did I say anything shameful. When the champagne was served everyone congratulated me, and I drank 'hands across' with Dmitri and Dubkov to our close friendship. Since I did not know to whom the bottle of champagne belonged (it was explained to me later that it was common property), I considered that, in return, I ought to treat my friends out of my own money, which I had never ceased to finger in my pocket. I stealthily extracted a ten-rouble note, and beckoning the waiter, handed him the money and told him in a whisper (yet not so softly but that everyone could hear me, seeing that they were staring at me in dead silence) to 'bring, if you please, another half-bottle of champagne.' At this Volodya reddened again, and began to fidget violently, and to gaze at me and everyone else with such a distracted air that I felt sure I had somehow put my foot in it. However, the half-bottle came, and we drank it with great gusto. After that, things went on merrily. Dubkov continued his unending fairy-tales, while Volodya also told funny stories – and told them well, too – in a way I should never have credited him: and we all laughed a great deal. Their best efforts lay in producing parodies and variants of a certain well-known joke. 'Have you ever been abroad?' one would say to the other. 'No,' the other would reply, 'but my brother plays the fiddle.' Such perfection had the pair attained in this species of comic absurdity that they altered the original reply to 'My brother never played the fiddle either.' They could answer any question by this means, or they would endeavour to unite two absolutely unconnected matters without a previous question having been asked at all, yet say everything with a perfectly serious face, producing a most comic effect. I too began to catch on, and tried to be funny myself, but as soon as I spoke they either looked embarrassed, or did not look at me until I had finished: so that my anecdotes fell flat. Yet, though Dubkov always remarked, 'Our *diplomat* is lying, brother,' I felt so exhilarated with the champagne and the company of my elders that the remark scarcely touched me. Only Dmitri, though he drank level with the rest of us, continued in the same severe, serious frame of mind – which put a certain check upon the general hilarity.

'Now, look here, gentlemen,' said Dubkov at last. 'After dinner we ought to take the *diplomat* in hand. How would it be for him to go with us to see Auntie? There we could put him through his paces.'

'Ah, but Nekhlyudov will not go there,' objected Volodya.

'O unbearable, insupportable man of quiet habits that you are!' cried Dubkov, turning to Dmitri. 'Just come with us, and you shall see what an excellent lady our dear Auntie is.'

'I will neither go myself nor let him go,' replied Dmitri, flushing.

'Let whom go? The *diplomat*? But you want to go, don't you, diplomat? Why, you yourself saw how he brightened up at the very mention of Auntie.'

'It is not so much that I *will not let* him go,' continued Dmitri, rising and beginning to pace the room without looking at me, 'as that I neither wish him nor advise him to go. He is not a child now, and if he must go he can go alone – without you. Surely you are ashamed of yourself, Dubkov? – ashamed of always wanting others to do all the wrong things that you yourself do?'

'But what is there so very wrong in my inviting you all to come and take a cup of tea with our Auntie?' said Dubkov, with a wink at Volodya. 'If you don't like us going, it is your affair; yet we are going all the same. Are you coming, Volodya?'

'Yes, yes,' assented Volodya. 'We can drive there, and then return to my rooms and continue our piquet.'

'Well, do you want to go with them or not?' said Dmitri, approaching me.

'No,' I replied, at the same time making room for him to sit down beside me on the divan. 'I did not wish to go in any case, and since you advise me not to, nothing on earth will make me go now. Yet,' I added a moment later, 'I cannot honestly say that I have *no* desire to go. All I say is that I am glad I am not going.'

'That is excellent,' he said. 'Live your own life, and do not dance to anyone's piping. That's the best thing.'

This little tiff not only failed to mar our hilarity, but even increased it. Dmitri suddenly reverted to the kindly mood which I liked best – so great (as I afterwards remarked on more than one occasion) was the effect which the consciousness of having done a good deed had upon him. At this moment the source of his satisfaction was that he had deterred me from going to 'Auntie's.' He grew extraordinarily gay, called for another bottle of champagne (which was against his rules), invited a perfect stranger into our room, plied him with wine, sang 'Gaudeamus igitur,' requested everyone to join him in the chorus, and proposed that we should take a drive out to Sokolniki, at which Dubkov remarked that he was becoming too sentimental.

'Let us enjoy ourselves tonight,' said Dmitri, smiling. 'It is in honour of his matriculation that you now see me getting drunk for the first time in my life. So be it.'

Yet somehow this merriment sat ill upon him. He was like some good-natured father or tutor who is pleased with his young charges and lets himself go for their amusement, yet at the same time tries to show them that one can enjoy oneself decently and in an honourable manner. However, his unexpected gaiety had an infectious influence upon me and my companions, and the more so because each of us had now drunk nearly half a bottle of champagne.

It was in this pleasing frame of mind that I went out into the main *salon* to smoke a cigarette which Dubkov had given me.

In rising I noticed that my head seemed to swim a little, and that my legs and arms retained their natural positions only when I bent my thoughts determinedly upon them. Otherwise my legs would deviate from the straight line, and my arms describe strange gestures. I concentrated my whole attention upon these members, commanded my hands first to raise themselves and button my tunic, and then to smooth my hair (though in doing so my elbows flew up extraordinarily high), and lastly commanded my legs to march me to the door – which they duly did though at one time with too much reluctance, and at another with too much *abandon* (the left leg, in particular, kept coming to a halt on tiptoe). A voice called out to me, 'Where are you going? They will bring you a cigarlight directly.' I guessed the voice to be Volodya's, and, feeling satisfied, somehow, that I had succeeded in divining the fact, merely smiled airily in reply and continued on my way.

XVI

THE QUARREL

IN the main *salon* I perceived sitting at a small table a short, squat gentleman of the professional type. He had a red moustache, and was engaged in eating something or other, while by his side sat a tall, clean-shaven individual with whom he was carrying on a conversation in French. Somehow the aspect of these two persons displeased me; yet I decided, for all that, to light my cigarette at the candle standing in front of them. Looking from side to side to avoid meeting their gaze, I approached the table and set about lighting my cigarette. When it was alight I involuntarily threw a glance at the gentleman who was eating and found his grey eyes fixed upon me with an expression of intense displeasure. Just as I was turning away his red moustache moved a little, and he said in French: 'I do not like people to smoke when I am dining, my good sir.'

I murmured something inaudible.

'No, I do not like it at all,' he went on sternly, and with a glance at his clean-shaven companion, as though inviting him to admire the way in which he was about to deal with me. 'I do not like it, my good sir, nor do I like people who have the impudence to puff their smoke up one's very nose. I do not like them at all.'

By this time I had gathered that it was myself he was scolding, and at first felt as though I had been altogether in the wrong.

'I did not mean to inconvenience you,' I said.

'Well, if you did not suppose you were being impertinent, *I* did! You are a lout, young sir!' he shouted in reply.

'But what right have you to shout at me like that?' I exclaimed, feeling that it was now *he* that was insulting *me*, and growing angry accordingly.

'This much right,' he replied, 'that I never allow anyone to fail in respect to me, and that I always teach young fellows like yourself their manners. What is your name, sir, and where do you live?'

At this I felt so hurt that my lips trembled, and I felt as though I were choking. Yet all the while I was conscious of being in the wrong, most likely for having drunk so much champagne; and so, instead of offering him any further rudeness, humbly told him my name and address.

'And *my* name, young sir,' he returned, 'is Kolpikov, and I will trouble you to be more polite in future. – You will hear from me again' (*Vous aurez de mes nouvelles* – the conversation had been carried on wholly in French), was his concluding remark.

To this I replied, 'I shall be delighted,' with as much firmness as I could muster in my tone. Then, turning on my heel, I returned with my cigarette – which had meanwhile gone out – to our own room.

I said nothing, either to my brother or my friends, about what had happened (and the more so because they were at that moment engaged in a dispute of their own), but sat down in a corner to think over the strange affair. The words, 'You are a lout, sir (*un mal élevé, monsieur*)' vexed me more and more the longer that they sounded in my ears. My tipsiness was gone now, and in considering my conduct during the dispute, the uncomfortable thought came over me that I had behaved like a coward. 'Yet what right had he to attack me?' I reflected. 'Why did he not simply say that I was annoying him? After all, it may have been *he* who was in the wrong. Why, too, when he called me a young lout, did I not say to him, "A lout, my good sir, is one who permits himself to be rude"? Or why did I not simply tell him to hold his tongue ? That would have been the best thing. Or why did I not challenge him to a duel? No, I did none of those things, but swallowed his insults like a wretched coward.'

Still the words, 'You are a lout, young sir,' kept sounding in my ears with maddening repetition. 'I cannot leave things as they are,' I at length decided as I rose to my feet with the intention of returning to the gentleman and saying something outrageous to him – perhaps, even, of breaking the candlestick over his head if occasion offered. Yet, though I considered this last measure with great pleasure, it was not without a good deal of trepidation that I re-entered the main *salon*. As luck would have it, M. Kolpikov was no longer there, but only a waiter engaged in clearing the table. For a moment I felt like telling the waiter the whole story and explaining to him my innocence in the matter, but for some reason I thought better of it, and once more returned, in a most dismal state of mind, to our own room.

'What is wrong with our *diplomat*?' said Dubkov. 'No doubt he is deliberating on the fortunes of Europe.'

'Oh, leave me alone,' I said, turning moodily away. Then, as I paced the room, something made me begin to think that Dubkov was not altogether a good fellow. 'There is nothing very much to admire in his eternal jokes and his nickname of "*diplomat*,"' I reflected. 'There is nothing kindly in that. All he thinks about is winning money from Volodya and going to see some "Auntie." There is nothing agreeable about him. Everything he says has a touch of blackguardism or vulgarity in it, and he is forever trying to make fun of people. In my opinion he is simply stupid when he is not absolutely a brute.' I spent about five minutes in these reflections, and felt my enmity towards Dubkov continually increasing. For his part, he took no notice of me, and that angered me the more. I actually felt vexed with Volodya and Dmitri because they went on talking to him.

'I tell you what, gentlemen: the *diplomat* ought to be sluiced down,' said Dubkov suddenly, with a glance and a smile which seemed to me derisive, and even treacherous. 'He is in a bad way! Lord, he is!'

'You yourself ought to be sluiced down, you are in a bad way yourself!' I retorted with spiteful smile, and actually forgetting to address him as 'thou.'[1]

This reply evidently surprised Dubkov, but he turned away unperturbed, and went on talking to Volodya and Dmitri. I tried to edge myself into the conversation, but, since I felt that I could not keep up the pretence of good humour, I soon returned to my corner, and remained there until we left.

When the bill had been paid and coats were being put on, Dubkov turned to Dmitri and said: 'Whither are Orestes and Pylades going now? Home, I suppose, to talk about love. Well, let *us* go and see my dear Auntie. That will be far more entertaining than your sour company.'

'How dare you speak like that, and laugh at us?' I burst out as I approached him, arms waving. 'How dare you laugh at feelings which you do not understand? I will not have you do it! Hold your tongue!' At this point I had to hold my own, for I did not know what to say next, and was, moreover, out of breath with excitement. At first Dubkov was taken aback, but presently he tried to smile, and to take it as a joke. Finally I was surprised to see him look worried, and lower his eyes.

'I am certainly not laughing at you or your feelings. It is merely my way of speaking,' he said evasively.

'Indeed?' I cried; yet the next moment I felt ashamed of myself and sorry for him, since his flushed, downcast face expressed genuine pain.

'What is the matter with you?' said Volodya and Dmitri simultaneously. 'No one was trying to insult you.'

'Yes, he *did* try to insult me!' I replied.

'What a desperate fellow your brother is!' said Dubkov to Volodya. At that moment he was passing out of the door, and could not have heard what I said.

---

1 In Russian, as in French, the second person singular is the form of speech used between intimate friends.

Possibly I should have flung myself after him and offered him further insult, had it not been that just at that moment the waiter who had witnessed my encounter with Kolpikov handed me my greatcoat, and I at once quietened down – merely making sufficient pretence of anger in front of Dmitri as was necessary to present my sudden appeasement from appearing odd. Next day when I met Dubkov at Volodya's the quarrel was not mentioned, yet he and I still addressed each other as 'you,' and found it harder than ever to look one another in the face.

The remembrance of my scene with Kolpikov – who, by the way, never sent me '*de ses nouvelles*,' either the following day or any day afterwards – remained for years a keen and unpleasant memory. Even so much as five years after it had happened I would begin fidgeting and muttering to myself whenever I remembered the unavenged insult, and could only comfort myself with the satisfaction of recollecting the sort of young fellow I had shown myself to be in my subsequent affair with Dubkov. It was only later still that I began to regard the matter in another light, and both to recall with comic appreciation my passage of arms with Kolpikov, and to regret the undeserved affront which I had offered 'that good fellow' Dubkov.

When, at a later hour on the evening of the dinner, I told Dmitri of my adventure with Kolpikov, whose appearance I described in detail, he was astounded.

'That is the very man!' he cried. 'Don't you know that this precious Kolpikov is a known scamp and sharper, as well as, above all things, a coward, and that he was expelled from his regiment by his brother officers because, having had his face slapped, he would not fight ? How did he manage such courage on this occasion?' he added, with a kindly smile and glance. 'So he said nothing worse to you than calling you a lout?'

'No,' I admitted with a blush.

'Well, it was not right, but there is no great harm done,' said Dmitri consolingly.

Long afterwards, when thinking the matter over at leisure, I came to the probable conclusion that Kolpikov, feeling that he could attack me with impunity, took the opportunity in the presence of the dark clean-shaven man of vicariously wiping off upon me the slap in the face which he had once received, just as I myself took the opportunity of vicariously wiping off the epithet 'lout' upon the innocent Dubkov.

XVII
I GET READY TO PAY SOME CALLS

ON awaking next morning my first thoughts were of the adventure with Kolpikov. Once again I muttered to myself and stamped about the room, but there was no help for it. Today was the last day that I was to spend in Moscow, and it was to be spent, by Papa's orders, in my paying a round of calls which he had written out for me on a piece of paper – his first solicitude on our account being not so much for our morals or our education as for our due observance of the *convenances*. On the piece of paper was written in his swift, broken handwriting: '(1) Prince Ivan Ivanych *without fail*; (2) the Ivins *without fail*; (3) Prince Mikhailo; (4) Princess Nekhlyudova and Madame Valakhina if time permits.' Of course I was also to call upon the university curator, the rector, and the professors.

These last-mentioned calls, Dmitri advised me not to pay: saying that it was not only unnecessary to do so, but not the thing. However, there were the other visits to be got through. It was the first two on the list – those marked as to be paid *'without fail'* – that most alarmed me. Prince Ivan Ivanych was a commander-in-chief, as well as old, wealthy, and a bachelor, so I foresaw that *vis-à-vis* conversation between him and myself, a sixteen-year-old student, was not likely to be interesting. As for the Ivins, they too were rich – the father being a departmental official of high rank who had only on one occasion called at our house during my grandmother's time. Since her death I had remarked that the younger Ivin had fought shy of us, and seemed to give himself airs. The elder of the pair, I had heard, had now finished his course in jurisprudence, and gone to hold a post in Petersburg, while his brother Sergei (the former object of my worship) was also in Petersburg, as a great fat cadet in the Corps of Pages.

When I was a young man, not only did I dislike having to do with people who thought themselves above me, but such contact was for me an unbearable torture, owing partly to my constant dread of being snubbed, and partly to my straining every faculty of my intellect to prove to such people my independence. Yet even if I failed to fulfil the latter part of my father's instructions, I felt that I must carry out the former. I paced my room and eyed my clothes ready laid out on chairs – the tunic, the sword, and the hat. Just as I was about to set forth, old Grap called to congratulate me, bringing with him Ilyenka. Grap *père* was a Russianised German and an intolerably effusive, sycophantic old man who was more often than not tipsy. As a rule he visited us only when he wanted to ask for something, and although Papa sometimes entertained him in his study, old Grap never came to dinner with us. With his servility and begging propensities went such a faculty of good-humour and a power of making himself at home that everyone looked upon his attachment to us as a great merit. For my part, however, I never liked him, and felt ashamed for him when he was speaking.

I was much put out by the arrival of these visitors, and made no effort to conceal the fact. Upon Ilyenka I had been so used to look down, and he so used to recognise my right to do so, that it displeased me to think that he was now as much a matriculated student as myself. It seemed to me too that he felt somewhat uneasy in my presence because of this equality. I greeted the pair coldly, and, without inviting them to be seated (since it went against the grain to do so, and I thought they could do so, if they wanted, without being invited by me), gave orders for the drozhki to be got ready. Ilyenka was a good-natured, extremely moral, and far from stupid young fellow, yet, for all that, what is known as a person of moods. For no apparent reason he was forever in some *pronounced* frame of mind – now lachrymose, now frivolous, now touchy over the smallest trifle. Today he appeared to be in the last-named mood. He kept looking with a disagreeable expression from his father to myself without speaking, except when directly addressed, at which times he smiled the self-deprecatory, forced smile under which he was accustomed to conceal his feelings, especially that feeling of shame for his father which he must have experienced in our house.

'So, Nikolai Petrovich,' the old man said to me, following me about the room as I went through the operation of dressing, while all the while his fat fingers kept turning over and over a silver snuff-box which my grandmother had once presented to him, 'as soon as I heard from my son that you had passed your examinations so well (though of course your abilities are well-known to everyone), I at once came to congratulate you, my dear boy. Why, I have carried you on my shoulders before now, and God knows that I love you all as though you were my own kin. My Ilyenka too begged me to come and see you: he too feels quite at home with you.'

Meanwhile Ilyenka remained sitting silently by the window, apparently absorbed in contemplation of my three-cornered cap, and every now and then angrily muttering something in an undertone.

'Now, I also wanted to ask you, Nikolai Petrovich,' his father went on, 'whether my son did well in the examinations? He tells me that he is going to be in the same faculty as yourself, and that therefore you will be able to keep an eye on him, and advise him, and so on.'

'Oh, yes, I believe he passed well,' I replied, with a glance at Ilyenka, who, conscious of my gaze, reddened violently and ceased to move his lips.

'And might he spend the day with you?' was the father's next request, made with a timid smile as though he stood in actual awe of me, and keeping so close to me wherever I went, that the fumes of drink and tobacco with which he was impregnated were constantly perceptible to me. I felt vexed at his placing me in such a false position towards his son, as well as at his distracting my attention from what was to me a highly important matter – the operation of dressing; while over and above all I was annoyed by the smell of liquor which followed me about. Accordingly I said very coldly that I could not have the pleasure of Ilyenka's company that day, since I should be out.

'Why, Father, you said you wanted to go and see your sister,' put in Ilyenka with a smile, but without looking at me. 'Well, I too have business to attend to.' At this I felt even more put out, as well as pricked with compunction; so, to soften my refusal a little, I hastened to say that the reason why I should not be at home that day was that I had to call upon *Prince* Ivan Ivanych, *Princess* Kornakova, and the Monsieur Ivin who held such an influential post, as well as, probably, to dine with *Princess* Nekhlyudova (for I thought that, on learning what important folk I was in the habit of mixing with, the Graps would no longer think it worth while pursuing their claims on me). Just as they were leaving I invited Ilyenka to come and see me another day; but he only murmured something unintelligible and gave me a forced smile. It was plain that he meant never to set foot in the house again.

I followed them out, and I set off on my round of calls. Volodya, whom I had asked that morning to come with me, so that I might not feel quite so shy as when altogether alone, had declined on the grounds that for two brothers to be seen driving in one drozhki would appear so horribly 'sentimental.'

XVIII
THE VALAKHIN FAMILY

ACCORDINGLY I set off alone. My first call, since it was the nearest, was to the Valakhins, in the Sivtsev Vrazhok. It was some three years since I had seen Sonya, and my love for her had of course long become a thing of the past, yet there still lingered in my heart a clear, touching recollection of my bygone childish affection. At intervals during those three years I had found myself recalling her memory with such force and vividness that I had actually shed tears, and imagined myself to be in love with her again, but those occasions had not lasted more than a few minutes at a time, and had been long in recurring.

I knew that Sonya and her mother had been abroad – for the past two years in fact. Also, I had heard that they had been in a carriage accident, and that Sonya's face had been so badly cut with the broken glass that her beauty was marred. As I drove to their house I kept recalling the old Sonya to my mind, and wondering what she would look like when I met her. Somehow I imagined that after her two years abroad she would be very tall, with a beautiful waist, and though sedate and imposing, extremely attractive. Somehow my imagination refused to picture her with her face disfigured with scars, but on the contrary, since I had read somewhere of a lover who remained true to his adored one in spite of her disfigurement by smallpox, strove to imagine that I was in love with Sonya, for the purpose of priding myself on holding to my troth in spite of her scars. As a matter of fact I was not really in love with her during that drive, but having once stirred up in myself old *memories* of love, felt *prepared* to fall in love, and the more so because for some time now I had been feeling ashamed to be left behind by all my friends, seeing that they were in love and I was not.

The Valakhins lived in a neat little wooden house approached by a courtyard. I gained admittance by ringing a bell (then a rarity in Moscow), and was received by a tiny, smartly-attired page. He either could not or would not inform me whether there was anyone at home, but leaving me alone in the dark hall, ran off down a still darker corridor.

For some time I waited in solitude in this gloomy place, out of which, in addition to the front door and the corridor, there opened a third door which at the moment was closed. Rather surprised at the dismal appearance of the house, I came to the conclusion that the reason was that its inmates had recently been abroad. After about five minutes the door leading into the *salon* was opened by the same page boy, who then conducted me into a neat but not richly furnished drawing-room, where presently I was joined by Sonya.

She was now seventeen years old, and very small and thin, as well as of an unhealthy pallor of face. No scars at all were visible, however, on her face, and the beautiful, prominent eyes and bright, cheerful smile were the same as I had known and loved in my childhood. I had not expected her to look at all like this, and therefore could not at once lavish upon her the sentiment which I had been preparing on the way. She gave me her hand in the English fashion (which was then as much a novelty as a door-bell), and bestowing upon mine a frank squeeze, made me sit down on the sofa by her side.

'Ah! how glad I am to see you, my dear Nicholas!' she said as she looked me in the face with an expression of pleasure so sincere that in the words 'my dear Nicholas' I caught the purely friendly rather than the patronising note. To my surprise she seemed to me simpler, kinder, and more sisterly in manner after her foreign tour than she had been before. True, I could now see that she had two small scars, one near her nose, the other on her brow, but her wonderful eyes and smile fitted in exactly with my recollections, and shone as of old.

'How greatly you have changed!' she said. 'You are quite grown up now. And I – I – well, what do you think of me?'

'I should never have known you,' I replied, despite the fact that at the moment I was thinking that I should have known her anywhere and always. I was feeling once again in that carefree, happy mood I had experienced five years ago, when dancing the *Grossvater* with her at Grandmamma's ball.

'Why? Am I grown so ugly?' she inquired with a shake of her little head.

'Oh, no, decidedly not!' I hastened to reply. 'But you have grown taller and older. As for being uglier, why, on the con- trary you are even——'

'Yes, yes; never mind. Do you remember our dances and games, and St Jérôme, and Madame Dorat?' (As a matter of fact, I could not recollect any Madame Dorat, but saw that Sonya was being led away by the joy of her childish recollec- tions, and mixing them up a little.) 'Ah! what a lovely time it was!' she went on – and once more there shone before me the same smile (perhaps even a better one) as I had always carried in my memory, and the same eyes sparkling before me. While she had been speaking I had been thinking over my position at the present moment and had come to the conclusion that I was in love. The instant, however, that I arrived at that result my careless, happy mood vanished, a mist seemed to arise before me which concealed even her eyes and smile, I felt ashamed of something and, blushing hotly, I became tongue-tied and ill-at-ease.

'But times are different now,' she went on with a sigh and a little lifting of her eyebrows. 'Everything seems worse than it used to be, and we ourselves too. Is it not so, Nicholas?'

I could return her no answer, but sat silently looking at her.

'Where are those Ivins and Kornakovs now? Do you remember them?' she continued, looking, I think, with some curiosity at my blushing, downcast countenance. 'What splendid times we used to have!'

Still I could not answer her.

The next moment I was relieved from this awkward position by the entry of old Madame Valakhina into the room. Rising, I bowed, and recovered my faculty of speech. On the other hand, an extraordinary change now took place in Sonya. All her gaiety and naturalness disappeared, her smile became quite a different one, and except for the point of her shortness of stature, she became just the lady returned from abroad whom I had expected to find in her. For this change there was no apparent reason, since her mother smiled every whit as pleasantly, and expressed in her every movement just the same gentleness, as of old. Seating herself in a large arm-chair, the old lady signed to me to come and sit in another beside her. She said something to her daughter in English, and Sonya at once left the room – a fact which still further helped to relieve me. Madame Valakhina then inquired after my father and brother, and passed on to speak of her bereavement – the loss of her husband. Presently, however, apparently feeling she had nothing more to speak to me about, she gave me a silent look as much as to say: 'If, now, my dear boy, you were to get up, to take your leave, and to depart, it would be well.' But a curious circumstance had overtaken me. Sonya returned to the room with her needle-work, and seated herself in a far corner – whence I was aware of her looking at me. While Mme Valakhina had been speaking of her bereavement I had recalled to myself not only the fact that I was in love, but the probability that the mother knew of it: whereupon such a fit of bashfulness had come upon me that I felt powerless to put any of my limbs to its proper use. I knew that if I were to rise and walk I should have to think where to plant each foot, what to do with my head, what with my hands. In a word, I felt very much as I had done the night before when I had drunk half a bottle of champagne, and therefore, since I felt uncertain of being able to manage myself if I *did* rise, I ended by feeling *unable* to rise. Madame must have felt some surprise as she gazed at my crimson face and noted my complete immobility, but I decided that it was better to continue sitting in that foolish position than to risk something ridiculous by getting up and leaving. Thus I sat on and on, in the hope that some unforeseen chance would deliver me from my predicament. That unforeseen chance at length presented itself in the person of an insignificant-looking young man who entered the room with an air of being one of the household and bowed to me politely as he did so: whereupon Madame rose, excused herself to me for having to speak with her '*homme d'affaires*,' and finally gave me a puzzled glance which said: 'Well, if you *do* mean to go on sitting there for ever, I shan't drive you out.' With a great effort I also rose, but finding that I was incapable of bowing, moved away towards the door, followed by the pitying glances of mother and daughter. On my way out I stumbled over a chair, although it was lying quite out of my route: the reason for my stumbling being that my whole attention was centred upon not tripping over the rug under my feet. Driving along in the fresh air, however – after muttering and fidgeting about so much that Kuzma, my coachman, asked me what was the matter – I soon found this feeling pass away, and began to meditate calmly enough on my love for Sonya and on her relations with her mother, which had appeared to me rather strange. When afterwards I told my father that mother and daughter had not seemed on the best of terms with one another, he said:

'Yes, Madame leads the poor girl an awful life with her dreadful meanness. Yet it is a strange thing,' added my father with a greater display of feeling than a man might naturally conceive for a mere relative, 'she used to be such an original, dear, charming woman! I cannot think what has made her change so much. By the way, you didn't notice a secretary fellow about, did you? Fancy a Russian lady having a male secretary!' he said angrily, walking away from me.

'Yes, I saw him,' I replied.

'And was he at least good-looking?'

'No, not at all.'

'It is incomprehensible!' concluded Papa, with a cough and an irritable jerk of his shoulder.

'Well, I am in love!' was my secret thought to myself as I drove along in my drozhki.

XIX

THE KORNAKOVS

MY second call lay at the Kornakovs', who lived on the first floor of a large mansion in the Arbat. The staircase of the building looked extremely neat and orderly, yet in no way luxurious − being lined only with a drugget pinned down with highly-polished brass rods. Nowhere were there any flowers or mirrors to be seen. The *salon*, too, with its polished floor, which I traversed on my way to the drawing-room, was decorated in the same cold, severe, orderly style. Everything in it looked bright and solid, but not particularly new, and pictures, curtains, and articles of *bric-à-brac* were wholly absent. In the drawing-room I found some of the young princesses seated − but seated with the sort of correct, 'company' air about them which gave one the impression that they sat like that only when guests were expected.

'Mamma will be here presently,' the eldest of them said to me as she seated herself by my side. For the next quarter of an hour this young princess entertained me with such an easy flow of small-talk that the conversation never flagged a moment. Yet somehow she made so patent the fact that she *was* just entertaining me that I did not altogether like her. Among other things, she told me that their brother Stepan (whom they called

Etienne, and who had been sent to the College of Cadets two years ago) had now received his commission. When she spoke of him, and more particularly when she told me that he had flouted his mother's wishes by entering the Hussars, she assumed a nervous air, and immediately her younger sisters, sitting there in silence, also assumed a nervous air. When, again, she spoke of my grandmother's death, she assumed a *mournful* air, and immediately the others all did the same. Finally, when she recalled how I had once struck St Jérôme and been expelled from the room, she laughed and showed her bad teeth, and immediately all the other princesses laughed and showed their bad teeth too.

Next, the Princess, their mother, herself entered – the same little dried-up woman, with a wandering glance and a habit of always looking at somebody else when she was addressing one. Taking my hand, she raised her own to my lips for me to kiss it – which otherwise, not supposing it to be necessary, I should not have done.

'How pleased I am to see you!' she said in her usual talkative manner as she gazed at her daughters. 'And how like his mother he looks! Does he not, Lise?'

Lise assented, though I knew for a fact that I did not resemble my mother in the least.

'And what a grown-up man you have become! My Etienne, you will remember, is your second cousin. No, not second cousin – what is it, Lise? My mother was Varvara Dmitrievna, daughter of Dmitri Nikolayevich, and your grandmother was Natalya Nikolayevna.'

'Then he is our *third* cousin, Mamma,' said the eldest princess.

'Oh, you always confuse things!' was her mother's angry reply. 'Not third cousin, but *issus de germains* – second cousins once removed – that is your relationship to my little Etienne. He is an officer now. Did you know? It is not well that he should have his own way too much. You young men need keeping in hand – oh yes! Well, you are not vexed because your old aunt tells you the plain truth? I always kept Etienne strictly in hand, for I believe it is necessary to do so.'

'Yes, that is how our relationship stands,' she went on. 'Prince Ivan Ivanych is my uncle, and your late mother's uncle also. Consequently I must have been your mother's first cousin – no, second cousin. Yes, that is it. Tell me, have you been to call on Prince Ivan yet?'

I said no, but that I was going to presently.

'Ah, is it possible?' she cried. 'Why, you ought to have paid him the first call of all! Surely you know that he stands to you in the position of a father? He has no children of his own, and his only heirs are yourself and *my* children. You ought to pay him all possible deference, both because of his age, and because of his position in the world, and because of everything else. I know that you young fellows of the present day think nothing of family relationships and are not fond of old men, yet do you listen to me, your old aunt, for I am fond of you, and was fond of your mother, and had a great – a very great – liking and respect for your grandmother. You must not fail to call upon him, must not fail on *any* account.'

I said that I would certainly go, and since my present call seemed to me to have lasted long enough, I rose, and was about to depart, but she restrained me.

'No, wait a minute,' she cried. 'Where is your father, Lise? Go and tell him to come here. He will be so glad to see you,' she added, turning to me.

Two minutes later Prince Mikhailo entered. He was a short, thick-set gentleman, very slovenly dressed and ill-shaven, yet wearing such an air of indifference that he looked almost stupid. He was not in the least glad to see me – at all events he did not intimate that he was; but the Princess (of whom he appeared to stand in considerable awe) hastened to say:

'Is not Voldemar here' (she had evidently forgotten my name) 'exactly like his mother?' and she gave her husband a glance, so that the Prince, having guessed what she wanted, approached me and with a most apathetic half-discontented expression held out to me an unshaven cheek, which I was obliged to kiss.

'Why, you are not dressed yet, though you have to go out soon!' was the Princess's next remark to him in the angry tone which she habitually employed in conversation with her domestics. 'It will only mean your offending someone again, and setting people against you.'

'In a moment, in a moment, my dear,' said Prince Mikhailo, and left the room. I also made my bows and departed.

This was the first time I had heard of our being Prince Ivan Ivanych's heirs, and the news struck me unpleasantly.

XX
THE IVINS

As for the prospect of my call upon the Prince, it now seemed even more unpleasant. However, the order of my route took me first to the Ivins, who lived in a large and splendid mansion in Tverskaya Street. It was not without some nervousness that I entered the great portico where a major-domo stood armed with his staff of office.

To my inquiry as to whether any one was at home he replied: 'Whom do you wish to see, sir? The General's son is at home.'

'And the General himself?' I asked bravely.

'I must report to him your business first. What may it be, sir?' said the major-domo as he rang a bell. Immediately the gaitered legs of a footman showed themselves on the staircase above; whereupon I was seized with such a fit of nervousness that I hastily told the footman to say nothing about my presence to the General, since I would first go and see his son. By the time I had reached the top of the long staircase I seemed to have grown extremely small (and not metaphorically, but in the literal sense of the word), and had very much the same feeling within me as had possessed my soul when my drozhki drew up to the great portico, namely a feeling as though drozhki, horse, and coachman had all of them become small. I found the General's son lying asleep on a sofa with an open book before him. His tutor, Monsieur Frost, under whose care he still pursued his studies at home, had entered behind me with his customary jaunty tread, and now awoke his pupil. Ivin evinced no particular pleasure at seeing me, and I noticed that while talking to me he kept looking at my eyebrows. Although he was perfectly polite, I conceived that he was 'entertaining' me much as the Princess Valakhina had done, and that he not only felt no particular liking for me, but even considered my acquaintance in no way necessary to one who possessed his own circle of friends. All this arose out of the idea that he was regarding my eyebrows. In short, his attitude towards me appeared to be (however disagreeable it is for me to admit it) very much the same as my own towards Ilyenka Grap. I began to feel irritated, and to interpret every fleeting glance which he cast at Monsieur Frost as a mute inquiry: 'Why ever has this fellow come to see me?'

After some conversation Ivin remarked that his father and mother were at home. Would I not like to go down with him and see them too?

'First I will go and dress,' he added as he departed to another room, although he had seemed to be perfectly well dressed (in a new frockcoat and white waistcoat) in the present one. A few minutes later he reappeared in his University uniform, buttoned up to the chin, and we went downstairs together. The reception rooms through which we passed were lofty and of great size, and seemed to be richly furnished with marble and gilding, things swathed in muslin, and mirrors. Just as we entered a little room off the drawing-room, Madame Ivina came in by another door. Welcoming me in very friendly fashion, she seated herself by my side and began to inquire with interest after my relations.

Closer acquaintance with Madame (whom I had seen only twice before, and that only in passing) impressed me very favourably. She was tall, thin, and very pale, and had a permanently sad and weary look. Yet, though her smile was a sad one, it was very kind, and her large, mournful eyes with a slight cast in them added to the pathos and attractiveness of her expression. Her attitude, while not precisely bent over, made her whole form seem limp, while her every movement was somehow drooping. Likewise, though her speech was languid, the *timbre* of her voice, and the manner in which she lisped her *r*'s and *l*'s, were very pleasing. She did not attempt to '*entertain*' me.

The answers which I returned to her questions about my relations seemed to afford her a painful interest, and to remind her sadly of happier days: with the result that when presently her son went off somewhere, she gazed at me in silence for a moment or two, and then burst into tears. As I sat there in mute bewilderment I could not conceive what I ought to do or say. At first I felt sorry for her as she sat there weeping with downcast eyes. Next I began to think to myself: 'Ought I not to try and comfort her, and how ought that to be done?' Finally I began to feel vexed with her for placing me in such an awkward position. 'Surely my appearance is not so moving as all that?' I reflected. 'Or is she merely acting like this to see what I shall do under the circumstances? Yet it would not do for me to go, for that would look too much as though I were fleeing to escape her tears.' Accordingly I began fidgeting about on my seat in order to remind her of my presence.

'Oh, how foolish of me!' she said at length, as she glanced at me for a moment and tried to smile. 'There are days when one weeps for no reason whatever.'

She felt about beside her on the sofa for her handkerchief, and then burst out weeping more violently than before.

'Oh dear! How silly of me to be forever crying like this! Yet I was so fond of your mother! We were such friends! We – we——'

She found her handkerchief, and burying her face in it, went on crying. Once more I found myself in the same embarrassing situation, which continued for some time. Though vexed, I felt sorry for her, since her tears appeared to be genuine – though I also had an idea that it was not so much for my mother that she was weeping as for the fact that she was unhappy, and had known happier days. How it would all have ended I do not know, had not her son reappeared and said that his father was asking for her. She rose, and was just about to leave the room when the General himself entered. He was a small, grizzled, thick-set man, with bushy black eyebrows, a grey, close-cropped head, and a very stern, austere expression about his mouth.

I rose and bowed to him, but General Ivin (who was wearing three stars on his green frockcoat) not only made no response to my salutation, but scarcely even looked at me; so that all at once I felt as though I were not a human being at all, but only some negligible object such as an arm-chair or a window; or, if I were a human being, as though I were quite indistinguishable from an arm-chair or a window.

'Then you have not yet written to the Countess, my dear?' he said to his wife in French, with an impassive yet severe expression on his face.

'Goodbye, Monsieur Irtenyev,' Madame said to me in her turn, as she inclined her head haughtily and looked at my eyebrows just as her son had done. I bowed to her once more, and again to her husband, but my second salutation made no more impression upon him than if a window had just been opened or closed. Nevertheless the student Ivin accompanied me to the door, and on the way told me that he was to go to the Petersburg University, since his father had been appointed to a post in that city (and young Ivin named a very high office in the service).

'Well, Papa may say what he likes,' I muttered to myself as I climbed into my drozhki, 'but at all events *I* will never set foot in that house again. The wife weeps like a cry-baby and looks at me as though I were some unfortunate wretch, while that old pig of a General does not even give me a bow. But I will get even with him some day.' How I meant to do that I do not know, but that is how my words came out.

Afterwards I frequently had to listen to the exhortations of my father, who said that I must cultivate the acquaintance of the Ivins, and not expect a man in the position of General Ivin to pay any attention to a boy like myself. But I held to my resolve for quite a long time.

XXI
PRINCE IVAN IVANYCH

'Now for the last call – Nikitskaya Street,' I said to Kuzma, and we started for Prince Ivan Ivanych's mansion.

Towards the end, the ordeal of a round of calls usually brought me a certain amount of self-assurance: consequently I was approaching the Prince's house in quite a tranquil frame of mind, when suddenly I remembered Princess Kornakova's words that I was his heir; besides which, I caught sight of two carriages waiting at the portico. Instantly my former nervousness returned.

Both the old major-domo who opened the door to me, and the footman who took my coat, and the three female and two male visitors whom I found in the drawing-room, and most of all, Prince Ivan Ivanych himself (whom I found clad in a 'civilian' frockcoat and seated on a sofa) seemed to look at me as at an *heir*, and so to eye me with ill-will. Yet the Prince was very gracious and after kissing me (that is to say, after pressing his cold, dry, flabby lips to my cheek for a second), asked me about my studies and plans, jested with me, inquired whether I still wrote verses of the kind which I had produced in honour of my grandmother's name-day, and invited me to stay to dinner. Nevertheless, in proportion as he grew the kinder, the more did I feel persuaded that his civility was only intended to conceal from me the fact that he disliked the idea of my being his heir. He had a custom (due to his false teeth, of which his mouth possessed a complete set) of raising his upper lip a little when he had spoken, and producing a slight snuffling sound from it, as if he were trying to draw the lip into his nostrils; and whenever on the present occasion he did so, it seemed to me that he was saying to himself: 'That boy, that boy: I don't need him to remind me. And my heir, too – my heir!', and so forth and so on.

When we were children we had been used to calling the Prince 'dear grandpapa'; but now, in my capacity of heir, I could not bring my tongue to the phrase, while to say 'Your Highness,' as did one of the other visitors, seemed derogatory to my self-esteem. Consequently never once during our conversation did I call him anything at all. The personage, however, who most disturbed me was the old Princess who shared with me the position of prospective inheritor, and who lived in the Prince's house. While seated beside her at dinner I felt firmly persuaded that the reason why she would not speak to me was that she disliked me for being her co-heir, and that the Prince for his part paid no attention to our side of the table for the reason that the Princess and I hoped to succeed him, and so were alike distasteful in his sight.

'You cannot think how I hated it all!' I said to Dmitri the same evening, in a desire to make a parade of disliking the notion of being an heir (somehow I thought it the thing to do).

'You cannot think how I loathed the whole two hours that I spent there! – Yet he is an excellent man, and was very kind to me,' I added – wishing, among other things, to disabuse my friend of any possible idea that my loathing had arisen out of the fact that I had been made to feel so small by the Prince. 'It is only the idea that people may be classing me with the Princess who lives with him, and who licks the dust off his boots. He is a wonderful old man, and good and considerate to everybody, but it is awful to see how he *maltreats* that Princess. Money is a detestable thing, and ruins all human relations.

'Do you know, I think it would be far the best thing for me to have it out with the Prince,' I went on; 'to tell him that I respect him as a man, but think nothing of being his heir, and that I desire him to leave me nothing, since that is the only condition on which I can in future visit his house.'

Instead of bursting out laughing when I said this, Dmitri pondered awhile in silence, and then said:

'You are wrong, you know. Either you ought to refrain from supposing that people may be classing you with this Princess of whom you speak, or, if you *do* suppose such a thing, you ought to tell yourself that you know quite well what people are thinking about you, but that such thoughts are so utterly foreign to your nature that you despise them and would never make them a basis for action. Suppose, however, that people *do* suppose you to suppose such a thing – well, to sum up,' he added, feeling that he was getting a little mixed in his pronouncements, 'you had much better not suppose anything of the kind.'

My friend was perfectly right, though it was not until long, long afterwards that experience of life taught me the evil that comes of thinking – still worse, of saying – much that seems very fine, but which should always be kept to oneself, since noble words seldom go with noble deeds. I am convinced that the mere fact of giving utterance to a good intention often makes it difficult, nay, impossible, to carry that good intention into effect. Yet how is one to refrain from giving utterance to the brave, self-satisfied impulses of youth? Only long afterwards does one remember and regret them, even as one regrets a flower one has incontinently plucked before its blooming, and subsequently finds lying withered and trampled on the ground.

The very next morning I, who had just been telling my friend Dmitri that money corrupts all human relations, and had squandered the whole of my cash on pictures and Turkish pipes, accepted a loan of twenty-five roubles in notes which he suggested should pay for my travelling expenses into the country, and remained a long while thereafter in his debt.

XXII

INTIMATE CONVERSATION WITH MY FRIEND

THIS conversation of ours took place in the phaeton on the way to Kuntsevo. Dmitri had dissuaded me from calling on his mother in the morning, but had called for me after dinner; the idea being that I should spend the evening, and perhaps also pass the night, at the summer residence where his family were living. Only when we had left the city and exchanged its grimy motley streets and the unbearably deafening clatter of its road-ways for the open vista of fields and the subdued grinding of carriage-wheels on a dusty high road (while the sweet spring air and open space enveloped us on every side) did I awake some-what from the new impressions and the sensation of freedom which over the past two days had totally unsettled me. Dmitri was in his kind and sociable mood. That is to say he was neither frowning nor blinking nervously nor twisting his neck to adjust his cravat. For my own part I was congratulating myself on those noble sentiments which I had expressed to him, in the belief that they had led him to overlook my shameful encounter with Kolpikov, and to refrain from despising me for it. Thus we talked together on many an intimate subject which even a friend seldom mentions to a friend. He told me about his family whose acquaintance I had not yet made – about his mother, his aunt, and his sister, as also about her whom Volodya and Dubkov believed to be his 'flame,' and always spoke of as 'the lady with the chestnut locks.' Of his mother he spoke with a certain cold and formal commendation, as though to forestall any further mention of her; his aunt he extolled enthusiastically, though with a touch of condescension in his tone; his sister he scarcely mentioned at all, as though averse to doing so in my presence; but on the subject of 'the lady with the chestnut locks' (whose real name was Lyubov Sergeyevna, and who was a middle-aged maiden lady living for family reasons with the Nekhlyudovs) he discoursed with animation.

'Yes, she is a wonderful woman,' he said with a bashful reddening of the face, yet looking me resolutely in the eyes. 'True, she is no longer young, and even rather elderly, as well as by no means good-looking; but as for loving a mere beauty – well, I never could understand that, for it is such a silly, idiotic, thing to do.' (Dmitri said this as though he had just discovered a most novel and extraordinary truth.) 'I am certain, too, that such a soul, such a heart and principles as are hers are not to be found elsewhere in the world of the present day.' (I do not know whence Dmitri had derived the habit of saying that good things were rare in the world of the present day, but he loved to repeat the expression, and it somehow suited him.)

'Only, I am afraid,' he went on quietly, after thus annihilating all such men as were foolish enough to admire mere beauty, 'I am afraid that you will not understand or appreciate her quickly. She is modest – even secretive, and by no means fond of exhibiting her beautiful and surprising qualities. Now my mother – who, as you will see, is a fine, sensible woman – has known Lyubov Sergeyevna for many years; yet even to this day she does and will not properly understand her. Shall I tell you why I was out of temper last evening when you were questioning me? Well, you must know that the day before yesterday Lyubov Sergeyevna asked me to accompany her to Ivan Yakovlevich's (you have heard of him, I suppose? the fellow who seems to be mad, but who in reality is a very remarkable man). Well, Lyubov Sergeyevna is extremely religious, and understands Ivan Yakovlevich to the full. She often goes to see him, and converses with him, and gives him money for the poor – money which she has earned herself. She is a marvellous woman, as you will see. Well, I went with her to Ivan Yakovlevich's, and felt very grateful to her for having afforded me the opportunity of exchanging a word with so remarkable a man; but my mother did not want to understand our action at all, and saw in it only superstition. Consequently last night she and I quarrelled for the first time in my life. A rather heated quarrel it was, too,' he concluded, with a convulsive jerk of his neck, as though the mention of it recalled the feelings which he had then experienced.

'And what do you think about it all?' I inquired, to divert him from such a disagreeable recollection. 'That is to say, how do you imagine it is going to turn out? Do you ever speak to her about the future, or about how your love or friendship are going to end?'

'Do you mean, do I intend to marry her eventually?' he inquired in his turn with a renewed blush, but turning and looking me boldly in the face.

'Well indeed, why not?' I thought, reassuring myself. 'We are both of us grown up, as well as friends, so we may as well discuss our future life as we drive along. Anyone would even enjoy overlooking or overhearing us now.'

'Why should I *not* marry her?' he went on in response to my reply in the affirmative. 'It is my aim – as it should be the aim of every sensible man – to be as good and as happy as possible; and with her, if she should still be willing when I have become entirely independent, I should be happier and better than with the greatest beauty in the world.'

Absorbed in such conversation, we hardly noticed that we were approaching Kuntsevo, or that the sky was becoming overcast and beginning to threaten rain. On the right the sun was already low behind the ancient trees of the Kuntsevo park –

one half of its brilliant disc obscured with grey, half-transparent cloud, and the other half sending forth spokes of flaming light which threw the old trees into striking relief as they stood there with their dense crowns of green showing motionless against a patch of clear blue sky. The light and shimmer of that region of the heavens contrasted sharply with the heavy violet cloud which lay massed above a grove of young birch-trees visible on the horizon before us.

A little further to the right, the parti-coloured roofs of the little houses around the Kuntsevo mansion could be seen behind a belt of trees and bushes – one side of them reflecting the glittering rays of the sun, and the other side taking on the more melancholy character of the other half of the heavens. Below us and to the left showed the still blue of a pond where it lay surrounded with pale-green willow-trees – its dull, convex-looking surface repeating the trees in more sombre shades of colour. Half-way up a hill beyond the water spread the black expanse of a fallow field, with the straight line of a dark-green ridge by which it was bisected running far into the distance, and there merging into the leaden, threatening horizon. On either side of the soft road along which the phaeton was swaying its way, bright-green juicy belts of rye were sprouting here and there into stalk. Not a motion was perceptible in the air – only a sweet freshness; and the green of the trees, the leaves and the rye was quite motionless, and looked extraordinarily clear and bright. It seemed as if every leaf, every blade of grass was alive with its own particular full and happy life. Near the road I could see a little brown path winding its way among the dark-green, quarter-grown stems of rye, and somehow that path reminded me vividly of our village, and somehow (through some con-nection of thought) the idea of that village reminded me vividly of Sonya, and of the fact that I was in love with her.

Notwithstanding my fondness for Dmitri and the pleasure which his frankness had afforded me, I now felt as though I desired to hear no more about his feelings and intentions with regard to Lyubov Sergeyevna, but to tell him about my own love for Sonya, which seemed to me an affection of a far higher order. Yet for some reason or another I could not make up my mind to tell him straight out how splendid it would seem when I had married Sonya and we were living in the country – of how we should have little children who would crawl about the floor and call me Papa, and of how delighted I should be when he, Dmitri, in a travelling suit, brought his wife, Lyubov Sergeyevna, to see us. And so instead of saying all that I pointed to the setting sun, and merely remarked: 'Look, Dmitri! How lovely!'

To this, however, Dmitri made no reply, since he was evidently dissatisfied at my answering his confession (which it had cost him much to make) by directing his attention to natural objects, to which he was in general indifferent. Upon him nature had an effect altogether different to the one it produced upon me, for it affected him rather by the interest it aroused in him than by its beauty – he loved it rather with his intellect than with his feelings.

'I am absolutely happy,' I went on, without noticing that he was altogether taken up with his own thoughts and oblivious of anything that I might be saying. 'You will remember how I told you about a girl with whom I used to be in love when I was a little boy? Well, I saw her again only this morning, and now I really am in love with her.'

Then I told him – despite his continued expression of indifference – about my love, and about all my plans for my future married happiness. Strangely enough, no sooner had I related in detail the whole strength of my feelings than I instantly became conscious that they were starting to diminish.

A shower of rain overtook us just as we were turning into the avenue of birch-trees which led to the house, but it did not really wet us. I only knew that it was raining by the fact that I felt a few drops fall, first on my nose, and then on my hand, and heard something begin to patter upon the young, sticky leaves of the birch-trees as, drooping their curly motionless branches overhead, they seemed to imbibe the pure, shining drops with an avidity which filled the whole avenue with scent. We descended from the phaeton so as to reach the house the quicker by running through the garden, but found ourselves confronted at the entrance-door by four ladies, two of whom were carrying their needle-work, one reading a book, and the fourth with a little dog, approaching rapidly from another direction. Thereupon Dmitri began to present me to his mother, sister, and aunt, as well as to Lyubov Sergeyevna. For a moment they stopped where they were, but almost at once the rain became heavier.

'Let us go to the gallery; you can present him to us again there,' said the lady whom I took to be Dmitri's mother, and we all of us ascended the entrance-steps.

XXIII
THE NEKHLYUDOVS

FROM the first, the member of this company who struck me the most was Lyubov Sergeyevna who, holding a lapdog in her arms and wearing thick knitted slippers, was the last of the four ladies to ascend the staircase and twice stopped to gaze at me intently and then kiss her little dog. She was extremely plain, red-haired, thin, short, and slightly lopsided in her appearance. What made her plain face all the plainer was the queer way in which her hair was parted to one side (a coiffure of the kind which women contrive to conceal their baldness). However much I should have liked to please my friend, I could not find a single comely feature in her. Even her hazel eyes, though expressive of good-humour, were small and dull – were, in fact, anything but pretty; while her hands (those most characteristic of features), were though neither large nor ill-shaped, red and rough.

As soon as we reached the gallery each of the ladies, except Dmitri's sister Varya, who only looked at me attentively out of her large, dark-grey eyes, said a few words to me before resuming her occupation, while Varya herself began to read aloud from a book which she held on her lap, keeping the place with her finger.

Princess Marya Ivanovna was a tall, graceful woman of about forty. To judge by the curls of half-grey hair openly displayed from beneath her cap one might have taken her for more, but as soon as one observed the fresh, extraordinarily tender, and almost wrinkleless face as well as, most of all, the lively cheerful sparkle of the large eyes, one involuntarily took her for less. Her eyes were brown and very frank, her lips too thin and slightly severe, her nose regular and slightly inclined to the left, and her hands ringless, large, and almost like those of a man, but with finely tapering fingers. She wore a dark-blue dress fastened to the throat and sitting closely to her firm, still youthful waist – a waist which she evidently liked to display. She sat very upright, sewing a garment of some kind. As soon as I entered the gallery she took me by the hand, drew me to her as though wishing to scrutinise me more closely, and said, as she gazed at me with the same cold, candid glance as her son's, that she had long known me by report from Dmitri, and that therefore, in order to make my acquaintance thoroughly, she was inviting me to stay until the next day in her house.

'Do just as you please here,' she said, 'and stand on no ceremony whatever with us, even as we shall stand on none with you. Pray walk, read, listen, or sleep if you would find that more amusing.'

Sophia Ivanovna was a maiden lady and the Princess's younger sister, though she looked the elder of the two. She had that oddly over-stuffed appearance which old maids always present who are short of stature, stout, and wear corsets. It seemed as though her physical vigour had shifted upwards so forcefully that it threatened at any moment to choke her. Her short, fat arms would not meet below the projecting peak of her bodice, and that tautly stretched peak of her bodice she could no longer see at all.

Notwithstanding that Princess Marya Ivanovna had dark hair and eyes, while Sophia Ivanovna had fair hair and large, vivacious and (a great rarity) tranquil blue eyes, there was a strong family likeness between the two sisters, for they had the same expression, nose, and lips. The only difference was that Sophia's nose and lips were a trifle fuller than Marya's, and when she smiled they inclined slightly towards the right, whereas Marya's inclined towards the left. Sophia Ivanovna, to judge by her dress and *coiffure*, did her best to look younger than her age, and would never have displayed grey curls, even if she had possessed them. At first her glance and bearing towards me seemed very proud, and made me nervous, whereas I at once felt at home with the Princess. Perhaps it was only Sophia Ivanovna's stoutness and a certain resemblance to portraits of Catherine the Great that gave her in my eyes a haughty aspect, but at all events I felt quite intimidated when she looked at me intently and said, 'Friends of our friends are our friends also.' I became reassured and changed my opinion about her only when, after saying those words, she fell silent and, opening her mouth, sighed deeply. It may be that she owed her habit of sighing after every few words – with her mouth open a little and a slight roll of her large blue eyes – to her stoutness, yet it was none the less one which expressed so much sweet good-humour that I at once lost all fear of her, and actually liked her very much. Her eyes were charming, her voice pleasant and musical, and even the extremely rounded lines of her figure seemed to my youthful vision not wholly lacking in beauty.

I had imagined that Lyubov Sergeyevna, as my friend's friend, would at once say something friendly and familiar to me; yet after gazing at me fixedly for a while, as though in doubt whether the remark she was about to make to me would not be *too* friendly, she at length broke her silence merely to ask me what faculty I was in. After that she stared at me as before, in evident hesitation as to whether or not to say something civil and familiar, until remarking her perplexity I besought her with a look to speak freely. Yet all she then said was, 'They tell me the Universities pay very little attention to science now,' and turned away to call her little dog, Suzette.

All that evening she spoke only in disjointed fragments of this kind – fragments which had no connection either with the matter under discussion or with one another; yet I had such faith in Dmitri, and he so often kept looking from her to me with an expression which mutely asked me, 'Now, what do you think of that?' that, though I entirely failed to persuade myself that in Lyubov Sergeyevna there was anything at all special, I could not bear to express the thought, even to myself.

As for the last member of the family, Varya, she was a well-developed girl of about sixteen. The only pretty features in her were a pair of large dark-grey eyes (which, in their expression of gaiety mingled with quiet attention, greatly resembled those of her aunt), a long coil of brown hair, and extremely delicate, beautiful hands.

'I expect, Monsieur Nicholas, you find it wearisome to hear a story begun from the middle?' said Sophia Ivanovna with her good-natured sigh as she turned over the pieces of the garment which she was sewing. The reading aloud had ceased for the moment because Dmitri had left the room for some reason.

'Or perhaps you have read *Rob Roy* before?' she added.

At that period I thought it incumbent upon me, in virtue of my student's uniform, to reply in a very 'clever and original' manner to every question put to me by people whom I did not know very well, and regarded such short, clear answers as 'Yes,' 'No,' 'I like it,' or 'I do not care for it,' as things to be ashamed of. Accordingly, glancing down at my new and fashionably-cut trousers and the glittering buttons of my coat, I replied that I had never read *Rob Roy*, but that it interested me greatly to hear it, since I preferred to read books from the middle rather than from the beginning.

'It is twice as interesting,' I added with a self-satisfied smirk; 'for then one can guess what has gone before as well as what is to come after.'

The Princess laughed what I thought was a forced laugh, but one which I discovered later to be her only one.

'Well, perhaps that is true,' she said. 'But tell me, Nicholas (you will not be offended if I drop the Monsieur) – tell me, are you going to be here long? When do you go away?'

'I do not know quite. Perhaps tomorrow, or perhaps not for some while yet,' I replied for some reason or another, though I knew perfectly well that in reality we were to go tomorrow.

'I wish you could stop longer, both for your own sake and for Dmitri's,' she said, looking into the distance. 'At your age friendship is a fine thing.'

I felt that everyone was looking at me and waiting to see what I should say – though certainly Varya made a pretence of looking at her aunt's work. I felt in fact as though I were being put through an examination, and that I ought to figure in it as well as possible.

'Yes, to *me* Dmitri's friendship is most helpful,' I replied, 'but to *him* mine cannot be of much use at all, since he is a thousand times better than I.' (Dmitri could not hear what I said, or I should have feared his detecting the insincerity of my words.)

Again the Princess laughed her unnatural, yet characteristic, laugh.

'Just listen to him!' she said. 'But *c'est* vous *qui êtes un petit monstre de perfection.*'[1]

' "*Monstre de perfection*," ' I thought to myself. 'That is splendid. I must make a note of it.'

'Yet, passing over the subject of yourself, he has been extraordinarily clever in *that* quarter,' she went on in a lower tone (which pleased me somehow) as she indicated Lyubov Sergeyevna with her eyes, 'since he has discovered in our poor little Auntie' (such was the pet name which they gave Lyubov Sergeyevna) 'all sorts of perfections which I, who have known her and her little dog for twenty years, had never suspected. – Varya, go and tell them to bring me a glass of water,' she added, letting her eyes wander again. Probably she had bethought her that it was too soon, or not entirely necessary, to let me into all the family secrets. 'Yet no; let *him* go, for he has nothing to do, you go on reading. Pray go to the door, my friend,' she said to me, 'and walk about fifteen steps down the passage, then halt and call out pretty loudly, "Pyotr, bring Marya Ivanovna a glass of iced water" ' – and she laughed her unnatural laugh once more.

'I expect she wants to say something about me in my absence,' I thought to myself as I left the room. 'I expect she wants to remark that she can see very clearly that I am a very, very clever young man.' Hardly had I taken a dozen steps when I was overtaken by Sophia Ivanovna, who, though fat and short of breath, trod with surprising lightness and agility.

'*Merci, mon cher*,' she said. 'I am going, so I will tell them myself.'

1 It is *you* who are the little monster of perfection.

XXIV

LOVE

SOPHIA Ivanovna, as I afterwards came to know her, was one of those rare, young-old women who are born for family life, but to whom that happiness has been denied by fate. All that store of their love which should have been poured out upon a husband and children is pent up in their hearts accumulating and growing ever stronger, until they suddenly decide to let it overflow upon a few chosen individuals. Yet sometimes so inexhaustible is that store of old maids' love that, despite the number of individuals so selected, there still remains an abundant surplus of affection which they lavish upon all around them – upon all, good or bad, whom they may chance to meet in their daily life.

Of love there are three kinds: (1) beautiful love, (2) self-denying love, and (3) practical love.

Of the love of a young man for a young woman, as well as of the reverse instance, I am not now speaking, for of such *tendresses* I am wary, seeing that I have been too unhappy in my life to have been able ever to see in such affection a single spark of truth, but rather a lying pretence in which sensuality, marital relations, money, and the wish to bind hands or to unloose them have rendered feeling such a complex affair as to defy disentangling. Rather am I speaking of that love for a human being which, according to the spiritual strength of its possessor, concentrates itself either upon a single individual, upon a few, or upon many – of love for a mother, a father, a brother, little children, a friend, a compatriot – of love, in short, for a fellow-being.

Beautiful love consists in a love of the beauty of the feeling itself and of its expression. People who thus love conceive the object of their affection to be desirable only in so far as it arouses in them that pleasurable sensation of which the consciousness and the expression delights the senses. Those who love with this beautiful love have little concern for reciprocity, since this is a consideration which has no bearing on the beauty and charm of their feeling. They change the object of their love frequently, since their principal aim consists in ensuring that the pleasant feeling of their adoration shall be constantly titillated. To maintain in themselves this pleasant feeling they talk unceasingly, and in the most elegant terms, on the subject of the love which they feel, not only to its immediate object, but also to people whom it does not concern at all. This country of ours contains many individuals of this well-known class who, cultivating the 'beautiful' form of love, not only discourse of it to all and sundry, but insist on speaking of it in *French*. It may seem a strange and ridiculous thing to say, but I am convinced that among us we have had in the past, and still have, a large section of society – notably women – whose love for their friends, husbands, or children would expire tomorrow if they were debarred from dilating upon it in French!

Love of the second kind – *self-denying love* – consists in a yearning to undergo self-sacrifice for the beloved, regardless of whether such self-sacrifice will benefit or injure the person in question. 'There is no unpleasantness which I would not endure to show both the world and him or her whom I adore, my devotion.' There we have the formula of this kind of love. People who thus love never look for reciprocity of affection, since it is a finer thing to sacrifice yourself for one who does not understand you. Also, they are always sickly, which again entrances the merit of their sacrifice; usually constant in their love, for the reason that they would find it hard to forgo the *kudos* of the deprivations which they endure for the beloved; always ready to die, to prove to *him* or to *her* the entirety of their devotion; but sparing of such small daily proofs of their love as call for no special effort of self-immolation. They do not much care whether you eat well, sleep well, keep your spirits up, or enjoy good health, nor do they ever do anything to obtain for you those blessings if they have it in their power; but to confront a bullet, or to fling themselves into fire or water, or to pine away for love – for all these things they are prepared if only the occasion would arise. Moreover, people addicted to love of such a self-sacrificing order are invariably proud of their love, exacting, jealous, distrustful, and – strange to tell – anxious that the object of their adoration should incur perils (that they may save him from them), misfortunes (that they may offer him consolation), and even be vicious (that they may reform him).

You are living alone in the country with a wife who loves you in this self-sacrificing manner. You may be healthy and contented, and have occupations which you like, while, on the other hand, your wife is too delicate to superintend the household work (which is left to the servants), or to look after the children (who are left to the nurses), or to put her heart into any activity which she might enjoy: and all because she loves nobody and nothing but yourself. She may be patently ill, yet she will say not a word to you about it, for fear of distressing you. She may be patently bored, yet for your sake she will be prepared to be so for the rest of her life. She may be patently depressed because you stick so persistently to your occupations (whether sport, books, farming, state service, or anything else) and see clearly that they are doing you harm; yet, for all that, she will keep silence, and suffer it to be so. Yet, should you fall sick – despite her own ailments and your entreaties that she will not distress herself in vain, your loving wife will remain sitting inseparably by your bedside. Every moment you will feel her sympathising gaze resting upon you and, as it were, saying: 'There! I told you so, but it is all one to me, and I shall not leave you.' In the morning you may be a little better, get up, and go into another room. The room, however, will be insufficiently warmed or set in order; the soup which alone you feel you could eat will not have been ordered from the kitchen; nor will any medicine have been sent for. Yet, though worn out with night watching, your loving wife will continue to regard you with the same expression of commiseration, to walk about on tiptoe, and to whisper unaccustomed and obscure orders to the servants. You may wish to be read to – and your loving wife will tell you with a sigh that she feels sure you will be unable to listen to her reading and only grow vexed with her, but she is used to that; and so you had better not be read to at all. You may wish to walk about the room – and she will tell you that it would be far better for you not to do so. You may wish to talk with a friend who has called – and she will tell you that talking is not good for you. At nightfall the fever may come upon you again, and you may wish to be left to doze; but your loving wife, though wasted, pale, and full of sighs, will go on sitting in a chair opposite you in the dim light of a candle, until her very slightest movement, her very slightest sound, rouses you to feelings of irritation and impatience. You may have a servant who has lived with you for twenty years, and to whom you are accustomed, and who would tend you well and to your satisfaction during the night, for the reason that he has had his sleep in the day and is moreover paid a salary for his services; yet she will not suffer him to wait upon you. No; everything she must do herself, with her weak, unaccustomed fingers (of which you follow the movements with suppressed irritation as those pale fingers do their best to uncork a medicine bottle, to snuff a candle, and spill your medicine, or touch you in a squeamish sort of way). If you are an impatient, hasty sort of man, and beg of her to leave the room, your irritated, ailing ears will hear her humbly sobbing and weeping behind the door, and whispering foolishness of some kind to the servant. Finally, if you do not die, your loving wife – who has not slept during the whole three weeks of your illness (a fact of which she will constantly remind you) – will fall ill in her turn, waste away, suffer much, and become even more incapable of any useful pursuit than she was before; while by the time that you have regained your normal state of health she will express to you her self-sacrificing affection only by shedding around you a kind of benignant dullness which involuntarily communicates itself both to yourself and to everyone else in the vicinity.

The third kind of love – *practical love* – consists of a yearning to satisfy every need, every desire, every caprice, nay, every vice, of the beloved person. People who love thus always love their life long, since the more they love, the more they get to know the object beloved, and the easier they find the task of loving – that is to say, of satisfying his or her desires. Their love seldom finds expression in words, but if it does so it expresses itself not with assurance or beauty, but rather in a timid, awkward manner, since people of this kind invariably have misgivings that they do not love enough. People of this kind love even the faults of their adored one, for those faults afford them the chance of constantly satisfying new desires. They look for their affection to be returned, and even deceive themselves into believing that it is returned, and are happy accordingly: yet they go on loving even if it is not, and they will still continue to desire happiness for their beloved one, and try by every means in their power – whether moral or material, great or small – to provide it.

Such practical love it was – love for her nephew, for her niece, for her sister, for Lyubov Sergeyevna, and even for me, because Dmitri loved me – that shone in the eyes, as well as in the every word and movement, of Sophia Ivanovna.

Only long afterwards did I learn to value her at her true worth. Yet even now the question occurred to me: 'What has made Dmitri – who throughout has tried to understand love differently to other young fellows, and has always had before his eyes the gentle, loving Sophia Ivanovna – suddenly fall so deeply in love with the incomprehensible Lyubov Sergeyevna, and declare that in his aunt he can find only *good qualities*? It is clearly a true saying that "a prophet hath no honour in his own country." It must be one of two reasons: either every man has in him more of bad than of good, or every man is more susceptible to bad than to good. Lyubov Sergeyevna he had not known for long, whereas his aunt's love he had known since the day of his birth.

XXV
I BECOME BETTER ACQUAINTED

When I returned to the gallery I found that they were not talking of me at all, as I had anticipated. On the contrary, Varya had laid aside her book and was engaged in a heated dispute with Dmitri, who was walking up and down the room with narrowed eyes and frowningly adjusting his cravat with his neck as he did so. The subject of the quarrel seemed to be Ivan Yakovlevich and superstition, but it was too animated a difference for its underlying cause not to be something which concerned the family much more nearly. Although the Princess and Lyubov Sergeyevna were sitting by in silence, they were following every word, and were evidently tempted at times to take part in the dispute; yet always, just when they were about to speak, they checked themselves and left the field clear for the two principals, Varya and Dmitri, to speak for them. On my entry Varya glanced at me with such an indifferent air that I could see she was wholly absorbed in the quarrel and did not care whether I heard what she said or not. The Princess too looked the same, and was clearly on Varya's side. But Dmitri began, if anything, to raise his voice still more when I appeared, and Lyubov Sergeyevna, for her part, seemed positively alarmed by my entry, and observed to no one in particular: 'Old people are quite right when they say, "*Si jeunesse savait, si vieillesse pouvait.*"'[1]

Nevertheless this quotation did not check the dispute, though it somehow made me feel that the side represented by Lyubov Sergeyevna and my friend was in the wrong. Although it was a little awkward for me to be present at a petty family disagreement, it gave me some pleasure to observe the real relations of the family as revealed in this discussion, and to feel that my presence did not prevent them from speaking their minds.

How often it happens that for years one sees a family cover themselves over with a conventional cloak of decorum, and preserve the real relations of its members a secret from every eye! How often, too, have I remarked that, the more impenetrable (and therefore the more decorous) is the cloak, the harsher are the relations which it conceals. Yet once let some unexpected question – often a most trivial one (the colour of a woman's hair, a visit, the husband's horses) – arise in that family circle, and without any visible cause there will also arise an ever growing difference, until in time the cloak of decorum becomes unequal to confining the quarrel within due bounds, and to the dismay of the disputants and the astonishment of those listening, the real and ill-adjusted relations of the family are laid bare, and

[1] If youth but knew, if old age but could.

the cloak, now useless for concealment, dangles uselessly between the contending factions, serving only to remind one how long it successfully deceived one's perceptions. Sometimes to strike one's head violently against the lintel of a door hurts one less than just to touch lightly upon some spot which has been hurt and bruised before: and in almost every family there exists some such raw and tender spot. In the Nekhlyudov family that spot was Dmitri's extraordinary affection for Lyubov Sergeyevna, which aroused in the mother and sister, if not a jealous feeling, at all events a sense of hurt family pride. This was the grave significance which underlay for all those present the seeming dispute about Ivan Yakovlevich.

'In anything that other people deride and despise you invariably profess to see something extraordinarily good!' Varya was saying in her clear voice, as she articulated each syllable with careful precision.

'Indeed?' retorted Dmitri with an impatient toss of his head. 'Now in the first place, only a most unthinking person could ever speak of *despising* such a remarkable man as Ivan Yakovlevich, while in the second place, it is *you* who invariably set out deliberately not to see the good which is before your very eyes.'

Meanwhile Sophia Ivanovna kept looking anxiously at us as she turned first to her nephew, then to her niece, and then to me. Twice she opened her mouth and drew a deep sigh, as though she had said somthing mentally.

'Varya, *please* go on reading,' she said at length, at the same time handing her niece the book and patting her hand kindly. 'I wish to know whether he ever found *her* again' (as a matter of fact, the novel in question contained no mention of anyone finding anyone else). 'And, Dmitri dear,' she added to her nephew, despite the glum looks which he was throwing at her for having interrupted the logical thread of his deductions, 'you had better wrap up your cheek, for it is chilly, and you will get toothache again.' The reading was resumed.

Yet this little quarrel had in no way dispelled the calm atmosphere of family peace and sensible harmony which enveloped this circle of ladies.

Clearly deriving its inspiration and character from the Princess Marya Ivanovna, it was a circle which for me had a wholly novel and attractive character of logicalness mingled with simplicity and refinement. That character I could discern in the daintiness, good taste, and solidity of everything about me, whether the handbell, the binding of the book, an arm-chair, or the table. Likewise I divined it in the upright, well-corseted pose of the Princess, in her unconcealed curls of grey hair, in the manner in which she had at our first introduction called me plain 'Nicholas' and 'he,' in the occupations of the ladies (the reading and the sewing of garments), and in the unusual whiteness of their hands. (Those hands showed a family feature common to all – that the flesh of the palm on the outer side was rosy in colour and divided by a sharp, straight line from the pure whiteness of the back of the hand.) Still more was the character of this feminine circle expressed in the manner in which the three ladies spoke Russian and French – spoke them, that is to say, with perfect articulation of each letter and ped-antic accuracy in finishing every word and sentence. All this, and more especially the fact that the ladies treated me as simply and as seriously as a real grown-up – telling me their opinions, and listening to my own (a thing to which I was so little accustomed that, for all my glittering buttons and blue cuffs, I was in constant fear of being told: 'Surely you do not think that we are talking *seriously* to you? Go away and get on with your homework') – all this, I say, caused me to feel an entire absence of restraint in this society. I ventured at times to rise, to move about, and to talk boldly to each of the ladies except Varya (whom at this first meeting I felt it was unbecom-ing, or even forbidden, for me to address unless she first spoke to me).

As I listened to her clear, pleasant voice reading aloud, I kept glancing from her to the path of the flower-garden, where the rain-spots were making small dark circles in the sand, and thence to the lime-trees, upon the leaves of which the rain was still pattering down in large detached drops shed from the pale, bluish shimmering edge of the thunder-cloud which hung suspended over us. Then I would glance at her again, and then at the last crimson rays of the setting sun throwing the thick old, rain-washed birches into brilliant relief. Yet again my eyes would return to Varya, and each time it struck me afresh that she was not nearly so plain as at first I had thought her.

'What a pity that I am in love already!' I reflected, 'and that Sonya is not Varya! How nice it would be if suddenly I could become a member of this family, and have the three ladies for my mother, aunt, and wife all at once!' All the time that these thoughts kept passing through my head I kept attentively regarding Varya as she read, until somehow I felt as though I were hypnotising her, and that presently she must look at me. At length she raised her head from her book, threw me a glance, and meeting my eyes, turned away.

'The rain does not seem to have stopped yet,' she remarked.

Suddenly a strange feeling came over me. I began to feel as though everything now happening to me was a repetition of some similar occurrence before – as though on some previous occasion a shower of fine rain had begun to fall, and the sun had been setting behind birch-trees, and I had been looking at her, and she had been reading aloud, and I had hypnotised her, and she had looked up at me. And I had even recollected that all this had already happened.

'Can she possibly be – *she*?' was my thought. 'Can *it* really be beginning?' However, I soon decided that Varya was not the '*she*' referred to, and that '*it*' was not beginning yet. 'In the first place,' I said to myself, 'Varya is not at all *beautiful*. She is just a girl whose acquaintance I have made in the ordinary way, whereas the *she* whom I shall meet somewhere and some day and in some *not* ordinary way will be anything but ordinary; and this family pleases me so much only because hitherto I have not seen anything yet. There must be many families like this one, and no doubt I shall see many more of them during my life.'

XXVI
I SHOW MYSELF TO ADVANTAGE

AT tea time the reading was broken off, and the ladies began to talk among themselves of persons and things unknown to me.

This I conceived them to be doing on purpose to make me conscious (for all their kind demeanour) of the difference which years and position in the world had set between them and me. When the conversation again became general, however, and I could take part, I sought to atone for my previous silence by exhibiting that extraordinary cleverness and originality to which I felt compelled by my University uniform. When the conversation touched upon country-houses, I said that Prince Ivan Ivanych had a villa near Moscow which people came to see from London and Paris, and that it contained balustrading which had cost 380,000 roubles, that the Prince was a very near relation of mine, and that, when lunching with him recently, he had invited me to go and spend the entire summer with him at that villa, but that I had declined, since I knew the villa well and had stayed in it more than once, and all those balustradings and bridges did not interest me, since I could not bear ornamental work, especially in the country, where I liked everything to be wholly countrified. After delivering this extraordinary and complicated invention I grew confused, and blushed so much that everyone must have seen that I was lying. Both Varya, who was handing me a cup of tea, and Sophia Ivanovna, who had been gazing at me throughout, turned their heads away and began to talk of something else with an expression which I later often encountered on the faces of good-natured people when a very young man looks them in the eye and tells them a manifest string of lies – an expression which says, 'Yes, we know he is lying, and why he is doing it, the poor young fellow!'

What I had said about Prince Ivan Ivanych having a country villa I had related simply because I could find no other pretext for mentioning both my relationship to the Prince and the fact that I had just dined with him; yet why I had said all I had about the balustrading costing 380,000 roubles, and about my having several times visited the Prince at that villa (I had never once been there – more especially since the Prince possessed no residences save in Moscow and Naples, as the Nekhlyudovs very well knew), I simply cannot explain. Neither in childhood nor in boyhood, nor in riper years did I ever remark in myself the vice of falsehood – on the contrary, I was, if any-thing, too outspoken and truthful; yet during this first stage of my adolescence I often found myself seized with a strange and unreasonable tendency to lie in the most desperate fashion. I say advisedly 'in the most desperate fashion,' for the reason that I lied in matters in which it was the easiest thing in the world to catch me out. On the whole I think that a vainglorious desire to appear different from what I was, combined with an impossible hope that the lie would never be found out, was the chief cause of this extraordinary impulse.

After tea, since the rain had stopped and the after-glow of sunset was calm and clear, the Princess proposed that we should go and stroll in the lower garden, and admire her favourite spot there. Following my rule to be always original, and conceiving that clever people like myself and the Princess must surely be above the banalities of politeness, I replied that I could not bear a walk with no object in view, and that, if I *did* walk, I liked to walk alone. I had no idea that this speech was simply rude; all I thought was that, even as nothing could be more degrading than empty compliments, so nothing could be more pleasing and original than a little blunt outspokenness. However, though much pleased with my answer, I set out with the rest of the company.

The Princess's favourite spot of all was at the very bottom of the lower garden, where a little bridge spanned a narrow piece of marsh. The view there was very restricted, yet very pensive and pleasing. We are so accustomed to confound art with nature that often enough phenomena of nature which are never to be met with in pictures seem to us unreal, and give us the impression that nature is unnatural, or *vice versa*; whereas phenomena of nature which occur with too much frequency in pictures seem to us hackneyed, and views which are to be met with in real life, but which appear to us too penetrated with a single idea or sentiment, seem to us fanciful. The view from the Princess's favourite spot was of that kind. On the further side of a small pond, overgrown with weeds round its edges, rose a steep ascent covered with bushes and with huge old trees, their many-coloured foliage mingling in a tangled mass, while overhanging the pond at the foot of the ascent stood an ancient birch-tree which, though partly supported by stout roots implanted in the marshy bank of the pond, rested its crown upon a tall, slender aspen, and dangled its curved branches over the smooth surface of the pond, which reflected in its surface both the branches and the surrounding greenery.

'How lovely!' said the Princess with a nod of her head, addressing no one in particular.

'Yes, marvellous!' I replied in my desire to show that I had an opinion of my own on every subject. 'Yet somehow it all looks to me so terribly like stage scenery.'

The Princess went on admiring the scene as though she had not heard me, turning to her sister and Lyubov Sergeyevna at intervals in order to point out to them its details – especially a twisted, pendant bough, with its reflection in the water, which particularly pleased her. Sophia Ivanovna observed that it was all very beautiful, and that her sister would sometimes spend hours together at this spot; yet it was clear that her remarks were meant merely to please the Princess. I have noticed that people who are gifted with the faculty of loving are seldom receptive to the beauties of nature. Lyubov Sergeyevna also seemed enraptured, and asked (among other things): 'How does that birch-tree manage to support itself? Will it go on standing there much longer?' Yet the next moment she kept glancing incessantly at her little dog Suzette, who, with her fluffy tail and crooked little legs went pattering to and fro upon the bridge, seeming to say by the restless expression on her face that this was the first time she had ever found herself out of doors. As for Dmitri, he fell to discoursing very logically to his mother on the subject of how no view can be beautiful of which the horizon is limited. Varya said nothing. Glancing round at her, I saw that she was leaning over the parapet of the bridge, her profile turned towards me, and gazing straight in front of her. Something seemed to be interesting her deeply, or even affecting her, since it was clear that she was oblivious to her surroundings, and thinking neither of herself nor of the fact that anyone might be regarding her. In the expression of her large eyes there was nothing but rapt attention and quiet, concentrated thought, while her whole attitude seemed so unconstrained and, for all her shortness, so dignified that once more some recollection or another touched me, and once more I asked myself, 'Is *it*, then, beginning?' Yet again I assured myself that I was already in love with Sonya, and that Varya was only an ordinary young lady, the sister of my friend. But she pleased me at that moment, and in consequence I somehow felt a vague desire to show her, by word or deed, some small unpleasantness.

'I tell you what, Dmitri,' I said to my friend as I moved nearer to Varya, so that she might overhear what I was going to say, 'it seems to me that even if there had been no mosquitoes here, there would have been nothing to commend this spot; whereas' – and here I slapped my forehead, actually squashing a mosquito – 'it is simply awful.'

'Then you do not care for nature?' said Varya to me without turning her head.

'I think it a foolish, futile pursuit,' I replied, well satisfied that I had said something slightly disagreeable to her, as well as original. Varya only momentarily raised her eyebrows a little with an expression of pity, and went on gazing in front of her as calmly as before.

I felt vexed with her. Yet for all that, the hand-rail of the little bridge on which she was leaning with its faded grey paint, the way in which the dark waters of the pond reflected the drooping branch of the overhanging birch-tree (it seemed as though the reflection was reaching up to join the branches above), the odour of the marsh, the feeling of crushed mosquito on my forehead, and her absorbed look and statuesque pose – many times afterwards did these things recur with unexpected vividness to my imagination.

XXVII
DMITRI

WHEN we returned to the house from our stroll, Varya declined to sing as she usually did in the evenings, and I was conceited enough to attribute this to my doing, in the belief that it was because of what I had said on the bridge. The Nekhlyudovs never had supper, and went to bed early, but tonight, since Dmitri had the toothache (as Sophia Ivanovna had foretold), he departed with me to his room even earlier than usual. Feeling that I had done all that was required of me by my blue collar and gilt buttons, and that everyone was very pleased with me, I was in a gratified, complacent mood, while Dmitri on the other hand was rendered by his quarrel with his sister and the toothache both taciturn and gloomy. He sat down at the table, got out a couple of notebooks – a diary and the copy-book in which it was his custom every evening to enter the tasks performed by or awaiting him – and, continually frowning and touching his cheek with his hand, continued writing for a while.

'Oh, *do* leave me alone!' he cried to the maid whom Sophia Ivanovna sent to ask him whether his teeth were still hurting him and whether he would not like to have a poultice made. Then, saying that my bed would soon be ready for me and that he would be back presently, he departed to Lyubov Sergeyevna's room.

'What a pity that Varya is not good-looking and in fact that she is not Sonya!' I reflected when I found myself alone. 'How nice it would be if, after I have left the University, I could come here to her and offer her my hand! I would say to her, "Princess, I am no longer young: I am unable to love passionately, but I will cherish you as a dear sister. And you," I would continue to her mother, "I greatly respect; and you, Sophia Ivanovna, believe me, I value very highly indeed. So tell me Varya, simply and directly: will you be my wife?" – "*Yes*." And she will give me her hand, and I shall press it and say, "Mine is a love which depends not upon words, but upon deeds." But suppose,' next came into my head, 'that Dmitri should fall in love with Lyuba (as Lyuba has already done with him), and should desire to marry her? Then either one or the other of us would have to resign all thought of marriage.[1] Well, that would

1 According to Russian law, marriage was not permitted between brother-in-law and sister-in-law.

be splendid too, for in that case I should act thus. As soon as I had noticed how things were, I should make no remark, but go to Dmitri and say, "It is no use, my friend, for you and I to conceal our feelings from one another. You know that my love for your sister will cease only with my life. Yet I know all; you have deprived me of all hope, and have rendered me an unhappy man; but do you know how Nikolai Irtenyev requites the misery which he must bear for the rest of his life? – Do you take my sister," and I should place Lyuba's hand in his. Then he would say to me, "No, not for all the world!" and I should reply, "Prince Nekhlyudov, it is in vain for you to attempt to outdo me in nobility. Not in the whole world does there exist a more magnanimous being than Nikolai Irtenyev." Then I should bow to him and depart. In tears Dmitri and Lyuba would pursue me and entreat me to accept their sacrifice, and I might consent to do so, and perhaps be happy ever afterwards – if only I were in love with Varya.' These fancies tickled my imagination so pleasantly that I felt as though I should like to communicate them to my friend; yet, despite our vow of mutual frankness, I also felt as though I had not the physical energy to do so.

Dmitri returned from Lyubov Sergeyevna's room with some toothache drops which she had given him, yet in even greater pain, and therefore even more morose, than before. Evidently no bed had yet been prepared for me, for presently the boy who acted as Dmitri's valet arrived to ask him where I was to sleep.

'Oh, go to the devil!' cried Dmitri, stamping his foot. 'Vaska, Vaska, Vaska!' he went on, the instant that the boy had left the room, with a gradual raising of his voice at each repetition. 'Vaska, lay me out a bed on the floor.'

'No, let *me* sleep on the floor,' I insisted.

'Well, it is all one. Lie anywhere you like,' continued Dmitri in the same angry tone. 'Vaska, why aren't you making up my bed?'

Evidently Vaska did not understand what was demanded of him, for he remained where he was.

'What is the matter with you ? Go and lay the bed, Vaska, I tell you!' shouted Dmitri, suddenly bursting into a sort of frenzy; yet Vaska still did not understand but, apparently fearful, stood there motionless.

'So you are determined to drive me to my – to drive me mad, are you?' – and, leaping from his chair and rushing upon the boy, Dmitri struck him on the head several times with the whole weight of his fist, until the boy rushed headlong from the room. Halting in the doorway, Dmitri looked round at me, and the expression of fury and cruelty which had sat for a moment on his countenance suddenly gave place to such a boyish, kindly, affectionate yet ashamed expression that I felt sorry for him, and gave up my intention of leaving him to himself. He said nothing, but for a long time paced the room in silence, occasionally glancing at me with the same expression as before, seeming to ask my forgiveness. Then he took his notebook from the table-drawer, wrote something in it, took off his jacket and folded it carefully, and stepping into the corner where the ikon hung, folded his large white hands upon his breast and began to say his prayers. So long did he pray that Vaska had time to bring a mattress and spread it, under my whispered directions, on the floor. Indeed, I had undressed and laid myself down upon the mattress before Dmitri had finished. As I contemplated his slightly rounded back and the soles of his feet (which somehow seemed to stick out in my direction in a sort of repentant fashion whenever he bowed to the ground), I felt that I loved him more than ever, and debated within myself whether or not I should tell him all I had been fancying concerning our respective sisters. When he had finished his prayers he lay down upon the bed near me, and propping himself upon his elbow, looked at me in silence with a kindly yet abashed expression. Evidently he found it difficult to do this, yet meant thus to punish himself. Then I smiled and returned his gaze, and he smiled back at me.

'Why do you not tell me that my conduct has been abominable?' he said. 'You have been thinking so, have you not?'

'Yes,' I replied; and although it was something quite different which had been in my mind, it now seemed to me that that *was* what I had been thinking. 'Yes, it was not right of you, nor should I have expected it of you.' It pleased me particularly at that moment to call him by the familiar second person singular. 'But how is your toothache now?' I added.

'Oh, much better. Nikolai, my friend,' he began, and so feelingly that it sounded as though there were tears in his eyes, 'I know and feel that I am bad, but God sees how I try to be better, and how I entreat Him to make me so. Yet what am I to do with such an unfortunate, horrible nature as mine? What am I to do with it? I try to keep myself in hand and to reform myself, but it is impossible for me to do so all at once – at all events, impossible for me to do so unaided. I need the help and support of someone. Now, there is Lyubov Sergeyevna; *she* understands me, and has helped me a great deal in this, and I know by my notebook that I have greatly improved in this respect during the past year. Ah, my dear Nikolai' – he spoke with the most unusual and unwonted tenderness, and in a tone which had grown calmer now that he had made his confession – 'how much the influence of a woman like her could do for me! Think how good it would be for me if I could have a friend like her when I am independent! With her I am a completely different person.'

And upon that Dmitri began to unfold to me his plans for marriage, for a life in the country, and for continual efforts to improve himself.

'Yes, I will live in the country,' he said, 'and you shall come to see me, and perhaps by then you will have married Sonya. Our children will play together. All this may seem to you stupid and ridiculous, yet it may very well come to pass.'

'Yes, it very well may,' I replied with a smile, yet thinking that it would be even nicer if I married his sister.

'I tell you what,' he went on presently after a brief silence; 'you only *imagine* yourself to be in love with Sonya, whereas I can see that it is all nonsense, and that you do not really know what love means.'

I did not protest, for, in truth, I almost agreed with him, and for a while we lay without speaking.

'Probably you have noticed that I have been in my old bad-humour today, and have had a nasty quarrel with Varya?' he resumed. 'I felt bad about it afterwards – more particularly since it occurred in your presence. Although she thinks wrongly on some subjects she is a splendid girl and very good, as you will soon recognise.'

His quick transition from telling me that I was not in love to praise of his sister pleased me extremely and made me blush, but I nevertheless said nothing more to him about his sister and we went on talking of other things.

Thus we chattered until the cocks had crowed twice. In fact, the pale dawn was already looking in at the window when at last Dmitri lay down upon his own bed and put out the candle.

'Well, now for sleep,' he said.

'Yes,' I replied, 'but——'

'But what?'

'It is good to be alive?'

'Yes, it *is* good to be alive,' he replied in a voice which, even in the darkness, enabled me to see the expression of his cheerful, kindly eyes and boyish smile.

XXVIII

IN THE COUNTRY

NEXT day Volodya and I departed with post-horses for the country. Turning over various Moscow recollections in my head as we drove along, I suddenly recalled Sonya Valakhina – though not until evening, and when we had already covered five stages of the road. 'It is a strange thing,' I thought, 'that I should be in love, and yet have forgotten all about it. I must start and think about her,' and straightway I proceeded to do so, but only in the way that one thinks when travelling – that is to say, disconnectedly, though vividly. And I thought so effectively that, for the first two days after our arrival home, I somehow considered it incumbent upon me always to appear sad and moody in the presence of the household, and especially before Katya, whom I looked upon as a great expert in matters of this kind, and to whom I threw out a hint of the state of my heart. Yet for all my attempts at dissimulation and assiduous adoption of such signs of love-sickness as I had occasionally observed in other people, I succeeded for only two days (and that at intervals, and

mostly towards evening) in reminding myself that I was in
love, and finally, when I had settled down into the new rut of
country life and pursuits, I forgot about my love for Sonya
altogether.

We arrived at Petrovskoye in the night time, and I was so
soundly asleep that I saw nothing of the house as we approached
it, nor yet of the avenue of birch-trees, nor of the household –
all of whom had long since gone to bed and to sleep. Only old
hunchbacked Foka – barefooted, clad in some sort of a wadded
jacket belonging to his wife, and carrying a candlestick –
unbolted the door to us. As soon as he saw who we were he
trembled all over with joy, kissed us on the shoulders, hurriedly
put away the piece of felt on which he slept, and started to dress
himself properly. I passed in a semi-waking condition through
the hall and up the stairs, but in the ante-room the lock of the
door, the catch, a crooked board in the flooring, the chest,
the ancient candlestick (splashed all over with tallow as of
old), the shadows thrown by the crooked wick of the cold,
just lighted, tallow candle, the perennially dusty double window which was never taken out, behind which I remembered a
moutain ash-tree to have grown – all these things were so
familiar, so full of memories, so harmonious with one another,
so, as it were, knit together by a single idea, that I suddenly
became conscious of a tenderness for this dear old house.
Involuntarily I asked myself, 'How have we, the house and I,
managed to remain apart so long?' and, hurrying from spot to
spot, ran to see if all the other rooms were still the same. Yes,
everything was unchanged, except that everything had become
smaller and lower, and I myself taller, heavier, and more filled
out. Yet, even as I was, the old house received me back into its
arms and aroused in me with every board, every window, every
step of the stairs and every sound the shadows of forms,
feelings, and events of the happy but irrevocable past. When
we entered our old night nursery all my childish fears lurked
once more in the darkness of the corners and doorways. When
we passed into the drawing-room I could feel the old calm
motherly love diffusing itself from every object in the room. In
the *salon* the noisy, careless merriment of childhood seemed

merely to be waiting to wake to life again. In the sitting-room (whither Foka led us, and where he had made up our beds) everything – mirror, screen, old wooden ikon, every irregularity of the walls covered with white paper – seemed to speak of suffering and of death and of what would never be again.

We got into bed, and Foka, bidding us good-night, retired.

'It was in this room that Mamma died, was it not?' said Volodya.

I made no reply, but pretended to be asleep. If I had said anything I should have burst into tears. On awaking next morning, I beheld Papa in his dressing-gown and slippers and smoking a cigar sitting on Volodya's bed and talking and laughing with him. Leaping up with a merry hoist of the shoulders, he came over to me, slapped me on the back with his great hand, and presented me his cheek and pressed it against my lips.

'Well done and thank you, *diplomat!*' he said in his most kindly jesting tone as he looked at me with his small bright eyes. 'Volodya tells me you have passed the examinations like the best of them, and that is a splendid thing. Unless you start and play the fool, I shall have another fine little fellow in you. Thanks, my dear boy, Well, we will have a grand time of it here now, and in the winter, perhaps, we shall move to Petersburg. I only wish the hunting was not over, or I could have given you some amusement in *that* way. Can you shoot, Voldemar? There is plenty of game, I will take you out with me some day. Next winter, if God pleases, we will move to Petersburg, and you shall meet people, and make contacts, for you are now my two young grown-ups. I have been telling Voldemar that you are just starting on your careers, whereas my job is done. You are old enough now to walk by yourselves, but, whenever you wish to ask my advice, pray do so, for I am no longer your nurse, but your friend. At least, I will be your friend and comrade and adviser as much as I can: and more than that I cannot do. How does that fall in with your philosophy, eh, Koko? Well or ill, eh?'

Of course I said that it fell in with it entirely, and, indeed, I really thought so. That morning Papa had a particularly winning, bright, and happy expression on his face, and these new relations between us, as of equals and comrades, made me love him all the more.

'Now, tell me,' he went on, 'did you call upon all our kinsfolk and the Ivins? Did you see the old man, and what did he say to you? And did you go to Prince Ivan Ivanych's?'

We continued talking so long that before we were fully dressed the sun had left the window of the sitting-room, and Yakov (the same old man as of yore, twirling his fingers behind his back and repeating his words) had entered the room and reported to Papa that the little carriage was ready.

'Where are you going to?' I asked Papa.

'Oh, I had forgotten all about it!' he replied, with a cough and an irritated jerk of his shoulder. 'I promised to go and call upon the Epifanovs today. You remember Epifanova – "*la belle Flamande*" – don't you, who used to come and see your mamma? They are nice people.' And with a self-conscious shrug of his shoulders (so it appeared to me) Papa left the room.

During our conversation Lyuba had more than once come to the door and asked, 'Can I come in?' but Papa had each time shouted to her that she could not do so, since we were not dressed yet.

'What of it?' she replied. 'Why, I have often seen *you* in your dressing-gown.'

'Never mind; you cannot see your brothers without their *inexpressibles*,' rejoined Papa. 'If each of them just raps on the door, let that be enough for you. Knock on the door, you boys. Even for them to *speak* to you in such a *negligé* costume is unbecoming.'

'How unbearable you are!' was Lyuba's parting retort. 'Well, at least hurry up and come down to the drawing-room, for Mimi wants so much to see you.'

As soon as Papa had left the room I hastened to array myself in my student's uniform and went to the drawing-room. Volodya on the other hand was in no hurry, but remained sitting on his bed and talking to Yakov about the best places to find snipe and plover. As I have said, there was nothing in the world he so much feared as to be suspected of any affection for his dear father, dear brother, and dear little sister, as he put it; so that to escape any expression of feeling he fell into the other extreme and affected a coldness which often hurt people who did not comprehend its cause. In the ante-room I collided with Papa, who was hurrying towards the carriage with short, rapid steps. He had a new and fashionable Moscow greatcoat on and smelt of scent. On seeing me he gave a cheerful nod, as much as to say 'Don't I look splendid?' and once again I was struck with the happy expression of face which I had noted earlier that morning.

The drawing-room looked the same lofty, bright room as of yore, with its English grand piano in yellow wood, and its large open windows and the green trees and yellowish-red paths of the garden looking cheerfully in. After kissing Mimi and Lyuba I was approaching Katya when it suddenly struck me that it might no longer be proper for me to exchange kisses with her. Accordingly I halted, silent and blushing. Katya, for her part, was quite at her ease as she held out her little white hand to me and congratulated me on my passing into the University. The same thing took place when Volodya entered the drawing-room and met Katya. Indeed, it was something of a problem how, after being brought up together and seeing one another daily, we ought now, after this first separation, to behave on meeting again. Katya blushed more deeply than any of us, yet Volodya seemed not at all confused as, with a slight bow to her, he crossed over to Lyuba, held a brief and lighthearted exchange with her, and then departed somewhere on a solitary walk.

XXIX

RELATIONS BETWEEN THE GIRLS AND OURSELVES

OF the girls Volodya took such a strange view that, although he wished that they should have enough to eat, should sleep well, be well dressed, and avoid making such mistakes in French as would shame him before strangers, he would never admit that they could think or feel like human beings, still less that it was possible to converse with them sensibly about anything.

Whenever they addressed to him a serious question (a thing, by
the way, which they had learned to avoid), such as asking his
opinion on a novel or inquiring about his doings at the
University, he invariably pulled a face and either turned away
without speaking or answered with some mangled French
phrase – '*Comme c'est très joli!*'[1] or the like. Or again, putting
on a serious and deliberately stupid face, he would say something absolutely meaningless and bearing no relation whatever
to the question asked him, or else suddenly exclaim, with a look
of pretended vacancy, the word '*bun*' or '*departed*' or '*cabbage*,'
or something of the kind. And when I happened to repeat
anything to him as having been told me by Lyuba or Katya,
he would always remark:

'Hm! So you actually care to talk to them, do you? I can see
you are a duffer still' – and one needed to see and hear him to
appreciate the profound, immutable contempt which was con-
veyed by this remark. He had been grown up now two years,
and was constantly falling in love with every good-looking
woman that he met; yet despite the fact that he came in daily
contact with Katya (who during those two years had been
wearing long dresses, and was growing prettier every day),
the possibility of his falling in love with her never entered his
head. Whether this proceeded from the fact that the prosaic
recollections of childhood – the schoolroom ruler, the bath
sheet, childish wilfulnesses – were still too fresh in his memory,
or whether from the aversion which very young people feel
for everything domestic, or whether from the common
human weakness which at a first encounter with anything
good and beautiful leads a man to say to himself, 'Ah! I
shall meet much more of the same kind during my life'; at
all events Volodya had never yet looked upon Katya as a
woman.

All that summer Volodya appeared to find things very
wearisome; his boredom arose out of that contempt for us all
which, as I have said, he made no effort to conceal. His
expression of face seemed to be constantly saying, 'Phew!

1 How very pretty that is.

how bored I am, and there's no one to talk to!' The first thing
in the morning he would go out by himself shooting, or sit
reading a book in his room, and not dress until dinner time.
Indeed, if Papa was not at home, he would take his book in to
that meal and go on reading it without addressing so much as a
single word to any one of us, who felt somehow guilty in his
presence. In the evening, too, he would lie with his feet up on a
settee in the drawing-room, and either go to sleep, propped on
his elbow, or with a most serious expression tell us farcical
stories – sometimes stories so improper as to make Mimi
grow angry and go red in patches, and ourselves die with
laughter. But he would not condescend to address a single
serious word to any member of the family except Papa or
(occasionally) myself. Quite unconsciously I reproduced my
brother's view of the girls, although I was not so afraid of
seeming affectionate as he, and moreover had by no means
such a profound and confirmed contempt for young
women. Yet several times that summer, when driven by lack
of amusement actually to try and engage Lyuba and Katya in
conversation, I always encountered in them such an absence
of any capacity for logical thinking and such an ignorance
of the simplest, most ordinary matters (as, for instance,
the nature of money, the subjects studied at Universities, the
nature of war, and so forth), as well as such indifference to
my explanations of such matters, that these attempts of mine
only ended in confirming my unfavourable opinion of the
girls.

I remember one evening when Lyuba kept repeating some
unbearably tedious passage on the piano about a hundred times
in succession, while Volodya, who was dozing on a settee in the
drawing-room, kept addressing no one in particular as he
muttered, 'Lord! how she murders it! *What* a musician!
What a Bithoven!' (he always pronounced the composer's
name with especial irony). 'Wrong again! Now – a second
time! That's it!' and so on. Katya and I were still at the tea-
table, and somehow she brought the conversation round to her
favourite subject – love. I was in the right frame of mind to
philosophise, and began by loftily defining love as the wish to

acquire in another what one does not possess in oneself, and so forth. To this Katya retorted that, on the contrary, love is not love at all if a girl desires to marry a man for his money, but that in her opinion wealth was a vain thing, and true love only the affection which can stand the test of separation (this I took to be a hint concerning her love for Dubkov). At this point Volodya, who must have been listening all the time, raised himself on his elbow and cried out in an interrogative tone: 'Katya! The Russians?'

'Oh, your eternal nonsense!' said Katya.

'Old pepper-pot?' continued Volodya, stressing each vowel. And I could not help thinking that he was quite right.

Apart from the general faculties (more or less developed in different persons) of intellect, sensibility and artistic feeling, there also exists (more or less developed in different circles of society, and especially in families) a private or individual faculty which I may call *apprehension*. The essence of this faculty lies in a shared sense of proportion, and in an accepted and identical view of things. Two individuals who belong to the same social circle or the same family and who possess this faculty, apprehend an expression of feeling up to a certain point, beyond which they both find in such expression merely empty phrases. They apprehend precisely where commendation ends and irony begins, where enthusiasm ceases and pretence begins – all of which appears quite otherwise to persons possessed of a different order of apprehension. Persons with the same apprehension view objects in an identically ludicrous, beautiful, or repellent light; and in order to facilitate such common apprehension between members of the same social circle or family, they usually establish a language of their own turns of speech, or terms to define such shades of apprehension which are non-existent for other people. In our family such apprehension was common between Papa, Volodya, and myself, and was developed to the highest pitch. Dubkov also approximated to our *coterie* in apprehension, but Dmitri, though far more intelligent than Dubkov, was obtuse in this respect. With no one, however, did I bring this faculty to such a pitch as with Volodya, who had grown up with me under identical conditions. Papa had long since fallen behind us, and much that was to us as clear as 'twice two are four' was to him incomprehensible. For instance, Volodya and I managed to establish between ourselves the following terms, with meanings to correspond. *Raisins* meant a desire to boast of one's money; *Cone* (on pronouncing which one had to join one's fingers together, and to put a particular emphasis upon the two *sh's* in the Russian word *shishka*) meant anything fresh, healthy, and comely, but not showy; a noun used in the plural meant an undue partiality for the object which it denoted; and so forth, and so on. At the same time, the meaning depended considerably upon the expression of the face and the context of the conversation; so that, no matter what new expression one of us might invent to define a shade of feeling, the other could immediately understand it by a hint alone. The girls did not share this faculty of apprehension, and this was the chief cause of our mental estrangement and of the contempt which we felt for them.

It may be that they too had their own private 'apprehension,' but it so little ran with ours that, where we already perceived the 'phrasing,' they still saw only the feeling – our irony was for them truth, and so on. At that time I had not yet learnt to understand that they were in no way to blame for this, and that absence of such apprehension in no way prevented them from being nice and clever girls, and so I looked down on them. Moreover, having once lit upon my precious idea of 'frankness,' and being bent upon applying it to the full in myself, I thought the quiet, confiding nature of Lyuba guilty of secretiveness and dissimulation simply because she saw no necessity for digging up and examining all her thoughts and spiritual impulses. For instance, the fact that she always made the sign of the cross over Papa before going to bed, that she and Katya invariably wept in the chapel where we went to attend requiem masses for Mamma, and that Katya sighed and rolled her eyes when playing the piano – all these things seemed to me sheer make-believe, and I asked myself: 'At what period did they learn to pretend like grown-up people, and how is it they are not ashamed to do it?'

XXX
HOW I EMPLOYED MY TIME

NEVERTHELESS, that summer I became better friends with the young ladies of our household than I had been in other years by reason of my new-found passion for music. In the spring a young neighbour presented himself to us who, as soon as he entered the drawing-room, fixed his eyes upon the piano and kept gradually edging his chair closer to it as he talked to Mimi and Katya. After discoursing awhile of the weather and the amenities of country life, he skilfully directed the conversation to piano-tuners, music, and pianos generally, and ended by saying that he himself played – and very soon he did sit down and perform three waltzes, with Mimi, Lyuba, and Katya grouped about the instrument, watching him. He never came to see us again, but his playing, and his attitude when at the piano, and the way in which he kept shaking back his long hair, and most of all, the manner in which he was able to execute octaves with his left hand, rapidly extending his thumb and little finger to span the octave, and then slowly bringing them together, and then quickly spreading them again, made a great impression upon me. This graceful gesture of his, together with his easy pose and his tossing of hair and successful winning of the ladies' attention by his talent, ended by firing me to take up the piano. Convinced that I possessed both talent and a passion for music, I set myself to learn, and in doing so acted just as millions of the male – still more, of the female – sex have done who try to teach themselves without a skilled teacher, without any real vocation for the art, and without the smallest understanding either of what the art can give or of what has to be done to obtain that gift. For me music (or rather, piano-playing) was simply a means of winning young ladies' good graces through their sensibilities. With the help of Katya I first learnt the notes, and having somewhat broken in my stubby fingers – which effort occupied two months or so of hard work, supplemented by ceaseless exercising of my rebellious fourth finger on my knee at dinner, and on the pillow in bed – went on to 'pieces,' which I played (so Katya assured me) 'with soul' ('*avec âme*'), but altogether regardless of time.

My range of pieces was the usual one – waltzes, galops, romances arranged for the piano, *etcetera*; all of them of the class of delightful compositions which anyone with a little healthy taste could pick out for you among the stacks of better-class works contained in any music shop and say, 'These are what you ought *not* to play, seeing that nothing more tasteless and sillier has ever yet been written down on music paper,' – but which (probably for that very reason) are to be found on the piano of every Russian lady. True, we also possessed Beethoven's 'Sonate Pathétique' and his C minor Sonata which have the misfortune to be forever murdered by young ladies in Russia (and which Lyuba used to play in memory of Mamma), as well as certain other good pieces which her teacher in Moscow had given her to play; but among that collection there were also compositions of the teacher's own in the shape of clumsy marches and galops – and these too Lyuba used to play. Katya and I cared nothing for serious works, but preferred, above all things, 'Le Fou' and 'The Nightingale,' which Katya would play so rapidly that her fingers were barely visible, and which I too was beginning to execute quite loudly and fluently. I had adopted the gestures of the young man of whom I have spoken, and frequently regretted that there were no strangers present to see me play. Soon, however, I began to realise that Liszt and Kalkbrenner were beyond me, and that I should never overtake Katya. Accordingly, imagining that classical music was easier (as well as, partly, for the sake of originality), I suddenly came to the conclusion that I loved abstruse German music. I began to go into raptures whenever Lyuba played the 'Sonate Pathétique,' and although (if the truth be told) that work had long since become deeply distasteful to me, I set myself to play Beethoven, and to pronounce his name with a long drawn-out first syllable – 'Bëethoven.' Yet through all this chopping and changing and pretence (as I now conceive) there may have run in me a certain vein of talent, since music sometimes affected me even to tears, and things which particularly pleased me I could strum on the piano afterwards (in a certain fashion) without the score; so that had anyone taught me at that period to look upon music as an end, a grace, in itself, and not merely as a means for pleasing womenfolk with the velocity and soulfulness of my playing, I might possibly have become a passable musician.

The reading of French novels (of which Volodya had brought a large store with him from Moscow) was another of my occupations that summer. At that period *Monte Cristo* and the various *Mystères* had just begun to appear, and I also plunged into stories by Sue, Dumas, and Paul de Kock. Even their most unnatural personages and events were for me as real as actuality, and not only was I incapable of suspecting an author of lying, but in my eyes there existed no author at all, and real, live people and real events paraded themselves before me on the printed page; and although I had never in my life met such people as I there read about, I never for a second doubted that I should one day do so.

I discovered in myself all the passions described in every novel, as well as a likeness to all the characters – heroes and villains impartially – just as a hypochondriac finds in himself the signs of every possible disease when reading a book on medicine. I took pleasure in the cunning designs, the glowing sentiments, the magical events, and the black-and-white character-drawing of these novels. A good man was of the goodness, a bad man of the badness, possible only to the imagination of early youth. Likewise I found very great pleasure in the fact that it was all written in French, and that I could lay to heart the noble words which the noble heroes spoke, and recall them for use some day when engaged in some noble deed. What quantities of French phrases I culled from those books for Kolpikov's benefit if I should ever meet him again, as well as for *hers*, when at length I should find her and reveal to her my love! For them both I prepared speeches which should overcome them as soon as spoken! Upon these novels, too, I founded new ideals of the moral qualities which I wished to attain. First of all, I wished to be *noble* in all my deeds and conduct (I use the French word *noble* instead of the Russian word *blagorodny* for the reason that the former has a different meaning – as the Germans well understood when they adopted the word as *nobel* and differentiated it from *ehrlich*); next, to be passionate; and lastly, to be what I was already inclined to be, namely as *comme il faut* as possible. I even tried to approximate my appearance and bearing to that of the heroes who possessed these qualities. In particular I remember how in one of the hundreds of novels which I read that summer there was an extremely passionate hero with heavy eyebrows, and that I so greatly wished to resemble him (I felt that I did so already in character) that one day, when looking at my eyebrows in the glass, I conceived the idea of clipping them in order to make them grow bushier. Unfortunately, after I had started to do so, I happened to clip one spot shorter than the rest and so had to trim down the rest to match it – with the result that, to my horror, I beheld myself eyebrow-less, and anything but presentable. However I comforted myself with the hope that my eyebrows would soon sprout again as bushy as my passionate hero's, and was only perplexed to think how I could explain the circumstance to the household when they saw my eyebrow-less condition. I borrowed some gunpowder from Volodya, rubbed it on my eyebrows, and set it alight. The powder did not fire properly, but I succeeded in singeing myself sufficiently so that no one found out what I had done. And indeed, afterwards, when I had forgotten all about the passionate hero, my eyebrows grew again, and much thicker than they had been before.

XXXI
'COMME IL FAUT'

SEVERAL times in the course of this narrative I have hinted at an idea corresponding to the French heading of this chapter, and now feel it incumbent upon me to devote a whole chapter to this idea, which was one of the most pernicious and false notions which ever became engrafted upon my life by my upbringing and social *milieu*.

The human race may be divided into numerous categories – rich and poor, good and bad, military and civilian, clever and stupid, and so forth. Yet each man has his own favourite, fundamental system of sub-division which he unconsciously applies to each new person he meets. At the time of which I am writing my own favourite, fundamental system of division in this respect was into people '*comme il faut*' and people '*comme il ne faut pas*' – the latter sub-divided again into people inherently not '*comme il faut*' and the lower orders. People '*comme il faut*' I respected, and looked upon as worthy to consort with me as my equals; the second of the above categories I pretended to despise, but in reality detested, and nourished towards them a kind of feeling of offended personality; while the third category had no existence at all so far as I was concerned, since my contempt for them was too complete. This '*comme il faut*'-ness of mine lay first and foremost in complete proficiency in the French language, especially in its correct pronunciation. A person who pronounced that language badly at once aroused in me a feeling of dislike. 'Why do you try to talk as we do when you haven't a notion how to do it?' I would mentally ask him with my most venomous irony. The second condition of '*comme il faut*'-ness was long nails that were well kept and clean; the third, ability to bow, dance, and converse; the fourth – and a very important one – indifference to everything, and a constant air of refined, supercilious *ennui*. Moreover, there were certain general signs which, I considered, enabled me to tell without actually speaking to a man the class to which he belonged. Chief among these signs (the others being the furnishings of his rooms, his signet-ring, his handwriting, his carriage, and so forth) were his feet. The relation of boots to trousers was sufficient to determine in my eyes the social status of a man. Heel-less boots with angular toes, wedded to narrow, unstrapped trouser-ends – these denoted the vulgarian. Boots with narrow, round toes and heels, accompanied either by tight trousers strapped under the instep and fitting close to the leg or by wide trousers similarly strapped, but projecting in a peak over the toe – these meant the man of *mauvais genre*; and so on, and so on.

It was a curious thing that I who lacked all ability to be '*comme il faut*,' should have assimilated the idea so completely as I did. Possibly it was the fact that it had cost me such enormous labour to acquire that caused it to take such deep root in my mind. It is dreadful to think how much of the best and most valuable period of existence – the time when I was about sixteen – I wasted upon its acquisition. Yet everyone whom I imitated – Volodya, Dubkov, and most of my acquaintances – seemed to acquire it easily. I watched them with envy, and silently toiled to become proficient in French, to bow gracefully and without looking at the person whom I was saluting, to gain dexterity in small-talk and dancing, to cultivate indifference and *ennui*, and to keep my finger-nails well trimmed (though I cut myself with the scissors in so doing). And all the time I felt that so much remained to be done if I was ever to attain my end. A room, a writing-table, an equipage I still found it impossible to arrange '*comme il faut*,' however much I fought down my aversion to practical matters in my desire to become proficient. Yet everything seemed to arrange itself properly with *other* people, just as though things could not be otherwise! Once I remember asking Dubkov, after much zealous and careful labouring at my finger-nails (his own were extraordinarily good), whether his nails had always been as now, or whether he had done anything to make them so: to which he replied that never within his recollection had he done anything to them, and that he could not imagine a gentleman's nails possibly being any different. This answer incensed me greatly, for I had not yet learnt that one of the chief conditions of '*comme il faut*'-ness was to hold one's tongue about the labour by which it had been acquired. '*Comme il faut*'-ness I looked upon as not only a great merit, a splendid accomplishment, an embodiment of all the perfection which I must strive to attain, but as the one indispensable condition without which there could never be happiness, nor glory, nor any good whatsoever in this world. Even the greatest artist or *savant* or benefactor of the human race would at that time have won from me no respect if he had not also been '*comme il faut*.' A man possessed of '*comme il faut*'-ness stood higher than, and beyond all possible equality with, such people, and might well leave it to them to paint pictures, to compose music, to write books, or to do good. He might even commend them for so doing (since why should not merit be commended wherever it be found?), but he could never stand *on a level* with them, seeing that he was '*comme il faut*' and they were not – a quite final and sufficient reason. In fact, I actually believe that, had I possessed a brother or a father or a mother who had not been '*comme il faut*,' I should have declared it to be a great misfortune, and announced that between myself and them there could never be anything in common. Yet neither waste of the golden hours which I consumed in constantly endeavouring to observe the many arduous, unattainable conditions of '*comme il faut*'-ness (to the exclusion of any more serious pursuit), nor dislike of and contempt for nine-tenths of the human race, nor disregard of all the beauty that lay outside the narrow circle of '*comme il faut*'-ness, constituted the chief evil which the idea wrought in me. The chief evil of all lay in the notion acquired that '*comme il faut*'-ness was a sufficient status in society, and that a man need not strive to become an official, a coachbuilder, a soldier, a scholar, or anything useful, so long only as he was '*comme il faut*' – that by attaining this quality he had done all that was demanded of him, and was even superior to most people.

Usually, at a given period in youth, and after many errors and excesses, every man recognises the necessity of taking an active part in social life and chooses some branch of labour to which to devote himself. Only with the '*comme il faut*' man does this rarely happen. I have known, and know, very, very many people – old, proud, self-satisfied, and opinionated – who to the question (if it should ever be asked of them in the next world) 'Who have you been, and what have you ever done?' would be unable to reply otherwise than by saying, '*Je fus un homme très comme il faut.*'[1]

Such a fate was awaiting me.

XXXII
YOUTH

DESPITE the confusion of ideas going on in my head, I was at least young, innocent, and free that summer – consequently almost happy.

---

1 I was an extremely respectable man.

Sometimes, fairly often, I would rise early in the morning, for I slept on the open verandah, and the bright, horizontal beams of the morning sun would wake me up. Dressing myself quickly, I would tuck a towel and a French novel under my arm, and go off to bathe in the river in the shade of a birch wood half a verst from the house. Next I would stretch out on the grass in the shade and read – raising my eyes from time to time to look at the surface of the river where it showed purple in the shade of the trees, at the ripples caused by the first morning breeze, at the yellowing field of rye on the further bank, and at the bright-red sheen of the morning sunlight as it struck lower and lower down the white trunks of the birch-trees which, ranged in ranks one behind the other, gradually receded into the remote distance of the thick forest. At such moments I was joyously conscious of having within me the same young, fresh force of life as nature was everywhere breathing forth around me. When, however, the sky was over-cast with grey clouds of morning and I felt chilly after bathing, I would often start to walk at random through the fields and woods, and joyously trail my wet boots in the fresh dew. All the while my head would be filled with vivid dreams concerning the heroes of my last-read novel, and I would imagine myself some leader of an army or some statesman or marvellously strong man or devoted lover or other, and looking round me in a nervous expectation that I should suddenly descry *her* somewhere near me, in a clearing or behind a tree. Whenever these rambles led me near peasants engaged at their work, all my ignoring of the existence of the 'common people' did not prevent me from experiencing an involuntary, overpowering sensation of awkwardness; so that I always tried to avoid being seen by them. When the heat of the day had increased it was often my habit – if the ladies had not come down for their morning tea – to go into the kitchen-garden or orchard and to eat whatever ripe vegetables or fruit were there. Indeed, this was an occupation which afforded me one of my greatest pleasures. Let anyone go into an apple-orchard, and dive into the midst of a tall, thick, sprouting raspberry-bed. Above is the hot clear, blue sky, and all around, the pale-green, prickly foliage of raspberry-canes where they grow mingled together in a tangle of overgrown weeds. From one's feet stretches gracefully upwards the dark-green nettle, with its slender crown of flowers, while the broad-leaved burdock with its curious bright-pink prickly blossoms overtops the raspberries (and even one's head) with its luxuriant masses until, with the nettle, it almost meets the pendant, pale-green branches of the old apple-trees where apples, round and lustrous as bone, but as yet unripe, are mellowing in the heat of the sun. Below, a young raspberry-bush, leafless and almost withered in appearance, twines itself round as it stretches its tendrils towards the sunlight, and green needles of grass and young burdocks peering through last year's dew-drenched leaves are growing juicily green in the perennial shade, as though unaware of the bright sunshine playing on the leaves of the apple-trees above them.

In this thicket there is always moisture – always a smell of confined, perpetual shade, of cobwebs, fallen apples turning black where they lie on the rotting leaf-mould, raspberries, and sometimes of those forest bugs of the kind which impel you to reach hastily for more fruit when you have unwittingly swallowed one of their number with the last berry. At every step your movements keep flushing the sparrows which make their home in these depths, and you hear their fussy chirping and the beating of their tiny, fluttering wings against the stalks, and catch the low buzzing of a bumble bee somewhere, and the sound of the gardener's footsteps (it is half-daft Akim) on the path as he hums his eternal sing-song to himself. Then you mutter under your breath, 'No! Neither he nor anyone in the world will find me here!' and you go on stripping juicy berries from their conical white centres, and cramming them into your mouth. At length – your legs soaked to above the knees as you repeat over and over again some rubbish which keeps running in your head, and your arms and nether limbs (despite the protection of wet trousers) thoroughly stung with the nettles – you come to the conclusion that the sun's rays are beating too straight upon your head for eating to be any longer desirable, and sinking down into the tangle of greenery, you remain there – looking and listening, thinking, and continuing in mechanical fashion to strip off one or two of the finer berries and swallow them.

Soon after ten o'clock – that is to say, when the ladies had taken their morning tea and settled down to their occupations – I would generally repair to the drawing-room. Near the first window with its unbleached linen blind lowered to exclude the sunshine, but through the chink of which the sun keeps throwing brilliant circles of light which hurt the eye to look at them, stands an embroidery frame, with flies quietly parading the whiteness of its covering. At the frame sits Mimi, shaking her head in an irritable manner, and constantly shifting from spot to spot to avoid the sunshine as at intervals it darts in upon her from somewhere, laying a streak of flame upon her hand or face. Through the other three windows the sun throws squares of light crossed with the shadows of the window-frames, and where one of these patches marks the unstained wood floor of the room there lies, in accordance with invariable custom, Milka, her ears pricked as she watches the flies promenading the lighted squares. Seated on a settee, Katya knits or reads aloud, from time to time giving her small white hands (looking almost transparent in the sunshine) an impatient shake to flick away the flies, or tosses her head with a frown to drive away some buzzing fly entangled in her thick auburn hair. Lyuba is either walking up and down the room (her hands clasped behind her) until the moment comes to go into the garden, or playing some piece on the piano, of which every note has long been familiar to me. For my part, I sit down somewhere and listen to the music or the reading until such time as I myself have an opportunity of taking my seat at the piano. After dinner I sometimes condescend to take the girls out riding (since to go for a mere walk at that hour seemed to me unsuitable to my years and position in the world), and these excursions of ours – in which I often take my companions through unaccustomed spots and ravines – are very pleasant. Indeed, on some of these occasions we meet with adventures which allow me to show off my many qualities, and the girls praise my riding and daring, and pretend that I was their protector. In the evening, if we have no guests with us, tea (served on the shady verandah) is followed by a walk round the homestead with Papa, and then I stretch myself on my usual arm-chair, and read and ponder as of old, listening to Katya or Lyuba playing the piano. At other times, alone in the drawing-room with Lyuba performing some old-time air, I find myself laying my book down, and gazing through the open doorway on to the balcony at the drooping, leafy branches of the tall birch-trees overshadowed by the coming night, and at the clear sky where, if one looks intently enough, misty, yellowish spots appear suddenly, and then disappear again. And as I listen to the sounds of the music wafted from the *salon*, and to the creaking of gates and the voices of the peasant women when the cattle return to the village, I suddenly think of Natalya Savishna and of Mamma and of Karl Ivanych, and become momentarily sad. But at that time my spirit is so full of life and hope that such reminiscences only touch me in passing, and soon flee away again.

After supper and (sometimes) a night stroll with someone in the garden (for I was afraid to walk down the dark avenues by myself), I would repair to my solitary sleeping-place on the verandah – a proceeding which, despite the countless mosquitoes which always devoured me, gave me the greatest pleasure. If the moon was full I frequently spent whole nights sitting up on my mattress, looking at the light and shadows, listening to the sounds or stillness, dreaming of one matter and another (but more particularly of the poetic, voluptuous happiness which, in those days, I believed was the acme of felicity) and lamenting that until now it had only been given to me to *imagine* it. No sooner had everyone dispersed, and I had seen lights pass from the drawing-room to the upper chambers (whence female voices would presently be heard, and the noise of windows opening and shutting), than I would go out on to the verandah and walk up and down there as I listened attentively to the sounds of the house as it sank into slumber. As long as I feel any expectation (no matter how small and baseless) of realising a fraction of some happiness of which I may be dreaming, I am still unable to give myself up calmly to imagining what the happiness is going to be like.

At the least sound of bare footsteps, or of a cough, or of a sigh, or of the rattling of a window, or of the rustling of a dress, I would leap from my mattress, and stand stealthily gazing and listening – thrown, without any obvious cause, into great excitement. But now the lights disappear from the upper rooms, the sounds of footsteps and talking give place to snores, the watchman begins his periodic tapping on his board, the garden grows both brighter and more mysterious as the streaks of red light vanish from the windows, the last candle passes from the pantry to the ante-room (throwing a glimmer into the dewy garden as it does so), and I glimpse the stooping figure of Foka in a blouse, and carrying the candle, on his way to bed. Often I would find a great and fearful pleasure in stealing over the wet grass in the black shadow of the house until I had reached the ante-room window, where I would stand listening with bated breath to the snoring of the boy, to Foka's gruntings (which he thought no one could hear), and to the sound of his aged voice as he drawled out very slowly his evening prayers. At length even his candle was extinguished, and the window slammed down, so that I found myself utterly alone; where-upon, glancing nervously from side to side, lest I should see a woman in white standing near a flower-bed or by my couch, I ran at full speed back to the verandah. Then, and only then, would I lie down with my face to the garden, and covering myself over so far as possible from the mosquitoes and bats, fall to gazing in front of me as I listened to the sounds of the night and dreamt of love and happiness.

At such times everything would take on for me a different meaning. The look of the old birch-trees, with the one side of their leafy branches showing bright against the moonlit sky and the other darkening the bushes and carriage-drive with their black shadows; the calm, rich glitter of the pond, ever swelling like a sound; the moonlit sparkle of the dewdrops on the flowers in front of the verandah; the graceful shadows of those flowers where they lay thrown upon the grey flower-bed; the cry of a quail on the far side of the pond; the voice of someone walking on the high road; the quiet, scarcely audible scraping of two old birch-trees against one another; the humming of a mosquito at my ear under the coverlet; the fall of an apple as it caught against a branch and rustled among the dry leaves; the leapings of frogs as they approached almost to the verandah-steps and sat with the moon shining mysteriously on their green backs – all these things took on for me a strange significance – the significance of overwhelming beauty and of unrealised happiness. Before me would rise *she*, with a long black plait of hair and a full bosom, always mournful in her fairness, with bare arms and voluptuous embraces. She loved me, and for one moment of her love I would sacrifice my whole life. – But the moon would go on rising higher and higher and shining brighter and brighter in the heavens; the rich sparkle of the pond would swell like a sound and become ever more and more brilliant, while the shadows grew blacker and blacker, and the sheen of the moon more and more transparent: until, as I looked at and listened to all this, something would say to me that even *she* with the bare arms and voluptuous embraces did not represent anything approaching *all* happiness, that love for her was far from being *all* bliss; so that the more I gazed at the full, high-riding moon, the higher would true beauty and goodness appear to me to lie, and the purer and purer they would seem – the nearer and nearer to Him who is the source of all beauty and all goodness. And tears of unsatisfied yet tumultuous joy would fill my eyes.

And yet I was still alone; and still it seemed to me that although great, mysterious Nature could draw the shining disc of the moon to herself, and somehow hold in some high, indefinite place the pale-blue sky, and be everywhere around me, and fill of herself the infinity of space, while I was but a lowly worm, already defiled with the poor, petty passions of humanity, yet endowed also with all the infinite mighty power of imagination and love – always it seemed to me that, nevertheless, Nature and the moon and I were one and the same.

XXXIII
OUR NEIGHBOURS

I was greatly astonished the first day after our arrival to hear Papa speak of our neighbours the Epifanovs as 'extremely nice people,' and still more so that he had been to call on them. The fact was that we had long been at law with this family over some land. When a child, I had more than once heard Papa raging over the litigation, abusing the Epifanovs, and sending for various people (so I understood him) to protect himself against them. Likewise I had heard Yakov speak of them as 'our enemies' and 'black people,' and could remember Mamma requesting that their names should never be mentioned in her presence, nor indeed in her house.

From these *data* I as a child had arrived at the clear and assured conviction that the Epifanovs were foemen of ours who would at any time stab or strangle both Papa and his son if they should ever come across them, and that they were 'black people' in the literal sense of the term. Consequently, when, in the year that Mamma died, I chanced to catch sight of Avdotya Vasilyevna Epifanova ('*la belle Flamande*') caring for my sick mother, I found it hard to believe that she came of a family of negroes. All the same, I had the lowest possible opinion of the family, and for all that we saw much of them that summer, continued to be strongly prejudiced against them. As a matter of fact their household consisted only of the mother (a widow of fifty, but a very well-preserved, cheery old lady), a beautiful daughter named Avdotya Vasilyevna, and a son, Pyotr Vasilyevich, a retired lieutenant, who was a stammerer, unmarried, and of very serious disposition.

For some twenty years before her husband's death Madame Epifanova had lived apart from him – sometimes in Petersburg, where she had relatives, but mainly in her village of Mytishchi, which was some three versts from ours. Yet the neighbourhood had taken to circulating such horrible tales concerning her mode of life that Messalina was by comparison a blameless child: which was why my mother had requested the very name of Epifanov never to be mentioned. As a matter of fact, not one-tenth part of the most cruel of all gossip – the gossip of country-houses – is worthy of credence; and although, when I first made Madame Epifanova's acquaintance, she had living with her in the house a clerk named Mitusha who had been promoted from a serf and who, curled, pomaded, and dressed in a frockcoat of Circassian pattern, always stood behind his mistress's chair at dinner, while from time to time she invited her guests in French to admire his handsome eyes and mouth, there was nothing in the least like what gossip continued to allege. I believe too that since the time – ten years earlier – when she had recalled her dutiful son Pyotr from the service, she had wholly changed her mode of living. Her property was not a large one – merely a hundred souls or so – and during her previous life of gaiety she had spent a great deal. So that some ten years ago those portions of the property which had been mortgaged and re-mortgaged had been foreclosed upon and compulsorily sold by auction. In this extremity Anna Dmitrievna had come to the conclusion that all these unpleasant details of trusteeship, distress upon and valuation of her property and the appearance of the bailiffs, had been due not so much to failure to pay the interest as to the fact that she was a woman: wherefore she had written to her son (then serving with his regiment) to come and save his mother from her embarrassments. He, like a dutiful son, conceiving that his first duty was to comfort his mother in her old age (as he quite sincerely wrote to her in his letters), had straightway resigned his commission (for all that he had been doing well in his profession, and was hoping soon to become independent) and had come to join her in the country.

Despite his plain face, uncouth demeanour, and his stutter, Pyotr was a man of unswerving principles and of an unusually practical mind. Somehow – by small borrowings, sundry strokes of business, petitions for grace, and promises to repay – he contrived to carry on the property, and having become a landed proprietor, donned his father's greatcoat (still preserved in a store-room), dispensed with horses and carriages, discouraged guests from calling at Mytishchi, dug drains, increased his arable land and curtailed that of the serfs, had his own timber felled by his serfs and sold profitably, and saw to matters generally. Indeed he swore, and kept his oath, that until all outstanding debts were paid he would never wear any coat than his father's greatcoat and a sail-cloth jacket which he had made for himself, nor ride in anything but a country waggon drawn by peasants' horses. This stoical mode of life he sought to apply also to his family, as far as the obsequious respect which he conceived to be his mother's due would permit; so that although in the drawing-room he would show her only stuttering servility and fulfil all her wishes, and blame anyone who did not do precisely as she bid them, in his study or his office he would sternly call to account anyone who killed a duck for the table without his orders, or anyone responsible for sending a serf (even though at Madame's own bidding) to inquire after a neighbour's health or for despatching the peasant girls into the wood to gather raspberries instead of setting them to weed the kitchen-garden.

Within four years or so every debt had been repaid, and Pyotr had gone to Moscow and returned thence in new clothes and a *tarantass*.[1] Yet despite this flourishing position of affairs he still preserved the stoical tendencies in which he took a certain vague pride before his own people and strangers, since he would frequently say with a stutter: 'Anyone who *really* wishes to see me will be glad to see me even in a peasant sheepskin, and to eat cabbage-soup and buckwheat porridge at my table. That is what I eat myself,' he would add. In his every word and movement spoke pride based upon a consciousness of having sacrificed himself for his mother and redeemed the property, as well as contempt for others who had done nothing of the kind.

The mother and daughter were altogether different characters from Pyotr, as well as altogether different from one another. The mother was one of the most agreeable, uniformly good-tempered, and cheerful women whom one

1 A two-wheeled carriage.

could possibly meet. Anything attractive and genuinely happy delighted her. Even the faculty of being pleased with the sight of young people enjoying themselves (it is only in the best-natured of elderly folk that one meets with that *trait*) she possessed to the full. On the other hand, her daughter Avdotya Vasilyevna was of a grave turn of mind, or rather she had that peculiarly careless, absent-minded, gratuitously distant bearing which commonly distinguishes unmarried beauties. When she tried to be gay her gaiety somehow seemed to be unnatural to her, so that she always appeared to be laughing either at herself or at the persons to whom she was speaking or at the world in general – a thing which she most likely had no real intention of doing. Often I asked myself in astonishment what she could mean when she said something like, 'Yes, I know how terribly good-looking I am,' or, 'Of course every-one is in love with me,' and so on. Her mother Anna Dmitrievna was a person always busy, since she had a passion for housekeeping, gardening, flowers, canaries, and pretty trinkets. Her rooms and garden, it is true, were not large or luxurious, yet everything in them was so neat and methodical, and had a general air of that gentle gaiety which one hears expressed in a pretty waltz or polka, that the word 'toy' by which guests often expressed their praise of it all exactly suited her surroundings. And Anna Dmitrievna herself was a 'toy' – being *petite*, slender, fresh-complexioned, small- and pretty-handed, and invariably gay and well-dressed. The only fault in her was that a slight over-prominence of the dark-blue veins on her little hands rather marred the general effect. On the other hand, her daughter Avdotya Vasilyevna scarcely ever did any-thing at all. Not only had she no love for trifling with flowers and trinkets, but she even neglected her personal appearance, and was always obliged to run away and change when guests happened to call. Yet on returning to the room in society costume, she always looked extremely handsome – save for that cold, uniform expression of eyes and smile which is com-mon to all very beautiful faces. In fact her strictly regular, beautiful face and shapely figure forever seemed to be saying to you, 'Yes, you may look at me if you wish.'

At the same time, for all the mother's liveliness of disposition and the daughter's air of indifference and abstraction, something told one that the former had never, either now or in the past, felt affection for anything that was not pretty and gay, but that Avdotya Vasilyevna, on the contrary, was one of those natures which, once they love, are willing to sacrifice their whole life for the one they adore.

XXXIV
MY FATHER'S SECOND MARRIAGE

MY father was forty-eight when he took as his second wife Avdotya Vasilyevna Epifanova.

I suspect that when, that spring, he had departed for the country with the girls, he had been in that restlessly happy, sociable mood in which gamblers usually find themselves who have retired from play after making large winnings. He had felt that he still had a good supply of unexpected luck left to him which, so long as he did not squander it on gaming, might be used for success in other things in life. Moreover it was springtime, he was unexpectedly well supplied with ready money, he was entirely alone, and he had nothing to do. As he conversed with Yakov on business matters and remembered both the interminable suit with the Epifanovs and the beautiful Avdotya Vasilyevna (it was a long while since he had seen her), I can imagine him saying: 'How do you think we ought to act in this suit, Yakov Kharlapych? My idea is simply to let that cursed bit of land go. Eh? What do you think about it?' I can imagine too how, thus interrogated, Yakov twisted his fingers behind his back in a deprecatory sort of way, and proceeded to argue that 'Furthermore, Pyotr Alexandrovich, we are in the right.'

Nevertheless Papa ordered the calash to be got ready, put on his fashionable olive-coloured driving-coat, brushed up the remnants of his hair, sprinkled his handkerchief with scent, and greatly pleased to think that he was acting in the style of a lord of the manor (and revelling even more in the prospect of soon seeing a pretty woman), drove off to visit his neighbours.

I only know that on his first visit Papa failed to find Pyotr Epifanov, who was out in the fields, and spent an hour or two in the company of the ladies. I can well imagine how he scattered compliments, how he charmed them, tapping on the floor with his soft boots as he spoke to them in his lisping voice with honeyed looks. I can imagine too how the cheerful older lady must have taken a sudden tender liking to him, and how her cold and beautiful daughter brightened up.

When a housemaid ran breathlessly to inform Pyotr Epifanov that old Irtenyev himself had arrived, I can imagine him answering angrily, 'Well, what if he has come?' and, how in consequence he walked home with as little hurry as possible, and perhaps even first went into his study to put on his dirty old jacket, and then sent down word to the cook that on no account whatever – no, not even if she were ordered to do so by the mistress herself – was she to lay on anything extra for dinner.

Since later I often saw Papa with Epifanov, I can form a very good idea of this first interview between them. I can imagine that, despite Papa's proposal to end the suit in a peaceful manner, Pyotr Vasilyevich was morose and resentful at the thought of having sacrificed his career to his mother, while Papa had done nothing of the kind – a by no means surprising circumstance, Pyotr Vasilyevich probably said to himself. And I can see Papa taking no notice of this ill-humour, but cracking quips and jests, Pyotr Vasilyevich treating him as a strange kind of humorist – by which Pyotr Vasilyevich felt offended one moment and inclined to be reconciled the next. Indeed, with his inclination to make fun of everything, Papa often used to address Pyotr Vasilyevich for some reason as 'Colonel'; and though I can remember Pyotr Vasilyevich once replying, with an unusually violent stutter and his face scarlet with vexation, that he had never been a c-c-c-colonel, but only a l-l-lieutenant, Papa called him 'Colonel' again before another five minutes were out.

Lyuba told me that up to the time of Volodya's and my arrival from Moscow they had been seeing the Epifanovs daily, and that things had been very lively, since Papa, who had a genius for arranging everything with a touch of originality and wit, and in a simple and refined manner, had devised shooting and fishing parties and fireworks for the Epifanovs' benefit. All these festivities – so said Lyuba – would have gone off even more splendidly but for the intolerable Pyotr Vasilyevich, who had spoilt everything by his puffing and stuttering.

After our coming, however, the Epifanovs visited us only twice, and we went over once to their house, while after St Peter's Day (on which, it being Papa's name-day, the Epifanovs called upon us in common with a crowd of other guests) our relations with that family for some reason came entirely to an end, and only Papa continued to go to see them.

During the brief period when I saw Papa and Dunyechka (as her mother called Avdotya) together, this is what I remarked about them. Papa remained unceasingly in the same buoyant mood as had so greatly struck me on the day after our arrival. So gay and youthful and full of life and happy did he seem that the beams of his felicity shone upon all around him, and involuntarily infected them with a similar mood. He never stirred from Avdotya's side so long as she was in the room, but either kept on plying her with sugary-sweet compliments which made me feel ashamed for him or, with his gaze fixed upon her with an air at once passionate and complacent, sat twitching his shoulder and coughing as from time to time he smiled and whispered something in her ear. Yet throughout he wore the same expression of raillery as was peculiar to him even in the most serious matters.

Avdotya herself seemed to have been infected by the happiness which I had noticed on Papa's face, and it shone almost continuously at this period in her large blue eyes; yet there were moments when she would be seized with such a fit of shyness that I, who knew the feeling well, was full of sympathy and compassion as I saw her embarrassment. At such moments she seemed to be afraid of every glance and every movement – to be supposing that everyone was looking at her, everyone thinking of no one but her, and that unfavourably. She would glance timidly from one person to another, the colour coming and going in her cheeks, and then begin to talk loudly and defiantly, but, for the most part, nonsense; until presently, realising this and supposing that Papa and everyone else had heard her, she would blush more painfully than ever. Yet Papa never noticed her nonsense, for he was too much taken up with coughing and with gazing at her with his look of happy, triumphant devotion. I noticed that although these fits of shyness attacked Avdotya Vasilyevna without any visible cause, they not infrequently followed the mention in Papa's hearing of one or another young and beautiful woman. Frequent transitions from depression to that strange, awkward gaiety of hers to which I have referred before; the repetition of favourite words and turns of speech of Papa's; the continuation with others of discussions which Papa had already begun – all these things, if my father had not been the principal actor in the matter and if I had been a little older, would have made clear to me the relations subsisting between him and Avdotya Vasilyevna. At the time, however, I never surmised anything – not even when Papa received in my presence a letter from her brother Pyotr Vasilyevich which so upset him that he did not call upon the Epifanovs again until the end of August.

Then, however, he began his visits once more, and ended by informing us, on the day before Volodya and I were to return to Moscow, that he was about to take Avdotya Vasilyevna Epifanova to be his wife.

XXXV

HOW WE RECEIVED THE NEWS

EVEN the day before the official announcement everyone in the house already knew of the matter, and reacted to it in a variety of ways. Mimi never left her room that day and wept copiously. Katya kept her company, and only came down for dinner, with a grieved expression on her face, manifestly borrowed from her mother. Lyuba on the other hand was very cheerful, and told us at dinner that she knew of a splendid secret, but was going to tell no one.

'There is nothing so splendid about your secret,' said Volodya, who did not in the least share her satisfaction. 'If you were capable of any serious thought at all, you would understand that it is on the contrary a very bad look-out for us.'

Lyuba stared at him in amazement and said no more. After the meal was over Volodya was on the point of taking me by the arm, and then, fearing that this would seem too much like 'affection,' nudged my elbow gently and nodded in the direction of the *salon*.

'You know, I suppose, what the secret is of which Lyuba was speaking?' he said when he was sure that we were alone. It was seldom that he and I spoke together in confidence about anything important: with the result that whenever it came about we felt a kind of awkwardness in one another's presence, and 'we began to see specks before our eyes,' as Volodya put it. On this occasion, however, he answered the embarrassment in my eyes with a grave, fixed look which said: 'You need not be alarmed, for we are brothers, and we have to consult on an important family matter.' I understood him, and he went on:

'You know, I suppose, that Papa is going to marry the Epifanov girl?'

I nodded, for I had already heard so.

'Well, it is not at all a good thing,' continued Volodya.

'Why so?'

'Why?' he repeated irritably. 'Because it will be so pleasant, won't it, to have this stuttering "colonel" and all his family for relations! Certainly *she* seems nice enough – as yet; but who knows what she will turn out to be later? It won't matter much to you or myself, but Lyuba will soon be making her *début* in society, and it will hardly be nice for her to have such a "*belle-mère*"[1] as this – a woman who speaks French badly and has no manners to teach her. She is a little fishwife, that is all she is – a kindly one no doubt, but still a little fishwife,' concluded Volodya, clearly much pleased with the appellation 'fishwife.'

1 Stepmother.

Although it seemed odd to hear Volodya criticising Papa's choice so coolly, I felt that he was right.

'Why does he want to marry her?' I asked.

'Oh, it is a hole-and-corner business, and God only knows why,' he answered. 'All I know is that her brother, Pyotr Vasilyevich, tried to talk him into the marriage, even insisted on it, and that although at first Papa would not hear of it he afterwards took some fancy or some sort of knight-errantry into his head. But it is a mysterious business altogether. I am only just beginning to understand my father' – the fact that Volodya called Papa 'my father' instead of 'Papa' hurt me deeply – 'and though I can see that he is a fine man, kind and clever, he is irresponsible and frivolous to a degree that – well, the whole thing is astonishing. He cannot so much as *look* upon a woman calmly. You yourself know how he falls in love with everyone that he meets. You know that it is so – even Mimi.'

'What do you mean?' I said.

'What I say. Not long ago I learnt that he was in love with Mimi herself when she was young, and that he used to send her poetry, and that there really *was* something between them. Mimi is heartbroken about it to this day' – and Volodya burst out laughing.

'Impossible!' I cried in astonishment.

'But the principal thing at this moment,' went on Volodya, becoming serious again and suddenly switching into French, 'is to think how delighted all our relations will be with this marriage! And she is bound to have children!'

Volodya's prudence and forethought struck me so forcibly that I had no answer to make. Just at this moment Lyuba came up to us.

'So you know?' she said with a joyful face.

'Yes,' said Volodya. 'Still, I am surprised at you, Lyuba. You are no longer a baby in long clothes. Why should you be so pleased because Papa is going to marry a piece of trash?'

At this Lyuba's face fell, and she became serious.

'Oh, Volodya!' she exclaimed. 'Why "a piece of trash," indeed? How can you dare to speak of Avdotya Vasilyevna like that? If Papa is going to marry her she *cannot* be "trash."'

'No, not trash, so to speak, but——'

'No "buts" at all!' interrupted Lyuba, flaring up.

'You have never heard *me* call the girl whom *you* are in love with "trash"! How, then, can you speak so of Papa and a respectable woman? Although you are my elder brother, I won't *allow* you to speak like that! You ought not to!'

'Mayn't I even express an opinion about——'

'No, you mayn't!' repeated Lyuba. 'No one ought to criticise such a father as ours. Mimi has the right to, but not you, however much you may be the eldest brother.'

'Oh, you don't understand *anything*,' said Volodya contemptuously. 'Try and do so. How can it be a good thing that some "Dunyechka" of an Epifanova should take the place of your dead mamma?'

For a moment Lyuba was silent. Then the tears suddenly came into her eyes.

'I knew that you were *conceited*, but I never thought that you could be so spiteful,' she said, and left us.

'Balderdash!' said Volodya, pulling a serio-comic face and make-believe-stupid eyes. 'That's what comes of arguing with them.' Evidently he felt that he was at fault in having so far forgotten himself as to condescend to discuss matters at all with Lyuba.

Next day the weather was bad, and neither Papa nor the ladies had come down to morning tea when I entered the drawing-room. There had been a cold autumnal rain in the night, and remnants of the clouds from which it had descended were still scudding across the sky, with the sun's luminous disc (already high in the heavens) showing faintly through them. It was a windy, damp, grey morning. The door into the garden was standing open, and pools left by the night's rain were drying on the damp-blackened floor of the terrace. The open door, fastened back on its iron hook, was shaking in the wind, and all the paths looked damp and muddy. The old birch-trees with their naked white branches, the bushes, the turf, the nettles, the currant-trees, the elder with the pale side of its leaves turned upwards – all were dashing themselves about and looking as though they were trying to wrench themselves free from their roots. From the avenue of lime-trees showers of round yellow leaves were flying through the air in tossing, eddying circles until, wet through, they came to rest on the wet road and the damp dark-green after-grass of the meadow. At the moment my thoughts were wholly taken up with my father's approaching marriage, which I saw from the same point of view as Volodya. The future seemed to me to bode no good for any of us, my father included. I felt distressed to think that a woman who was not only a stranger but a *young* woman should be going to associate with us in so many relations of life, without having any right to do so — nay, that this *young* woman was going to usurp the place of our dead mother. I felt depressed, and kept thinking more and more that my father was to blame in the matter. Just then I heard his voice and Volodya's speaking together in the pantry, and not wishing to meet Papa just then, I stepped outside, but I was pursued by Lyuba, who said that Papa wanted to see me.

He was standing in the drawing-room, with one hand resting on the piano, gazing in my direction with an air at once grave and impatient. His face no longer wore the youthful, gay expression which had struck me for so long, but on the contrary, looked sad. Volodya was walking about the room with a pipe in his hand. I approached my father and wished him good morning.

'Well, my friends,' he said resolutely, with a lift of his head and in the peculiarly hurried manner of one who wishes to announce something obviously unwelcome, but no longer admitting of reconsideration, 'you know, I suppose, that I am going to marry Avdotya Vasilyevna.' He paused a moment. 'I never intended to marry anyone else after your mother, but...' — and again he paused — 'it — it is evidently my fate. Dunyechka is an excellent, kind-hearted girl, and no longer in her first youth. I hope, my children, that you will come to love her, and she, I know, is sincerely fond of you, for she is a good woman. And now,' he went on, addressing himself more particularly to Volodya and myself, and apparently speaking hurriedly to prevent us from interrupting him, 'it is time for you to depart, while I myself am going to stay here until the

New Year, and then to follow you to Moscow with' – again he
hesitated a moment – 'my wife and Lyuba.' It hurt me to see my
father standing as though abashed and guilty before us, so I
moved a little nearer him, but Volodya only went on walking
about the room with his head down, and smoking.

'So, my friends, that is what your old father has planned
to do,' concluded Papa – reddening, coughing, and holding
out his hands to Volodya and me. Tears were in his eyes as
he said this, and I noticed too that the hand which he held out
to Volodya (who at that moment was at the far end of
the room) was shaking slightly. The sight of that shaking
hand gave me a painful shock, for I remembered that Papa
had served in the 1812 campaign, and had been, as everyone knew, a brave officer. Seizing his large hand with its
prominent veins, I kissed it and he squeezed mine hard in
return. Then, with a sob amid his tears, he suddenly threw
his arms around Lyuba's dark head and kissed her again and
again on the eyes. Volodya pretended that he had dropped his
pipe, and bending down, wiped his eyes furtively with the
back of his hand. Then, trying to be inconspicuous, he left
the room.

XXXVI

THE UNIVERSITY

THE wedding was to take place in two weeks' time, but as our
lectures were starting Volodya and I returned to Moscow at
the beginning of September. The Nekhlyudovs had also
returned from the country, and Dmitri (with whom, on parting, I had made an agreement that we should correspond
frequently, and of course we had never once written to one
another) came to see us immediately after our arrival and
arranged to escort me to the University for my first lecture on
the morrow.

It was a beautiful sunny day.

No sooner had I entered the auditorium than I felt
my personality disappearing amid the swarm of lighthearted youths who were seething tumultuously through

every doorway and corridor in the brilliant sunlight pouring in through the great windows. I found the sense of being a member of this huge community very pleasing, yet there were few among the throng whom I knew, and that only on terms of a nod and a 'How do you do, Irtenyev?' All around me men were shaking hands and chatting together; from every side came expressions of friendship, laughter, jests, and *badinage*. Everywhere I could feel the tie which bound this youthful society in one, and everywhere, too, I could feel that it left me out. Yet this impression lasted for a moment only and was succeeded, together with the vexation which it had caused, by the idea that it was best that I should *not* belong to all that society, but keep to my own circle of *gentlemen*; wherefore I proceeded to seat myself upon the third bench, with, as neighbours, Count B, Baron Z, Prince R, Ivin, and some other young men of the same class – of whom I was acquainted with Ivin and Count B. Yet the look which these young gentlemen threw at me at once made me feel that I was not of their set, and I turned to observe what was going on around me. Semyonov, with grey, tousled hair, white teeth, and frock-coat flying open, was seated a little distance off, leaning forward on his elbows as he nibbled a pen, while the gymnasium student who had come out first in the examinations had established himself on the front bench, and still with a black stock tied round his cheek, was toying with the silver watch-key which hung on his satin waistcoat. On a bench in a raised part of the hall I could descry Ikonin (who had contrived to enter the University somehow), and hear him fussily proclaiming, in all the glory of blue piped trousers which completely hid his boots, that he was now seated on Parnassus. Ilyenka – who had surprised me by giving me a bow not only cold, but supercilious, as though to remind me that here we were all equals – was just in front of me, with his thin legs resting in free and easy style on another bench (for my benefit, I thought), and conversing with a student as he threw occasional glances in my direction. Ivin's set by my side were talking in French, yet these gentlemen seemed to me terribly stupid. Every word which I overheard of their conversation appeared both silly and incorrect, not French at all ('*Ce n'est pas français,*' I thought to myself), while all the attitudes, utterances, and doings of Semyonov, Ilyenka, and the rest struck me as uniformly coarse, ungentlemanly, and not '*comme il faut.*'

Thus, attached to no particular set, I felt isolated and unable to make friends, and so grew resentful. One of the students on the bench in front of me kept biting his nails, which were all hangnails already, and this so disgusted me that I edged away from him. In short, I remember finding my first day a most depressing affair.

When the professor entered and there was a general stir and a cessation of chatter, I remember throwing a scornful glance at him, also that he began his discourse with a sentence which I thought made no sense. I had expected the lecture to be from first to last so clever that not a word could have been taken from or added to it. Disappointed in this, I at once proceeded to draw beneath the heading 'First Lecture' which I had inscribed in my beautifully-bound notebook no fewer than eighteen faces in profile, joined together in a sort of chaplet, and only occasionally moved my hand along the page in order to give the professor (who, I felt sure, must be greatly interested in me) the impression that I was taking notes. In fact, at this very first lecture I came to the decision which I maintained to the end of my course, namely that it was unnecessary and even stupid to take down every word said by every professor.

At subsequent lectures, however, I did not feel my isolation so strongly, since I made several acquaintances and got into the way of shaking hands and entering into conversation. Yet for some reason or another no real intimacy ever sprang up between us, and I often found myself depressed and only feigning cheerfulness. With the set which comprised Ivin and 'the aristocrats,' as they were generally known, I could not make any headway at all, for as I now remember, I was always unsociable and churlish to them and bowed to them only when they bowed to me; so that they evidently had little need of my acquaintance. With most of the other students, however, this arose from quite a different cause. As soon as I discerned friendliness on the part of a comrade, I at once gave him to understand that I dined with Prince Ivan Ivanych and kept my own drozhki. All this I said merely to show myself in the most favourable light in his eyes, and to induce him to like me all the more; yet almost invariably the only result of my communicating to him the information about the drozhki and my relationship to Prince Ivan Ivanych was that, to my astonishment, he at once adopted a cold and haughty bearing towards me.

Among us we had a Crown scholarship student named Operov – a very modest, industrious, and clever young fellow, who always offered one his hand like a slab of wood (that is to say, without closing his fingers or making the slightest movement with them); with the result that his comrades often did the same to him in jest, and called it the 'deal board' way of shaking hands. He and I nearly always sat next to one another, and often conversed. In particular he pleased me with the freedom with which he would criticise the professors as he pointed out to me with great clearness and acumen the merits or demerits of their respective ways of teaching, and even made occasional fun of them. Such remarks I found exceedingly striking and diverting, uttered in his quiet voice from his diminutive month. Nevertheless he never let a lecture pass without taking careful notes of it in his fine handwriting, and eventually, starting to became friends, we decided to join forces and to do our preparation together. Things had progressed to the point of his always turning his small grey, myopic eyes towards me and looking pleased when I took my usual seat beside him until, unfortunately, I one day found it necessary to inform him that my mother, on her death bed, had besought my father never to allow us to enter for an institution supported by the government, and that I myself considered Crown scholars, no matter how clever, to be – 'well, *ce ne sont pas des gens comme il faut*,'[1] I concluded, though beginning to flounder a little and feeling myself grow red. At that moment Operov said nothing, but at subsequent lectures he ceased to greet me first or to offer me his board-like hand, and never

1 They are not *gentlemen*.

attempted to talk to me, but as soon as I sat down he would lean his head upon his arm and purport to be absorbed in his notebooks. I was surprised at this sudden inexplicable coolness, but looked upon it as *infra dig*. '*pour un jeune homme de bonne maison*'[1] to curry favour with a mere Crown scholar like Operov, and so left him severely alone – though I confess that his aloofness hurt my feelings. On one occasion I arrived before him, and since the lecture was to be delivered by a popular professor whom students came to hear who did not usually attend such functions, I found almost every seat occupied. Accordingly I secured Operov's place for myself by spreading my notebooks on the desk before it; after which I left the room again for a moment. When I returned I saw that my notebooks had been relegated to the bench behind, and the place taken by Operov himself. I remarked to him that I had already secured it by placing my notebooks there.

'I know nothing about that,' he replied sharply, yet without looking up at me.

'I tell you I put my notebooks there,' I repeated, purposely trying to bluster in the hope of intimidating him with my hostility. 'Everyone saw me do it,' I added, including the students near me in my glance. Several of them looked at me with curiosity, yet none of them spoke.

'Seats cannot be booked here,' said Operov. 'Whoever first sits down in a place keeps it,' and settling himself angrily where he was, he flashed at me a glance of defiance.

'Well, that only means that you are a cad,' I said.

I have an idea that he murmured something about my being 'a stupid young idiot,' but I decided not to hear it. What would be the use, I asked myself, of my hearing it? That we should brawl like a couple of *manants*[2] over less than nothing? (I was very fond of the word *manant*, and often used it as an answer and a solution in many awkward situations.) Perhaps I should have said something more had not, at that moment, a door slammed and the professor (dressed in a

1 For a young man of good family.
2 Louts.

blue frockcoat, and shuffling his feet as he walked) ascended the rostrum.

Nevertheless, when the examination was about to come on and I had need of someone's notebooks, Operov remembered his promise to lend me his, and we did our preparation together.

XXXVII
AFFAIRS OF THE HEART

Affaires du cœur occupied me a good deal that winter. In fact, I was in love three times. The first time I became passionately enamoured of a very buxom lady whom I used to see riding at Freitag's riding-school; with the result that every day when she was taking a lesson there (that is to say, every Tuesday and Friday) I used to go to gaze at her, but always in such a state of trepidation lest I should be seen that I stood a long way off, and bolted directly I thought her likely to pass the spot where I was standing. Likewise I used to turn round so carelessly whenever she appeared to be glancing in my direction that I never even saw her face properly, and to this day do not know whether she was really beautiful or not.

Dubkov, who was acquainted with her, surprised me one day in the riding-school, where I was lurking concealed behind the lady's footmen and the fur wraps which they were holding, and having heard from Dmitri of my infatuation, frightened me so terribly by proposing to introduce me to this Amazon that I fled headlong from the riding-school, and was prevented by the mere thought that possibly he had told her about me from ever entering the place again, or even going as far as the place where the footmen waited, lest I should encounter her.

Whenever I fell in love with ladies whom I did not know, and especially married women, I experienced a shyness a thousand times greater than I had ever felt with Sonya. I dreaded beyond measure that my divinity should learn of my passion, or even of my existence, since I felt sure that once she had done so she would be so terribly offended that I should never be forgiven for my presumption. And indeed, if the Amazon referred to above had ever come to know how I used to stand behind the footmen and dream of seizing her and carrying her off to some country spot – if she had ever come to know what I should have done to her there, it is probable that she would have had very good cause for indignation. But I always failed to consider that even if she were to get to know me, she would not at once be able to divine these thoughts, and that there could, therefore, be nothing shameful in merely being introduced.

As my second *affaire du cœur* I fell in love once more with Sonya when I saw her at her sister's. My second passion for her had long since come to an end, but I became enamoured of her this third time through Lyuba giving me a copy-book in which Sonya had copied some extracts from Lermontov's *The Demon*, with certain of the more gloomily amorous passages underlined in red ink and marked with pressed flowers. Remembering how Volodya had been wont to kiss his *lady-love's* purse last year, I essayed to do the same thing now; and really, when alone in my room in the evening and engaged in dreaming as I looked at a flower or occasionally pressed it to my lips, I would feel a certain pleasantly lachrymose mood steal over me, and remain genuinely in love (or suppose myself to be so) for at least several days.

Finally, my third *affaire du cœur* that winter was connected with the lady with whom Volodya was in love, and who used occasionally to visit at our house. Yet in this damsel, as I now remember, there was not a single attractive feature to be found – or, at all events, none of those which usually pleased me. She was the daughter of a well-known Moscow lady of wit and learning and, *petite* and slender, wore long flaxen curls after the English fashion, and could boast of a limpid profile. Everyone said that she was even cleverer and more learned than her mother, but I was never in a position to judge of that, since, overcome with craven bashfulness at the mere thought of her intellect and accomplishments, I never spoke to her alone but once, and then with unaccountable trepidation. Volodya's enthusiasm, however (for the presence of an audience never prevented him from giving vent to his rapture), communicated itself to me so strongly that I also became passionately enamoured of the young lady. Yet, conscious that he would not be pleased to know that *two brothers were in love with the same maiden*, I never told him of my condition. On the contrary, I took special delight in the thought that our love was so pure that, though its object was in both cases the same charming being, we should remain friends and be ready, if ever the occasion should arise, to sacrifice ourselves for one another. Yet I have an idea that, as regards self-sacrifice, he did not quite share my views; for he was so passionately in love with the lady that once he was for giving a member of the diplomatic corps, who was said to be going to marry her, a slap in the face and a challenge to a duel; but for my part I gladly sacrificed my feelings for his sake, possibly because it cost me no great effort, seeing that the only remark I had ever addressed to her had been on the subject of the merits of classical music, and that my passion, for all my efforts to keep it alive, expired the following week.

XXXVIII
SOCIETY

As regards those social delights to which I had intended, on entering the University, to surrender myself in imitation of my brother, I underwent a complete disillusionment that winter. Volodya danced a great deal, and Papa also went to balls with his young wife, but I appeared to be thought either too young or unfitted for such delights, and no one invited me to the houses where balls were being given. In spite of my vow of frankness with Dmitri, I never told him (nor anyone else) how much I should have liked to go to those balls, and how I felt hurt at being forgotten and (apparently) taken for the philosopher that I consequently pretended to be.

Nevertheless a reception was to be given that winter at the Princess Kornakova's, and she personally called to invite us all – myself among the rest! Consequently I was to attend my first ball. Before starting, Volodya came into my room to see how I was dressed – an act on his part which greatly surprised me and took me aback. In my opinion (it must be understood) solicitude about one's dress was a shameful thing, and should be kept under, but he seemed to think it a thing so natural and necessary that he said outright that he was afraid I might be put out of countenance on that score. Accordingly he told me to be sure to put on my patent-leather boots, and was horrified to find that I wanted to put on suede gloves. Next he adjusted my watch-chain in a particular manner and carried me off to a hairdresser's near the Kuznetsky Bridge to have my locks coiffured. That done, he withdrew to a little distance, and surveyed me.

'Yes, he looks right enough now,' he said to the hairdresser. 'Only – *couldn't* you smooth down those tufts of his a little?' Yet, for all that Monsieur Charles treated my forelocks with some sticky essence, they persisted in rising up again whenever I put on my hat. In fact, my curled head seemed to me to look far worse than before. My only hope of salvation lay in an *affectation* of casualness. Only in that guise would my appearance be anything like satisfactory.

Volodya was apparently of the same opinion, for he begged me to get rid of the curls, and when I had done so and still looked unpresentable, he ceased to regard me at all, but throughout the drive to the Kornakovs remained silent and depressed.

I entered the Kornakovs' mansion boldly enough alongside Volodya, but when the Princess had invited me to dance, and I, for some reason or other (though I had driven there with no other thought in my head than to dance well), had replied that I never danced, I quite lost my nerve, and left solitary among a crowd of strangers, became plunged in my usual insuperable and ever-growing shyness. I remained silent on that spot almost the whole evening.

While a waltz was in progress one of the young princesses came up to me and asked me, with the sort of formal kindness common to all her family, why I was not dancing. I can remember my alarm at the question, but at the same time – for all my efforts to prevent it – a self-satisfied smile stole over my face as I began talking, in the most inflated and long-winded

French, such rubbish as even now, decades later, it shames me to recall. It must have been the effect of the music, which, while exciting my nervous sensibility, drowned (as I supposed) the less intelligible portion of my utterances. I went on speaking of the exalted company present, and of the futility of men and women, until I had got myself into such a tangle that I was forced to stop short in the middle of a word of a sentence which I found myself unable to conclude.

Even the innately urbane young Princess was shocked by my conduct, and gazed at me in reproach; I smiled. At this critical moment Volodya, who had remarked that I was conversing with great animation and was probably curious to know how I was making up by brilliant conversation for not dancing, approached us with Dubkov. Seeing my smiling face and the Princess's startled mien, and hearing the appalling rubbish with which I concluded my speech, he went red in the face and turned away again. The Princess rose and left me. I continued to smile, but in such a state of agony from the consciousness of my stupidity that I felt ready to sink into the floor. I felt that, come what might, I must move about and say something, in order to effect a change in my position. I approached Dubkov and asked him if he had danced many waltzes with *her* that night. This I feigned to say in a gay and jesting manner, yet in reality I was imploring help of the very Dubkov to whom I had cried 'Hold your tongue!' on the night of the matriculation dinner. By way of answer he made as though he had not heard me, and turned away. Next I approached Volodya, and said with a desperate effort and in a similar tone of assumed gaiety: 'Hullo, Volodya! Are you played out yet?' He merely looked at me as much as to say, 'You don't speak to me like that when we are on our own,' and left me without a word, in the evident fear that I might continue to hang about his person.

'My God! Even my own brother deserts me!' I thought.

Yet somehow I had not the courage to depart, but remained standing where I was until the very end of the evening. At length, when everyone was leaving the room and crowding into the ante-room, and a footman slipped my greatcoat on to

my shoulders in such a way as to tilt up the brim of my hat,
I gave a sickly, half-tearful smile, and remarked to no one in
particular: '*Comme c'est gracieux!*'[1]

XXXIX
THE STUDENTS' CAROUSAL

ALTHOUGH as yet Dmitri's influence had kept me from indulging in those traditional student festivities known as *kutyozhi* or
'wines,' that winter saw me participate in one such function,
and carry away with me a not over-pleasant impression of it.
This is how it came about.

At a lecture soon after the New Year Baron Z – a tall, fair-
haired young fellow of very serious demeanour and regular
features – invited us all to spend a sociable evening with him.
By 'us all' I mean all the men more or less '*comme il faut*' of our
course, and exclusive of Grap, Semyonov, Operov, and com-
moners of that sort. Volodya smiled disdainfully when he heard
that I was going to a 'wine' of first-year men, but I looked to
derive great and unusual pleasure from this, to me, novel
pastime. Accordingly, punctually at the appointed hour of
eight I presented myself at Baron Z's.

Our host, in an open tunic and white waistcoat, received his
guests in the brilliantly lighted *salon* and drawing-room of the
small mansion where his parents lived – they having given up
their reception rooms to him for the evening for the purpose of
this party. In the corridor could be seen the heads and skirts of
inquisitive maids, while in the dining-room I caught a glimpse
of a dress which I imagined to belong to the Baroness herself.
The guests numbered a score and were all of them students
except Herr Frost, who had come with the Ivins, and a tall,
red-faced gentleman in mufti who was superintending the feast
and who was introduced to everyone as a relative of the Baron's
and a former student of the University of Dorpat. At first the
excessive brilliancy and formal arrangement of the reception
rooms had such a chilling effect upon this youthful company

1 How pleasant!

that everyone involuntarily hugged the walls, except a few bolder spirits and the ex-Dorpat student, who, with his waist-coat already unbuttoned, seemed to be in every room and in every corner of every room, at once, and filled the whole place with his resonant, agreeable, never-ceasing tenor voice. The remainder of the guests preferred either to remain silent or to talk in discreet tones about professors, faculties, examinations, and other serious and uninteresting matters. Yet everyone, without exception, kept watching the door of the dining-room, and while trying to conceal the fact, wearing an expression which said: 'Come! It is time to begin.' I too felt that it was time to begin, and awaited the beginning with pleasurable impatience.

After footmen had handed round tea among the guests the Dorpat student asked Frost in Russian:

'Can you make punch, Frost?'

'Oh *ja*!' replied Frost with a joyful wriggle of his calves, and the other went on:

'Then do you set about it' (they addressed each other in the second person singular, as former comrades at Dorpat). Frost accordingly departed to the pantry with great strides of his bowed, muscular legs, and after some walking backwards and forwards from drawing-room to pantry deposited upon the drawing-room table a large soup-tureen, accompanied by a ten-pound sugarloaf supported above it on three students' swords placed crosswise. Meanwhile the Baron had been going round among his guests as they sat regarding the soup-tureen, and addressing them one by one, with a face of immut-able gravity, in the formula: 'I beg of you all to drink of this cup in student fashion to *Bruderschaft*,[1] that there may be good-fellowship among the members of our course. Unbutton your waistcoats, or take them off altogether, as you please.' Already the Dorpat student had divested himself of his coat and rolled up his white shirt-sleeves above his elbows, and now, planting his feet firmly apart, he proceeded to set fire to the rum in the soup-tureen.

1 Brotherhood.

'Gentlemen, put out the candles!' cried the Dorpat student with a sudden shout so loud and insistent that we seemed all of us to be shouting at once. However, we still went on silently regarding the soup-tureen and the white shirt of the Dorpat student, and feeling that the moment of great solemnity had arrived.

'*Löschen Sie die Lichter aus, Frost!*'[1] the Dorpat student shouted again, this time in German, no doubt because he was over-excited. Accordingly everyone helped to extinguish the candles, until the room was in total darkness save for a spot where the white shirts and hands of the three students support- ing the sugarloaf on their crossed swords were lit up by the bluish flames from the bowl. The Dorpat student's tenor voice was not the only one to be heard, for in different quarters of the room resounded chattering and laughter. Many had taken off their coats (especially students whose shirts were of fine cloth and perfectly clean), and I now did the same, with a conscious- ness that '*it*' had 'begun.' There had been no great festivity as yet, but I felt assured that things would go splendidly when once we had begun drinking tumblers of the potion that was now in course of preparation.

The punch was ready and the Dorpat student, with much bespattering of the table as he did so, ladled the liquor into tumblers and cried: 'Now, gentlemen, come along!' When we had each of us taken a brimming sticky tumbler of the stuff, the Dorpat student and Frost sang a German song in which the word '*Juche!*'[2] kept occurring again and again, while we joined in discordant fashion in the chorus. Next we clinked glasses together, shouted something in praise of punch, linked arms, and took our first drink of the sweet, strong mixture. After that there was no further waiting; the 'wine' was in full swing. The first glassful consumed, a second was poured out. Yet, for all that I began to feel a throbbing in my temples, that the flames seemed to be turning blood-red, and that everyone around me was laughing and shouting, things seemed lacking in real gaiety,

1 Put out the lights, Frost!
2 Hurrah!

and I somehow felt that as a matter of fact we were all of us finding the affair rather dull, only for some reason found it necessary to *pretend* that we were enjoying it. The Dorpat student may have been an exception, for he continued to grow more and more red in the face and more and more ubiquitous as he filled up empty glasses and spilled more and more of the sweet, sticky stuff on the table. The precise sequence of events I cannot remember, but I can recall feeling terribly fond of Frost and the Dorpat student that evening, learning their German song by heart, and kissing them each on their sticky-sweet lips; also that that same evening I conceived a violent dislike for the Dorpat student, and was for throwing a chair at him, but restrained myself; also that, besides feeling the same sensation of the independence of all my limbs that I had felt on the night of the matriculation dinner, my head ached and swam so badly that I thought each moment would be my last; also that for some reason or other we all of us sat down on the floor and imitated the movements of rowers in a boat as we sang in chorus, 'Down our mother stream the Volga'; also that I conceived this procedure on our part to be uncalled for; also that I lay prone upon the floor, wrestling gipsy-fashion with legs interlocked; also that I ricked someone's neck, and came to the conclusion that I should never have done such a thing if I had not been drunk; also that we had some supper and another kind of liquor, and that I kept going outside to get some fresh air; also that my head seemed suddenly to grow chill, and that I noticed, as I drove home, that it was terribly dark and that the step of the vehicle was sharply aslant and slippery, and that it was impossible to hang on to Kuzma because he seemed to have turned all flabby and to be waving about like a dish clout. But what I remember best is that throughout the whole of that evening I never ceased to feel that I was acting with excessive stupidity in pretending to be enjoying myself, to like drinking a great deal while being in no way drunk, as well as that everyone else present was acting with equal stupidity in pretending those same things. All the time I had a feeling that each one of my companions was finding the festivities as distasteful as I was myself; but in the belief that he was the only one doing so, felt himself bound to pretend that he was very merry in order not to mar the general hilarity. Also, strange to state, I felt that I ought to keep up this pretence for the sole reason that into a soup-tureen there had been poured three bottles of champagne at ten roubles the bottle and ten bottles of rum at four roubles – making seventy roubles in all, exclusive of the supper. So convinced of my folly did I feel that when, at next day's lecture, those of my comrades who had been at Baron Z's party seemed not only in no way ashamed to remember what they had done, but even talked about it so that other students might hear of their doings, I felt utterly astonished. They all declared that it had been a splendid 'wine,' that Dorpat students were just the fellows for that kind of thing, and that there had been consumed at it no fewer than forty bottles of rum among twenty guests, some of whom had been left senseless under the table. That they should care to talk about such things seemed strange enough, but that they should care to slander themselves seemed absolutely unintelligible.

XL

MY FRIENDSHIP WITH THE NEKHLYUDOVS

THAT winter I saw a great deal both of Dmitri, who often looked us up, and of his family, with whom I was beginning to stand on intimate terms.

The Nekhlyudovs (that is to say, mother, aunt, and daughter) spent their evenings at home, at which time the Princess liked young men to visit her – at all events young men of the kind whom she described as able to spend an evening without cards or dancing. Yet such young fellows must have been few and far between, for although I went to the Nekhlyudovs almost every evening I seldom found other guests present. Thus I came to know the members of this family and their various dispositions well enough to be able to form clear ideas as to their mutual relations, and to be quite at home amid the rooms and furniture of their house. Indeed, so long as no other guests were present I felt entirely at my ease, except on occasions when I was left alone in the room with Varya. I could not rid myself of the idea that, not being a particularly pretty girl, she wanted me to fall in love with her; but in time this embarrassment of mine began to lessen. She managed so naturally to give the impression that it was all the same to her whether she was talking to me or to her brother or to Lyubov Sergeyevna, that I came to look upon her simply as a person to whom it was in no way dangerous or wrong to show that I took pleasure in her company. Throughout the whole of our acquaintance, although she appeared to me at times a plain girl, and at other times not at all bad-looking, I never once asked myself the question, 'Am I, or am I not, in love with her?' Sometimes I would talk to her direct, but more often I did so through Dmitri or Lyubov Sergeyevna; and it was the latter method which gave me the most pleasure. I gained considerable enjoyment from discoursing when she was there, from hearing her sing, and in general, from knowing that she was in the room with me; but it was seldom now that any thoughts of what our future relations might ever be, or that any dreams of self-sacrifice for my friend if he should ever fall in love with my sister, came into my head. If any such ideas or fancies occurred to me I felt satisfied with the present, and drove away all thoughts about the future.

Yet in spite of this intimacy I continued to look upon it as my bounden duty to keep the Nekhlyudovs in general, and Varya in particular, in ignorance of my true feelings and tastes, and strove always to appear altogether another young man than I really was – to appear, indeed, such a young man as could never possibly have existed. I affected to have a passionate nature, and would go off into raptures and exclamations and impassioned gestures whenever I wished it to be thought that anything pleased me, while, on the other hand, I tried always to seem indifferent towards any really unusual circumstance which I myself perceived or which I was told about. I aimed always at figuring both as a sarcastic cynic who held nothing sacred, and as a shrewd observer. I tried to appear logical in all my conduct, precise and methodical in all my ways of life, and at the same time contemptuous of all materiality. I may safely say that I was far better in reality than the strange being into whom I tried to convert myself; yet, whatever I was or was not, the Nekhlyudovs took to me greatly, and (happily for me) evidently took no notice of my play-acting. Only Lyubov Sergeyevna, who, I believe, really believed me to be a great egoist, atheist, and cynic, had no love for me, but frequently disputed what I said, flew into tempers, and left me stunned by her disjointed, irrelevant utterances. Yet Dmitri held always to the same strange, something more than friendly, relations with her, and used to say not only that she was misunderstood by everyone, but that she did him a world of good. This, however, did not prevent the rest of his family from being distressed by his friendship with her.

Once, when talking to me about this incomprehensible attachment, Varya explained the matter thus:

'You see, Dmitri is a vain person. He is very proud, and for all his intellect, very fond of praise, and of amazing people, and of always being *first*, while little Auntie' (the general nickname for Lyubov Sergeyevna) 'is innocent enough to admire him, and at the same time devoid of the tact to conceal her admiration. Consequently she flatters his vanity – not out of pretence, but sincerely.'

This *dictum* I laid to heart, and when thinking it over afterwards could not but come to the conclusion that Varya was very clever; so that I was glad to raise her thenceforth in my regard. Yet, though I was always glad enough to assign her any credit which might arise from my discovering in her character any signs of good sense or other moral qualities, I did so with strict moderation, and never ran to any extreme pitch of enthusiasm in the process. Thus, when Sophia Ivanovna (who was never weary of discussing her niece) related to me how, four years ago in the country, when still a child, Varya had suddenly given away all her dresses and shoes to some peasant children without first asking permission to do so, so that they had subsequently to be recovered, I did not at once accept the fact as entitling Varya to elevation in my opinion; in fact I ridiculed her in my own mind for her unpractical view of things.

When other guests were present at the Nekhlyudovs' (among them, sometimes, Volodya and Dubkov) I used to withdraw myself to a remote plane, and with the complacency and quiet consciousness of strength of an *habitué* of the house, listen to what others were saying without putting in a remark myself. And everything that they said seemed to me so immeasurably stupid that I used to feel inwardly amazed that such a clever, logical woman as the Princess, with her equally logical family, could listen to and respond to such rubbish. Had it, however, entered into my head to compare what others said with what I myself said when there alone, I should probably have ceased to feel surprise. Still less should I have continued to feel surprise had I believed that the women of our own household – Avdotya Vasilyevna, Lyuba, and Katya – were exactly like the rest of their sex and in no way inferior, and remembered the kind of things over which Avdotya and Katya would laugh and jest with Dubkov from one end of an evening to the other; how Dubkov seldom let an evening pass without having seized upon the occasion and read out with deep feeling either some verses beginning '*Au banquet de la vie, infortuné convive . . .*'[1] or extracts from *The Demon*. In short, I should have remembered what nonsense they used to chatter for hours at a time.

It need hardly be said that when guests were present Varya paid less attention to me than when we were alone, and I was deprived of the reading and music which I so greatly loved to hear. When talking to guests she lost, in my eyes, her principal charm – that of quiet seriousness and simplicity. I remember how strange it used to seem to me to hear her discoursing on theatres and the weather to my brother Volodya! I knew that of all things in the world he most despised and shunned banality, and that Varya herself used to make fun of forced conversations on the weather and similar matters. Why then, when meeting in society, did they both of them talk such intolerable nothings, and, as it were, shame one another? After talks of this kind I used to feel silent rage against Varya, as well as next day to poke fun at yesterday's visitors. Yet one result of it was that I derived all the greater pleasure from being alone with the Nekhlyudovs' family circle.

1 At life's banquet, an ill-starred guest . . .

At all events, I began to prefer meeting Dmitri in his mother's drawing-room to being with him alone.

XLI

MY FRIENDSHIP WITH DMITRI NEKHLYUDOV

AT this period indeed, my friendship with Dmitri hung by a hair. I had been criticising him too long not to have discovered faults in his character, for it is only in first youth that we love passionately and therefore love only perfect people. As soon as the mists engendered by love of this kind begin to dissolve, and to be penetrated by the clear beams of reason, we see the object of our adoration in his true shape and with all his virtues and failings exposed. Some of those failings strike us with the exaggerated force of the unexpected, and combine with the instinct for novelty and the hope that perfection may yet be found in a fellow-man, to induce us not only to feel coldness, but even aversion towards the late object of our adoration. Consequently, desiring it no longer, we usually cast it from us with no regret, and pass onwards to seek fresh perfection. If that was not what occurred in my own relationship with Dmitri, I owed it to his stubborn, punctilious, and more critical than impulsive attachment to myself – a tie which I should have felt ashamed to break. Moreover, our strange vow of frankness bound us together. We were afraid that if we parted we should leave in one another's power all the incriminatory moral secrets of which we had made mutual confession. At the same time, our rule of frankness had long ceased to be faithfully observed, but proved a frequent cause of constraint and brought about peculiarly strained relations between us.

Almost every time that winter that I went to see Dmitri, I used to find there a University friend of his named Bezobyedov, with whom he studied. Bezobyedov was a small, slight fellow, with a face pitted over with smallpox, tiny, freckled, hands, and a great mass of red hair much in need of the comb. He was invariably dirty, shabby, uncouth, and not even a hard worker. To me Dmitri's relations with him were as unintelligible as his relations with Lyubov Sergeyevna, and the only reason he could have had for choosing such a man for his associate was that in the whole University there was no worse-looking student than Bezobyedov. Yet that alone would have been enough to make Dmitri defy everybody and extend him his friendship, and as a matter of fact, in all his intercourse with this fellow he seemed to be saying proudly: 'I care nothing who a man may be. In my eyes everyone is equal. I like him, and therefore he is all right.'

Nevertheless I could not imagine how he could bring himself to do it, nor how the wretched Bezobyedov ever contrived to maintain his awkward position. To me the friendship seemed a most distasteful one.

One night I went round to Dmitri's to persuade him to come down for an evening's talk in his mother's drawing-room, where we could also listen to Varya's reading and singing, but Bezobyedov had forestalled me there, and Dmitri answered me curtly that he could not come down, since as I could see for myself, he had a visitor.

'Besides,' he added, 'what is the fun of sitting there? We had much better stay *here* and talk.'

I scarcely relished the prospect of spending a couple of hours in Bezobyedov's company, yet could not make up my mind to go down alone; so, cursing my friend's vagaries, I seated myself in a rocking-chair and began rocking myself silently to and fro. I felt vexed with them both for depriving me of the pleasures of the drawing-room, and my only hope as I listened irritably to their conversation was that Bezobyedov would soon take his departure. 'A nice guest indeed to be sitting with!' I thought to myself when a footman brought in tea and Dmitri had five times to beg Bezobyedov to have a glass, for the reason that the bashful guest thought it incumbent upon him always to refuse the first and second glasses and to say, 'No, help yourself.' I could see that Dmitri had to put some restraint upon himself as he resumed the conversation. He tried several times to inveigle me also into it, but I remained glum and silent.

'There's no point in putting on a face that dares anyone to suspect that I am bored,' was my mental remark to Dmitri as I sat quietly rocking myself to and fro with measured beat. As the moments passed I found myself – with a certain satisfaction – stoking up more and more my feeling of inward hostility to my friend. 'What a fool he is!' I thought. 'He might be spending the evening agreeably with his charming family, yet he goes on sitting with this brute! – will go on doing so, too, until it is too late to go down to the drawing-room!' Here I glanced at him over the edge of my chair. His hand, his general posture, his neck (particularly the back of it), and his knees all seemed so offensive and repellent that at that moment I could gladly have done something to him – even something really unpleasant.

At last Bezobyedov rose, but Dmitri could not easily let such a delightful friend depart, and asked him to stay the night; fortunately Bezobyedov declined the invitation and departed.

Having seen him off, Dmitri returned, and smiling a faintly complacent smile as he did so, and rubbing his hands together (partly, no doubt, because he had sustained his character for eccentricity, and partly because he had got rid of a bore), started to pace the room, with an occasional glance at me. I felt more offended with him than ever. 'How dare he go on walking about the room and grinning like that?' I thought.

'What are you so angry about?' he asked me suddenly as he halted in front of my chair.

'I am not in the least angry,' I replied (as people always do answer under such circumstances). 'I am merely vexed that you should play-act to me, and to Bezobyedov, and to yourself.'

'What rubbish!' he retorted. 'I never play-act to anyone.'

'I have in mind our rule of frankness,' I replied, 'when I tell you straight out that I am certain you cannot bear this Bezobyedov any more than I can. He is an absolute cad and goodness knows what besides, yet it pleases you to give yourself airs before him.'

'Not at all! To begin with, he is a splendid fellow, and——'

'But I tell you it *is* so. I also tell you that your friendship for Lyubov Sergeyevna is founded on the same basis, namely, that she thinks you a god.'

'And I tell *you* once more that it is not so.'

'But I tell you that it is. I know it for myself,' I retorted with the heat of suppressed anger, and trying to disarm him by my frankness. 'I have told you before, and I repeat it now, that I always seem to like people who say pleasant things to me, but that as soon as I come to examine the matter properly, I invariably find that there is no real attachment between us.'

'Oh, but you are wrong,' said Dmitri, irritably straightening his collar with a jerk of his neck. 'When I like people, neither praise nor blame can make any difference to my feeling towards them.'

'That is not true. You know that I confessed that when my father called me a good-for-nothing I hated him for a time, and wished that he was dead. In the same way, you——'

'Speak for yourself. I am very sorry that you could ever have been so——'

'No, no!' I cried as I leapt from my chair and faced him with the courage of exasperation. 'What you are saying is wrong. Didn't you tell me about my brother? I won't go into that, for it would be dishonourable, but surely you said . . . Anyway, I will tell *you* what I think of you.'

And, burning to wound him even more than he had wounded me, I set out to prove to him that he was incapable of feeling any real affection for anybody, and that I had the best of grounds (as in very truth I believed I had) for reproaching him. I took great pleasure in telling him all this, but at the same time forgot that the only conceivable purpose of my doing so – to force him to confess to the faults of which I had accused him – could not possibly be attained at the present moment, when he was in a rage. Had he, on the other hand, been in a condition to make a clean breast of it, I should probably never have said what I did.

The dispute was verging upon an open quarrel when Dmitri suddenly became silent and left the room. I pursued him, and continued what I was saying, but he did not answer. I knew that his failings included a hasty temper, and that he was now fighting it down. I cursed his list of good resolutions even more in my heart.

This, then, was what our rule of frankness had brought us to – the rule that we should 'tell one another everything in our minds, and never discuss one another with a third person!'

Many a time we had exaggerated frankness to the pitch of making the most disgraceful mutual confessions, and of shaming ourselves by voicing to one another speculations and fancies as if they were real desires and feelings, as I had just been doing with him; yet those confessions had not only failed to draw closer the tie which united us, but had dissipated sympathy and thrust us further apart, until now pride would not allow him to expose his feelings even in the smallest detail, and we employed in the heat of our quarrel the very weapons which we had previously handed one another – weapons which could strike the most painful blows.

XLII

OUR STEPMOTHER

ALTHOUGH Papa had not meant to return with his wife to Moscow before the New Year, he arrived in October, when there was still good riding to hounds to be had in the country. He gave as his reason for changing his mind that his suit was shortly to be heard in the Senate, but Mimi told us that Avdotya Vasilyevna had found herself so bored in the country, and had so often talked about Moscow and pretended to be unwell, that Papa had decided to accede to her wishes.

'You see, she never really loved him – she only kept buzzing in everyone's ears about her love because she wanted to marry a rich man,' added Mimi with a pensive sigh which said: 'To think what a certain other person could have done for him if only he had valued her!'

Yet that 'certain other person' was unjust to Avdotya Vasilyevna, seeing that the latter's affection for Papa – the passionate, devoted love of self-abandonment – revealed itself in her every word and look and movement. At the same time, that love, and the desire never to leave her adored husband's side, in no way hindered her from desiring to visit Madame Annette's and order there a lovely cap, a hat trimmed with a magnificent blue ostrich feather, and a blue Venetian velvet gown which was to expose to the public gaze the snowy, well-shaped breast and arms which no one had yet gazed upon except her husband and maids. Of course Katya sided with her mother, and in general there grew up between our stepmother and ourselves, from the day of her arrival, the most extraordinary and burlesque order of relations. As soon as she stepped from the carriage, Volodya assumed an air of great seriousness and ceremony, and advancing towards her with much bowing and scraping to kiss her hand, said as though presenting someone for the first time:

'I have the honour to greet the arrival of our dear mamma, and to kiss her hand.'

'Ah, my dear little son!' she replied with her beautiful, unvarying smile.

'And do not forget the second little son,' I said as I also approached her hand, with an involuntary imitation of Volodya's voice and expression.

Had our stepmother and ourselves been certain of any mutual affection, that expression might have signified contempt for outward display of affection. Had we already been ill-disposed towards one another, it might have denoted irony, or contempt for pretence, or a desire to conceal from Papa (standing by the while) our real relations, as well as many other thoughts and sentiments. But in the present case that expression (which well consorted with Avdotya Vasilyevna's own spirit) simply signified nothing at all – simply concealed the absence of any definite relations between us. In later life I have often observed, in the case of other families whose members anticipated among themselves relations not altogether harmonious, the same sort of false, burlesque relations; and it was just such relations as those which now became established between ourselves and our stepmother. We scarcely ever strayed beyond them, but were artificially polite to her, conversed with her in French, bowed and scraped before her, and called her '*chère Maman*'[1] – a term to which she always responded in a tone of similar jocularity and with her beautiful, unchanging smile. Only Lyuba the cry-baby, with her goose feet and artless prattle, really liked our stepmother, or tried, in her naive and

1 Dear Mamma.

frequently awkward way, to bring her into closer touch with the rest of the family: so that the only person in the world for whom, besides Papa whom she loved passionately, Avdotya Vasilyevna had a spark of affection, was Lyuba. Indeed, she always treated her with a kind of grave admiration and timid deference which greatly surprised me.

From the first Avdotya Vasilyevna was very fond of calling herself our stepmother and hinting that since children and servants usually adopt an unjust and hostile attitude towards a stepmother, her own position was likely to prove a difficult one. Yet though she foresaw all the unpleasantness of her predicament, she did nothing to escape from it by (for instance) conciliating this one, giving presents to that other one, and not grumbling – the last a precaution which it would have been easy for her to take, seeing that by nature she was in no way exacting, as well as very good-tempered. Yet, not only did she do none of these things, but her expectation of difficulties led her to adopt a defensive attitude before she had been attacked. Supposing that the entire household was designing to show her every kind of insult and annoyance, she would see evil intent in everyone, and consider that her most dignified course was to suffer in silence – an attitude of passivity as regards gaining affection which of course led to her gaining dislike. Moreover, she was so totally lacking in that faculty of 'apprehension' to which I have already referred as being highly developed in our household, and all her customs were so utterly opposed to those which had long been rooted in our establishment, that those two facts alone were bound to count severely against her. Her mode of life in our tidy, methodical household was that of a person who had only just arrived there. Sometimes she went to bed late, sometimes early; sometimes she appeared at dinner, sometimes she did not; sometimes she took supper, sometimes she dispensed with it. When we had no guests with us she more often than not walked about the house half-dressed, and was not ashamed to appear before us – even before the servants – in a white chemise with only a shawl thrown over her shoulders and her arms bare. At first this simplicity pleased me, but before very long it led to my losing the last shred of respect which I felt for her. What struck us as even more strange was the fact that, according as we had or had not guests, she was two different women. The one (when visitors were present) was a young and healthy, but rather cold, beauty, a person richly dressed, neither stupid nor clever, but cheerful. The other woman (when no guests were present) was considerably past her first youth, languid, depressed, slovenly, and bored, though affectionate. Frequently, as I looked at her when, smiling, rosy with the winter air, and happy in the consciousness of her beauty, she came in from a round of calls and, taking off her hat, went to look at herself in a mirror; or when, rustling in her rich, *décolleté* ball dress, at once shy and proud before the servants, she passed to her carriage; or when, at one of our small receptions at home, she was sitting dressed in a high silken gown finished with some sort of fine lace about her soft neck, and flashing her unvarying but lovely smile around her – as I looked at her at such times I could not help wondering what would have been said by persons who had been ravished to behold her thus, if they could have seen her as I often saw her, namely when, waiting in the lonely midnight hours for her husband to return from his club, she would wander like a shadow from room to room, with her hair dishevelled and her form clad in a sort of dressing-jacket. At such times she would sit down to the piano and, her brows puckered with the effort, play over the only waltz that she knew; or she would pick up a novel, read a few pages some-where in the middle of it, and throw it aside; or else, repairing in person to the pantry so as not to disturb the servants, she would get herself a cucumber and some cold veal and eat them standing by the pantry window – then once more resume her weary, aimless, gloomy wandering from room to room. But what above all other things caused estrangement between us was that lack of understanding which expressed itself chiefly in the peculiar air of indulgent attention with which she would listen when anyone was speaking to her concerning matters of which she had no knowledge. It was not her fault that she acquired the unconscious habit of bending her head down and smiling slightly with her lips only, when people spoke to her on topics which did not particularly interest her (which meant any topic except herself and her husband); yet that smile and that inclination of the head, when incessantly repeated, could become unbearably wearisome. Also, her peculiar gaiety – which always sounded as though she were laughing at herself, at you, and at the world in general – was *gauche* and anything but infectious; her sympathy was too evidently forced. Worst of all, she knew no reticence with regard to her ceaseless rapturising to all and sundry concerning her love for Papa. Although she only spoke the truth when she said that her whole life was bound up with her husband, and although she proved it her life long, we considered such unrestrained, continual insistence upon her affection for him revolting, and felt more ashamed for her when she was descanting thus before strangers even than we did when she was perpetrating bad blunders in French.

She loved her husband more than anything else in the world, and he too had a great affection for her, especially at first, and when he saw that others besides himself admired her beauty. The sole aim of her life was to retain the love of her husband; yet it seemed as though she purposely did everything most likely to displease him – simply to prove to him the strength of her love, her readiness to sacrifice herself for his sake.

She was fond of display, and my father too liked to see her in society as a beauty who excited praise and admiration; yet she sacrificed her weakness for fine clothes to her love for him, and grew more and more accustomed to remain at home in a plain grey blouse. Papa considered freedom and equality to be indispensable conditions of family life, and hoped that his favourite Lyuba and his kind-hearted young wife would become sincere friends; yet Avdotya Vasilyevna sacrificed herself by considering it incumbent upon her to pay the 'real mistress of the house,' as she called Lyuba, an amount of deference which only shocked and annoyed my father. He played cards a great deal that winter, and lost considerable sums towards the end of it – and, unwilling as usual to let his gambling affairs intrude upon his family life, he began to pre-serve complete secrecy concerning his play; yet Avdotya Vasilyevna again insisted on sacrificing herself, and though often ailing, and towards the end of the winter pregnant, considered herself bound always to sit up (in her grey blouse, and with her hair dishevelled) for my father when, at four or five o'clock in the morning, he returned home from the club ashamed at having had to pay an eighth fine,[1] depleted in pocket, and weary. She would ask him absent-mindedly whether he had been fortunate in play, and listen with indulgent attention, little nods of her head, and a faint smile upon her face as he told her of his doings at the club and begged her for the hundredth time never to sit up for him again. Yet though Papa's winnings or losings (upon which his substance practically depended) in no way interested her, she continued to be the first to meet him when he returned home from the club. This she was incited to do, not only by her passion for self-sacrifice, but by a certain secret jealousy from which she suffered in the highest degree. No one in the world could have persuaded her that it was *really* from his club, and not from a mistress's, that Papa came home so late. She would try to read love secrets in his face, and discerning none there, would sigh with a sort of enjoyment of her grief and give herself up once more to the contemplation of her unhappiness.

As the result of these and many other constant sacrifices which occurred in Papa's relations with his wife during the latter months of that winter (a time when he lost much, and was therefore out of spirits), there gradually grew up in Papa's relations with her an intermittent feeling of tacit hostility – of that restrained aversion to the object of one's devotion of the kind which expresses itself in an unconscious eagerness to show that person every possible species of petty annoyance.

XLIII
NEW COMRADES

THE winter had passed imperceptibly and the thaw begun when the list of examinations was posted at the University,

---

1 A fine was imposed for players who stayed at clubs after the normal closing time of midnight, and was doubled every half-hour.

and I suddenly remembered that I had to return answers to questions in eighteen subjects on which I had heard lectures delivered without listening to them, and with regard to which I had taken no notes and made no preparation whatever. It seems strange that the question 'How am I going to pass?' should never have entered my head, but the truth is that all that winter I had been in such a state of haze through the delights of being both grown up and '*comme il faut*,' that whenever the question of the examinations had occurred to me, I had mentally compared myself with my comrades and thought to myself, 'They are certain to pass, and as most of them are not even "*comme il faut*," and I am therefore their personal superior, I am bound to come out all right.' In fact, the only reason why I attended lectures at all was that I had become accustomed to doing so, and Papa did not permit me to stay at home. Moreover, I had many acquaintances now and often enjoyed myself vastly at the University. I loved the racket, talking, and laughter in the auditorium, the opportunities for sitting on a back bench and letting the measured voice of the professor lure one into dreams as one contemplated one's comrades, the occasional runnings across the way to Materne's for a snack and a glass of vodka (sweetened by the fearful joy of knowing that one might be hauled before the professor for so doing), the stealthy creaking of the door as one returned to the auditorium, and the participation in 'course *versus* course' scuffles with laughing students who thronged the corridors. All this was great fun.

By the time, however, that everyone had begun to put in a better attendance at lectures, and the professor of physics had completed his course and taken his leave of us until the examinations came on, and the students were busy collecting their notebooks and arranging to do their preparation in parties, it struck me that I too had better prepare for the ordeal. Operov, with whom I still continued on bowing terms, but with whom I was otherwise cool, as I have already mentioned, suddenly offered not only to lend me his notebooks, but to let me do my preparation with him and some other students. I thanked him, and accepted the invitation – hoping by that conferment of honour to make amends for our old misunderstanding; but at the same time I requested that the gatherings should be held at my home, since my quarters were so splendid.

To this the students replied that they meant to take turn and turn about – sometimes to meet at one fellow's place, sometimes at another's, wherever might be most convenient. The first of our sessions was held at Zukhin's, who had a small room behind a partition in a large building on the Trubnoy Boulevard. The opening day I arrived late, and entered when the reading aloud had already begun. The little apartment was thick with tobacco-smoke, not of high-quality tobacco, but of the coarse shag which Zukhin smoked, while on the table stood a bottle of vodka, a glass, bread, salt, and a shin-bone of mutton. Without rising, Zukhin asked me to have some vodka and to take off my coat.

'I expect you are not accustomed to such refreshments,' he added.

They were all wearing dirty cotton shirts and false shirt-fronts. Endeavouring not to show my contempt for the company, I took off my coat and lay down in a comradely manner on the sofa. Zukhin went on reading aloud and occasionally referring to his notebooks, while the others stopped him to ask questions, which he always answered with ability, correctness, and precision. I began to pay careful attention, and as there was much that I did not understand, since I had not been present at what had gone before, soon interpolated a question.

'Hullo, old fellow! It will be no good for you to listen if you do not know the subject,' said Zukhin. 'I will lend you my notebooks, and then you can read it up by tomorrow; otherwise there is no point in trying to explain.'

I felt ashamed of my ignorance. Also, I felt the truth of what he said; so I gave up listening and amused myself by observing my new comrades. According to my classification of humanity into persons '*comme il faut*' and persons not '*comme il faut*,' they evidently belonged to the latter category, and so aroused in me not only a feeling of contempt, but also a certain sensation of personal hostility, for the reason that though not '*comme il faut*,' they accounted me their equal, and actually patronised me in a good-humoured fashion. What in particular excited in me this feeling was their feet, their dirty hands and bitten-down finger-nails (and one long talon on Operov's obtrusive little finger), their pink shirts and false shirt-fronts, the abuse which they good-naturedly threw at one another, the dirty room, a habit which Zukhin had of continually half-blowing his nose, pressing a finger to one nostril, and above all, their manner of speaking – that is to say, their use and intonation of certain words. For instance, they said 'blockhead' for fool, 'precisely' for exactly, 'magnificent' for splendid, and so on – all of which seemed to me bookish and disagreeably vulgar. Still more was my '*comme il faut*' detestation aroused by the accents which they put upon certain Russian – and, still more, upon foreign – words. Thus they said *máchine* instead of *machíne*, *áctivity* instead of *actívity*, *déliberately* instead of *delíberately*, *mantelpiéce* instead of *mántelpiece*, *Shákespeare* instead of *Shakespéare*, and so forth.

Yet for all their insuperably repellent exterior I could detect something good in these people and envied them the cheerful good-fellowship which united them. I began to feel attracted towards them, and made up my mind that, come what might, I would become one of their number. The kind and honourable Operov I knew already, and now the *brusque* and exceptionally clever Zukhin (who evidently took the lead in this circle) began to please me greatly. He was a dark, thick-set little fellow, with a perennially glistening, somewhat puffy face, but one that was extremely lively, intelligent, and independent in its expression. That expression it derived from a low but prominent forehead, deep black eyes, short, bristly hair, and a thick, dark beard which looked as though it stood in constant need of trimming. Although, too, he seemed to think nothing of himself (a *trait* which always pleased me in people), it was clear that his mind was never idle. He had one of those expressive faces which, a few hours after you have seen them for the first time, change suddenly and entirely to your view. Such a change took place, in my eyes, with regard to Zukhin's face towards the end of that evening. Suddenly I seemed to see new wrinkles appear upon its surface, its eyes grow deeper, its smile become a different one, and the whole face assume such an altered aspect that I scarcely recognised it.

When the reading was ended, Zukhin, the other students, and I manifested our desire to be 'comrades all' by drinking a glass of vodka apiece until little remained in the bottle. Zukhin asked if anyone had a quarter-rouble to spare, so that he could send the old woman who looked after him to buy some more; yet, on my offering to provide the money, he made as though he had not heard me, and turned to Operov, who pulled out a purse sewn with beads, and handed him the sum required.

'And mind you don't get drunk,' added Operov, who himself had not partaken of the vodka.

'No fear!' answered Zukhin as he sucked the marrow out of the mutton bone (I remember thinking that it must be because he ate marrow that he was so clever). 'No fear!' he went on with a slight smile (and his smile was of the kind that one involuntarily noticed, and somehow felt grateful for), 'even if I did get drunk, there would be no great harm done. I wonder which of us two could look after himself the better – you or I? Anyway I am willing to make the experiment,' and he slapped his forehead with mock boastfulness. 'But Semyonov needs to look out. He has been drinking hard.'

Sure enough, the grey-haired Semyonov who had comforted me so much at my first examination by being uglier than I was, and who after passing the second examination had attended his lectures regularly during the first month, had taken to hard drinking even before revision had started, and had not been seen at the University throughout the latter part of the course.

'Where is he?' asked someone.

'I don't know,' replied Zukhin. 'He has escaped my eye altogether. Last time I was with him we smashed up the Lisbon together. That was a great evening. After that, I heard, he got himself into a mess . . . What fire there is in the man! and what an intellect! I should be sorry if he has come to grief – and come to grief he probably will, for he's not the sort of chap to stick at his University course, not with his wild outbursts.'

After a little further conversation, and agreeing to meet again the next night at Zukhin's, since his quarters were the most central point for us all, we began to disperse. As one by one we left the room, my conscience started pricking me because everyone seemed to be going home on foot, whereas I had my drozhki. So with some hesitation I offered Operov a lift. Zukhin came to the door with us, and after borrowing a rouble from Operov went off to make a night of it with some friends. As we drove along Operov told me a good deal about Zukhin's character and mode of life, and on reaching home it was long before I could get to sleep for thinking of the new acquaintances I had made. For many an hour as I lay awake I kept wavering between the respect which their knowledge, simplicity, and sense of honour, as well as the poetry of their youth and courage, excited in my mind, and the distaste which I felt for their unseemly exterior. In spite of my desire to do so, it was at that time literally impossible for me to associate with them, since our ideas were too wholly at variance. For me life's meaning and charm contained an infinitude of nuances of which they had not an inkling, and *vice versa*. The greatest obstacles of all, however, to our better acquaintance I felt to be the twenty-rouble cloth in my frockcoat, my drozhki, and my white cambric shirt; and they appeared to me most import-ant obstacles, since they made me feel as though I had unwit-tingly insulted these comrades by displaying such indications of my prosperity. I felt guilty in their eyes, and now humbling myself, now rebelling against my undeserved humiliation and swinging over into arrogance, I was quite unable to enter into equal and unaffected relations with them. Yet to such an extent did the stirring poetry of the courage which I could detect in Zukhin (in particular) overshadow the coarse, vicious side of his nature, that the latter made no unpleasant impression upon me.

For a couple of weeks I visited Zukhin's almost every night for purposes of work. Yet I did very little there, since, as I have said, I had lost ground at the start, and not having sufficient grit in me to catch up my companions by solitary study, was forced merely to *pretend* that I was listening to and taking in all they

were reading. I have an idea, too, that they divined my pretence, since I often noticed that they passed over points which
they themselves knew without first inquiring of me whether
I knew them too.

Yet day by day I was coming to regard the vulgarity of this
circle with more indulgence, to feel increasingly drawn
towards its way of life, and to find in it much that was poetical.
Only my word of honour to Dmitri that I would never indulge
in dissipation with these new comrades kept me from deciding
also to share their diversions.

Once I thought I would make a display of my knowledge of
literature, particularly French literature, and so led the conversation to that theme. To my surprise I discovered that
although my companions pronounced the foreign titles with
a Russian accent, they had read far more than I had, and knew
and could appraise English, and even Spanish, writers, and
Lesage, of whom I had never so much as heard. Likewise,
Pushkin and Zhukovsky were to them *literature* (and not, as
to myself, little books in yellow covers which I had once read
and studied as a child). For Dumas, Sue and Féval they had
equal contempt, and in general were competent to form much
better and clearer judgements on literary matters than I was, as I
could not but acknowledge. In knowledge of music, too,
I could not beat them, and was astonished to find that
Operov played the violin, and another student the 'cello and
piano, while both of them were members of the University
orchestra, and possessed a wide knowledge of music and could
appreciate what was good. In short, with the exception of their
French and German pronunciation, my companions were better posted at every point than I was in everything I would have
liked to boast about, yet not the least proud of the fact. True, I
might have plumed myself on my position as a man of the
world, but Volodya utterly excelled me in that. Wherein then
lay the height from which I presumed to look down upon these
comrades? In my acquaintance with Prince Ivan Ivanych? In
my French accent? In my drozhki? In my cambric shirt? In my
finger-nails? 'Surely this is all rubbish,' was the thought which
would begin dimly to pass through my mind under the

influence of the envy excited in my breast by the good-fellow-ship and kindly, youthful gaiety displayed around me. They were all close friends addressing one another in the second person singular. True, the familiarity of this address almost approximated to rudeness, yet even the boorish exterior of the speaker could not conceal a constant endeavour never to hurt another one's feelings. The terms 'brute' or 'swine,' when used in this good-natured fashion, grated only on me, and gave me cause for inward ridicule, but in no way did they offend the person addressed or prevent the company at large from remaining on the most sincere and friendly footing. In all their treatment of one another these youths were delicate and forbearing in a way that only very poor and very young men can be. And above all I sensed something unconstrained and dashing in Zukhin's character and in his exploits at the Lisbon. I had a feeling that his revels were of a very different order to the puerility with burnt rum and champagne in which I had participated at Baron Z's.

XLIV
ZUKHIN AND SEMYONOV

ALTHOUGH I do not know what class of society Zukhin belonged to, I know that he had matriculated from the S Gymnasium, was without means, and apparently not of the gentry. At that time he was about eighteen – though he looked much older. He was very clever, especially in his powers of assimilation: to him it was easier to survey the whole of some complicated subject, to foresee its various parts and deductions, than to use that knowledge, when gained, for reasoning from the laws to which those deductions were due. He knew that he was clever, and of that he was proud; and in consequence of it he treated everyone with unvarying simplicity and good-nature. His experience of life must have been considerable, for love, friendship, activity, and money had all already made their mark on his ardent, receptive nature. Though it had only been on a small scale and in the lower ranks of society, there was nothing he had attempted which he did not look upon with the disdain, the indifference, and disregard which were bound to result from his attaining his goal too easily. He seemed to apply himself to each new pursuit with such ardour, only to despise it as soon as his purpose had been achieved; and his abilities always led him to success, and therefore to a certain right to despise it. With the sciences it was the same. With little work and taking no notes, he knew mathematics thoroughly, and was uttering no vain boast when he said that he could beat the professor himself. Much of what he heard said in lectures he thought rubbish, yet with the habit of unconscious practical cunning which was native to him he feigned to subscribe to all that the professors required, and all the professors liked him. True, he was outspoken to the authorities, but they none the less respected him. Besides disliking and not respecting the sciences, he despised those who laboured to attain what he himself had mastered so easily. The sciences, as he understood them, did not occupy one-tenth of his powers. In fact his life as a student contained nothing to which he could devote himself wholly, and his impetuous, active nature (as he himself often said) demanded life *complete*: thus he frequented the drinking-bout in so far as he could afford it, and surrendered himself with passionate enthusiasm to dissipation chiefly out of a desire to wear himself out 'to the limits of my strength.' Consequently, just as the examinations were approaching, Operov's prophecy to me was fulfilled, for Zukhin disappeared for two whole weeks, and we had to do the latter part of our preparation at another student's. Yet at the first examination he reappeared with pale, haggard face and tremulous hands, and passed brilliantly into the second year.

The company of roisterers of which Zukhin had been the leader since its formation at the beginning of the term consisted of some eight students, among whom at first had been numbered Ikonin and Semyonov; but the former had left under the strain of the continuous revelry in which the band had indulged in the early part of the year, and the latter seceded later because he found even this too tame. In its early days this band had been looked upon with awe by all the fellows on our course, and had had its exploits much discussed.

Of these exploits the leading heroes had been Zukhin and, towards the end of the term, Semyonov, but the latter had come to be generally shunned, and he created a considerable stir on the rare occasions when he attended a lecture.

Just before the examinations began, Semyonov rounded off his drinking exploits in a most energetic and original fashion, as I myself had occasion to witness (through my acquaintanceship with Zukhin). This is how it was. One evening we had just assembled at Zukhin's, and Operov, reinforcing the candlestick with a second candle stuck in a bottle, had just plunged his nose into his notebooks and begun to read aloud in his thin little voice from his minutely-written notes on physics, when the landlady entered the room, and informed Zukhin that someone had brought a note for him.

Zukhin went out and soon returned, his head bent and a reflective expression on his face, holding in his hands an unfolded note written on a piece of grey wrapping-paper, together with two ten-rouble notes.

'Gentlemen! An extraordinary event,' he said, looking up and surveying us in a serious and solemn manner.

'What, have you received some money for your private tutoring?' said Operov, leafing through the pages of his note-book.

'Well, let's get on with our reading,' said someone.

'No, gentlemen! I am not going on,' continued Zukhin in the same tone of voice. 'An incredible event, I tell you! Semyonov has sent a soldier with these twenty roubles which he borrowed from me some time, and he writes that if I want to see him, I should come to the barracks. You know what that means?' he added, looking round at us all. No one replied. 'I am going to him right away,' Zukhin continued, 'and anyone who wants to can come with me.'

In a trice we had all put on our overcoats and were ready to go and see Semyonov.

'Won't it be rather embarrassing,' said Operov in his thin little voice, 'if we all go and gaze at him, as if he were some sort of curiosity?'

I entirely agreed with Operov's remark, particularly as it referred to myself, who was almost completely unacquainted with Semyonov, yet it was so agreeable to me to feel that I was involved in a common comradely enterprise, and I wanted so badly to see Semyonov, that I said nothing in reply to his observation.

'Nonsense!' said Zukhin. 'What is there embarrassing about our all going to say goodbye to a comrade, wherever he may be? Stuff and nonsense! Come on, whoever wants to.'

We found ourselves cabs and set off, taking the soldier with us. The non-commissioned officer on duty was at first reluctant to let us into the barracks, but Zukhin somehow talked him round, and the same soldier who had brought the note led us into a large, half-dark room feebly lit by a few nightlights, along the sides of which recruits with shaven fore-heads and wearing grey greatcoats were sitting or lying on plank beds.

As I entered the barracks I was struck especially by the strong smell and the sound made by hundreds of men snoring; and walking behind our guide and Zukhin, who stepped firmly between the plank-beds, I peered nervously into the space occupied by each recruit, attempting to impose on each man my memory of Semyonov's worn, wiry figure with its long, tousled, almost grey hair, white teeth and brilliant but gloomy eyes. In the farthest corner of the barracks, by the very last earthenware bowl filled with black oil in which the burned-down wick hung smokily over the edge, Zukhin quickened his pace and suddenly halted.

'Hullo, Semyonov,' he said to a recruit with a shaven fore-head like the others, wearing thick army underwear and a grey greatcoat across his shoulders, sitting with his feet up on his plank-bed and chatting to another recruit, while he ate some-thing. It was *he*, with his grey hair close-cropped, his shaven forehead showing a blue tinge, and his ever melancholy, restless and vigorous expression. I was afraid that he might be offended by my staring at him, and I turned away. Operov, evidently of the same opinion as I, stood behind everyone else; but the customary jerky intonation of Semyonov's voice as he greeted

Zukhin and the others completely reassured us, and we hurried forward to offer him – I, my hand, and Operov his 'deal board,' but Semyonov had already forestalled us by holding out his large blackened hand, thereby saving us from any uncomfortable feeling we might have had that we were doing him an honour. He spoke quietly and as if reluctantly, as he always did.

'How do you do, Zukhin. Thank you for dropping in. Well, gentlemen, please be seated. You, Kudryashka, move over,' he said to the recruit to whom he had been chatting over supper, 'we can talk afterwards. Do sit down now. Well, Zukhin, did I surprise you, eh?'

'Nothing has ever surprised me from you,' replied Zukhin, sitting down beside him on the plank-bed with something of the same expression with which a doctor sits down on the bed of his patient. 'But it would have surprised me if you turned up for the examinations, that I can say. But tell us, where did you get to, and how did this happen?'

'Where did I get to?' he replied in his rich, powerful voice. 'I have been in taverns and pot-houses and such-like establishments. Come, sit down all of you, gentlemen, there is plenty of room. Just shift your legs up, you,' he shouted imperiously, with a flash of his white teeth, to a recruit on the plank-bed to his left, who was lying with his head on his arm and watching us with idle curiosity. 'Well now, I have been having a fling. I've been a bad fellow. And I've enjoyed it,' he went on, the expression on his energetic face changing at each abrupt utterance. 'You know about that business with the shop-keeper: the scoundrel went and died. They wanted to expel me. As for money – I squandered the lot. But none of that would have mattered. I was left with a heap of debts – bad ones into the bargain. And nothing to settle them with. Well, that's all of it.'

'But however did you get the idea of doing such a thing?' said Zukhin.

'It was like this: I was having a binge one time at Yaroslavl, you know, at Stozhenko's. I was drinking with some gentleman merchant or other. He was a recruiting agent. I said to him: "Give me a thousand roubles, and I'll join up." So I went.'

'But all the same, how can you, a gentleman———', said Zukhin.

'Stuff and nonsense! Kirill Ivanov set it all up.'

'What Kirill Ivanov?'

'The one who bought me' (and at this his eyes flashed in a curiously mocking, ironic way, and he almost smiled). 'Made a decision about it in the Senate, they did. I did a bit more drinking, paid off my debts, and then I came and joined up. That's all there is to it. Anyway, at least they're not allowed to flog me . . . I've got five roubles left. And perhaps there will be a war . . .'

Then he began to recount to Zukhin his strange and extraordinary adventures, constantly varying the expression on his restless face as he did so, his melancholy eyes burning.

When it was impossible for us to stay any longer in the barracks, we began to take our leave of him. He extended his hand to each of us in turn, shook ours vigorously, and without rising to see us off, said:

'Please drop in again some time, gentlemen. They say that we are not going to be moved before next month,' and again he half-smiled.

Zukhin, however, having taken a few steps, came back to him again. Wishing to see their parting, I too hung back, and saw Zukhin take some money from his pocket and offer it to Semyonov, but Semyonov thrust his hand away. Then I saw them embrace and heard Zukhin, as he caught up with us, cry out in quite a loud voice:

'Goodbye, old boy. Of course I probably shan't graduate – but you will be an officer.'

Whereupon Semyonov, who never laughed, burst into unwonted, ringing laughter, which made an exceptionally painful impression upon me. We went out.

All the way home, as we walked along, Zukhin remained silent and kept half-blowing his nose, pressing a finger now to one nostril, now to the other. When we had got back he immediately took his leave of us, and from that very day drank steadily until it was time for the examinations.

XLV
I COME TO GRIEF

At length the first examination – on the differential and integral calculus – drew near, but I continued in a strangely befogged state and was unable to form any clear idea of what was awaiting me. Every evening, after consorting with Zukhin and the rest, the thought would occur to me that there was something in my convictions which I must change – something wrong and mistaken; yet every morning the daylight would find me again satisfied to be '*comme il faut*,' and desirous of no change whatsoever.

Such was the frame of mind in which I attended for the first examination. I seated myself on a bench on the side where the princes, counts, and barons were sitting, and began talking to them in French, and (strange to relate), I never gave a thought to the answers which I would shortly have to return to questions in a subject of which I knew nothing. I gazed composedly at other students as they went up to be examined, and even allowed myself to chaff some of them.

'Well, Grap,' I said to Ilyenka, when he returned from the examiner's table, 'have you got over your fright?'

'We'll see how you get on,' said Ilyenka, who, from our first entry into the University, had shaken off my influence, had ceased to smile when I spoke to him, and always remained ill-disposed towards me.

I smiled contemptuously at Ilyenka's retort, although the doubt which he had expressed had given me a momentary shock. Once again, however, the fog of indifference soon overlaid that feeling, and I remained so entirely absent-minded and supine that, the very moment after I had been examined (as if it were a mere formality for me) I was promising Baron Z to go and have a snack with him at Materne's. When called out with Ikonin, I smoothed the coat-tails of my uniform and walked up to the examiner's table with perfect *sang-froid*.

True, a slight shiver of apprehension ran down my back when the young professor – the same one as had examined me for my matriculation – looked me straight in the face as I reached across to the letter-paper on which the question slips were written. Ikonin, though taking a slip with the same lunge of his whole body as he had done at the previous examinations, did at least return some sort of an answer this time, though a poor one. I, on the contrary, did just as he had done on the previous occasion, or even worse, since I took a second slip, yet for a second time returned no answer. The professor looked me compassionately in the face, and said in a quiet but determined voice:

'You will not pass into the second course, Mr Irtenyev. You had better not complete the examinations. The faculty must be weeded out. The same with you, Mr Ikonin.'

Ikonin implored leave to be re-examined, as a great favour, but the professor replied that he was not likely to do in two days what he had not succeeded in doing in a year, and that he had not the smallest chance of passing. Ikonin renewed his humble, piteous appeals, but the professor again refused.

'You may go, gentlemen,' he remarked in the same quiet, but resolute voice.

Only then did I bring myself to do so, and I felt ashamed of seeming by my silent presence to be joining in Ikonin's humiliating entreaties. I have no recollection of how I threaded my way through the students in the hall, nor of what I replied to their questions, nor of how I passed into the vestibule, nor of how I got home. I was aggrieved, humiliated, and genuinely unhappy.

For three days I never left my room, and saw no one, but as in my childhood found relief in copious tears. I looked for pistols to shoot myself in case I should really want to. I thought that Ilyenka Grap would spit in my face when he next met me, and that he would have the right to do so; that Operov must be rejoicing at my misfortune, and telling everyone of it; that Kolpikov had justly shamed me that night at Yar's restaurant; that my stupid speeches to Princess Kornikova had had their fitting result; and so on, and so on. All the moments in my life which had been for me most difficult and painful recurred to my mind. I tried to blame someone for my calamity, and thought

that someone must have done it on purpose – must have con-
spired a whole intrigue against me. I murmured against the
professors, against my comrades, Volodya, Dmitri, and Papa
(the last for having sent me to the University at all). I railed at
Providence for having let me live to see such ignominy. At last,
believing myself ruined for ever in the eyes of all who knew me, I
besought Papa to let me go into the Hussars or go to the
Caucasus. Naturally, Papa was anything but pleased at what
had happened; yet on seeing my terrible distress he comforted
me by saying that, though it was a bad business, it might yet be
mended by my transferring to another faculty. Volodya, who
also saw nothing very terrible in my misfortune, added that at
least in a new faculty I should not be put out of countenance,
since I should have new comrades there.

As for the ladies of the household, they neither knew nor
cared what either an examination or not passing one meant,
and condoled with me only because they saw me in such
distress. Dmitri came to see me every day, and was very kind
and consolatory throughout; but for that very reason he seemed
to me to have grown colder than before. It always hurt me and
made me feel uncomfortable when he came up to my room and
seated himself in silence beside me, much as a doctor might seat
himself by the bedside of a seriously sick patient. Sophia
Ivanovna and Varya sent me books via him for which I had
expressed a wish, as also an invitation to go and see them, but in
that very thoughtfulness of theirs I saw only proud, humiliating
condescension to one who had fallen beyond forgiveness.
Although in three or four days' time I grew calmer, it was not
until we departed for the country that I left the house, but spent
the time in nursing my grief and wandering, fearful of all the
household, through the various rooms.

I thought and thought, until late one evening, as I was sitting
downstairs alone and listening to Avdotya Vasilyevna playing
her waltz, I suddenly leapt to my feet, ran upstairs, got out the
copy-book on which I had once inscribed 'Rules of Life,' opened
it, and experienced my first moment of repentance and moral
resolution. True, I burst into tears once more, but they were no
longer tears of despair. Pulling myself together, I decided to set

about writing a fresh set of rules, in the assured conviction that never again would I commit a wrong action, waste a single moment on frivolity, or alter the rules which I now decided to frame.

How long this moral impulse lasted, what it consisted of, and what kind of new start it gave me for my moral growth, I will relate when speaking of the ensuing and happier portion of my youth.

ABOUT THE TRANSLATORS

CHARLES JAMES HOGARTH (b. 1869) translated works by, among others, Tolstoy, Dostoevsky, Gogol, Erckmann-Chatrian and Sienkiewicz, all of which were published by Everyman's Library earlier this century.

NIGEL J. COOPER read French and Russian at Christ Church, Oxford. He has recently retired from Middlesex University where he was a Principal Lecturer in Modern Languages, teaching French and Russian language and literature, and European literature in translation.

ABOUT THE INTRODUCER

Journalist, novelist and biographer A. N. WILSON has been Literary Editor of both the *Evening Standard* and *The Spectator*. He has written lives of Tolstoy and Hilaire Belloc, and studies of Jesus and St Paul.

This book is set in BEMBO which was cut
by the punch-cutter Francesco Griffo
for the Venetian printer-publisher
Aldus Manutius in early 1495
and first used in a pamphlet
by a young scholar
named Pietro
Bembo.